CARRY YOUR HEART

a novel by
K. Ryan

For everyone who told me I could do this when I thought I couldn't.
I guess you can say I told you so now.

CHAPTER ONE
Crossroads

Isabelle

The parking lot of Sawyer Auto Repair, lined with rows of motorcycles and cracked, ashen pavement, wasn't even half full yet.

This wasn't part of the plan.

This was the *opposite* of the plan.

Given that it was already almost noon and the fact that the Iron Horsemen's clubhouse was just a few hundred yards away from the shop's office, I'd hoped the place would be crawling with customers in need of an oil change or whatever else they came here for. A crowded parking lot meant I could just slip in and out unnoticed.

No big deal.

No real risk if everyone around was too busy to notice.

But the longer I sat here in my mom's Trans Am, the faster the little bit of courage I had left slipped right through my fingertips.

Laughter choked in my throat and I shook my head in an almost desperate grasp for control that would never come.

What was the worst that could happen? Skyler Sawyer could just choose not to hire me? What did I really have to lose?

Working at a repair shop run by the local MC in my hometown wasn't exactly my first choice in employment, but hey, beggars can't be choosers, you know?

I needed a job the way a fish needs water and Sawyer Auto Repair was hiring.

After a disastrously short tenure at Aimee's Diner and my dad's threats breathing down my neck, my choices were limited. I needed to find something *now*. So, when my best friend not-so-discreetly informed me that Claremont's only real successful auto shop was on the lookout

3

for some help in the office, it was either sink or swim. Do or die trying.

Of course, Becca was only privy to this inside information because she was currently hot and heavy with one of the Horsemen's patches, Eli, but at this point, I was willing to take any job that didn't involve stripping my clothes for crumpled up dollar bills.

All I needed was a job to prove that throwing his tuition money away and breaking his heart in the process wasn't for nothing. And if he kicked me out, he'd be in that house all by himself. I just couldn't let that happen.

So, with a renewed sense of determination, I stepped out into the sweltering North Carolina heat, ambivalent towards this new direction. Basking in the sunlight and feeling that warmth spreading over my bare shoulders used to be something I found comforting. Now, that same heat suffocated me and pinned me down like a glaring spotlight, leaving nowhere to hide and nowhere to run except straight ahead.

As I ambled closer to the main office, some bangs and crashes echoed from inside the garage. Loud rock music bounced off the pavement as voices sang along really off-key, probably on purpose. Nothing out of the ordinary for an auto repair shop, but it was still completely foreign.

And scary as hell.

Walking past the long row of motorcycles sent a little shiver of anxiety snaking down my spine. My entire life had basically been spent steering clear of the Horsemen's clubhouse and everyone in it more out of fear of the unknown than anything.

My dad had told me once that the Horsemen were a cancer.

Always in and out of prison for engaging in various illegal activities and he'd spent just as much time cursing their existence as he did the law enforcement for allowing it to happen. He had no shortage of criticisms for the club, complete with conspiracy theory after conspiracy theory that the shop and The Oval Office, a rather notorious strip club about twenty miles outside of town, were all just a cover for the Horsemen's other *enterprises*.

But for all his ranting and raving about *the criminals*, I'd still never seen anything personally that suggested his assumptions were correct. It just wasn't a life I knew anything about, or even really cared to know about, but now, out of necessity, I just had to suck it up and step inside.

Using the last shred of courage I could muster, I knocked on the office door.

"Yeah?" A muffled voice yelled from the inside.

I shuffled nervously from one side to the other, not sure where I was supposed to go from here. I didn't want to be rude and just walk inside uninvited, but I couldn't exactly convince Skyler Sawyer to hire me if I just stood outside the door either. Before I could talk myself out of it, I pushed the door open and stuck my head inside.

"Is it alright if I come in?" I asked, praying the light tremor in my voice didn't betray just how scared shitless I was right now.

Skyler Sawyer peered down her nose through her reading glasses and leaned back in her chair, appraising me with black-rimmed eyes and a few taps of painted acrylic nails on the desk. I'd only ever really seen Skyler around town in passing, but there'd always been an aura of tough superiority surrounding the older woman that made me feel uneasy.

Maybe being the matriarch of a supposed lawless motorcycle club just brought it out in her and Skyler Sawyer had been embedded in that life since...well, since probably her entire life.

Even though I wasn't exactly an expert on the inner-workings of the so-called *organization*, the history of the club was more widely known. My mom had told me once, covertly of course when my dad wasn't around, that Skyler married the club's much older president, Connor Sawyer, when she was just 18 and already six months pregnant with her first and only son. Apparently, it was quite the scandal, especially for a small town like Claremont, where everyone had their noses shoved so far down everyone else's business the whole place reeked of crap.

When Connor keeled over in the middle of the shop's parking lot from a heart attack 10 years ago, the whole town, surprisingly enough, fell into mourning.

That day still lingered in my memory—fifth grade, social studies, and Principal Moreland coming in to bring Caleb to the office. The room went still, nobody made a sound, and even if he couldn't have possibly known the news he was about to receive, 11-year-old Caleb Sawyer's face crumbled with dread and my heart plummeted into my stomach.

But since my own dad never would've allowed me anywhere near Caleb outside of school, there hadn't been much my 11-year-old self could really to do to help, even though I'd wanted to. Who knew we'd ever have something so awful in common?

It was just too bad those feelings of sympathy and compassion quickly devolved into something much different as we grew up.

Some point after Connor's death, Skyler hooked up with the current club president, Marcus Hoffman, and had been with him ever since, but as my mom correctly predicted, she'd still never remarried.

My attention drifted back to the front of the office to find Skyler Sawyer, the Iron Horsemen's matriarch, scrutinizing me from head to toe. When it seemed like I'd passed this initial test, and Skyler waved her hand with a flick of her wrist, I exhaled a giant sigh of relief.

"Come on in," Skyler told me easily, gesturing for me to sit down across from her. "You were in Caleb's grade, right?"

I nodded, still feeling a little queasy at the way Skyler's dark, almost shark-like eyes seemed to slice right through me. "Yeah. I'm Isabelle Martin."

Recognition flickered over Skyler's hard-lined, world-weary face and she was nodding almost immediately.

"That's right. I heard you were back in town, but haven't really seen you around. What do you need? An oil change or somethin'?"

"Uh, no. Actually, Becca told me you were looking for some help here in the office and I was hoping I could apply."

Skyler frowned and her chair squeaked as she leaned forward. "Okay. Summer's almost over. Don't you have to go back to school soon?"

Right.

It wouldn't make sense to hire somebody that was going to be leaving town so soon. Luckily for us both, that wasn't a problem.

"I'm not going back," I shook my head.

Skyler's eyebrows shot into her forehead in surprise, but I figured that was as good a reaction as any. "Not going back, huh? You were at law school, weren't you? Where were you going again?"

"Duke," I barely bit back a wince as I said it, knowing exactly how it must sound to this powerful, regal woman who had probably never thrown an opportunity away in her life.

"Huh," Skyler leaned back into her chair and then abruptly rose, resting a hand against her hip. "Well, you definitely heard right. I *am* looking for someone to help me in the office. So let's talk then. Why are you lookin' to work here? I'm sure there are plenty of other places in town you'd probably rather work at."

"Aimee and I parted ways yesterday, if that's what you're asking," I offered quietly. "It was a mutual decision."

Skyler lifted an eyebrow in amusement. "Waitressing didn't agree with ya?"

"Something like that, yeah," I nodded.

It wouldn't help my case to disclose the countless dishes I'd dropped and all the orders I'd inexplicably lost track of. To say I'd been a horrible waitress would be the understatement of the year. In fact, the only reason Aimee probably put up with me for so long was because she felt sorry for me.

Color me grateful for all this pity and sympathy.

Thanks, universe. Generous as usual.

Sympathy could really only get a girl so far. All those whispers over my shoulder, those pained, uncomfortable expressions when people didn't know what else to say to me after apologizing for my loss—I didn't need any of that.

What I needed was a *job*.

Take that and suck it, universe.

"So the shop is your next choice?" Skyler was asking me now and the judgment underneath the weight of her stare was really starting to make me anxious.

Before my sanity could catch up with me, I jutted a hand on my hip and laid it all out on the table.

"Look, Mrs. Sawyer, I may not have been a very good waitress, but I *am* good with numbers. I'm good with bookkeeping, and although my last job didn't end so well, I *was* good with the customer service part. Everything else not so much. I just really need a job—this job—because if I don't have a job, my dad is going to kick me out and I don't have enough money saved up to afford to live on my own yet."

There. I didn't know what else I could say now. Part of me wanted to clamp my hand over my mouth. Skyler stared back at me with surprise, shock, and a hint of suspicion all flickering across her face. Then, in a

7

flash, her expression shifted into a resigned, albeit respectful, smile.

"Alright, then. I'll start you at part-time, $8.50 an hour, 20-25 hours a week, and then, depending on how you do here, we can talk about raises and maybe even full-time, if that's something you want," Skyler offered diplomatically.

At first, I wasn't sure I'd heard her correctly.

"Really? You—"

Skyler lifted an eyebrow. "You really wanna finish that sentence or do you just wanna take the job already?"

Yeah. Way to screw this up before it even started.

"Uh," I stalled a little so I could shake myself out of it. "Thank you so much! When do you want me to start?"

"How about tomorrow? I can break down the books for you and we'll go over customer check-in and check-out, give you a feel for the job."

"Great!"

I winced at how eager, how desperate that sounded and then that wince curled into a full-blown grimace.

I really *was* desperate. My life really *did* depend on this.

If this didn't work out...

"See you tomorrow, Isabelle," my new boss was telling me now, waving dismissively to shoo me out of the office. "Be here at 10, alright?"

"Okay. Thank you so much. You have no idea how much I appreciate this, Mrs. Sawyer."

"Hey, call me Skyler, alright? Mrs. Sawyer makes me feel old."

"Sure...thanks, Skyler."

I tried not to stumble too much over her name, but it just felt strange to be on a first name basis with someone so goddamn scary and intimidating.

But as I headed out the door, stepping back onto the pavement and into the warm sunlight, I felt like for once, my life was finally about to start heading in the right direction.

CHAPTER TWO
Stalemate

Caleb

My phone buzzed from the back of my work pants and I grunted, setting both my tools and my frustration aside to dig for it.

Finally in the groove and this sudden interruption was not helping me keep my shit together. If I was being completely honest with myself, the whole morning had been off and it felt like I was working on this engine completely submerged underwater from the deep end of a pool.

Sleep was pretty much a lost cause last night, but after the epic shit show that was my life exploded into one giant, catastrophic disaster, that was probably to be expected. Working on basically no sleep was not a good recipe for working on an engine, especially an expensive as hell one, but my hands were tied.

My mom would skin me alive if I missed a shift, but then again, she never really took into account just how much you actually needed to be mentally present in order to do this job and not completely screw it up.

Bracing myself for what was waiting, I flipped open my phone, and a glimmer of hope stuttered and waned with just one glance at the name.

Ariel.

Our fight last night was a vicious one, the worst we'd had since she'd first dropped the hammer and told me she'd gotten into a social work program at UCLA. In California. On the other side of the damn country. Without even bothering to tell me she'd applied in the first place.

This most recent screaming match erupted into a fit of fiery, blinding rage in front of the entire clubhouse, and ended with my fist smashing through the wall in my dorm. Maybe I might've been impressed with my ability to still maneuver around this engine despite the throbbing in my right hand if I just wasn't so goddamn miserable.

So, because I was a glutton for punishment, I glanced down at what she'd texted:

I'm sorry about last night. Can we talk about it when u get off today?

As much as I hated myself for it, and as much as I knew we probably needed some space to cool off, I knew I wouldn't be able to say no. I loved her. That was the problem.

I *loved* her and she wanted to leave me.

She didn't understand why I couldn't come with her, why I couldn't abandon everything I knew and everything I loved. She didn't understand what the club—my goddamn family—meant for the course of my life and I couldn't understand why she would ever ask me to leave them behind.

We were at a stalemate now.

Neither of us would budge until the other shoe finally dropped. The clock was quickly running out and I didn't know what else I could say, what else I could do, to convince her that leaving me would be the worst mistake of our lives.

Short of getting her pregnant—which I shuddered just to think about, let alone seriously consider—I was all out of hands to play. All I could do now was wait for some sort of absolution. The sick dread pooling in the pit of my stomach told me I wouldn't like how this all played out.

I'd just rather tie myself to a chair and let myself get waterboarded than admit it out loud.

I thought we had our lives ahead of us. We were young, in love, and had the world, at the very least the town, at our feet. Ariel saw it as a prison and I was just another shackle weighing her down, holding her back. If she didn't leave now and try to make something of herself, she'd told me, she never would. And then she'd be stuck here with me in miserable limbo for the rest of our lives.

Maybe she hadn't worded it exactly like that, but the resentment lingered in her eyes, was written across her face—hell, even her cold, detached body language told me everything I needed to know.

Five years.

Five years I'd given her. Sure, we'd even been on and off for a little while too, but I never thought I'd have to actually contemplate a life without her. I'd always known she was unhappy in Claremont, how suffocated she'd felt in this small town, but just had never known what to do about it. Instead of dealing with something so heavy, I'd just assumed I would be enough for her to stay.

What a mistake that was.

Despite the crippling dread, I knew I had to swallow my pride.

I wasn't throwing in the towel yet. This could be saved. This could be *stopped*. I just needed to keep reminding her what she would be leaving behind and pray she would ultimately make the right decision for both of us.

My fingers flew over the keys in a quick response: *Sure, babe. I'll call ya when I'm done. Love u.*

I quickly turned my phone off and slid it back into my pocket. I didn't need to add to my self-inflicted suffering by waiting to see how she responded—to see if she told me she loved me back.

Right about now, I wasn't so sure she actually did.

"Hey, Caleb?"

Ordinarily, I'd probably sigh at the sound of my mom's voice and dread whatever one-sided argument was about to start. Lately, the only reason she wanted to talk to me was to tell me to stop being such a pussy-whipped baby about Ariel and just let her go already.

My mom hadn't hidden her general distaste for my old lady pretty much from day one and that shit had gotten old fast. But now, today, her voice was a welcome respite from the voices in my head.

"Yeah, Ma?" I called back over my shoulder.

"Can I talk to you in the office for a second?"

Great.

What now?

The woman wouldn't let up until she got what she wanted, so I nodded over my shoulder and grabbed a towel to wipe the grime from my hands. As I turned on my heel to head towards the office, a flash of shiny blonde hair and long, tanned legs caught my eye. The figure was walking towards a black, vintage Trans Am and just as my head turned away from the girl in the parking lot, my eyes slammed right back to her.

Holy shit—was that? It couldn't be.

The girl turned to open the car door, giving me an eyeful of her face

11

to confirm my suspicions. What the hell was Isabelle Martin doing at the shop? And where did she get that kick-ass classic beauty of a car?

Even from a distance, she looked good. *Real* good. Her hair was a little shorter than I remembered, a little curlier too, but it fit her. Made her look older, more mature.

Visions of seeing her bounce around the halls in that tiny cheerleading skirt danced in my head and she clearly hadn't lost the body she'd somehow squeezed into that sorry excuse for a skirt. That same skirt also got me punched in the head after I'd watched Isabelle doing some high kicks a little too closely at the one pep rally Ariel managed to drag me to. I gotta say...facing down Ariel's wrath was worth it just for the memory alone.

As a senior in high school, I'd yet to learn that for Ariel, just even looking at another girl constituted cheating. It sure as shit wasn't fair because even by that point, I'd made my commitment pretty clear. Isabelle Martin was just pretty hallway decoration as far as I was concerned, but my old lady didn't exactly see it that way.

Still, I didn't really learn that lesson until after a few action-packed nights at the clubhouse after finally patching in as a Horseman. It had taken an all-girl all-out smackdown to do it, and while seeing Ariel rolling around on the floor with another girl was probably the hottest thing I'd ever seen in my life, when the dust settled, I'd gotten the message loud and clear.

Not that it really mattered much where Isabelle was concerned. We hadn't exactly run in the same circles and hell if I could count on one hand the number of classes I even remembered having with her in high school.

One class, in particular, stood out. I'm pretty sure—okay, 100 percent sure—I'd relied heavily on her intellect to get through the American Lit final and you know you're pretty stupid when the teacher pity-seats you next to the smartest person in the room.

Honestly? I'd rather walk through hell covered in gasoline, roll around in a whole nest of fire ants, and eat an entire urinal cake than read poetry again.

But Isabelle just ate it up. First one to raise her hand. Last one to turn in her essays because she was too busy poring over every word.

Me? I sparknoted that shit and bullshited my way through the rest.

It was funny—I'd all but forgotten that we'd sat next to each other every day during our last semester of high school, but her sudden appearance in the shop's parking lot brought the memories right along with it.

The flashbacks were hazy, but from what I did remember, we'd engaged in some pretty entertaining banter from time to time as she'd rolled her eyes or scoffed at my antics in class. All I had to do was mention her cheerleader skirt and her feathers ruffled up before I even finished the sentence.

It almost made me wish I'd taken the time to get to know her sooner than just during our last semester of school.

Now, I figured we wouldn't have a whole lot to say to each other. I didn't really know anything about her, save for our time together as table partners, and couldn't say that I ever really had. What I did know about her...I just wished it was something other than the fact that her mom died about six months ago from lung cancer.

I'd never really known Katherine Martin either, but whenever we ran into each other in town—which wasn't often—she'd always been so friendly, so talkative, so warm, which was a nice change of pace from the way some of Claremont's residents tended to treat club members, like her husband, for instance.

My mom passed around a sympathy card for the family and I'd signed it out of respect. She also sent some flowers with the card, courtesy of the Horsemen and the shop, and everything was probably just thrown into a pile with all the other condolences from people who had no idea what Isabelle's family was really going through.

My mom and I, on the other hand, knew a little something about that kind of loss. If we'd ever actually been friends, I might've tried to contact her somehow, for all the good it would do, but instead, my sympathies went unspoken and therefore, unnoticed.

And now here she was in the shop's parking lot.

Wasn't she supposed to be in law school or something like that?

"Caleb."

My mom's voice jerked me right out of my thoughts and kick-started me back into action. The last thing I needed right now was for her to realize what, or rather who, I'd been looking at. Closing the door behind me, I found her waiting impatiently behind her desk and tapping her nails on a file folder spread out in front of her.

"What's up, Ma?"

She just shrugged. "I just hired Isabelle Martin to help me out in the office."

When she just cocked an amused eyebrow my way, I knew there was a pretty good chance I wasn't actually being punked right now. Well, at least that explained what she was doing here, even if that explanation left a shitload of other questions in its wake.

"Okay."

"You know I've been wanting some help around here. Frees me up to do some other things, anyways. So I hired her. Not gonna pass up an opportunity to hire someone here who could've gone to law school."

I could see her point and just lifted a shoulder. "Alright, so what did you wanna talk to me for?"

"Well," my mom leveled a hard stare my way. "Seeing as how you two went to school together, I just wanted to make sure there wasn't any *history* I needed to know about."

She sure didn't waste any time. I wasn't sure who I was more disgusted with—my mom or myself.

"I never messed around with her," I informed her, shaking my head. "That's what you wanted to know, right?"

She held her hands up in defense. "Sorry, I had to ask. She's a good girl, smart too, and it would really be a shame if it didn't work out just because you couldn't keep it in your pants back then. I'd like to keep her around for awhile, ya know?"

"Yeah, I guess, Ma."

My mom's mouth crinkled up in amusement. "Didn't she used to be a cheerleader?"

I nodded, tugging a hand through my overly-long, tangled hair. Jesus, I really needed to start giving more of a shit.

"Yeah, I mean, a smart cheerleader is kind of an oxymoron, right? Kinda weird she'd end up workin' here of all places."

"I think she has her reasons. Can't imagine what she must be going through right now. She said somethin' about her dad wanting to kick her out if she didn't have a job and I heard he's been hittin' the bottle pretty hard too. Bet he didn't take his little princess not following in his footsteps too well either."

"So she quit school?"

"That's what she said."

"Shit," I exhaled.

She nodded the same sentiment. "Yeah, shit is right. Hey, did she ever come to the clubhouse when you kids were in school? I don't remember ever seeing her around."

"Uh, well," I bit back a smile. "I just saw her there once. That was it."

I didn't see the need to elaborate that I'd found Isabelle puking her guts out in a dark corner outside the clubhouse right before graduation four years ago. The one time her and her friend Becca had managed to sneak in they both overdid it with a few too many tequila shots and I was still willing to bet that was the first time Isabelle had ever really drank like that, at least up until then.

Stepping outside for a quick cigarette had afforded me the best surprise of my life, so much that I'd nearly shit myself when I found her crouched down in the darkness and moaning in agony.

Watching Claremont High's reigning cheerleader princess brought down a few notches wasn't a sight I was going to pass up. Not to mention that I'd gotten a healthy eyeful of her cleavage, too.

Always a bonus.

And it had been funny right up until she threw up all over my brand new Nikes.

But instead of getting pissed, I did the gentlemanly thing and held back her hair as she emptied the rest of her stomach onto the grass. Then I helped her back inside the clubhouse to find Becca and stood outside with them as we waited for Isabelle's jackass boyfriend to pick them up and that had been that.

Even now, how many years later, I still wasn't entirely sure why I didn't just walked away from her after her epic display. Maybe it was the humiliation in her voice as she apologized or the way she'd looked up at me with wide, mortified eyes, but I just hadn't been able to leave her out there like that.

And despite the high I got from teasing her, I never mentioned a word about it to her the following Monday or any other day, for that matter. I still don't really know why I did that.

"Huh," she huffed a little at my lack of disclosure, obviously sensing there was more to the story, but she wasn't going to hear it from me.

"I guess the clubhouse wasn't exactly her scene," I offered with a shrug.

"Yeah, I guess not. Well, don't give her too hard a time, alright? Be nice."

"What makes you think I won't be nice?" I frowned.

The least she could do was *pretend* she didn't think I was a total and pathetic pile of garbage.

"I don't know. You've been more than a little moody lately," her eyes widened when I narrowed my own right back at her. "Well, Caleb, you know what I mean and you know it's true. Just don't take your shit out on the new girl."

"Alright, alright," I conceded, wanting to sidestep any mention of Ariel as much as possible. I didn't need another lecture about how selfish she was being or how it was time to finally move on with my life. "You don't have to worry about anything. I'm not a complete asshole, a'ight?"

"Just figured I'd throw it out there," she replied with a shrug that was a little too easy for her, given that she was also my mother.

"Wow," I put my hand over my heart to fake some pain. "Thanks, Ma."

She just grinned and leaned forward to peck me on the cheek. "You know I still love ya."

"Yeah. Right."

"Get back to work. Hey, you gonna be by the house later for dinner?"

And here I'd almost made it out the door. So close yet so far. "Uh, probably not. I'm gonna see Ariel when I get off."

My mom's face slipped into an icy, hard mask and I shook out a shutter.

"Really, Caleb? After all that drama last night, you're just gonna go running back to that girl like some kind of pussy-whipped puppy?"

There were more than a few things about what she'd just said that tasted really bitter. Referring to Ariel as *that girl* for starters. Calling me a pussy-whipped puppy didn't really help either.

One of us needed to be the adult in this relationship. Since it looked like it wasn't going to be my mom, I just shrugged my shoulders and headed out the door to get back to work.

CHAPTER THREE
Impasse

Isabelle

I pulled into the coffee shop's parking lot with a heavy sigh, parking the Trans Am right next to Becca's car. How I'd managed to go toe-to-toe with Skyler Sawyer without running away and screaming my head off was the miracle of miracles.

That woman was nothing short of terrifying with her regal posture, heavy makeup, and spiky high heels. Of course the fact that she just oozed influence and power had done nothing for my nerves.

Yeah, a little caffeine and some food was exactly what I needed right now to settle down.

At least I could take comfort in the fact that our meeting went better than I could've hoped for. I got the job and that was all that mattered.

Becca was already sitting at our usual table with a coffee mug and a cookie when I walked in and she waved me over with a bright smile. "Belle! Get over here and tell me everything!"

I grinned at my long-time friend as I dropped into the chair across from her, grateful to still have this connection. We'd been best friends since sharing crayons and a Disney princess coloring book in kindergarten. Since then, we'd shared just about everything with each other, from trading lunches and friendship bracelets in middle school, to trading worries about boys, homework, and bitchy girls in high school.

Although we'd more or less gone our separate ways after graduation, me to following in my family's footsteps at Duke and Becca to the local beauty school here in Claremont, we'd never lost touch and six months ago, I'd needed my best friend in a way neither of us ever anticipated. And now, with the ashes of that tragedy still glowing bright, I found myself leaning on my best friend for the support I wasn't getting from the only living family member I had left.

"I told you Skyler would hire you," Becca stated matter-of-factly before taking a sip of her latte.

"Well," I shot back quickly. "It wasn't exactly a slam dunk either. It's not like I have the best track record in terms of employment as of late."

Becca just waved a hand in dismissal. "Who cares? You have a new, better job now and you don't have to worry about anything anymore."

Yeah, like worrying about getting kicked out for smashing my dad's already broken heart.

At this point, he was in such bad shape I figured he was just looking for a reason to implode altogether and there was no point in handing him the detonator myself.

"I start tomorrow and everything. I just can't believe she went for it. For a second there, I thought she was about to scratch out my eyes or something."

Becca just smirked with an easy shrug. "Yeah, that's just how she is. She must've liked you enough to hire you on the spot. But you never can tell though. Just be glad your name isn't Ariel. Then she'd *really* hate you."

"You know," I tilted my head to the side in thought as I spoke. "I gotta say I'm kinda surprised those two are still together."

"What do you mean? They've always been pretty hot and heavy."

"I don't know," I just shrugged. "I guess Ariel never seemed like the type who'd want to stay here her whole life."

"I wouldn't have pegged you as someone who would come *back*, so there's that."

I lifted a shoulder and took a sip from my cup. "People change. Circumstances change."

"Yeah, well, she probably won't be sticking around for too much longer anyways, so I guess that's a moot point. And let me tell you, the after-shocks of that are not gonna be pretty."

The big, glaringly obvious change in my best friend was her involvement with the Horsemen. Well, more like *partying* with the Horsemen. And I could only guess that since Becca was currently sleeping with one of the new patches, the inner-workings of an organization neither of us had cared too much about when we were younger was probably the biggest, if not only, excitement in Becca's life.

"Just prepare yourself. That's all I'm sayin'," she went on, clearly enjoying the gossip. "Caleb is gonna be a trainwreck after she moves to California."

"So it's a done deal, then? I thought he was still trying to talk her out of it?"

"I heard they've been fighting a lot and Ariel isn't budging. Besides, she's supposed to leave in, like, a week, so I don't think there's a whole lot left he can do."

"We really shouldn't be talking about this," I shook my head again. "You know it isn't really any of our business, right?"

"You know I've always been a sucker for some good gossip. It's not like I ever get anything good from you, so I gotta get my kicks somewhere else. Speaking of which, the clubhouse is throwing a party again on Friday. You should come, being a new employee and all," Becca winked conspiratorially.

"Oh, no," I rolled my eyes with a groan. "And watch you hump what's-his-name the whole night? No thanks."

"Come on," Becca pouted. "I've been trying to get you to come for weeks. Skyler said I could bring a friend anytime, so it wouldn't be a big deal or anything."

"I don't think I would be very comfortable there. It'd be hard to let loose, you know? Especially since I'm going to be working there now. The last thing I want to do is go there, start drinking because I'm so nervous, and throw up all over the bar...or someone's shoes again."

"Hey," Becca giggled. "We can laugh about that now. That happened, like, what? Four years ago? I'm sure he doesn't even remember anyways. Wait, is that really why you've been avoiding the clubhouse since then?"

"No," I replied a little too quickly. "I guess it's just that I don't really know any of them. I've *never* really known any of them. It would be weird to just show up how many years after high school and try to party with them, don't you think?"

"I guess I see your point," Becca conceded with a sigh and passed me her leftover cookie. "But maybe it would be good for you to try something new. Broaden your horizons. You're all about that now anyways, right?"

Well, I had to give her that one. But I'd never really been friends with any of them in that group—Caleb, Ariel, Dominic, or even Lexie, who'd always been pretty nice to me—and I wasn't sure how my attendance would be received, by Ariel and Caleb especially. It was strange how you could know *of* people you'd spent a good part of your life going to school with, but never really *know* them at the same time.

"Do you really think your dad would actually...?" Becca trailed off, like she wasn't quite sure how to phrase something so terrible and hopefully, not an inevitability.

"Kick my ass out?" I offered.

"I don't know," she shrugged. "That just seems so harsh. So final. I can't believe he'd really do it, Belle. You're still his daughter."

"Yeah, try reminding him of that and see what happens. And I don't really see the point in taking the chance, especially since I basically have no money right now."

"I know," she sighed. "You could still stay with me, you know."

"I know, I know," I told her. "But I don't know how much rent money I'd be able to give you this month and even after I've been working at the shop for awhile, I don't know where I'll be at money-wise. I don't want to have to do that to you, Becs. It'll be fine. I'll figure it out."

We'd been over this already and I couldn't take a handout, not even from my best friend. I just didn't know how to tell her that me living at home was about more than being short on rent money.

"I don't care about that though. You could just stay with me until you get your feet off the ground. Save up enough money for your own place. It's really not a big deal, Belle. I'm happy to help you."

I swallowed tightly. "And I appreciate that. I'll just...I'll figure out another way."

And make sure my dad's still breathing on a nightly basis.

"I just hope you like working at the shop," Becca went on quietly. "You deserve that."

"Thanks," I shot her a weak smile. "But I swear to God, if he starts to call me you-know-what I'll...I don't know what I'll do. I'll do *something* though."

I shook my head at the memory as Becca just laughed. While Caleb Sawyer and I never had our lockers by one another, never sat near each other during lunch, hardly ever saw each other in the halls, and barely had any classes together, he never wasted an opportunity to piss me off by calling me...Iz.

It wasn't so much the name itself, but the *way* he said it, especially coming from the big, bad biker-boy, that grated on every nerve in my body.

It made me cringe a little just thinking about it. His taunts usually went something like, *lookin' smokin' today, Iz...you got a shirt to go with that skirt, Iz...hey, Iz, when do I get to see some of those high kicks*...he knew exactly what to say to get under my skin and I'd fallen right into his trap every single time.

And I was about 99 percent sure he'd cheated off me on our American Lit final senior year. Anyone that couldn't appreciate a poet like ee cummings was sorely missing out and he'd just bluffed his way through it. That pissed me off too.

"He's not the same person he was in high school and neither are you," Becca offered diplomatically.

I could only hope that was true. Otherwise, this was going to be a very long, trying tenure at Sawyer Auto Repair.

"So what are you doing later tonight?" Becca asked quietly from across the table. "You up for a *Project Runway* marathon or something?"

"I don't know. I'll have to see how things are when I get home."

Becca nodded sympathetically. "Bad night yesterday?"

Having to pick up your falling-down drunk father, who was letting grief and disappointment eat him alive, from a dirty, grungy bar on a pretty rough side of town and somehow manage to get his drunk ass into bed before he passed out was more than just a bad night.

But someone had to be there, someone had to make sure he was alright, even if alright meant passing out in his own bed instead of on a dive bar's sticky floor. I just had to hope that things would get better, that he'd find a way to forgive me, and that he'd find something to live for now that my mom was gone.

"Something like that, yeah," I pushed out with an exhale.

"You know you can call me, right? If you need some help, I could bring Eli along for an extra pair of hands in case he's too..." Becca trailed off quietly, realizing her error and I was grateful for it.

"It's fine. I'm fine. He's gonna be fine. He's just going through a rough time right now. That's it."

"You shouldn't have to be his caretaker though, Belle. You're the daughter. That shouldn't be your job right now. You should be..." Becca's voice stalled, knowing she was crossing into dangerous territory yet again.

I knew exactly what she was about to say next: I should be finishing school instead. But the closer it came to September, the less I wished I really was going back to Duke. Sure, I'd loved being on campus and everything that went along with it at one point, but when my mom got sick, all that just fell by the wayside.

Although my mom kept telling me to stay, to have fun with my friends, that I didn't need to be spending all my time in a hospital, the freedom and excitement of college vanished into thin air. That wasn't where I needed to be and now that my mom wasn't here to force my hand, I didn't see a reason to continue.

Truth be told, I'd never really been all that crazy about law school in the first place, but law school had also been in the plan since I was a baby. For the past 21 years of my life, it had all been about making my dad proud and following in his footsteps.

There was just no point anymore. It hadn't felt right before my mom died and it sure as hell didn't feel right now.

Life was too short to spend your whole life trying to make other people happy.

But my reasons for being back in Claremont were more complicated than that. I was on the fast track towards losing another parent, a reality that was as horrifying as it was an actual possibility, and if that was true, this time around, I couldn't have any other distractions like school getting in the way of being where I needed to be.

"Well," Becca sighed, "I guess I should be getting back to the salon. My break's just about over. Text me if you change your mind about tonight, okay?"

"Sure, Becs," I smiled back. "Hey, thanks again for telling me about the job at the shop. I don't know what I would've done if I hadn't been able to find something so quickly."

"Don't worry about it," Becca waved it off as she rose from her seat. "What kind of friend would I be if I didn't?"

"True."

I watched her best friend exit the diner and sunk a little deeper into my chair. I probably needed to go back now to check on him and make sure he was still breathing after last night, but I was already dreading what I would find. It was always a crapshoot of how the house would look after he'd spent the night drinking: sometimes it was his office that he completely destroyed, sometimes it was his bedroom or the kitchen and sometimes he just passed out on the couch with an empty bottle in his hand.

The grief counselor told me after the funeral that this kind of behavior wasn't entirely abnormal after a loss of this magnitude and that it would pass. Granted, the grief counselor was also unaware how that behavior had escalated and if that counselor got wind of even half of what was really going on, my dad would be in some sort of facility faster than a Nascar crew in the pit and he'd raise hell, kicking and screaming as that race car dragged him away.

My mom was the love of his life and if I'd hit rock bottom by quitting school, throwing away years of tuition, blood, sweat, and tears in the process, I could only imagine the pit of despair he'd succumbed to.

After the funeral, some space and some time was what we both needed and so, I'd more or less given him the space and time he needed. The problem was that he was getting worse, progressively worse, and I had no idea what to do when the bottom finally dropped out because I felt like maybe it already had.

As agonizing as it was to watch him slowly drink his way into an early grave, my hands were tied.

Any talk of rehab ended with screaming, doors slamming, and finally, radio silence. I hadn't been there for my mom like I should have been and so I couldn't abandon my sole living parent now—not when he threatened to kick me out, not when he threatened to cut me off, and not when he bitterly spat in my face how much of a disgrace I was.

This new job at the shop had to be the start of something new, something *good*.

Maybe this time away from school would clear my head enough to pick up the pieces of my life and for my dad to steer away from the path of complete destruction.

I didn't want to think about the alternative.

CHAPTER FOUR
Asshole

Isabelle

"So, the last thing you need to do is just get the customer's signature, give them the yellow copy, and then give them their keys. Oh, and always make sure you walk them out the door and show them where their car is parked," Skyler explained, gesturing towards the parking lot as she spoke.

Well, so far so good.

I was picking things up pretty quickly and even though it was still just my first day, this job seemed like it was going to be something I might enjoy. There was always something to file, always something to order or ship, always a customer to help or call, and I hadn't realized how much I thrived on always having something to do.

Busyness and I were BFFs now.

Awesome.

"So," Skyler went on. "You think you got it? There's a customer coming soon. Caleb is just about finished with the BMW and I think you could handle it, if you think you're ready."

"Yeah, absolutely," I nodded.

There was no *way* I was ready, but I wasn't about to tell her that. I was the model employee now. Nod. Smile. Nod again. That's all there was to it.

When Skyler handed off the print-out, I went over the mental check-list that had been drilled into my head all day and put my initials where they needed to go, acutely aware that my new boss was still hovering over my shoulder.

"That looks great, Isabelle."

That hint of surprise in Skyler's voice, with a little bit of pride too, swept away some of the lingering doubt over my ability to fit in here. It was a relief to finally have a good feeling about something again instead of always wondering when things were going to smash headfirst into some concrete. All that goodwill skidded out the window when the door from inside the shop swung open.

Caleb Sawyer sauntered through with that easy, smug swagger I remembered from high school. If he had, in fact, changed since I'd vaguely known him, he sure as hell wasn't demonstrating any sort of maturity and growth now. From what I could tell, he hadn't changed a bit.

The blonde scruff on his chin was coming in a little thicker now and his shoulders seemed broader, filling out that blue work shirt in ways I *definitely* didn't remember, but he still somehow managed to pull off that overly-long surfer-boy hair he'd always had. When those piercing blue eyes zeroed in on me and his lips twisted into that cocky smirk that had made all the girls swoon, I felt a familiar stirring in my stomach.

As much as I'd hated the way he taunted me, I'd never been completely immune to his well-honed charms either. He was so good-looking it had to be some sort of crime. Any girl with a pair of ovaries was susceptible and I'd forgotten how easy it was to get lost in those clear, ocean-blue eyes.

"Hey," Caleb's lips curved as he spoke, his eyes glimmering with mischief. "Long time no see, huh, Iz?"

And there it was.

Whatever spell he'd just had me under was broken with one stupid word. Hearing it from his lips again might as well have been nails on a chalkboard.

"Looks like I'll be seein' ya around here," he drawled as he walked up to the desk. He passed a pair of keys to his mother, but his eyes never left their target.

"Yeah, I guess so," I replied, all gritted teeth and grimaces.

Two seconds in his presence again and it was like no time had passed.

In light of recent events in my life, Sawyer Auto Repair was the glue that basically held everything together for me right now. So, if working here also meant I had to work with him, I figured I might as well make an effort to remain civil, even if it looked like he wasn't game for that.

"BMW's all set, Ma," Caleb's eyes flitted over to his mother for a brief moment before settling his warm gaze once again on me and God help me, something inside me curled under the weight of it.

As he turned to leave, he waved two fingers in a cocky, mock-salute and I had a sudden vision of myself winding back, slamming my fist into his smug, beautiful face, and sending him flying right through the door.

Ugh. If only it were that easy.

"Nice seein' you, Iz. I take my break in about 20, you in?"

He was still the immature asshole he'd always been and he still knew exactly what to say to burrow under my skin and have me spitting fire in his wake.

Because any way I could possibly respond would make me look like a huge bitch in front of Skyler, the only real option I had was to act like an adult and hold my tongue. Nothing had ever been harder. Seriously.

Caleb was still the boss's son and painting myself in a negative light on my first day was a terrible idea from any angle.

But apparently, my silence was just the answer he was looking for and he winked—he *winked*—as he strolled back out into the shop. When he was finally gone, I huffed out an angry breath, shoving some hair out of my face in a failed attempt at pretending he hadn't just thrown me completely off-balance.

"Same old shit, different day, huh?" Skyler laughed at my side, clapping a comforting hand on my shoulder.

"He's exactly the same as I remembered," I exhaled and my eyes widened in horror as my brain caught up to my mouth. There were only so many ways she could take that...

"You're absolutely right," Skyler just laughed heartily. "My son hasn't changed much and I suspect I'm gonna be apologizing for him a lot. But, you know, your honesty is pretty damn refreshing. I like that about you."

I wasn't exactly sure how I was supposed to take all that so I fell into employee of the month mode. Nod and smile. Nod and smile.

"His break isn't really in 20 minutes, by the way," Skyler shook her head. "I don't know why he said that just now. Probably just trying to ruffle your feathers or somethin'."

Consider my feathers officially ruffled.

"Yeah, he liked to do that when we were in high school," I replied, running a hand through my hair with escalating anxiety. "I probably shouldn't make it so easy on him."

Skyler just shrugged and flipped her auburn hair over her shoulder. "Best just to ignore him. He's been a moody son of a bitch lately and I have a feeling it's about to get worse."

I nodded, not really wanting to get into the Ariel subject. Skyler's dislike for her son's girlfriend practically oozed from her pores and if our roles were reversed, I'd probably feel the same way. Any girl who tried to convince your only son into moving across the country would be an enemy in my book too.

On the other hand, I couldn't blame Ariel for wanting to leave, even if it meant leaving Caleb behind — the small-town mentality here sucked the life out of anyone who wanted to break out of Claremont and I'd left nothing but skid marks in my wake when I busted out of this town four years ago. But like I'd told Becca the day before, circumstances had changed. This was where I needed to be and in spite of the memories attached to it, this town still felt like home.

If Ariel needed to leave, for whatever the reason may be, I guess I couldn't really fault her for that either.

.   .   .

About an hour later, Skyler practically kicked me out the door to take a break. My head was swimming with new information and procedures and it probably showed. A little air and some Mountain Dew definitely wouldn't kill me.

After grabbing my purse, I hit up the snack and soda machine on my way out and headed straight for the empty picnic table sitting on the small lawn right outside the shop. My shift was barely half over and even though all this new training would take a little while to digest, I could do this. Actually, I kind of liked working here. Skyler, in spite of the rough exterior, was patient, generous, and from what I could tell, not the monster my dad painted in all those horror stories he'd ever told me.

So far, the paperwork part of the job was coming pretty easy, which was a far cry from my last outing in part-time employment. Customer service was a breeze and that probably had something to do with being surrounded by lawyers my entire life. For the most part, this job was just the placeholder I needed until I figured out where the hell to go from here.

With a sigh, I cracked open my soda can and ripped open the bag of pretzels, happily snacking away until flashing from inside my purse caught my attention. Yanking my phone out, I swiped across the screen to flip through my messages: two from Becca and one from my dad, which was a surprise, and then my eyes fell on three new messages from Nick.

My fingers itched to toss the phone across the table.

Why couldn't he just take the hint? We were over and I'd thought that was perfectly clear when I left Duke after my last final in May. I just didn't have the room or the energy in my life right now for a long distance relationship that would never work anyways.

Avoiding him hadn't worked because he was relentless. He just didn't understand why we had to break up in the first place and I was too chickenshit to tell him that other than my life unravelling six months earlier, I just didn't love him. Maybe I might've had feelings for him in the beginning, when things were complication-free, but when push came to shove and my mom lay dying in a hospital bed, Nick wasn't the person I wanted to call. And deep down, that wasn't entirely a surprise.

When I read his messages, it was hard not to bang my head into the damn picnic table.

Give me a chance. I just want to talk.

Please, Isabelle. Just call me back.

I still love u. Please call me.

The pleas of a desperate ex-boyfriend were exactly that—desperate. And exasperating. And a little pathetic.

All I could do was try to placate him long enough so he could just move on with his life and forget me. Deep down, I knew Nick probably was stupid enough to drive up here from Atlanta, where he was staying with his parents for the summer. I just had to figure out a way to make sure that didn't happen.

Some movement to my left caught my eye and I glanced up, startled to see Ariel walking towards the garage. While she looked a little bit harder and a little bit more world-weary than I remembered, she still looked almost exactly the same. Same dark chestnut hair, same tight jeans, same high heels. She was pretty the way expensive strippers were pretty—tan, fake, heavily pancaked, and just a little bit trashy. Okay, more than a little bit trashy.

It was like she'd been frozen in time, like a record on continual replay, and for a moment, it was painful, almost unnerving even, because she just looked so absolutely *miserable*.

Ariel's dark eyes widened as she drew closer to the picnic table and I wasn't sure if it was out of shock or horror to see me sitting there. Pure judgment weighed down from Ariel's stare and it was obvious what she was thinking.

For someone who seemed to want to leave Claremont more than anything, regardless of who drowned in her wake, I imagined Ariel was having a difficult time figuring out why the hell I would ever come back here. It was probably a fair question, too. Not like Ariel would ever ask.

"Hey, Isabelle," Ariel started slowly, hesitation lining her face as she approached the picnic table.

It was a sign of goodwill, even it was an artificial one, and for now, it seemed like she was willing to play nice for a change.

"Hi, Ariel," I nodded back.

Just as the words, *how are you*, were about to fall from my lips, I quickly caught myself. That was the kind of sentiment between, at the very least, acquaintances and that was definitely not what we were. Besides, the answer was pretty obvious.

Ariel shifted uncomfortably and shoved her hands in her back pockets. "So, um, Caleb told me you were working here now. Today's your first day, right? Everything going okay so far?"

Annoyance prickled up the back of my neck. I could only imagine the conversation they'd had about me working here...probably laughing gleefully about the poetic justice of the cheerleader's fall from grace. There'd always been a careful, passive-aggressive line in the sand between Ariel and me—I just never really knew what I'd ever done to deserve the coldness.

I'd liked to believe Ariel probably didn't mean anything by it, at least not this time. Combining her chronic self-involvement with all the drama between her and Caleb, she probably couldn't care less what was actually going on with me.

And that was totally fine.

"Uh, yeah, thanks for asking," I offered, playing with the edge of my pretzel bag to deflect the awkwardness permeating the air between us.

Ariel chewed the side of her cheek like she didn't really want to keep this conversation going either, but was too polite to just bail. "That's good to hear. So, um, I'm looking for Caleb. Is he in the shop right now?"

"Yeah," I nodded. "I'm sure he was going to take his break soon anyways."

Ariel didn't know if her own boyfriend was working today? Seriously?

Her face brightened a little and the first genuine expression I'd had seen from her flickered across her face. "Okay, thanks."

She'd already turned to head towards the garage when she stopped short and angled back to me.

Great.

What now?

"Hey, Isabelle, I'm really sorry about your mom. I've never gotten a chance to tell you..."

She trailed off nervously and started chewing on her bottom lip again.

I'd heard it a million times, the same old, meaningless words of condolence spoken by pretty much everyone since my mom's funeral, but every time, those words stung just the same. Every time those words came my way, I knew they always came with the best of intentions, and still, every time I either wanted to slap the person who'd said them or run and hide.

"Thanks, Ariel," I just nodded back to her, hoping she got the hint that she really could leave now and not feel guilty about it.

Ariel forced a smile across her face and turned on her heel to head back towards the garage in search of Caleb. When she disappeared inside, I finally felt myself relax and blew out an agitated breath. It was just small talk, and to be fair, this seemed like a legitimate attempt on Ariel's part to be friendly unlike other times we'd interacted in the past, but past experience had also taught me not to trust that girl any farther than I could throw her.

Maybe it was the fact that we'd never been friends and anytime we did interact, it always seemed like Ariel was trying too hard to be cool, to be a bitch, especially if Caleb was around and those two were basically connected by some body part all the time anyways.

It was gross.

Only a few minutes later, when my attention slid back to the frustrating texts glaring at me from my phone, Ariel practically sprinted out of the shop and charged blindly for her car. Bracing myself for Caleb to come barreling out after his girlfriend, I sunk a little lower on the bench to hide, but no explosions erupted in Ariel's wake.

Caleb did appear about 30 seconds later, but it wasn't to chase Ariel down or leap in front of her car to stop her.

Instead, he hung back a little from the garage's entrance, observing her car pull out of the parking lot with a mask of ice shielding his true emotions from any onlookers. He shoved a hand into his back pocket, groping deep inside until he pulled out a pack of cigarettes. Puffing away anxiously until it was just a nub between his fingers, he flicked the burning cherry away like it was somehow the cause of all his current drama.

I slouched even further down on the bench, my cheeks flushing with embarrassed heat at having witnessed this whole intimate scene. But I still had 10 minutes left of my break and I had just as much a right to be there as anyone. It wasn't my fault they chose to play out their exhausting breakup for the whole world to see.

When Caleb's cold gaze flickered to the picnic table, I immediately looked down at my hands, my heart dropping down into my stomach.

Caught red-handed.

Great.

More attention on myself. Just what I needed.

This was absolutely none of my business and we weren't friends, so shock was about all I could register when he swung a leg over the side of the bench to join me at the picnic table.

"What up, Iz."

It wasn't really a question and he probably didn't really care about the answer either.

"Hey, Caleb," I offered softly, my eyes focused on the Mountain Dew can in front of me.

His sudden nearness was a little unsettling and I couldn't figure out why he'd even bothered to come over here. What did he expect me to do? Coddle him and tell him everything was going to be fine when it clearly wasn't?

Without any other straws to grasp, I figured I might as lay it all out on the table. If he was already in a bad mood, maybe it wouldn't take much to get him to leave me alone today so I could finish out my break, and the rest of my first shift, in peace.

"Hey, Caleb?"

He glanced up at me with expectant, hard eyes, almost daring me to challenge him with something—anything—to get his mind off the heartache eating away at him.

"Yeah, Iz?"

"You think you could do me a favor?"

"Shoot."

"I would really appreciate it if you didn't call me that, okay?"

He frowned, leaning forward to grab a handful of my pretzels. "Iz? What's wrong with calling you Iz?"

"I just don't like it. I really never have and I would appreciate it if you stopped. Like...now."

His eyebrows shot up in surprise, and then that cocky, self-righteous grin curled his lips. "Well, shit, if you didn't like it that much, you should've said somethin' a long time ago. Guess that means deep down, Iz, you actually kinda like it. You just don't wanna admit it."

My eyes narrowed. "That's not what I said."

"I know what you said," Caleb just shrugged. "I just don't think you really meant it."

"Sure. Whatever. You're the expert in feelings today, right?"

When he just huffed out a resentful, bitter laugh, my fists curled into tight, white balls underneath the table and my feet itched to kick him right in the shin.

Why did I let him do this to me? He knew he was pissing me off and he was *enjoying* it too. All he wanted from me right now was a distraction and he was willing to take it anyway he could get it, no matter the consequence. It was like he was bipolar or something, hot and cold, sullen and then cocky.

Screw him and his mood swings. I didn't have to be his victim today or any other day.

When he reached for his cigarette pack, drawing one out and closing his lips around it, that was it. If it'd been any other day and if I'd been sitting across from anybody else, I might've been able to look the other way, but this was the one thing I couldn't tolerate from him right now. The one thing that triggered just about every bitter, guilt-ridden, and devastated bag of emotions I desperately tried to keep out of reach.

Bitch mode engaged.

"Do you mind not lighting that up?" I spat hotly.

His face twisted into a snarl and he tugged a hand through his hair, shaking his head with mirthless laughter. "What, I can't light up a smoke now, too?"

"I'd prefer it if you didn't," I shot back.

Caleb was leaning forward on his elbows now, his eyes hard and calculating. "So I guess this is the part where you tell me I should quit, too, huh?"

I just lifted a shoulder and folded my arms across my chest. "You wanna kill yourself, go right ahead. You're a big boy. Just don't blow your smoke in my face."

"Wow, you're really off to a great start here, aren't you?" he snapped. "It's a free fucking country, you know."

In light of recent events in both our lives, I really wished I could overlook everything that was wrong with this scenario. But because I was pissed and because I felt like being a bitch to go right along with his shitty attitude, I scrambled to my feet and snatched my pretzel bag off the table to stalk back towards the office. Smiling and nodding was the last thing on my mind right now.

As I stomped past him, I just couldn't help myself and muttered over my shoulder, "Asshole."

First day on my new job?

Screw it.
He deserved that.

CHAPTER FIVE
Olive Branch

Caleb

The venom in her voice was unmistakable as Isabelle stormed away. My eyes lifted to the clear sky above me, the only calm thing in my life right now, and I wondered if I was going to have to deal with women stomping around, pissed off and disappointed with me my whole life.

If this was all I had to look forward to, a long life looked real ugly right now.

But as I brought the cigarette to my lips again, the truth of my error rammed its way down to my stomach—Isabelle's mom had literally just died from lung cancer.

I really *was* an asshole.

A huge, gaping, pile of shit-eating asshole.

For the last few weeks, I'd felt like I was hovering over my own body, watching my life scatter into a thousand pieces right before my eyes. And because I had no idea how to salvage it, I'd been saying and doing a lot of shit lately I didn't really mean.

What I'd just done to Isabelle, the way I'd talked to her—it was just completely uncalled for. This messed up situation with Ariel, which was free-falling out of my control, had completely messed with my head.

And now?

Now, I'd taken it out on someone who'd just been in the wrong place at the wrong time. Right about now, asshole should be my middle name.

I scrambled off the bench, almost tripping over it and landing on my ass, and called out to her: "Hey, Iz! Shit, Isabelle..."

Her shoulders tensed at the sound of my voice. It was going to take more than a simple apology to make amends for this particular screw-up in a long line of screw-ups. When she just kept on the path back towards the office, I jogged after her.

All I wanted to do was apologize, even if she didn't want to listen. Not that I'd blame her right about now.

"Isabelle, wait up," I huffed out as I hustled to get alongside her, panting from the effort. Maybe it really was time to quit smoking.

My hand reached for her shoulder, but she jerked away from my grasp. Her lips were set in a firm, grim line, but it was her icy blue eyes that held all her emotions—she looked like she was seriously debating whether or not to punch me in the face.

Part of me almost wished she would.

"What do you want?" she spat back.

"Look," I started quickly, holding my hands up in the air in defense. "I'm sorry, okay? I shouldn't have said that and..."

I trailed off, realizing that we were currently standing in front of the garage and in complete view of everyone inside it. Since the intense, but brief, argument with Ariel minutes before had already humiliated me enough, the last thing I needed was for the entire shop to see me get into it with not just one, but *two* women today, even if I had this one coming.

"Can you just come back to the table, please?" I pleaded, gesturing with my head towards the picnic table. "I'm an asshole. I'm a jackass. I know, I know. Just—I don't need you pissed at me too, okay?"

I winced a little when the words flew out of my mouth. How many damned times was I going to have to apologize today?

"Can I buy you another Mountain Dew or something?" I offered to force her hand. "You still have some time left on your break, right? Don't waste it just because I'm a dumbass."

She shifted anxiously from side to side, clearly torn on how to play this. The expression on her face shifted from pissed to confused to weary all in the span of about two seconds and then she sighed, blowing a piece of blonde hair out of her eyes. That little movement drew my attention right to her glossy lips and as messed up as this whole thing was, I was a little in awe at how something so simple could be so...

"Well, I *was* eyeing up a bag of Gardetto's too," she told me softly, graciously pulling me from my current train of thought and she looked away at the cracks in the pavement to avoid eye contact.

I grinned even though I knew she couldn't see it. "Gardetto's it is then."

I jogged back inside the shop to grab her request and when I rushed back outside, she was already settling back into her spot at the picnic table. Relief washed over me at the sight of her sitting there, waiting for me to make my amends and willing to accept it, and it had been way too long since I'd felt anything remotely like that.

If we were going to have to work together, I didn't want her to hate me. Maybe if this olive branch worked, we could go back to the old banter I'd happily engaged in with her all those years ago.

That kinda sounded fun.

As I approached the picnic table, she was looking at something on her phone and my lips twisted a little at this avoidance tactic—I'd become pretty familiar with it myself lately, too. But then her fingers pounded furiously over the keys and I wondered if she was taking everything out on her phone instead of me.

Good thing I'm not her phone. Christ.

Isabelle tossed her phone back into her purse with a frustrated huff. Gingerly setting the bag in front of her, almost as if I was approaching a wild animal, I gestured towards the bench in front of me.

"Is it alright if I sit?"

"It's a free country," she shrugged dismissively as she tore open the bag and popped a pretzel into her mouth.

Yeah, I deserved that and then some.

But this was probably as good as I was going to get from her right now.

Yeah, probably in my best interest to take it, too.

But when I swung my legs over the side of the bench and positioned myself directly in front of her, all I could come up with was...nothing. I'd planned everything out all the way to sitting down on this bench with her and after that?

I had no idea where we went from here.

"I'm sorry I freaked out on you back there," she told me quietly, playing with the edge of her soda can a little so she wouldn't have to look at me. "Look, my mom smoked like two packs a day and—"

"Isabelle," I cut in quickly. She didn't need to do this and I wasn't going to let her. "You don't have to explain, okay? I get it. And I'm sorry. It won't happen again."

She smiled sadly. "Can't say I'm sorry for calling you an asshole though."

"Yeah, I sorta deserved that one."

Her phone buzzed loudly from inside her purse and thankfully, gave us something else to focus on. Mild amusement, an emotion I also hadn't felt in awhile, had me biting back a smirk as her lips pressed into a grimace and she gritted her teeth.

"Crap," she muttered, quickly reading over whatever text message had shifted her mood like this.

"Everything alright over there?" I tossed out, figuring I might as well try to have a civil conversation with her.

Another agitated breath blew out of her nose and she chewed anxiously on her bottom lip as she read over the text again, too deep in her own little world to even hear me.

"It's nothing," she replied finally and tossed her phone back into her purse.

"Sure didn't look like nothin' to me," I pressed on with an easy shrug.

"Well, that's what it was," Isabelle informed me and then she promptly shifted her attention to the snack bag in her hands.

A few moments of silence later and I thought my head was going to explode. The fact was I just didn't really know what to say to her. I'd completely shoved my head up my ass before and now I didn't know how the hell I was supposed to come back from that.

What were we were supposed to talk about now? There was no way I was touching her recent family tragedy, especially not after the way I'd epically stuck my foot in my mouth before.

Although my dad had been dead and gone for almost 10 years and the emptiness didn't necessarily feel like it was going to swallow me whole anymore, I remembered what it was like to lose a parent with brutal clarity.

Anytime someone told me how sorry they were about my dad—how good of a guy he was, how much they missed him—it was just one more reminder in a long list of what I'd lost and would never get back. I wouldn't make that mistake with her, especially since the wound was still so goddamn fresh. Throw in her dropping out of school and that was probably a recipe for a disaster of epic proportions, at least in terms of us attempting to play nice.

By now, I figured she probably wanted to move forward more than anything and it was pretty hard to do that when everyone kept bringing your shit up all the time.

So if I couldn't bring up her mom or school, which I wasn't going to, I was just treading water in the deep end of the pool again, barely keeping my head above the surface.

"So," she broke the silence with a tiny smile and I grinned back, grateful for the respite. "What else is new around here? I heard Dominic and Lexie are getting married soon. She's pregnant too, right?"

I rubbed my chin and nodded, grinning at the memory of my best friend finding out life as he knew it was over. Dom's face had shifted hilariously from pale to green to pale again and finally red-hot when he realized the entire shop was staring at them, open-mouthed and wide-eyed, after Lexie blurted out the news in front of everyone.

"Yeah, she is," I laughed.

"That's pretty crazy. I mean, I can't even imagine getting married right now let alone having to be responsible for another human being," she shook her head.

"Yeah, you and me both, Iz," my eyes widened when I realized what I'd just done. "Shit, I mean, Isabelle. Sorry, sorry...it's a habit. Won't happen again, darlin'."

Her pretty blue eyes narrowed warily at me. "I'm not sure which is worse. You calling me Iz or *darlin'*."

"Aw, come on," my mouth twisted a little. "I gotta call you somethin' and I honestly didn't know that bothered you so much. I mean, sure, I knew it pissed you off, but not like that. You should've said somethin' a long time ago."

She jerked an eyebrow up at me. "You really expect me to believe you would've stopped?"

I didn't even need to take a second to consider it. "Yeah, you're probably right. I would've been all over that like white on rice."

She flung a pretzel at me and I ducked down, laughing as I got out of harm's way. Well, at least she wasn't putting her fist through my jaw. This was an improvement. This was something I could live with.

When Isabelle's phone buzzed again in her purse, her facial expression was priceless. It was somewhere in between frustrated and horrified and I bit back a laugh when she squeezed her eyes shut before sliding the offensive object back out of her purse with a wince. Her eyes scanned the new message and then lifted to the sky with a shake of her head.

"Come on," I grinned, leaning forward against the table to get a closer look at the text. "That's not nothin'. You gotta tell me now."

She sighed as she flipped her phone back into her purse without sending off a response. "It's just a guy who can't take a hint."

Ah. Now that made sense. It looked like relationship troubles were floating around in abundance these days.

"Ex-boyfriend or just one who wants to be?" I asked, surprising myself at how genuinely curious I was about her personal life. There was no real reason for my curiosity, but it was there just the same.

"Ex," Isabelle informed me flatly, her frustration evident just from the tight tone of her voice. "He doesn't really get why I broke up with him or why I won't come back to school, for that matter."

Although her words were a potential opening into her departure from Duke—of all places—it was best not to push her. With my recent track-record with her, I figured I should probably quit while I was at least a little ahead. Besides, I'd learned through experience that a person will only tell you something when they're ready to and trying to coax it out of them will only get you shoved away.

Instead, I chose to steer my focus on this guy who clearly couldn't understand that no meant no.

"So, what's he sayin'?"

She exhaled deeply before turning her weary eyes back towards me and I couldn't help but smile. This was the first time, I realized, that we'd ever really sat down and had a real conversation that didn't start with commentary on her insanely short, barely existent cheerleading skirt.

It was kind of nice. When I wasn't being a complete asshole, of course.

"The usual, I guess," she sighed. "He thinks we can work it out, but there's nothing to work out. It's done and I'm not going back to school. He just won't listen to me."

There was a hint of something in her voice—a hint of worry or fear, maybe—that triggered an overprotectiveness for her that surprised the hell out of me.

"You're not scared of this guy, right?"

Her face twisted down in a frown and her mouth slipped open a little as she considered my words. "What do you mean?"

"Well, he never hurt you anything like that, right? I don't know. You just seem like you're nervous or somethin' about this guy."

Recognition flickered across her features and then she let out a low laugh. "Oh, no. No. I don't think Nick has an aggressive bone in his body. He's more of the...non-violent type."

I nodded, relieved that I'd jumped to conclusions. "Good. For a second there, I thought I was gonna have to go beat the shit out of him or somethin'."

"Oh really?" she replied slyly with a cocked eyebrow. "Yeah, he shows up here and you tackle him to the ground. I can just see it now. I'm sure you guys would get along just great, but I really don't think *that* will be necessary."

"Well," I shrugged. "Gotta protect a fellow co-worker, you know."

"Thanks, I guess."

"Sure. All you gotta do is ask, Iz."

She flung another chip at me and I playfully held up my hands in defense.

"Alright, alright, that one was on purpose. That was the last time, I promise."

"Good," she laughed. "I really hated that damn nickname, you jerk."

"Wow," I chuckled. "I think that was the first time I've ever heard you say that."

"What? I swear," she retorted, biting back a snicker. And when I arched an eyebrow at her, she insisted, "I do! Just not where people can hear it most of the time."

I snatched up the chip she'd just tossed my way and snapped it back at her, enjoying this interaction way more than I had any right to.

"So, what are you gonna do about this guy, then?" I nodded towards her phone.

"I honestly don't know. Nothing I say seems to get the point across and then when I ignore him altogether, it just makes it worse."

"Did you try telling him you're with a new guy now? Even if that's not true, it would probably make me back off if I were him."

She shifted uncomfortably on the bench and I found myself rubbing the back of my neck a little to shake off my own uneasiness. Putting myself in her ex-boyfriend's shoes was an awkward position to be in. I hadn't meant for it to get weird. I was just grateful she was still here talking to me and instead of being helpful, I'd once again stuck my foot directly up my ass.

"I don't know," she replied finally. "I'm not sure if he'd buy that and I don't really wanna have to lie to him either."

"Short of tellin' him to screw off completely, maybe it's worth a try, ya know?"

"Yeah, maybe," Isabelle replied absentmindedly, glancing at her phone from inside her purse. "Hey, well, my break's just about done. Thanks for the chips, Caleb. You didn't have to do that."

My eyes followed her as she rose from the bench and gathered her purse from the table. When she set off towards the office, I called after her: "No problem, Isabelle. It was nice talkin' to you."

Her head turned back to me for only a second, but it was long enough to see she shared the feeling. A brief smile crossed her lips as she waved back to me and then a moment later, she was walking through the office door, headed back for another installment of training with my mom.

I squared my shoulders back to where she'd been sitting and then the short relief I felt was long gone. There was no one here to talk to, no one to take my mind off the growing panic I felt with each day that passed.

It really had been nice to talk to her. There was no judgment or even sympathy brimming in those clear blue eyes. Just normal conversation about her relationship woes, instead of my own, and her anger and frustration towards both me and that dipshit ex of hers was refreshing. Maybe we could reach some sort of mutual understanding and actually be civil towards each other.

Right about now, I really needed a little civility.

CHAPTER SIX
Interlude

Isabelle

I pushed through the front door, my head pounding from a long day of information overload, and a pile of mail in my hands. Gratefully kicking off my shoes, I tossed my keys and my purse onto the kitchen table and flipped through the envelopes in my hand.

I was stalling.

But lately, I found myself dreading coming home and making up every excuse in the book to put it off for fear of what I would find.

A loud crash echoed from down the hall and my heart just about dropped into my stomach. I took off down the hallway and sped across the house until I was skidding into the bathroom, finding my dad keeled over with one hand still resting on the toilet seat. Immediately taking an inventory of his condition—I'd gotten used to gauging how bad it was with just a quick appraisal—I noted his shallow breathing right away.

He was asleep.

I squeezed my eyes shut and ran a hand over my face, trying to decide if I should attempt to move him, but I was probably more likely to throw out my back than actually get him anywhere by myself.

Right about now, it really would be nice to have an extra pair of hands.

So with a heavy, sick feeling churning in my stomach, I grabbed some pillows and a blanket from the hall closet. My dad still hadn't moved when I stepped through the bathroom's threshold again and the jury was still out if that was good or bad.

With careful movements, I gingerly lifted his leaden head and shifted the pillow underneath him, draping the fleece blanket around him and tucking it all the way up to his neck. He'd most likely be out like this for at least a few more hours, if not the rest of the night, and he didn't need to wake up shivering on the bathroom floor. At least he'd be warm now.

I just knew, deep down to the ebbing sickness in my stomach, that this was only going to get worse. And short of screaming at him pull himself together and forcing him into rehab, both of which I'd tried and failed at already, there wasn't much else I could do for him other than to just be there and hope it would pass on its own.

Wouldn't he eventually realize what he was doing to himself? Wouldn't he eventually realize that this would've broken Mom's heart to see the way he was destroying himself?

Being around my dad was like watching a train about two minutes before it ran off the rails. You knew what was coming and you knew there was nothing you could do about it, but you just couldn't look away.

It was for the best I'd found him like this, already out cold on the floor. If he'd been awake when I came home, I would've just had to listen to him slur out all the ways I'd disappointed him.

How I'd thrown away my future, how I had zero respect for him and for his colleagues who'd wasted their time writing letters of recommendation for me, how I had absolutely no sense of responsibility or ownership towards anything, and how if I didn't get my life together, he was going to throw me out of his house and onto the street.

Well, isn't that just the pot calling the kettle black.

It would be easy to toss all those things right back in his face, but he wouldn't hear it, wouldn't even register the truth. The only way he was ever going to get healthier was if he admitted what he was doing to himself, but when was that going to actually happen? He was swallowed up by grief and barely resembled the man I'd grown up desperately trying to emulate.

And what about my grief? What about my loss? He might've lost the love of his life, but I'd also lost my mom. Didn't that matter too?

But despite all the ranting and raving he shoveled my way, I could never bring myself to disrespect him by saying any of that to his face.

For the last six months, our father-daughter relationship had deteriorated into empty silences and whiskey-fueled outbursts. No family counseling, no life coaching, nothing. Somewhere along the way, he'd just stopped being a father altogether. It was just a title in name only now, one he certainly hadn't earned since the day we'd buried my mom.

He was just existing, a shell of his old self, drowning in whiskey and desolation, and tossing everything I suggested out the window like it was the most half-brained idea he'd ever heard.

He didn't need anyone to tell him how to live and he didn't need anyone to tell him how epically he'd screwed up his life either. He already knew it, he'd told me.

In spite of all the ways I'd tried and failed, the only thing I couldn't do was allow anyone to see him like this. It would destroy what little was left of his law career—how he still had one was beyond me—and it wasn't like it would do much good anyways. He'd probably never speak to me again, too, and then I might as well be an orphan for real.

With a deep sigh, I retreated back out into the hallway and fell onto the couch. Knowing a little noise wouldn't stir him, I turned on the TV and flipped mindlessly through the channels—nothing really interested me, nothing that could take me mind off the sleeping shell of a man in the bathroom anyways.

It would be really freaking great if it was just tomorrow already so I could get out of this house and back to the shop. At least being there gave me something to do instead of just sitting here, waiting around for the inevitable.

And despite the initial tension with Caleb, he'd actually been decent to talk to...eventually, which surprised me more than anything else that happened today. He'd genuinely seemed to care that he'd upset me and hadn't just blown it off with a lame apology.

Instead, he'd made an effort to actually make amends. Having a conversation with him wasn't so bad either and he'd proven he was capable of going more than two seconds without making an asshole comment, even if it was more towards the end of our conversation than the beginning.

Maybe he really had grown up a little after all and there was something about him that was different than I remembered.

More mature, maybe. A little more grown-up.

Maybe it had something to do with the fact that he was finally patched into the Horsemen like he'd always been bragging about, but I suspected it had more to do with the fact that his relationship was crumbling right before his eyes. It was only a matter of time before Ariel finally left. Everyone seemed to walk on eggshells around him and even his own mother wasn't above the tip-toeing act.

With only literally a few days, maybe a week, left before Ariel would have to choose once and for all if she was going to stay or go, I had a sinking feeling Caleb was just chasing a mirage, a fantasy that didn't really exist, and everyone seemed to know it but him.

But maybe he did know, even if he just couldn't bring himself to admit it. Maybe that was why he'd chosen not to chase after her today because he knew she was already on her way out regardless of what he said or did.

Something about that broke my heart.

Ariel just needed to shit or get off the pot already and put Caleb out of his misery. There was only so much drama a person could stand in life and by my count, both Caleb and I had just about reached our limit.

CHAPTER SEVEN
Gone

Caleb

It felt like someone had reached down into my stomach, twisted it up into a ball, and pulled it out through my spine.

I was on fire.

No, I was dying.

Everything hurt. Every blink, every breath, every movement and I felt myself die a little more inside.

For three days, I'd sat on the floor of my dorm at the clubhouse and stared at the wall like a zombie. No interest in any of the food my mom had been leaving for me. No interest in sleep since all that came with it were visions I couldn't stomach seeing.

I'd barely moved long enough to even *feel* alive.

At first, I hadn't believed her. Couldn't believe she was really leaving, that everything I'd been dreading had finally, abruptly become my living nightmare.

Every time I closed my eyes, all I could see was Ariel's face when she told me there was a cab waiting outside to take her to the airport. The anger, the hurt, and the disappointment eroded away into a flash of hope. A last flicker of a chance that I might change my mind and follow her.

And for a second, I almost did.

I *almost* reached for her.

My fingers practically tingled I'd wanted to touch her so bad. But then I remembered what she was asking me to do, what she was demanding I leave behind, and then, the moment was gone. And the anger, the hurt, and the disappointment reflected in her heartbroken brown eyes again.

That last flicker, that last chance, was just our relationship's death rattle.

I couldn't go with her.

It was as simple as that.

This was my home and the only thing I'd ever known. The only place I would ever feel like I belonged. I couldn't desert them. I couldn't just up and leave because Ariel couldn't make her life work here.

If you can't be here, I'd screamed in her face, *you can't be with me.*

That must've been the nail in the coffin, the push she'd needed to propel herself into drive. I hadn't really intended to shove her away, but I'd needed to push her to do something because her indecision was literally killing me.

Someone had to make a decision. *Someone* had to be proactive here because all of this inaction was running both of us head first into concrete.

But at the same time, I hadn't forced her hand. She wanted an out and all I did was give it to her.

I wanted to hate her. I wanted to tear my room apart, raging at all she'd destroyed, but I just didn't have it in me.

Instead, my phone lay in pieces at my feet.

At least I couldn't call her now. I was terrified at what I might say if I was actually able to talk to her, of what I might do to somehow make everything the way it used to be when she still loved me. Now I was just sitting here in the darkness, ruminating over how I'd let everything spin so disastrously out of control.

I was pathetic. I was useless. I was completely destroyed.

Even at that last moment, when she was walking out the door forever, she'd turned back with tears streaming down her face and whispered that she'd always love me.

That was the biggest pile of bullshit I'd ever heard.

The problem was that I'd never had control over the situation to begin with. She'd applied for a social work program almost 2,500 miles away without telling me. She'd accepted a scholarship without telling me. She'd lied right to my face when she said she was going on a weekend shopping trip with Lex when they were really going to L.A. to look at apartments around campus. She'd been planning this exit for a long time and deep down, I wondered if me coming along was just an afterthought in her plans.

If only I'd been able to send her on her way when she'd first laid this on me at the beginning of the summer. Then I would've been able to hate her. Then I would've been able to tell her off to her face.

But you didn't do that to the person you loved.

So I couldn't send her on her way and I couldn't hate her—I'd just clawed and scratched and fought for her until there was nothing left but a bloody, hollowed-out shell of what we used to be.

Of what I used to be.

It was all for nothing anyways.

She was always leaving...whether I was coming along or not. I was just too stupid to see it. I knew Ariel was selfish—a part of me had always known that—I just never imagined it would all one day come back and bite me in the ass.

I didn't need the *I told you so* stares or the pitying, embarrassed looks from my club brothers. It was just easier to sit here in this room, in the darkness, and wallow.

That black hole just widened, sucking me down deeper, but I really didn't give a shit. My mom knocked on my door a few more times, but she wasn't getting in. She'd see me when I wanted her to see me.

With that thought, I tossed the empty bottle of Jack to the floor and staggered up to my closet where more bottles of Jack waited. It was the only thing that numbed the pain right now and I didn't care how I felt later. All I cared about was how I felt right *now* and that I just wanted to feel better. Besides, there was no way it could ever get any worse than this.

As I stumbled back to my spot on the carpet, a jarring image of Ariel assaulted my brain. We'd had sex right here where I sat many, many times, mainly because Ariel was always worried about everyone else in the clubhouse hearing us, and I could almost picture the way her eyes practically rolled back into her head and sighed as I slid her panties down those smooth, creamy legs.

How could she tear me to pieces like this? Didn't she know that I would've done just about anything for her, anything she asked, to keep her? But the one thing she asked, the one thing she wanted—that was the one thing I couldn't give. I just couldn't do it.

And now as I sat in the exact spot that had given me so many hours of blissful, sated ecstasy, I wondered why I'd ever bothered in the first place. Settling down with an old lady wasn't ever something I'd wanted. When I'd first gotten my prospect patch, the endless revolving supply of women, both in school and at the clubhouse, was something to be enjoyed and I appreciated that they never left anything in their wake.

No attachments. No expectations. No relationships. And no commitments.

With Ariel, it had never been that way from day one. Getting involved with her meant I would have to do the attachments, expectations, and relationships. That I would have to commit to her or forget her and I hadn't been able to forget her.

She got under my skin and crawled around like she owned the damned place. No matter what I did or how hard I tried, her face was always there and those big, brown eyes were always beckoning to me like the siren call they were. So I'd slipped into those uncharted waters, followed my siren, and drowned.

This was my life now.

It sucked worse than a black hole.

As I slumped against my bed, that darkness began to clear, giving way to loud, vibrating music and the low murmur of chatter over the noise. The usual Friday night bash at the clubhouse had probably already started over an hour ago, but I'd just been too deep wallowing in self-pity to notice.

I took another long pull from the bottle of Jack nestled in between my hands and each drop that slipped down my throat told me it was time to get up, move around, and forget a little.

Maybe I'd wallowed in despair, away from civilization for long enough and the last thing I needed right now was to worry my club brothers. If I didn't show tonight, my absence would undoubtedly be noted and I didn't need to add that to my ever-growing list of unsolvable, hopeless problems.

This was something I could fix. This was something I could do to prove I wasn't a complete dickhead.

The club didn't necessarily need me to show up tonight. No one had said it and since, the soft knocking on my door had ceased hours ago, I was willing to bet the club would probably let it slide just this one time in light of recent events. But I needed them to know I was still the same guy I'd always been and that a girl wouldn't be the thing that broke me, even it was all a goddamn lie.

And as I staggered to my feet, my hands reaching out for the door knob, I wondered if maybe tonight I'd be able to forget what I'd lost, if even it was just for a few moments.

That was worth the effort and the stares and the questions. What I needed now was just to forget Ariel ever existed and it was the only way I had a prayer of coming out of this on the other side.

Yeah.

I was a delusional, sorry bastard.

Time to go numb the pain.

CHAPTER EIGHT
Behind Blue Eyes

Isabelle

"There's really no way I can get out of this, is there?"

"Nope," Becca replied curtly and just continued applying yet another layer of black mascara.

I watched, more than a little miffed, while Becca put the finishing touches on her eye makeup and ran a long finger underneath her eye to pick up the excess. I huffed a little, hoping that would garner some sort of reaction from my best friend and all I got was a whole lot of silence.

At this point, I was willing to do just about anything to get myself out of going to the Horsemen's clubhouse tonight. I'd just been minding my own business, listening to Becca squeal about just how *awesome* Eli was in bed when she suddenly turned the tables and informed me I was coming to the party whether I liked it or not.

When Becca had her mind set on something, come hell or high water, it was happening and that was what worried me.

The clubhouse was the last place I wanted to be tonight for a number of reasons. But no matter how much I protested, no matter how much I begged and pleaded, the fact remained that I just didn't have a legitimate excuse to get out of it. Well, if I was going down, might as well go down swinging.

"Seriously, though, Becca," I attempted again. "I really don't think this is such a good idea tonight."

"Why?" Becca turned to me abruptly and wagged a tube of lip gloss in front of my face. "Because you've only been there once before and it was, like, ages ago? Or because you're worried you might actually have some fun for once?"

I just rolled my eyes and slumped down on the toilet seat for added

54

dramatic effect, even if this was an argument I wouldn't be winning. "Well, for starters, there's the whole Caleb situation. I'm not so sure I wanna be around for that tonight."

Becca's hand froze in mid-air as she brought the lip gloss wand to her lips like she'd just remembered the hurricane that had raged through the Iron Horsemen's property. It was actually pretty difficult to forget, but maybe that had more to do with me working at the shop, which gave me a clear view of the impact, albeit from a safe distance away. But Becca's reaction told me this might be an angle worth playing.

"Oh yeah, I kinda forget about all that. It might make for an interesting night, but that's no reason why you shouldn't come with me. In fact, I think it's even *more* reason. Don't you wanna see Caleb falling down drunk on his ass?"

"No, actually, I don't," I replied simply.

It was the honest truth. I didn't want to have anything to do with whatever was going down at the clubhouse tonight.

"I thought you guys didn't really get along..." Becca trailed off as if she was trying to wrap her head around it. "So why does it matter?"

"That has nothing to do with it," I waved a hand dismissively at Becca's suggestion. "Why would *anyone* wanna see that? His girlfriend just deserted him, what, literally *three* days ago? It's gonna be horrible and...I've seen enough of that already to last me a lifetime, okay?"

Although just about everyone in Claremont had seen it coming, watching Ariel actually go through with leaving was still a bit of a shock. Part of me expected Ariel to board the plane, realize her mistake at the last possible moment, chicken out, and then rush back to the shop and jump into Caleb's arms just like a movie.

But it wasn't a movie, at least not for Caleb. Ariel slammed the door to the clubhouse one last time, ducked her head into the waiting cab, and never looked back.

That was three days ago and according to the murmuring around my new workplace, Caleb had yet to surface from his clubhouse dorm for longer than minutes at a time. Becca had told me, after hearing it from Eli, that Caleb only answered his door once, just for Skyler, and had promptly thrown her out after about two minutes.

"Yeah, I guess I see your point," Becca conceded quietly and she looked down into the sink for a moment. A second later, her sparkling brown eyes snapped back up to stare me down through the mirror.

"Don't get me wrong. I understand your concern. I really do. But what's the alternative for you, huh? It's a *Friday night* for God's sake. You need to live a little bit, Belle. Let your frickin' hair down, ya know? And don't give me that crap about not wanting to party where you work. Almost everyone who parties at the clubhouse either works for the Horsemen or is connected to them somehow. You might as well jump in and have some fun for a change."

This little pep talk was intended to rile me up, to convince me to embrace whatever was left of my youth, and as much as I hated to admit it, Becca was right. If I fought and scratched my way out of tagging along, the alternative was waiting for my dad to call for a ride home from whatever fine establishment he chose to park it at tonight.

To add insult to injury, I knew all too well what time he would call — right at bar close as usual — and I would still have plenty of time to spend at the clubhouse before he made the call. There really wasn't a way out and I knew it. Still, one last try...

"Well," I pushed out hurriedly. "What happens when my dad calls me needing a ride home? You know I can't let him call a cab and —"

"Maybe Eli will be able to get someone to pick him up for you so you don't have to worry about it."

Wow, Becca was just on a problem-solving roll today. Time to put my foot down. Like yesterday. We'd had this conversation before and Becca was very aware *I* needed to be the one to take him home, even if it was just so that I could see for myself that he was still breathing.

"No, you know I can't do that, Becs. Maybe I'll just stay for a little bit and then go home and then —"

"No!" Becca practically shouted in me face. "Just stay long enough to have some fun, let loose, relax a little, and when you get that call, I'll come with you if you want."

"I wouldn't dream of stealing you away from your boy-toy," I waved it off. I knew defeat when it was staring me right in the face.

Becca's face lit up. She'd clearly realized she'd just won. "So I take it that means you've officially resigned to a night of awesomeness?"

I just shrugged and took the tube of lip gloss from Becca's

outstretched hand. "I'm not sure I would go that far, but I don't see a way out of this."

"Yay!" Becca squealed and tossed her arms around her in victory.

I didn't even bother returning the hug. Resistance was futile anyways.

"Will you just promise me you'll try to have fun?" Becca was whispering in my ear now. "I mean, you look smokin' hot tonight, you're rockin' those heels you stole from my closet, and showing just enough cleavage to have some serious fun, Belle. You gotta embrace that, ya know?"

I glanced down at my attire with a cocked eyebrow, still unsure about the ensemble I'd haphazardly pieced together. With four-inch nude heels, black skinny jeans, and a shiny silver top, I looked like ready for a night at the *club* and not the club*house*. Even though it had been over four years since I'd stepped foot inside the clubhouse, it wasn't easy to wipe the images of the girls there from my mind.

Smeared makeup, barely-there skirts and too-tight tank tops seemed to be the accepted uniform there for...what were they called again? Mamas? Sweetbutts? As disgusting and misogynistic as that was, the terminology, unfortunately, was an accurate description of the women who frequented the clubhouse.

I'd made it my mission to wear as much clothing tonight as possible so there would be no confusion over what I was and what I definitely wasn't. While Becca was right, there was no way I was going to let myself get *that* loose and my outfit needed to send that message loud and clear.

So, maybe, even as I'd chosen my outfit, I'd known exactly where this night was headed after all.

Crap.

"I'm not gonna make any promises I can't keep," I stated matter-of-factly. "I'll go to the clubhouse with you, have a drink or two, and when my dad calls, I'm going to leave, alright?"

"Yes, ma'am," Becca mock-saluted. "Wouldn't dare hope you'll actually have fun."

I just rolled my eyes. "Right."

A half hour later, I was parking the Trans Am in the shop's parking lot and Becca was bouncing next to me, unable to conceal her elation. Well, at least one of us was excited.

As we stepped out onto the pavement, it took me a second to remind my feet how to walk in high heels. I hadn't worn a pair of high heels since my mom's funeral and my feet were already screaming in protest.

Adding concern over my ability, or rather inability, to walk wasn't going to help me loosen up any time soon. Still, I dutifully followed Becca up to the main entrance, my senses immediately assaulted by ear-splitting music and the stomach-churning stench of smoke and alcohol that wafted from underneath the door.

Even though I'd spent the last week here, I'd never really thought too much about what went on in the clubhouse at night. It was just easier to put it out of sight, out of mind in order to concentrate on the job at hand and then all the excitement, or catastrophe, of Ariel's exit had disturbed the generally peaceful environment I'd previously enjoyed in the office.

But now as the clubhouse loomed treacherously at my high-heel clad feet, it was absolutely terrifying. This definitely wasn't like anything I'd ever been to in college, and let's just say I didn't exactly remember much from the last time I'd been to a Horsemen party.

This was a whole different kind of beast and as my stilettos toed along the threshold of the entrance, I might as well have been stepping inside a foreign country. It didn't matter that I'd spent a week with most of the people inside already—that was different. That was work. That was a job.

At night, these people inside probably transformed into something else entirely. Or maybe they were just enhanced a little more. A little more larger than life than they already were.

Despite all that, I still knew there was nothing to be afraid of inside the clubhouse walls. I just needed to have a good time, unwind, let loose, just like Becca said. With a deep breath, I glanced down one more time at my outfit, even though it was far too late to make any changes to it now.

I looked good tonight. I was ready to have fun tonight. I was ready to finally live a little tonight.

So, I walked through the door.

. . .

The air in the clubhouse billowed around me in a swarm of must, ripe body odor, smoke, and alcohol. My eyes needed more than a few moments to adjust to this new onslaught of an environment and my senses still hadn't adapted. Everything seemed to pass by in a blur, a whirlwind of leather cuts, short skirts, booze, and weed.

At five minutes in, I still wasn't sold on this whole idea.

Becca was a few steps ahead of me, probably because she was on the look-out for her very own plate of man-meat, and just that little bit of space made me feel even more self-conscious — and isolated — than I already was.

I wasn't even all the way inside and already I'd set myself up for failure with this kind of attitude. This was supposed to be a fun night. This was supposed to be a night to let my hair down, to live a little. And I just needed to keep telling myself that.

"I'll be right back," Becca called over her shoulder as she weaved around the sweaty bodies.

To my surprise, she headed straight for the bathroom, completely ignoring Eli on the other side of the clubhouse.

Huh.

I'd expected her to make a beeline for him the second she saw him, but whatever. At this point, I was more concerned about the fact that she'd left me alone, standing in the middle of this room, when she knew I didn't really want to be here in the first place.

What the hell, Becca?

I stepped over to the bar area, desperate to hide just as much as I needed some liquid courage.

"Get the lady whatever she wants, prospect," a gruff, but familiar voice called out behind me.

I turned around on my heel only to come face to face with Dominic Fletcher, who had his girlfriend, Lexie Wright, tucked safely under his arm. Both of them were smiling at me, but it wasn't just their presence or their smiles that threw me off-guard. It was the genuine happiness and the bright, warm welcome in their eyes that had me wondering if this was a case of mistaken identities.

"Hey, Isabelle!" Lexie's grin just grew wider as she spoke, her tiny pregnant belly ever so slightly protruding out in front of her. "It's so great to see you. It's been, what, four years?"

I barely had a chance to register her words when Lexie reached up and enveloped me in a quick embrace. Although the hug was over just as quickly as it started, it still shocked the hell out of me. But then again, out of everyone connected to the Horsemen, Lexie had always been the one who seemed the most *normal*, for lack of a better word.

She was consistently unfazed by the world her soon-to-be husband lived in and if anything, seemed annoyed by it more often than not. Here I'd always thought that the women who hung around the Horsemen were the type that liked the danger, the violence, the sex, the rush, and everything else that went with it, Ariel included.

Lexie, however, just seemed to tolerate it because she loved Dominic.

"Hi," I replied with a grin. "It's really good to see you, too."

And it really was. Especially now, here in the clubhouse, where I felt like such an outsider, and already been abandoned by Becca. For all of Becca's grandstanding about how I needed to let loose and have some fun, horniness sure trumped solidarity any day of the week.

"How's it going at the shop so far? Those guys treating you alright over there?" Lexie asked.

I just shrugged and nodded gratefully to the guy behind the bar when he slid me a vodka and soda. "Ah, things are going pretty well actually. I'm liking it so far."

Lexie nodded emphatically. "Good, I'm glad to hear it. I'm sure having to be around all those greasy, smelly guys isn't exactly ideal."

I grinned back at Lexie and batted a hand in the air. "Nah, they've all been pretty nice actually. Can't say I wasn't surprised, but..."

As a familiar blonde head weaved in and out through the leather cuts and scantily-clad women, those words died in my throat. Even though I was on the opposite side of the clubhouse, Caleb's stringy, greasy hair and the way he staggered unsteadily on his feet all pointed to signs that the show was about to start.

The second I got a good look at his face, any wayward feelings of annoyance at this situation dissipated. Gone was the cocky, confident, swaggering young prince of the clubhouse and in his place was a broken, shattered man, finally resurfacing from three days of self-imposed exile. He looked so haggard, older somehow too, and just like that day back in fifth grade when Principal Moreland called him out of class, I felt my heart free-fall into my stomach.

"Shit," Dominic exhaled.

"Jesus..." Lexie muttered under her breath, her eyes sweeping worriedly from Caleb to Dominic and back to Caleb.

"What the hell is he doin' out here?" Dominic said, his voice barely audible above the blaring music. "He's just gonna make shit worse for himself, being out here."

The expression on Caleb's face was one I knew well. Even from the distance between us, the bags underneath Caleb's eyes told me he hadn't slept in days. The way his eyelids drooped down into his eyelashes meant he would be having some serious problems standing upright pretty soon and the half-empty bottle of Jack dangling from his fingertips made my eyes narrow.

Yeah, this was an image I was familiar with.

"Dom," Lexie was pleading now. "Maybe you should try to talk to him before he does something stupid."

"I can't imagine anything I have to say will change his mind," Dominic cut in quietly.

"Just try, Dom," Lexie pleaded a little more forcefully this time.

He turned towards both of us with his lips set in a firm, grim line. I swallowed nervously as Dominic and Lexie seemed to be engaging in some sort of telepathic communication, feeling like I was intruding on a moment meant to be shared just between the two of them.

A few moments later, Dominic stalked over to the other side of the clubhouse with long, purposeful strides. The entire exchange seemed to happen in slow motion as Dominic tried in vain to grab him by the shoulders, but Caleb just kept shrugging him off, wrapping his free arm around some dark-haired girl that snuck up to his side instead of acknowledging his best friend.

It was hard not to watch this in between my fingers—I knew exactly what was going to happen next, especially since this train was already on its collision course. All that remained was the inevitable crash.

When Dominic tried yet again to force Caleb's attention, all he got was the same, nonchalant response. Finally, with defeat mirrored in his eyes and a frustrated downward sweep of his hands, his head swayed from side to side as he stepped around the crowd and moved back to the bar. The confrontation had gone exactly like I thought it would, but part of me still held out hope that Caleb would listen.

My eyes widened when Caleb wasted no time in escorting the tiny brunette bimbo glued to his side down the hallway and presumably to a more private room.

As his blonde head evaporated into the hallway, I tore my eyes away and back to Lexie's troubled face. Lexie tried to make some friendly small talk after that, and God bless her for it, but my thoughts were still swimming somewhere in that dark hallway. Whatever Caleb was doing in there was his own business. I just couldn't shake the feeling that someone was standing on top of my shoulders, cementing me into the floor below.

I was frozen, held underwater, and strangled for air. Everything seemed to buzz around me in a haze. My heart thundered in my chest and I knew exactly what this was, exactly what had me rooted to this sticky floor with dread.

That ashen, gaunt look on Caleb's face was one I'd seen reflected in the mirror for months after my mom died. Seeing that twin emotion riddled all over his face was like reliving the devastation, the shock, and the emptiness all over again. Even though the loss was something that would never go away, normal functionality was slowing becoming more of a daily reality, or, at least that's what I had to tell myself.

The same, however, could not be said for my dad and that probably had everything to do with why I couldn't move now.

Grief wasn't something you could just *get over* and everything would magically go back the way it used to be. No amount of self-help books, grief counseling, or therapy could speed the process any faster, but at some point, I think my mind was just ready to let go and to find that normalcy again.

Eventually, little by little, the emptiness didn't hurt as much. It just lingered like a dull ache that showed up every once and awhile to nag at me. That wasn't the case for my dad. He was still stuck in reverse and he was still drowning.

When I looked at Caleb now, I saw the same heaviness that lingered in my dad's eyes and that scared the crap out of me. His eyes held the same haunted, tormented, and tired expression of a man that barely made it from one day to the next. Was that Caleb's fate? Was he headed down the same black highway as my dad?

I shook myself out from underwater and forced myself to swim back up to the surface. I was trying to be a different person, trying to be my *own* person.

It wasn't like I was Caleb's keeper or could even call myself a friend, so why did any of this even matter? Besides, Becca would kill me if I spent the entire party standing at the bar, staring at an empty hallway.

Still, when my phone buzzed in my pocket a little after one, I was overwhelmingly grateful, which was an abnormal feeling at best. All I had to do was hold my phone up and Becca nodded to the door, knowing me well enough to understand I wasn't accepting any help tonight, or any night for that matter. The idea of Becca, or anyone else, seeing what I saw every night made my stomach roll.

So without another word, or another thought to the darkness mirrored in Caleb's cobalt eyes, I left the clubhouse to go help the person I was actually responsible for.

.   .   .

Once I heard soft snores from inside my dad's bedroom, I tiptoed to my own room and shut the door behind me. Sleep was probably going to be an impossible feat tonight and I tossed and turned, eventually throwing the covers completely off me as I willed myself to shake the image of Caleb's empty eyes out of my head.

It just wouldn't leave. I wondered if it would *ever* leave.

Nothing else would work, not reading on my iPad, watching TV, or even listening to music, and finally, I slid out of bed to pad nervously over to my closet. Reaching up to my tiptoes, my fingers grazed the long-forgotten box on the highest, dustiest shelf.

It was telling that I knew exactly where to find it...like some sort of divine intervention. Like it was the universe's way of telling me this was the way it had to be whether I liked it or not.

At least maybe I'd be able to get some sleep tonight once it was all said and done.

When my sketchbook lay open on my lap, my fingers itched to sift through the worn, smudged pages, but I brushed that nagging aside. It wouldn't be any different than slicing through a wound that finally scabbed over and I didn't feel like putting myself through that, especially not at three in the morning.

Maybe some other night.

With a sharp inhale and trembling fingers, the pencil began to dance around the blank page, almost as if it had a life of its own. My fingers angled and curved until I got the shading just right and then I brushed a feather-light touch down an edge to finish the line.

Almost an hour passed, but I barely noticed. I'd forgotten how easily I could be swept away in a sketch, just lost in my own little world where everything else around me just faded away.

Since leaving my childhood bedroom behind for a college dorm, this sketchbook was tucked away on my shelf, out of sight, but not completely out of mind. Law school called for maturity, focus, and drive in order to succeed, which left no time for *doodling in a notebook*, at least that was what my dad had told me every time he caught me sketching.

God, I'd missed this.

And I knew I'd never get to sleep tonight if I didn't exorcise this demon out of my mind. It was as if something just tugged me to that box in the closet.

Now that the image of Caleb's empty eyes stared back at me on the page and the demon was put decidedly in its place, a calm flowed through me, something I hadn't felt in far too long. Now that it was back, I doubted I'd be able to just toss it aside like I had before leaving for Duke.

And it was that thought that propelled me back into bed and sleeping soundly with the haunting image of hollow navy-blue eyes tucked safely away and out of my dreams.

Something good *had* come from this night. I'd let loose, not in the way Becca had planned, but it was *something*...a rediscovery of what I'd buried, of what I'd forced myself to tuck away high on a dusty shelf.

Gone, but not completely forgotten.

It was a start.

CHAPTER NINE
Word Vomit

Isabelle

On Monday, I felt like I was sleep-walking through my shift. Part of me wondered if last Friday night was all just a figment of my imagination. Then again, I had the proof in my sketchbook, carefully hidden away inside my over-sized purse.

Skyler was already shuffling around the office when I reported for duty and when my boss wordlessly handed over a thick folder of invoices, the workload was a welcome relief. Distraction, in any form, was absolutely imperative today. As I slid into the chair directly across from Skyler, a quick survey through the open blinds told me the shop was still mostly empty.

Mondays typically tended to be slower business days, so the number of mechanics on hand would be few and far between, even though Skyler purposefully scheduled Mondays light so the staff always had a little recovery time from a weekend of partying. I knew that because Skyler, having judged me ready and able to take on more responsibility, had let me help make the schedule for the week.

The rest of the morning passed by without much of a hitch, a few customers here and there, but for the most part, I dove into the paperwork, letting my brain flip the switch it needed to forget everything else.

It wasn't until around noon that a nagging twitch settled into my chest. I was nervous. Anxious. And the cause of said anxiousness materialized from the clubhouse and jogged through the parking lot until he skidded into the garage.

Caleb was running late.

It wasn't so much that I was nervous about seeing him specifically. It had more to do with my anxiousness about how this first shift after Hurricane Ariel would fare for him and everyone around him.

A loud exhale behind me made me jump in my seat and my head curved to the side to see Skyler hovering over the desk, watching every move Caleb made with narrowed dark eyes, her hands fisted into her hips.

"Well," Skyler muttered under her breath. "Look what the cat dragged in."

Frustration, worry, with just a hint of disappointment, too, enveloped Skyler's already scratchy voice and it was hard not to feel the same way. Seeing Caleb's head-first downward spiral into oblivion was not something I had taken lightly and the evidence practically burned a hole through my purse.

"At least he looks a little better," I offered weakly. "I think he showered."

Skyler chuckled. "Well, I suppose that is an improvement."

The smile I tried to press to my face wouldn't quite stick. Making light of our mutual concern just didn't feel right.

"He's been scaring the hell out of me," Skyler murmured now. "I'm not sure what else to do. Everything I say, whatever I do, he just slams the door in my face."

Skyler hesitated for a moment, like she was trying to put her thoughts together, her eyes still trained on her son.

"It's not so much the women," she continued softly. "That comes with the territory. It's the drinking that scares me."

I nodded and whispered, "I've seen worse."

It wasn't a lie for Skyler's benefit. Caleb was well on the path to self-destruction, but he was only a couple miles in. My dad, on the other hand, had a few thousand miles on him.

Skyler eyes flicked over to me and for a moment, I wondered if Skyler had forgotten I was even in the office. But then, as clear understanding swept over her face, Skyler's eyes clouded in sympathy— which was unfortunate because that wasn't really what I was going for.

"If things ever get bad," Skyler offered quietly. "You know, with your dad, we'll help you anyway we can. You know that, right?"

I blinked back, my mouth opening slightly as the weight of Skyler's words echoed around me. It was way too early in the morning for such a heavy conversation.

"Now, I know you haven't been workin' here all that long," Skyler went on, striding up closer as she spoke. "But we're a loyal breed, you know? We don't let one of our own fall by the wayside if we can help it. You've been a terrific employee and you're a good girl. If you need something, all you gotta do is ask."

As much as I wanted to feel grateful for that promise, it was hard to feel anything but the way I always felt whenever anyone regarded with me even a minuscule dose of pity: bitter. That wasn't Skyler's fault. It was just nature taking its course.

So instead of saying thank you, all I could do was swallow the lump of bitter-tasting anxiety and nod.

"Well," Skyler sighed, her eyes quickly finding Caleb's blonde head. "At least he's got something to keep him occupied today."

My gaze ventured out into the garage and found Caleb hunched underneath the hood of a beat-up Mercury Sable. Even from where I stood, sleep deprivation and hangovers were written all over him. The bloodshot eyes, hanging head, clenched shoulders—all postmarked signs I knew well.

"I think it's a good thing he's even here today after..." I trailed off, knowing I didn't need to rehash those particular details with his mom. "I mean, he's here. He's working. That's gotta mean something, right?"

A glimmer of a smile crept across Skyler's face and she nodded. I almost jumped when I felt a hand ghost over my shoulder.

"Thanks, Isabelle," Skyler grinned. "Have I told you yet today how glad I am I hired you?"

"Not yet," I shrugged.

"Well, in that case, I think maybe you should get back to the morning paperwork then."

An echo of laughter bounced off the office walls as I took off for the desk and Skyler swatted me lightly on the shoulder. I was still smiling to myself when I sat down in my chair and got to work on the mountain of invoices my boss had so generously left for me. For the most part, this place was really starting to feel like it could be somewhere I belonged, somewhere that made sense, even if it wasn't long-term.

Years ago, just the very idea of going to the Horsemen for anything would've made me balk. But now, if push came to shove, it wasn't outside the realm of possibility that I might actually have to take Skyler up on her offer. And as much as the thought almost paralyzed me, I knew that Skyler also hadn't been exaggerating before. I'd been around the club matriarch long enough at this point to know she never said or did anything without a reason and she definitely wouldn't offer up the Horsemen's services if she wouldn't really deliver the goods.

The next hour seemed to fly by as a steady stream of customers made their way in and out of the office. Because of that, there wasn't much down time to even really glance out of the office window, let alone really observe what was happening outside it.

That was probably for the best though—what Caleb was going through was none of my business. Curiosity or no, I didn't really want to immerse myself too deeply in the revolving door of drama that always seemed to follow the Horsemen wherever they parked their Harleys.

So when I headed out towards the picnic tables for my break, the last thing I expected to see was Caleb sitting at my normal break table. My feet halted in the pavement, feeling stuck with indecision. But in the split second it took me to begin weighing the pros and cons of high-tailing it back into the office, Caleb's somber, haunted eyes flicked up from the spot on the table he'd been searing a hole into.

I couldn't move if I tried—his cold blue eyes held me right where I stood. And then the choice was simple. There really wasn't any other choice to make.

Clutching my lunch in one hand and shifting my purse with the other, I trekked across the pavement and stopped a few feet away from the table's bench. His cigarette, which had been nestled securely in between Caleb's fingers just a few seconds before, flew through the air towards the grass, a trail of ashes sparking behind it.

That quick flick of his wrist startled me, but if he noticed, his eyes didn't register it. His eyes didn't really register much of anything.

"Is it alright if I sit?" I asked hesitantly, almost afraid of the answer. *Might as well call this what it really is...I'm terrified.*

"Free country," he muttered, dipping his chin down towards the empty space across the table.

I pressed a tight, awkward smile to my face in response and swung my legs over the side of the bench, settling in across from him, shoving the fear of the unknown aside. My eyes flitted up to him and found his eyes were firmed locked on his folded hands at the table, so I silently unpacked my lunch and unwrapped a granola bar.

The silence, the inability to come up with anything worthwhile to say, the drooped, hunched over figure sitting across from me—it was all a little too much to handle. I needed to come up with something to talk about and quick. The awkwardness of just sitting here in complete silence weighed me down with each second that ticked by.

Something. Anything. Please, God, I can't take this anymore...

"So, it's September and I don't even really feel like I should be in school right now."

I almost wanted to clamp my hand around my mouth. Of all the things I could've said, what the hell made me say that? Pure, unadulterated word vomit.

But I was not prepared to see that his attention had now shifted away from his hands, and his gaze was observing me with clear, calculating precision like he was trying to figure me out. A moment later, his eyes slid back down to his hands. It was like he shut down again right in front of me.

"I thought I might feel differently when this came around. You know, when everyone is going back to school and settling in for classes?" I paused to gauge his reaction.

Maybe bringing up the subject of leaving for school was too close to home.

But he didn't respond and he didn't look away from his hands again. So, I did the only thing I could do in a shot to crap situation like this: I just kept talking.

"Well, anyways," I went on with a shaky laugh. God, what was I *doing*? "All my friends from school told me I would feel...I don't know, maybe sad or disappointed in myself when September came and I wasn't at Duke. I kinda believed them. You know, I thought maybe I would start to get antsy or bored without anything to do. But now that it's here, I don't feel any of that. I just feel—I don't know what the right word is. Relieved, maybe?"

My eyes flicked back to him and found his eyes still focused downward. Might as well keep talking. He probably wasn't even really listening anyway.

"I bet you're wondering why I didn't go back in the first place. I mean, that's what everyone wants to know. It's just that no one will ask. Well, besides my dad. I guess, if you're wondering," I gestured out to him with my hands even though I was sure he hadn't noticed. "The simple answer is that I don't think I've ever wanted to be a lawyer."

A weight—one that I hadn't had the courage to acknowledge before now—magically evaporated from my shoulders with those words.

I never wanted to be a lawyer. Ever.

And it was that renewed sense of strength and self that propelled me to keep talking. At this point, it didn't matter if Caleb was even paying attention. The dam had broken and now it just felt so good to finally say it all out loud.

"It was just something that was always shoved down my throat, you know? Ever since I was a little girl, that was just always the expectation. It was like the path to law school was laid out for me the second I was born. There was never an alternative. And then..."

This was the part that was going to hurt. This was the part that I had never told anyone before. This was the moment when everything started to catch up to me—why now? And why him of all people?

"And then," I took in a shaky inhale for courage. "My mom got sick. That just...changed everything. No, that's not right. It didn't just change everything. It upended my entire life. Tore everything apart. Nothing just...nothing made sense to me anymore. Nothing about being at school felt right. I mean, how could I sit there and laugh and hang out with my friends when my mom was lying in a hospital bed with six months to live? Everything that was important to me before—grades, studying, partying—it was like all that just disappeared."

I needed to take a moment to re-group. This one-sided conversation was too heavy and when I hesitantly shifted my gaze over to Caleb, my brain froze completely when I realized his eyes were on me. It *almost* seemed like he was listening.

Whatever fire had been lit under was almost toppled completely by that distraction. But then again, I'd already started. Why stop now?

What difference did it make? Still, I had to shift my eyes to anywhere but directly in front of me before pushing on.

"I couldn't stay there," I whispered, my eyes settling on a crack in the pavement. "I couldn't keep doing what I was doing and feel good about it. And then she was gone. She really put up one hell of a fight, too. Did you know the doctors told us she would only make it six months, and even that was pretty generous, but she toughed it out for eight?"

I swallowed as my brought my eyes back up to the table. Caleb shook his head and a small smile touched his lips. He was listening. For some reason, knowing someone, *anyone*, was not just hearing me, but actually *listening*...tears burned my eyes and I had to swallow them back.

"When she was gone," I sighed. "I guess I just sort of hit rock bottom. I didn't see a reason for going back to school because there was no point, you know?"

I looked to him now as I asked the question and he nodded solemnly, his eyes still fixed carefully on me, but it didn't unnerve me now the way it did before. Just seeing the understanding and the acceptance of my story in his eyes kept me on this crazy truth train and now I had no intention of getting off.

"If it didn't feel right before my mom...before she died," my breath caught on that last word because saying it out loud still felt foreign and strange. "It definitely didn't feel right after. I just don't see the point in wasting your life doing something you have no interest in and never will just to make other people happy. I mean, don't get me wrong—I broke my dad's heart when I told him I wasn't going back this semester. I spent the whole summer feeling like complete crap because of it."

Caleb's voice floated softly across the table, but the sound of it still shocked me. "But you still think you did the right thing though."

I nodded, feeling a smile tugging at my lips. He got it. He understood what I was thinking. What I was *still* thinking.

"I know I did."

His eyes softened a little at those words and his head dipped down in a nod. He shifted his weight around on the bench and he just seemed more relaxed since I started talking, like my words were the distraction, the temporary balm he needed to forget his own problems for a while. Maybe my rambling had done some good for both of us.

"So what are you gonna do now? I mean, let's face it, you're not gonna work here forever," he gestured toward the shop as he spoke.

"I have no idea," I shrugged. "I'm not in a rush. I guess I figured I just spent the last eight years doing everything my dad wanted me to do, so I don't feel like I have to have it all figured out right now."

"Yeah," he offered quietly. "I guess you earned that right."

I shot him a weak smile and shifted my gaze back down to that crack in the pavement. After a few beats and a few moments of silence, a cold shiver crawled up the base of my neck, as the reality of how much I'd just shared with him crept over my skin. That was some seriously heavy crap to tell someone I could barely call an acquaintance. Especially an acquaintance who had just had his entire life turned upside down.

"Hey," I started slowly. "I'm sorry about spilling all this on you. I'm sure you didn't really want to hear—"

His eyes darted back to me and he cut in with a frown, "You don't have anything to be sorry about, Isabelle."

"Okay, but still. Thanks for listening. It just...it felt good to say it. I don't know why I did, but it just felt good to finally say that out loud."

He nodded, a touch of smile curving into his lips. For a split second, I felt a surge of something in my stomach. Somewhere, deep down, I knew *exactly* what that was, but my subconscious knew better than to go there.

"Don't worry about it."

"Okay," I rose from the bench as I spoke. "I should probably head back to the office. Your mom's got a pile of paperwork waiting for me and I figured the only way to get on her good side today is just good ol' fashioned punctuality."

"Nice dig," Caleb chuckled lightly. He stretched his hands over his head with a yawn before shoving his hands into his front pockets. "Have fun with that."

"Thanks for..." I called over my shoulder. "Well, thanks."

A ghost of a smile traced his lips and then I turned back towards the office, my whole body feeling lighter with every step than it had in a very long time.

Purged. That's what this feeling was.

Catharsis. Much-needed catharsis.

And it felt *really* good.

CHAPTER TEN
The Land of the Living

Caleb

She had been gone for two weeks.

Two weeks since my life spun off its axis. Two weeks since everything just went black. Today was the first day I think I actually acknowledged how different everything felt.

I still felt like I was standing outside my body, watching myself go from point A to point B, just going through the motions like I was on autopilot. Programmed to eat, sleep, drink, work, and repeat. That was it.

My tired eyes fell on a random, slightly soiled, pair of panties and I scrubbed a hand over my face with a heavy sigh. That shit wasn't really helping things either.

All it—or more accurately, they—were doing was numbing me for a few moments. That was really it. I forgot her for those few moments. I forgot what she felt like, what she tasted like—I couldn't even *think* her name anymore.

This passage of time had at least granted me the gift of clarity. Once the fog lifted, the situation settled itself into something I could make more sense of: she'd betrayed my trust and then she'd abandoned me.

No amount of bullshitting myself into believing otherwise would help me. I wanted to hate her. I wanted to tear my room apart and shred every last reminder of her, but it just wasn't that simple. Not when I still saw her everywhere and in everything and because of that, it was pretty much impossible to ever acknowledge the degree of torment her betrayal had caused. So, as much as I wanted to, returning to the land of the living just wasn't in the cards for me right now.

Part of me wondered if it would ever be.

Glancing sideways at the clock, I gingerly picked up the evidence of my latest midnight indiscretion and discarded it underneath a pile of trash on my floor. Then my fingers flew over the buttons on my garage T-shirt as I stumbled out into the hallway. My shirt was still half-unbuttoned when I heard a familiar chuckle behind me.

"Running late again, brother?"

"Nah, Dom," I just shrugged. "I'm early."

Dom snatched the beanie off his head and tugged a hand through his tangled, overly-long hair with poorly-hidden exasperation. Even if I hadn't known Dom his entire life, I wouldn't have needed anything longer than a heartbeat to know something was up.

"Everything alright, Dom?"

It took my best friend a moment before he spoke again. "Everything's fine. Hey, listen, how do you feel about a change of scenery tonight? You know, get out of the clubhouse?"

I frowned and crossed my arms over my chest. "You sure everything's alright?"

His eyes lifted briefly to the ceiling before settling back down. "Yeah, brother. I just thought...I don't know. Maybe you'd want to leave the damn compound for awhile? Breathe a little bit?"

Well, I figured I couldn't blame him for feeling that way. After all, Dom had dutifully watched over my sorry ass for the last two weeks while I buried myself in Jack, weed, and sex. A change of scenery was only fair.

"Besides," Dom went on quietly. "Lex has been buggin' me about goin' somewhere that isn't so smoky. You know, with the kid, and all. I guess it's a miracle I can even get her to come along to the clubhouse anymore. I think she's just coming because she's worried about—"

And there it was.

No problem. Just keep piling on the guilt. Big deal.

"Sorry, brother," Dom stared back at me solemnly. "I didn't mean it like that."

A forced smile, if only for the sake of my best friend, pushed itself across my face and I slapped him on the shoulder.

"Don't worry about it, Dom. I didn't realize any of that was bothering her. I kinda had some, uh, arrangements for tonight though."

"Oh sure, *arrangements*," he made air-quotes with a laugh. "Whatever you wanna call it."

I already had a long-standing—meaning two days—agreement with...what the hell was her name? Alyssa? Elena? Yeah, Elena. That was it. Hot little Latina with dark hair all the way down to a pretty fine ass. Yeah.

At least I remembered her name. Sort of.

Supposedly, we'd agreed on a round two, as she'd put it, but seeing as how I couldn't even completely remember round one, I figured I could probably renege on that little agreement no problem. Still, it was easy, I was lazy, and with Elena, I would have to put zero effort into warming my bed tonight and that was good enough for me.

"You think maybe we could pencil this change of scenery in for another night?" I asked, figuring I already knew the answer.

"Saturday?" Dominic offered hopefully. "Lex was talking about hittin' up Graffiti's. Apparently, it's retro night on Saturday and she's all hard-up about listening to some shitty 80s music."

"Saturday it is."

Dominic clapped me on the shoulder and pushed me towards the end of the hallway. "Sounds good. Now get your ugly ass to work before your ma shoves her heel up your ass."

I was still chuckling to myself when I stepped into the office to clock in. My mom, of course, was anxiously awaiting my arrival, toe-tapping and all.

What a shocker.

Instead of acknowledging her helicopter-esque parenting skills, I opted to sidestep her in order to get closer to the desk so I could punch my time card and get on with this already.

"Nice to see you, too, Caleb," my mom bit out. "What's the excuse this time?"

To be fair, I'd been barely getting to work on time since I started working bitch-and clean-up duty at the shop when I was 12. Even then, Skyler was already on my case about the importance of character-building. How being on time for a job reflected work ethic and some more bullshit like that. I'd never completely bought into it and sometimes, I showed up for my shift right on the dot just to piss her off.

The last two weeks, however, fell under slightly different circumstances and my mother was well-aware of those circumstances. So, it was only fair that she laid off for awhile.

"Sorry," I held my hands up in the air in defense. "I was talkin' to Dom. Lost track of time. Sorry, Ma. It won't happen again, alright?"

She just eyed me warily. "You really think I'm stupid enough to believe that?"

"Alright, fine," I conceded with a shrug. "It won't happen again for at least a full week."

She rolled her eyes, a little bit too dramatically for my taste, and shook her head. "Well, at least you're knee-deep in something else instead of pussy."

"Thanks, Ma," I shot back. "Love you too."

Some shuffling to my left caught my attention and my eyes widened when I realized Isabelle was in the office, now scrambling to her feet and towards the nearest exit.

"I think, uh, maybe I'll just take my break now," Isabelle exhaled in a rush, barely grabbing hold of her purse as she backpedalled until her back hit the door behind her.

When I turned my attention back to my mom, her arms were crossed over her chest and she was shaking her head at me. Up until now, I'd done a decent job by-passing her impatience and frustration. My mother wanted me to just get over it already and move on with my life.

Two weeks was more than enough time to mourn, she'd told me yesterday. And while I didn't exactly appreciate her use of the term *mourn*, I also didn't agree with her logic.

Two weeks and I was just finally starting to feel somewhat human again. Of course, I used the term, *somewhat*, pretty loosely. Who the hell was she to tell me how and when to feel? Being 21-years-old should at least give me the right to wallow in self-pity for as long as I wanted.

"Caleb," my mom sighed, raking a hand through her hair. "I'm sorry if I..."

"Jumped the gun?" I finished for her, crossing my arms over my chest to mirror her current stance.

"Sure," she waved a hand. "Look, I'll try not to..."

I cocked an eyebrow at her. "Hover?"

"Sure," she rolled her eyes. "Look, what I've been *trying* to say is that I'm worried about you, alright? It puts me a little on edge and then I fly off the handle."

"I know, Ma," I offered quietly. "I'm trying. I really am. I know what you all want me to do and I'm trying..."

My mom lifted an eyebrow. "Weed, Jack, and all those girls helpin' you out with that?"

"A little," I shrugged. "So what?"

She put a hand on my shoulder and squeezed it gently. "I just wanna see you happy again. That's all. I just wanna see things go back to normal for you. I don't think that's so unreasonable."

"No," I shrugged again. Jesus, was I always going to be fighting an uphill battle with her? "It's not. But you gotta give me some space, alright? I'm fine. I really am. But you just gotta let me deal with this on my own, okay?"

The room was silent for a moment as she studied me, like she was trying to gauge just how much bullshit I'd just thrown at her.

It was all bullshit. I'd just said what she needed to hear.

That didn't make me a criminal even though I knew she wouldn't hesitate to use that as an excuse to smother me a little more. Sure, she was worried. I got that. I wanted to move on and forget just as much as anybody, but that didn't make it any less complicated. This crash-course in heartbreak really drove that point home.

Forgetting, moving on, and living was a hell of a lot easier said than done.

Suddenly, my mom was wrapping me up in a warm embrace and it took all my remaining willpower not to struggle right out of it.

"I just can't stand seeing you like this...looking like you haven't really eaten or showered in a week," she whispered into my ear. "I love you and all I want is to see you come out of the other side of this."

"I will, Ma. I will."

I didn't know who I was trying to convince more.

"I know, baby," she smiled, touching a hand to my cheek. "Why don't you head outside for a few minutes? You know, have a smoke or something, clear your head. The shop is pretty slow right now anyways and I think everyone else can handle it without you a little longer."

I nodded and forced a weak smirk on my face. Even if I didn't believe all the bullshit I'd just spat left and right, it was absolutely necessary that my mother did because she'd never leave me alone if she didn't.

She pushed me gently towards the door and I had to admit, taking a breather was a welcome distraction. The sudden ambush the second I stepped foot in the office wasn't really that big of a surprise. It was in her nature to meddle, but I liked to believe I was doing at least an okay job of hiding everything rattling my brain right now.

Guess I needed to work on that.

.   .   .

The warm North Carolina sun enveloped my face and now I could finally take a breath. If my dorm felt smaller, the office was like a closet. My feet padded out towards the usual picnic table only to find it already occupied.

A light smile curved my lips as I took in Isabelle, who was facing me but too busy hunched over the table to notice, and what was she...was she writing in a notebook or something? Curiosity getting the better of me, I edged closer to the table until I could see that she wasn't writing, but drawing in the notebook.

Huh.

This was new.

As I shuffled over to the bench, Isabelle looked up sharply, snapped the notebook shut and shoved into her purse.

"How's it goin', Isabelle?" I called over to her. "Alright if I sit?"

This seemed to be our routine lately. One of us would get there first and then the other would ask if it was okay to sit down. At this point, we both had to know it was perfectly acceptable to share a table, but courtesy was pretty much the only thing keeping the formality going.

Isabelle stretched her arms out wide and leaned back into the empty space behind her. "Free country, Caleb."

I chuckled softly and plopped down across from her, jutting my chin out towards her purse. "What were you doin' over there? Anything you wanna show me?"

When her expression shifted from mere confusion to wide with awareness and then flushed with embarrassment, a sly grin slipped across my face. It felt so good to just feel *something* again. The emotion didn't quite have a name, but it was there and I guessed that was all that mattered.

"Um, no."

If I didn't know any better, I thought I detected a little playfulness underneath that prissy exterior.

I held my hands out in defense, the smile still lingering on my lips. "Don't you worry. I'd never try to steal that notebook you were drawin' in or anything."

"Shut up, you jerk. And I'm not drawing. I'm sketching. Drawing is for two-year-olds. If you're gonna make fun of me, at least make sure you know what you're talking about."

My eyebrows shot up in amusement and I liked this little game we were playing. This time, the sarcasm and good-natured grin on her face was unmistakable. Seeing her doing something in a notebook, let alone sketching, was a fascinating little kernel of intel and this might be the only opportunity I would ever get.

"Sorry, okay? Thanks for the vocabulary lesson. Jesus," I laughed, holding my hands up one last time. "So, maybe you could show me just one sketch?"

Her blue eyes sparked and I hoped it was because I'd gotten the terminology right this time. A moment later, she shrugged as if it didn't matter. "Why do you want to see my sketches so bad?"

"I don't know," I admitted. At this point, I was really itching for a cigarette, but I'd learned my lesson about smoking around her the hard way. "Just curious is all. I didn't mean to pry or anything."

She shifted anxiously in her seat, like she was waging some sort of mental battle with herself and again, I found myself grinning as a knee-jerk reaction. The truth was, ever since she'd spilled out all the dirty details surrounding her current residence in Claremont, I'd looked at her a little differently.

In fact, Isabelle had become about twenty times more interesting and a thousand times more complicated all at once. Half the time, I sat across from her at our picnic table just wondering what she was going to say next. And when she'd sat right where she was now, brimming with tears, and still finding the strength to say the words that must've felt like a sucker punch to the gut, I'd felt a spike of something vaguely familiar.

I'd had the sudden urge to call her Iz then too, but not because I wanted to piss her off.

That had been the start.

On the other hand, I couldn't help but wonder why she'd chosen me of all people. There was no doubt in my mind she'd never told that story like that for anyone else before and I just couldn't wrap my head around it. I just couldn't imagine a situation right now that would ever put me in a position to be a friend to anyone, let alone a *good* one.

But she'd still chosen me. Even if the only reason was because I was there and she was finally ready to talk, the conversation brought me another millimeter closer to feeling like a human being again.

Some soft ruffling in front of me yanked me out of my reverie and my eyes widened when I realized Isabelle was sliding the notebook across the picnic table.

Before I could say anything or protest her decision, she quickly shook her head, like she could read my mind.

"Just don't look at the pages in the front. That's, um, that's private," she flipped open the notebook and pointed down at a page. "Start here, okay?"

I nodded, groping aimlessly for the protocol in a situation like this and came up empty. This wasn't exactly the first time I'd been in this position with her, but this felt different. She wasn't trying to fill an empty silence—she was just...I didn't know what this was. So I just swallowed tightly and slid the notebook closer, peering down at the page.

Delicate black lines outlining an image of her Trans Am stared up at me. At first, the subject itself caught me off guard but then, as my eyes studied each stroke of her pencil, each curve and shape of shading—it was like I was seeing the same car she drove to work in everyday for the first time. It was somehow more beautiful, more captivating on paper than it was in person and the fact that it had come from *her*, from *her* pencil and *her* creativity made me feel like she'd just shared something with me that most people, if any, didn't get to see.

That's what this was. That's what she was doing. The problem was I just didn't know what I could give back, what I had to offer in return.

"Wow," I exhaled, turning the notebook a little to see it from a different angle. "This is...I don't even know what to say here, Isabelle. This is so amazing."

"Thanks," she murmured softly with a hint of anxiousness.

"You know, I've been meaning to ask you," my eyes didn't leave the page as I spoke.

"Where did you get that little beauty anyways?"

"It was my mom's."

My eyes jumped back up to her in apology and she laughed nervously.

"Well, technically, it was my grandpa's, who gave it to my mom, who left it to me."

That made sense. And that definitely explained her dedication in committing the image to paper. Nothing I could come up with seemed good enough — there really wasn't a response that matched everything she'd just shared with me. So instead, I just nodded and hoped that was enough.

It probably wasn't enough.

A soft smile played across Isabelle's lips and she gestured back to the notebook. "You can turn the page. It's really okay."

I took the direction and flipped the page. And then another and another. Each new page pushed me deeper into awestruck fascination. There was a couple embracing in the shop's parking lot, a pair of wrinkled hands, a figure standing off into the shadows, a mother walking hand-in-hand with her child, a twinkling Christmas tree, a wave-filled beach, the inside of my mom's immaculate office, and a pair of intertwined hands.

Snapshots of life captured perfectly on the page.

I wished I could step inside one of those pages so I could remember what that felt like.

"Wow, Isabelle," I murmured, finally drawing my eyes back to her. "These are just...you're an amazing artist, you know that, right?"

"Oh no," she laughed lightly. "I wouldn't exactly say that."

"I would."

"Okay, well," she laughed again. "If you say so."

I nodded firmly before carefully closing the notebook and sliding it back across the table. She swept it off the top and promptly shoved it back into her purse. We sat there in complete silence for a few moments, her playing nervously with her cell phone and me staring a hole into the table.

The problem was that there just wasn't anything I could really say that would accurately explain what I was feeling. The fact that I was feeling at all was enough to completely destroy this carefully constructed mask of indifference I pulled on lately whenever people were around. That mask wouldn't help me now because I had a feeling she could see right through it.

So I just blurted out the first stupid thing that popped into my head.

"So you comin' to the clubhouse tonight?"

Isabelle hid her surprise pretty well, her eyebrows just jumping up into her forehead. "What?"

"Well, you've been comin' the last few times with Becca, right?" I recovered quickly, wanting to smack myself in the face even as I spoke. "I just figured you'd be comin' tonight too."

I wasn't even sure why this was worth bringing up in the first place. In fact, I could only vaguely remember seeing her at the clubhouse over the past few weeks. Those nights, when I got completely, numbingly shit-faced, were hazy at best.

"I don't know," she replied quickly, her brow still furrowed into a confused frown. "I'm not really sure what I'm doing tonight."

"Okay," I nodded.

Even after she waved goodbye and headed back into the office, I was still shaking my head. Of all the things I could've said to her after she once again shared something so incredibly personal, asking her if she was going to another debauchery-filled night at the clubhouse probably should've been on the bottom of that list.

That was not an appropriate response to this situation. And now I'd heard my mother's voice in my head, which was bad for me on pretty much every level.

Well, maybe there was one good thing about sitting alone at the picnic table.

    At least now I could finally have a cigarette.

CHAPTER ELEVEN
Karma

Isabelle

Despite my better judgment, I found myself dutifully following Becca inside the smoky, alcohol-drenched clubhouse. Not like I was really in the mood for yet another round of depraved revelry, but it was getting more and more difficult to come up with arguments.

It was, however, getting a little bit easier to dress for the environment. A few trips to the clubhouse and my inner party-girl was slowly crawling her way out. High heels were a little bit easier to throw on and I didn't mind showing a little bit more cleavage than I would just about anywhere else.

The jury was still out on whether or not that was a good thing.

In general, though, the inside of the clubhouse was getting easier to manage. My senses were no longer immediately assaulted and I didn't exactly feel the need to cover my ears anymore at the attack of crashing heavy-metal music. Not that I was running out to download an entire library of Metallica or Black Sabbath on my iPod, but it was becoming tolerable, to say the least.

As we rounded the corner to sidle up to the bar, we came face to face with a club member planted face first under the skirt of some random girl. While I wasn't quite sure on his name—Casey, maybe...it was difficult to keep track sometimes with all the comings and goings around here, my stomach churned at the display right next to me.

I didn't want to see that, especially not on a regular basis. Okay, so maybe I wasn't acclimating as well as I wanted to, but seriously, the average person does *not* see all this everyday and honestly? The average person really shouldn't have to, but then again, average wasn't exactly a word thrown around the clubhouse, or even the shop, very often.

Still, it was difficult not to stare. The girl looked like she was having the time of her life — never mind that the entire clubhouse was around to witness it.

Becca nudged me in the side with a sly grin. "Party's started without us, huh? Just pretend like they're not there. Let's get a drink."

Once I had a drink in hand and a little bit of necessary liquid courage, my body started to feel less rigid and more relaxed. I was even bobbing my head a little to the music. Somewhere along the way, Becca cozied herself up to Eli and I was the third wheel — again.

That was my cue to leave them alone because they were bound to end up in a dark hallway sometime tonight and Becca would've long forgotten about me by then anyways. Not that I could really blame her though; Eli was hot and being part of an MC gave him a dangerous edge I think Becca had always secretly craved.

A few more nights like this and I might find myself in a dark hallway somewhere, too.

Who was I kidding?

I didn't have the balls, figuratively, of course, to be that brazen, that uninhibited, that spontaneous and impulsive. The fact that I worked with these people was always bubbling up to the surface of my mind.

Never crap where you eat. That was a pretty big argument against doing anything remotely humiliating, let alone potentially self-destructive, at my workplace.

So when Becca predictably disappeared, casting me a quick apologetic glance as Eli pulled her away, I had to stand there, like an idiot without a cause, until my savior came sauntering through with her growing baby bump leading the way. I was almost immediately drawn into a tight embrace and now, maybe I'd finally found an ally in the midst of all this chaos.

"Hey, Isabelle!" Lexie had to practically shout to be heard over the ear-splitting beat of the song screaming from the sound system. "I'm so glad you're here. For some reason, this place is particularly annoying tonight."

"Must be the music," I replied just as loudly and pointed up in the air.

"You're right. That's gotta be it," she laughed over the music and took a quick sip from her water bottle. "It's really goddamn stuffy in here."

"Where's Dom?" I asked. He was around here somewhere; of all the times I'd been to the clubhouse, Dominic and Lexie were never too far apart from each other.

Lexie shrugged and glanced around a few times before her eyes lit up, signaling she had found what she was looking for. "He's just playing some pool over there."

There was something about the way Dominic and Lexie looked at each other, like each was the axis the other's entire world spun around, that made me a little jealous. It was the kind of unconditional, all-encompassing love that inspired poets like Keats and my personal favorite, ee cummings. It wasn't something you came across everyday, not even in passing.

On occasion, Nick had looked at me like his world would crumble without me in it, but there was nothing either of us could do to force me to feel the same way. Seeing the real thing in such close proximity just ignited a long-dormant yearning for that kind of mutual commitment and devotion.

"You don't mind just kinda hanging out here by yourself?" I asked her now.

When Lexie just shrugged again, I figured I hadn't hit on a sore subject.

"Nah, it's fine. I honestly don't mind it all that much anymore. I guess I'm just sort of used to it by now. If Dom and I were just starting out, then maybe it would be a different story," she gestured towards the bar, where two scantily-clad girls were currently grinding together on top of it. "I guess nothing really shocks me anymore. Once you've been here a few times, you've seen it all, you know?"

"Yeah," I nodded. "I guess I can see how you'd feel that way."

"It just comes with the territory," Lexie continued, waving her hand in the air dismissively. "It does help to have someone to hang out with, especially when you're new to all this."

Just when I was about to open my mouth to ask who Lexie had had with her when she was new to the clubhouse, I snapped it shut. The answer was obvious. Ariel. Of course it was Ariel. But speaking that name around here right now seemed like a pretty ill-advised idea.

As if on cue, a familiar blonde head weaved its way in and out of the crowd and suddenly, I felt like an even bigger idiot for being there. I didn't know what his motive was for asking me if I was going to be here tonight, but giving him such a tentative 'I don't know' was awkward.

I didn't want him to think I'd shown up because I'd misinterpreted our conversation earlier today at our picnic table. But, on second thought, what were the odds he was really thinking about anything right now, let alone even realized I was standing on the other side of the clubhouse? His attention was currently preoccupied by the redhead and brunette flanking both sides of him, so I guess the answer was in the question.

Lexie's heavy sigh next to me jerked me from that thought. When I turned back to face her, Lexie's entire demeanor had completely changed on a dime. Gone was the relaxed, perpetually good-natured, and suspiciously cheerful pregnant woman and in her place was a troubled, almost disturbed, sad one instead.

That reaction was probably about right.

Lexie and Caleb had known each other for years. She was getting married to his best friend and I'd had heard, through Skyler, that Dominic and Lexie already asked Caleb to be the godfather of their unborn child. Lexie had every right and every cause to be more than concerned for the guy currently hooking an arm over not one but two different women she'd never seen before.

At least the stringy, greasy hair was long gone. But his cheeks were more hollow and his clothes hung more loosely on his body than before. He wasn't the same person I remembered even from I started working at the shop three weeks ago. That person clearly left the building the same time Ariel did.

"Jesus Christ," Lexie muttered under her breath. "Please don't tell me he's going to take both of them back to his room."

There wasn't much I could say or do other than whole-heartedly agree.

"I just still can't believe she did that," Lexie continued, fire seeping into her eyes as she spoke. "I just never thought that she would...that she would actually leave him, especially not like that."

The words just came tumbling out before I could stop them: "Do you really think she would've changed her mind though?"

Now I just wanted to clamp my hand over my stupid, thoughtless mouth. If I was lucky, I might be able to actually call Lexie a friend and here I was, running my mouth about things I had no idea about, things that were painful, things that had obviously caused Lexie a lot of pain. After all, Caleb wasn't the only person Ariel abandoned, but I doubt if Ariel even really considered that notion when she'd left Claremont in her rearview mirror. She didn't deserve that much credit.

And even though plenty of assorted curses were reserved for Ariel here at the clubhouse, that still didn't mean it was acceptable to say it out loud, especially not when the two people her abandonment affected the most were standing within earshot.

But yet, despite my outburst, no flashes of anger, disappointment, or frustration crossed Lexie's face. There was just nothing on her face but sadness.

"I ask myself that everyday, you know?" Lexie finally answered, even though it came out barely above a whisper. "I asked her to be maid of honor and everything. Sometimes I wish I could just take that back. Then he wouldn't have to see her again in a few months."

"If you don't mind me asking...do you ever talk to her? I mean, is she at least still talking to you if not...?" I wasn't sure if I was overstepping here, but I just couldn't stop myself from asking and I didn't really know why I even cared in the first place.

Lexie just shrugged and sighed heavily. "I got a few phone calls, a couple of texts, things like that right after she left. Now? Not so much. I guess she's off putting her new life together in the big city."

"I'm sorry."

There wasn't much else to say because even though Lexie hadn't said it, the pain of losing her best friend was evident in her swimming brown eyes. Ariel hadn't just left one person devastated in her wake. Right about now, it seemed like a ten-car pile-up of destruction. The selfishness of Ariel to just take off like that when her best friend needed her the most—first baby, getting married—those were situations I couldn't imagine going through without Becca.

"Don't worry about it," Lexie was saying now. "What's done is done.

Other than getting her skinny ass back here for my wedding, she's never coming back."

Movement flashing from across the clubhouse's main floor caught both our attention. Caleb and his newly-formed harem were making their way through the crowd, clearly headed towards his dorm room. The problem was, in their effort to get to Caleb's dorm as quickly as possible, their path had them on a shortcut directly past Lexie and me.

Caleb sauntered lazily towards us, both arms draped around the redhead and brunette's shoulders to keep himself upright. As they ambled closer, the glassy, dazed look in Caleb's eyes sent a cold shiver down my spine.

Yeah, that looked familiar.

Lexie was already shaking her head in disgust when Caleb and his future bedmates were only a few feet in away. That movement must have caught his attention because his steps skidded to a halt, nearly bringing the two equally drunk ladies down.

"Oh, hey, Lex," Caleb slurred, a lazy, barely cognizant smile slipping across his features. "How's it goin'?"

Lexie blew out an exasperated breath and clenched her jaw. "Oh, *hi*. Looks like your night is off to a *great* start."

Caleb clearly missed the sarcasm in her voice—the disoriented, sleepy expression on his face said as much—and he just nodded with a shit-eating grin.

Looks like he's at least coherent enough to know he's about to get laid. Nice.

His lips parted when his gaze landed on me long enough to finally realize I was standing there too. "Hey, Iz—shit, I mean, Isabelle. I didn't think you were comin' tonight."

I just shrugged, not wanting him to stand there with his arms wrapped around two barely-clothed women any longer than necessary. "I guess I changed my mind."

Teetering unsteadily on his feet, he managed to nod. "Cool."

He stood there for a moment longer, just enough to make me feel uncomfortable, until the redhead tugged impatiently on the arm draped around her shoulder and motioned with her head towards the hallway.

"See ya, Lex. Later, Isabelle," he called out over his shoulder as the girls led him away and down that dark hallway.

After a few moments of staring at the empty space left behind by Caleb, Lexie shook her head again in complete frustration. There really wasn't anything left to be said and truth be told, Caleb's little appearance had really sucked any fun out of the night I might've had. Lexie shifted anxiously next to me and I turned to see her tugging a hand through her dark hair in exasperation.

"Well," Lexie exhaled. "I'm not sure my night could get any worse than that. Might as well quit while I'm ahead. I'm think I'm gonna go find Dom and see if he can take me home."

"Sure," I nodded.

Right about now, I really wished there was a way I could follow Lexie's lead.

Unfortunately, I'd miscalculated how this night was going to go and actually let Becca drive us there. Fool me once, shame on you. Fool me twice...

I figured Lexie and Dominic would probably give me a ride if I asked, but I didn't want to come off looking like some needy, helpless girl they used to know in high school.

"Hey, you know, I was thinking," Lexie leaned in closer to me so I could hear her. "We should go out for lunch sometime. Do some shopping, something like that. What do you think?"

I didn't need any time to consider my answer. "Yeah, absolutely. Maybe sometime next week?"

"Sure," she nodded excitedly. "I can pick you up during your lunch break. I usually come during Dom's break, but he'll get over it."

After we exchanged numbers, Lexie leaned forward and whispered in my ear: "Don't stay too long, alright? If you need a ride or something, just text me and we can bring you home."

Then Lexie was gone and I was on my own.

In the clubhouse.

Fun.

A few spilled drinks later and I was officially ready to leave. Stickiness seemed to saturate every inch of my clothes and my skin and even in a crowded room full of sweaty people, I just felt cold. What I really needed right now was a pair of pajamas, a blanket, a good book, and maybe a fireplace, but that wasn't happening anytime soon.

It wouldn't do me any good to go looking for Becca either; I knew I'd get a text message when Becca and Eli were, ah, *finished*. Seeing as how they'd been gone about an hour already, I probably had some more time to kill.

People were drinking, laughing, dancing, playing pool, and just having a good time. Well, everyone was having a good time but me. I guess I had no one to blame for that but myself, too. Becca was in a room somewhere doing God knows what with her boy toy. Caleb was in a room somewhere doing God knows what with those two skanks.

So why the hell was I standing here, all by myself, and feeling like crap?

And now, I was pissed.

How many times had I seen the same old song and dance from Caleb? Get falling down wasted, bang some random chick, pass out, and repeat. That seemed to be his life now and who could actually be happy living like that?

It had only been two weeks since Ariel left and his nights were just a revolving door of nameless girl after nameless girl. Each empty hookup sunk him another inch further into the sandpit he was already waist-deep in.

I saw enough of that with my dad and I didn't need to see that here, too. Not when it was a Friday night and I was supposed to be letting loose and having fun for once in my life and not when I was supposed to be preoccupied with figuring my own life out, too.

Worrying about someone else's wasn't exactly on my to-do list tonight or ever.

If I was being completely honest with myself, the worse part was that it seemed like Caleb was with a different girl every night. That really shouldn't bother me. It was his business, his life to screw up, his dirty laundry.

Did it bother me because he was slowly killing himself? Because the endless cycle of empty sex was so far removed from anything I would ever do? There were a few other options darting around in my head, but I didn't want to touch those with a 10-foot pole.

Ugh.

Regardless, I was sick of watching this sad show play out. Suddenly, the air in the clubhouse felt thick and stuffy. It was goddamn stifling. I just couldn't stand to be in this room another minute. Not when I knew exactly what was happening just a few rooms away.

My tired feet carried me through the crowd and pushed me outside the clubhouse doors. The cool breeze hit my face and I finally felt like I could breathe. Now that I had some space, the suffocation I'd been struggling to smother didn't feel like such a menace.

There was a crowd of people inside, many of whom I worked with on a daily basis, and here I was, happier outside and alone.

If that wasn't antisocial, then I didn't know what was.

The clubhouse doors creaked behind me and I whirled around to find Caleb, alone, stumbling out onto the pavement with unsteady feet. His eyes were focused intently on the lighter in his hands and he struggled for a few moments to bring his cigarette to the flame.

Then he inhaled deeply, blowing out the smoke through his nostrils, as he ambled further down the clubhouse's walkway.

When his eyes finally shifted away from the pavement and to where I stood a few feet away, Caleb's cloudy blue eyes widened as his brain finally seemed to catch up to him. He fumbled around in his pockets, trying to shove the lighter away, and promptly stomped the cigarette out on the pavement in front of him.

He'd done that every time we'd been around each other since I'd not-so-nicely asked him not to blow his smoke in my face, but that still didn't erase the rest of the night's events. And I was tired and my feet hurt from these stupid heels I'd tried to squeeze into and I just wanted to crawl into my bed and forget everything and everyone.

In other words, I was in no mood for his crap tonight.

"That was quick," I bit out.

He just shrugged and shoved his hands into his front pockets. "Yeah, well, I guess it was a pretty poor showing on my part."

"I'm sure Thing 1 and Thing 2 are crying into their beers right now."

His eyebrows rose in amusement and a grin twisted into his lips as he shuffled closer to me. Wait a minute, that wasn't exactly the reaction I was going for. The closer he got, the more my heart thundered anxiously in my chest.

For a moment, that glassy look in his eye veered towards something else — not exactly threatening, but not exactly friendly either. And that did nothing for my nerves because he just kept coming closer.

Caleb's whole body suddenly seemed to jerk backwards like he'd just smacked into an invisible wall and his knees buckled underneath them. Instinct sent my arms immediately out to his shoulders to keep him steady on his feet and just as it felt like he'd regained his balance, his head jerked forward and his stomach emptied violently out in front of him.

All over my studded stilettos.

Wow. Karma really was a big, fat bitch.

There wasn't much I could do but jump into damage control mode as he sunk lower, still heaving, and a last second shift of our weight was the only thing that kept us both from sliding down into the mess he'd just made all over the grass. And on my studded stilettos.

With a wince, I kicked off my ruined shoes and turned my attention back to the more pressing matter at hand.

"Shit," Caleb panted as he gasped for air, his hands fisted into his knees. "Sorry, Iz, I—"

Another rush of vomit interrupted those words and I had to look away, grimacing as he heaved out into the grass. All I could do was hold his shoulders and hope it was helping. At some point, I found myself rubbing a hand on his leathered back until he came up for air, his head still hovering in between his knees.

"Fuck my life," he sputtered and I winced again as he spit into the grass a few more times.

He straightened up a little bit, but I kept my hands firmly glued to his shoulders just in case. After he wiped his mouth and his watering eyes, he was standing completely upright with both hands scrubbing across his face.

"Caleb," I started softly. One hand fell from his face at the sound of my voice. "Let's get you back inside. Should we go through the front door or...?"

He immediately shook his head, still teetering a little too unsteadily on his feet.

"There's a back door," he mumbled in between deep inhales. "You don't have to...you don't have to do anything. I'll be fine. I'll just go find

Dom or somethin'."

Even as he spoke, his knees started to buckle again and my arms shot out to his chest to help him balance his weight.

"Dominic took Lexie home a little while ago, so it looks like you're stuck with me," I whispered loudly, grabbing hold of his arms to keep him upright. "Come on, let's go. Just try to stay on your feet, okay? You go down, I go down."

Somehow, he managed to chuckle under his breath in spite of our current predicament and swung an arm around my waist to balance himself. When his fingers brushed the space between my tank top and my jeans, way too close for comfort, I grabbed his hand and shoved it back up my waist.

"I swear to God, Caleb," I muttered harshly because I was *really* not appreciating the turn this had taken. "If your hands move any lower, I will punch you in the face."

His hands immediately shot up in defense, his bloodshot eyes wide with surprise. "No touching. Got it, Iz. I promise."

This was going to be a long night.

CHAPTER TWELVE
Iz

Caleb

Puking my guts out on the sidewalk and all over Isabelle's shoes had, at the very least, sobered me up pretty quickly. Splashing some cold water on my face helped too and now I was standing in my bathroom, hands splayed over the sink, staring into the mirror.

Hell if I even recognized the reflection staring back at me. This entire night was a new low and that was really saying something.

First, I'd gotten so plastered I could barely see two feet in front of me, then I hadn't been able to keep it up for Elena and her friend, or Thing 1 and Thing 2, as Isabelle had so aptly called them, and now this —throwing up all over Isabelle's feet.

Honestly, I've never felt so ashamed in my entire life. And here I thought I'd hit rock bottom a long time ago.

Shows what I know. Christ.

Thank God I'd been coherent enough to remember the back entrance otherwise the entire club would've been witness to this, too. I'd had to rely heavily on Isabelle's much smaller frame to get myself through the door and into my dorm, which was pretty damn shameful.

Now she was waiting for me out in my room and all I wanted to do was just crawl down onto the cold floor and shut everything else out. And maybe throw up again.

She didn't have to do what she did tonight. She could've easily just left me out there to my own pathetic devices, but she'd practically pushed me into the clubhouse herself. There were clearly better things she could've been doing with her night and that made me just want to hide even more. But I figured I owed it to her to get my ass out of this bathroom after everything she'd dealt tonight with because of me.

When I cracked the bathroom door open, she was shuffling through some trash on my desk. Damn, I really needed to do a better job of cleaning this hole up.

"Hey, I was just looking for a cup or something to get you some water," she held up a coffee mug with a sheepish grin.

"Sure."

I stepped aside as she slid past me towards the sink. When my shins hit the side of the bed, something told me that sitting on my bed right now would be the wrong choice. I'd literally just had not one but two girls in this same bed and here I was now with yet another one in my bathroom. It didn't even matter that nothing much had happened with those two girls tonight.

Because the two circumstances were so wildly different, my stomach churned just at the thought of Isabelle coming anywhere near this bed. So I slid down to the floor until I was resting sort of comfortably with my back against the edge of my bed.

A water-brimmed coffee mug appeared in front of my face and after I took it from her, I patted the ground next to me, my eyebrows lifting at her understandable indecision.

Isabelle shifted a little from side to side, like she was weighing whether or not this was a good idea. Truth be told, as much as my head was pounding right now, I just didn't want to be alone. I'd been alone, really in every sense of the word, for the last two weeks and found myself needing her company tonight more than anything inside the clubhouse.

There was something about her that I couldn't put my finger on, something about the conversations we'd had that made me feel...*something*.

Maybe it was just because I knew more personal details about her than I probably really knew about anybody—real pain and real loss— and that she'd come out of it on the other side. Maybe I just needed to see the evidence for myself that things would eventually get better for me, too.

And I really, really needed her to sit down right now.

Finally, she dropped down next to me, careful to keep a safe distance away, which was just fine because that wasn't what this was about.

"Thanks, Isabelle," I murmured softly.

"No problem," she replied, her voice barely above a whisper. "It's not a big deal, Caleb, especially seeing as how I kinda owed you anyways...and it's not like I had anything else going on tonight, you know?"

I knew she'd meant it as a joke, but the hitch in her voice had me wondering what she was even doing at the clubhouse tonight in the first place.

"Aw, come on," I shook my head. "Don't you have to avoid what's-his-name's texts or somethin' like that?"

"I actually haven't heard from him in a few days. I took your advice, by the way, and told him I'm seeing someone else now. I can't say I liked lying to him, but I guess it worked. At least I hope it did."

I held up two twisted fingers with a grin. "Fingers crossed?"

"Yeah," she laughed. "So no desperate ex-boyfriend. My best friend's having some alone time with Eli and so I'm stuck in the clubhouse for awhile anyways. What else did I have going on that was so pressing I couldn't help carry your sorry ass in tonight?"

I nodded, but that was still besides the point. "I mean, a girl like you has gotta have something better to do than hang out with assholes like us, right?"

"What do you mean?"

"I guess I just figured someone that's got their shit together like you would have better things to do," I shrugged. "And I don't mean anything by that. I just..."

What I wanted to say was that someone like her was just wasting her time being anywhere near someone like me. I was a train wreck, off the rails and all. Besides, it wasn't like I stood a snowball's chance in hell of ever...

There were miles in between her and the girls that were literally just in this same room because she wasn't that type of girl. She was better. In a way, she reminded me of Lex, who was barely tolerant of the club simply because of who she'd chosen to be with. If not for Becca, Isabelle would've been somewhere else tonight and it was as simple as that.

"I just," I started again. "I just feel like — I feel like shit."

It felt good to finally say that to someone.

Everyone around me was already thinking it, and I knew I looked exactly like I felt too, but no one would say it to my face. At least now, I had the satisfaction of beating everyone else to the punch.

I waited for her to say something, but maybe her silence was giving me permission to say whatever I needed to say.

"I guess I haven't felt like myself for awhile now and I'm sorry you had to put with me tonight."

When she was still silent next to me, I wondered if I'd shared too much. Some things just aren't meant to be spoken out loud and the words stung worse than I thought they would. It was that kind of dull ache that probably wasn't going to go away anytime soon.

"Hey, Caleb?"

My head jerked at the sound of her voice. "Yeah?"

"I hope this isn't too out of line, but I'm gonna say it anyways, okay?" she waited for my nod of approval before continuing. "My mom used to tell me that if a guy really wanted to be with you, I mean if he *really* loved you, he would move heaven and earth to be with you. He wouldn't let anything stand in the way of being with you and would do whatever it took to make things work. I think that goes both ways, too."

It took me a moment to really process everything she'd just said. And for some reason, it was almost a relief to hear someone finally say that out loud, too.

"So you're saying if Ariel had really wanted to be with me, she never would've left in the first place?"

Her eyes widened slightly, like she'd just realized that maybe she'd overstepped.

"I just think you've been spending all this time and energy mourning something that was probably never going to work anyways," she told me in a soft voice I almost didn't recognize. "I know I don't know the first thing about your relationship, but from what I do remember about you and Ariel, it was probably always headed this way, you know? You're never going to leave Claremont and there's nothing wrong with that. This is your home. This is where your family is. This is where the club is. But I guess Ariel just wanted something different. Not necessarily more, just...different. Maybe you were always headed in opposite directions. You just couldn't see it right away."

"Doesn't make it hurt any less," I mumbled.

"I never said it doesn't."

At this point, she'd shifted her body so that her entire head was turned towards me. Her sky blue eyes seemed to glimmer in the soft lamplight just above her head and I had a sudden urge to sweep a wayward piece of hair off her face to tuck it behind her ear, but that was a line I wasn't going to cross with her—especially her.

"It's hard to watch you do this to yourself," she went on quietly. "Random girls aside, I'd be willing to bet that the only time you're not drinking is when you're on the clock. Don't ask me how I know that...it's just that, God, Caleb, you're not taking care of yourself. I've never seen you eat a full meal at work these last two weeks and you look like you haven't gotten a full night's sleep in days. You just, well, you look like shit. And I guess that makes sense if that's the way you feel. But for what it's worth, and you can be mad at me later for saying this, but...nobody is worth that, Caleb. I don't care who they are or what you think they mean to you, nobody is worth killing yourself over and anybody that would willingly put you in this position doesn't deserve you anyways."

Her words sliced through my chest, a direct hit on her target. Hearing all of that—everything I knew the people around me were thinking, but wouldn't say to my face—was a hard slap of reality. The sting still lingered long after Isabelle turned her tired blue eyes back to the carpet.

She was right. I knew she was right. If she'd put money down on that bet, I would've had to pay up. The worst part was she really didn't know me well enough to be able to just assume all this just by looking at me, but she still knew it all anyways.

Words failed. It just didn't make any sense. She knew all this from what, observation? We were tentative acquaintances at best. We shared a lunch table together and talked sometimes while we ate. That was really it.

Yet she still understood something so basic, so raw about me. It was like she took one look at this haphazardly constructed wall of booze and empty one-night stands and saw me exactly for what I was: lost, broken, damaged, and completely pathetic.

The thing was...Isabelle didn't look at me like I was beyond repair. She looked at me like maybe I had a shot at actually gluing myself back together. And as that reality wove its way into my consciousness, the request fell out of my mouth before I could stop myself.

"You know, I really am sorry I've pissed you off so much," I whispered hoarsely, staring into the mug clenched in between my hands. "I never meant to—look, do you think it'd be okay if I still called you Iz?"

She blinked back at me. "What?"

"I don't know," I started to explain, but for the life of me, couldn't grasp the words. "I know you don't like it, but I guess that's just who you are to me. It's weird to call you anything else and I swear to God I'm not tryin' to be an asshole. I mean it."

She said nothing and gave away nothing.

"I've been tryin' to figure out what this is," I was fumbling now. After everything that had happened tonight, I needed her to understand, but I also needed her to not take this the wrong way. "When I'm talkin' to you, I feel normal again. Like this isn't the end of the world. I didn't mean that you're not normal...that's not what I'm tryin' to say. I don't think that. I just mean that *you* make me feel normal. Like I'm not some sort of goddamn freak that everyone needs to tip-toe around and whisper about like I'm not standing right there."

It hadn't come out as eloquent as what she'd said to me, but it would have to be good enough. Isabelle had relaxed a little bit more and a ghost of a smile lifted her lips. Well, at least she didn't look like she wanted to slap the hell out of me. Maybe the message was delivered as I'd intended, which was probably a first for me.

"So..." I prompted, waiting for the answer to my not-so-articulate question.

She chewed on her bottom lip in thought, scrutinizing me with careful, clear blue eyes. Finally, her lips curved up and for the first time in months, I was about to finally get something I wanted.

"I guess I could live with it," Isabelle allowed. "As long as you promise to start eating normal meals again. And take a shower. Seriously. You stink."

"Got it. Thanks, Iz," I grinned victoriously, relishing the feel of saying that name again. I hadn't realized how much I'd missed it until I had it back again.

"For the record," she grinned back. "I really *don't* have my shit together."

"Sure you do."

She just shrugged, leaning forward to hug her knees into her chest. "Well, I don't. I don't think anybody really does."

I wanted to say that someone like her, who'd been through just as much pain and destruction in her life as me, if not more, to not be falling down drunk, in some sort of rehab, in bed with some random guy, or doing anything else that could be labeled self-destructive, well, she was doing okay. A helluva lot better than me, that's for sure.

Quitting school and working at the shop didn't qualify as reckless in my book. And it was easy to just sit there next to her and enjoy this feeling, this normalcy for a little bit longer because soon, her cell phone buzzed in her pocket and she stepped out of my dorm to meet up with Becca.

Then I was alone again, lost in the emptiness surrounding my room and what was left of my pathetic, miserable life.

Great.

CHAPTER THIRTEEN
FML

Two Weeks Later

Isabelle

"Come on, now," Dominic yelled, thumping his fist against the counter. "One more! You can do it! I know you got it in you!"

"Oh God, no!" Becca cried out. "I can't look! Oh my God, I think I'm gonna be sick."

"Do you not see that I'm goddamned pregnant here?" Lexie demanded, one hand fisted into her hip and the other resting firmly on her stomach.

"I don't care," Caleb shot back with a wide grin. "She's doin' it whether she likes it or not."

I gulped and then had to squeeze my eyes shut when swallowing down phlegm did nothing for my courage. Crap, that didn't work either. One eye flipped open and all four of my bar companions at Graffiti's tonight were staring at me with either eager expectancy or disgusted hesitancy.

My current nemesis glared up at me and I met it head-on. When someone dares you to take a Three Wise Men shots, you can't turn him or her down, especially when that someone's name is Caleb Sawyer.

You just suck it up and you do it.

I blew out a breath, more for strength than anything else, gripped the cold glass in between my shaky hands, and then downed the entire contents. Nothing but sheer willpower kept it all from coming right back up.

Just as the room seemed to twirl on its axis, a pair of strong hands ghosted across my back to hoist me up just enough to keep my balance.

Given that Dominic and Eli were to the right of me and the hands came from the left, even my current dizzy, alcohol-leaden state couldn't confuse whose hands were on me now.

Don't shiver and definitely don't stare at him like you want him to keep touching you in other places, too.

"Easy there, killer," Caleb laughed softly, keeping a hand lightly on my back to make sure I wouldn't sway again. A second later, his hands shot up in defense. "Sorry, no touching. I forgot about that, Iz."

I smacked him on his leather-clad chest and shrugged. Lexie slid a tall glass of water over to me with a mirthless cringe and I knew it was only because I'd just made us both literally and figuratively sick. If anything, it was a good distraction from all feelings Caleb kicked up with that nickname.

"Don't worry about it, Caleb," I replied, my eyes widening when I realized how much my words were slurring.

If I didn't take it easy for the rest of the night, I was going to be face down in a bathroom somewhere before I knew it. That water couldn't go down fast enough. There was a small part of me that whispered words like *hypocrite* and *idiot*. Here I was, doing the very same thing that was basically destroying what was left of my family.

You're allowed to have fun with your friends, I told myself. *Seriously. You're 21-years-old. And you're not him. You're not the one with the problem. Quit your bitching.*

"I never lost faith in ya," Caleb leaned in a little closer so I could hear him over the buzzing crowd behind us.

"Well, thanks," I laughed. "Now that I know I'm capable of such an amazing feat, I'll finally get to sleep tonight."

Caleb's head fell back as his shoulders shook with laughter. "Good, I was worried about that, Iz."

His calloused hand grazed over my skin and gently squeezed my shoulder before snatching his hand back almost as quickly as he started. I couldn't decide where the fluttering in my stomach was coming from: that whisper-like touch or the copious amount of alcohol I'd just consumed.

Probably both.

Although it had completely snuck up on me, our interactions had subtly shifted since the night he'd emptied his stomach and his dignity all over my studded stilettos. The next morning at the shop, Caleb wordlessly set a bag of Gardetto's and an ice cold can of Mountain Dew on my desk and walked out of the office with a sly wink.

On the outside, he pulled on this persona of the careless and cool bad boy. Maybe that worked when we were in high school, but now, I knew better.

Sure, he had swagger in spades, but the facade just crumbled whenever we were alone. The carefree asshole I thought I'd known, the same one who buried himself in whiskey and women just because it was fun and because he could, didn't exist.

He wasn't an asshole. He was just...complicated.

A walking, talking, cocky, and sweet contradiction.

In the two weeks since that night at the clubhouse, when I'd bluntly told him exactly what I thought of she-who-shall-not-be-named, an easy understanding had blossomed between us. The more time I spent with him, the easier it was be around him.

The conversations at our shared picnic table carried on and our interactions had become — dare I say it — friendly. I had, above all odds and circumstance, become friends with Caleb Sawyer and I knew this because I'd told him things about myself I'd never told anyone before.

And I couldn't even begin to wrap my head around his reaction to my sketches. No one had ever taken my sketching seriously before and no one had ever called me an artist before. He'd just taken one look and that was it. No arguing. No room for judgment. He'd just accepted me as I was without questioning it.

I didn't know what to do with that.

It was that thought that propelled me towards the bathroom for a break. Those shots of tar and sludge must have really went straight to my brain. Some splashes of water woke me up a little more and I quickly reapplied some powder so I wouldn't look so scary. A little more lip gloss didn't hurt either and with a deep breath, I pushed through the bathroom door only to collide into a mass of solid muscle.

"Oh crap, I'm so sorry!"

My hands immediately thrust out to steady myself and when I looked up, a familiar pair of chocolate brown eyes stared down at me.

"Brandon?"

"Isabelle?"

Brandon Davis was gaping back at me in happy surprise, a beer in hand, and a cigarette dangling between his fingers. For a moment, I think I forgot where I was. Right before the start of our freshmen year of college, we'd parted ways, having the foresight to realize that a long-distance relationship wouldn't last longer than a few months once we settled into colleges hours away from each other.

A beat later, I was enveloped into the strong arms I used to know so well.

"What the hell are you doin' here?" he practically shouted into my ear he seemed so happy. "I thought you were back in town. How are you?"

Ah. Such a loaded question. But this wasn't the time or the place to saddle him with any of that, if ever.

"I'm good," I pushed out quickly, wrapping my arms around his neck to hug him back. "It's so great to see you."

"You too, Isabelle. Who ya here with?"

I pointed over his shoulder to where Becca was waving with a loopy smile on her face.

"Wait—is that? Caleb Sawyer and Dominic Fletcher?" Brandon frowned, gripping his beer bottle a little tighter. "You're here with *them*? When the hell did that happen?"

"I actually work at the shop now. Becca's dating one of the Horsemen too and I guess it's all kinda relative there, you know?"

"Yeah. Sure. So, you're working there now. Cool. Hey—"

"Yo, Brandon, you comin' or what?"

He turned his head and now I had a clear view of the guys who were yelling and waving him over. They were the exact same burly, preppy, dumb football players Brandon had hung with in high school.

Now, I'd known Becca since kindergarten, and we'd seen each other almost every day since I'd been back in town, but I couldn't bite back the twinge of disappointment seeing that, at least on the surface, not much had changed since the last time I saw him, as hypocritical as it was.

"Yeah, just give me a second, okay?" Brandon called over his shoulder. When he turned back to me, he rubbed a hand nervously over the back of his neck. "So, uh, I was wondering if you wanted to maybe, I don't know, get together sometime. I could take you for coffee or dinner or something so we can catch up...shit, it's just so *good* to see you. I must sound like a real asshole right now."

I laughed lightly with a smile and just shrugged. "No, you don't. It's really good to see you, too."

"So..." he flashed me that boyish, dimpled, shy grin that had always sent a warm rush directly to my abdomen.

"I would tell you to call me, but I have a new number since we last saw each other."

"Well," he grinned widely. "We should take care of that, huh?"

In spite of the fact that we were standing right next to a grimy bathroom and standing on the sticky floor of a dive bar neither of us would've come within a mile of four years ago and despite the fact that I hadn't spent all that much time wondering what would've happened if we'd tried to stay together, I found myself smiling back at him.

He looked exactly the way I remembered—dark hair mussed up messily with gel, a little bit of stubble, and lean, strong muscles peeking out from his shirt. It wasn't like we'd split because our relationship crumbled—it was more like we'd had a realistic understanding of what long distance would do to us.

At the time, it was the right decision for both of us. We were young and I'd wanted to experience college just as much as he did, but circumstances were different now and college was in our rear view mirror.

So I gave him my number.

After another quick hug, he left to meet up with his party and I headed back towards mine. Becca wasted no time before she descended.

"Hey!" she untwisted herself from Eli long enough to grab my arm with a wickedly mischievous grin. "Was that Brandon Davis?"

"Um, yeah," I replied, my eyes flying to the audience at our table.

"So..." Becca trailed off, her eyebrows lifting impatiently as she waited for me to answer.

"He asked for my number. I think we might get together sometime soon or something," I shrugged noncommittally in an effort to sound unfazed by the whole thing.

If I was being completely honest with myself, it probably had something to do with the fact that Caleb had visibly stiffened less than a foot away from me. Given our history, I had no idea why this new development even mattered to him.

"Okay," Becca nodded quickly. "So, what now? Are you guys gonna...?"

"Geez, Becs, give me a second, alright?" I exhaled in exasperation.

We had literally just reconnected and already, Becca was jumping to delusions of grandeur.

Was it too much to ask for a little breathing room?

"Okay, okay," Becca's eyes widened as she spoke. "Geez, simmer down, will ya? I just forgot how hot he was and I got all excited for you. So sue me."

"Hey," Eli interjected. "I'm standing right here."

"Aw, come on," Becca smacked him playfully in the chest. "You know this has nothing to do with you."

Of course, it wasn't helping that all eyes and ears were directed towards our conversation. All I wanted at this point was for Becca to just let it go. We could talk about it later as soon as our current company's attention was occupied elsewhere.

All four of them were watching this play out with a varied mix of interest, mostly from Lexie, and annoyance, mostly from Dominic and Eli. Caleb was a harder read, landing somewhere in the middle as he stood a little too close for comfort with his arms folded tightly across his chest.

When Eli started nuzzling Becca's neck, I had to look away before my eyes started bleeding. Unfortunately, when I turned my head, my eyes collided with Caleb and the cloudy glint in his eyes sent a shiver down my spine. I smiled tightly, more so to reassure myself than anything else, and nearly closed my eyes with relief when the gesture was returned.

"So, Iz," a coldly detached voice called out to me from the left. "That asshat looked pretty happy to see you."

I rolled my eyes dramatically, more to downplay his animosity than anything. "C'mon, Caleb."

He just shrugged nonchalantly. "What?"

"Why don't you just go over there and have your stupid pissing contest already? And you know what? I bet one of the bartenders could probably find us a ruler too. Might as well get it all over with in one shot and find out whose dick is bigger once and for all."

I hadn't meant for that all to come out so...bitchy, but something about this dark, brooding attitude from him—and directed at me—had me sharpening my claws. Since I barely said a word about his weekend conquests at the clubhouse, it really wasn't too much to ask that he extend the same courtesy.

If I'd been expecting some sort of declaration of lifelong hatred towards Brandon Davis, something that wasn't exactly a secret anyways, I wasn't going to get it tonight. Instead, the cloudiness simmering in his eyes faded away. Now, Caleb's ocean-blue eyes glimmered with cocky mischief as he draped his arm over my shoulder once again with that crooked grin spreading across his lips.

"Wouldn't you like to know?" he murmured in my ear and leaned back with a sly wink.

Yes. I think I would.

Wait, what?

Heat flushed through my entire body, starting right where his mouth had just been and shooting all the way down to my toes. My eyes widened as his words and my thoughts finally caught up to my brain. When my head snapped to the right, only to find the rest of our table watching the scene with varied degrees of confusion and cocked eyebrows, that heat rushed right to my cheeks.

Caleb's arm slipped from my shoulders and the sudden loss of contact had me sucking in a breath.

What the hell?

Then he reached for the neck of his beer bottle like he hadn't just knocked me completely off-kilter, like he hadn't just sent shockwaves through my entire body with his little innuendo.

Asshole.

Against my better judgment, I dared one last glance to the other side of the table, only to find Becca and Lexie watching us with curious interest and Dom and Eli looking anywhere but at me.

Great.

CHAPTER FOURTEEN
Back-Up

Caleb

The stupid part just wouldn't slide in. I'd triple-checked to make sure I'd sized and greased it and the damn thing still wouldn't go where I needed it to go.

Story of my life.

Great, now I was thinking in metaphors and analogies and turning into a melodramatic chick.

One more turn of my wrench and finally, the damn thing slid into place. Just in time for my break too.

I'd spent way too much time and energy on one project and my mom was probably about ready to rip me a new one judging from the way she kept pacing around the office and flying daggers my way.

Speed and efficiency, she always drilled into my head, and today, it was painfully obvious my job performance wasn't exactly up to the auto mechanic Nazi's standards. But then again, my mom didn't exactly have realistic standards for just about anything.

I tossed a spent towel into a bin and headed straight for the parking lot, careful to keep my head down. Part of me just wanted to talk to Isabelle. The rumor floating around was that she'd been out with that asshole Brandon Davis a few times already and that they were getting back together.

Although I didn't typically make a habit of giving a shit about other people's personal lives, this new development was particularly unsettling.

Did I want to see Isabelle happy?

Of course I did.

But did that mean she had to get back together with a dipshit loser like Davis in order to do it?

Absolutely not.

It really wasn't any of my business to begin with, but I couldn't forgo the need to find out what exactly was happening there.

As I rounded the corner of the garage and stepped out onto the pavement, I almost skidded to a stop.

The picnic table was empty.

Huh.

Since the day she'd started here, it was like clockwork. My breaks almost always coincided with Isabelle's and I was positive we were scheduled to take the same break today. So where the hell was she?

Maybe Skyler or some customer was throwing her off schedule but from what I'd seen, Isabelle was punctual to a fault.

She hated being late for anything.

With a shrug, I plopped down on the bench and dug into my back pocket for my cigarettes. The good news—I could have a cig and not feel like a piece of garbage for smoking in front of Isabelle. The idea of her seeing me with a cigarette even in my *hand*, let alone lighting one up...Jesus, I think I'd rather take a nail gun to the face than put either of us through that.

The bad news—I had to sit here by myself. Lunch was really going to suck today.

I'd just dug a sandwich out of my bag when the office's front door slapped open and Isabelle practically tripped out the door, her phone clenched in a nasty death-grip. Her eyes frantically scanned the parking lot and just as I was about to wave her down, a silver Camaro pulled into the lot. Judging by the horrified, white-as-a-sheet expression on Isabelle's face, this all added up to no good.

Isabelle stood rooted to the ground as the Camaro's car door opened and a clean cut, gelled hair, preppy as shit dude slid out of the driver's seat.

And from the way Isabelle's panicked blue eyes darted over to me, she didn't need to tell me who this guy was. Her alarm said it all.

Snapping into action, I swung my legs over the side of the bench and headed for the middle of the parking lot, which would set me right in between them. The only way to play this scenario was to treat it just like any other club business.

Play it cool. Don't show any unnecessary emotion. Never back down. Protect your own.

My feet didn't stop until I was just close enough to respect Isabelle's space, yet in prime position to jump in if necessary. When Isabelle flashed me a grateful smile, I knew I'd made the right call.

"Nick," she started, her hands up in front of her to appease him and she was closing the distance between them now. "I told you not to do this."

"Yeah, Isabelle?" he called out to her. "I guess I didn't listen."

There were a few things about this that already set me on edge and had me inching even closer with every second that ticked by. One—I really didn't like the way this guy was looking at her, like she was some sort of prize to be won. From as much as she'd told me, this guy just didn't know how to take a hint and now, he had the balls to show up at her work to—what? Convince her to do something she obviously didn't want to do? What the hell was this guy's endgame here?

And two—I really didn't appreciate the condescending tone. And the possessive way he said her name that had me ready to pounce, like he expected her to just drop everything and come running to him because he'd shown up here after she'd obviously told him not to.

Hell if I'd let that happen.

"Nick," Isabelle tried again, her voice taking on a more desperate edge. "I think you should go. We've been over this already. I still feel the same way I did before summer started and it's not going to change. I'll call you when you get back and we can talk then if that's what you want, but not here, not at my work, okay?"

Nick just shook his head and took one too many aggressive steps closer. "And I told you that I'm not gonna let you make the worst mistake of your life."

That was my cue to step in.

"Look, man," I jumped in, matching the jerk's steps tit for tat. "Iz clearly doesn't want you here and I don't appreciate you showin' up on my property like this uninvited. So, do yourself a favor and head back to wherever it is you came from."

The ex did a double-take, recognition and maybe a little self-awareness dawning on him as his dark eyes narrowed my way and he shot a glare back at Isabelle. "Is *this* the new guy you've been seeing?"

I stepped forward, ready to take one for the team, and opened my mouth to say as much, when Isabelle scrambled to get in between us, her hands pushing into us both to force some space.

"No, Nick, he's not," Isabelle told him and shot me an exasperated glance. "He's not. I *am* seeing somebody, but he doesn't work here."

There it was. The confirmation I'd been looking for. Fucking Brandon Davis. I just hadn't expected this overwhelming urge to either vomit or put my fist through something at hearing the words.

"Isabelle," Nick took another step closer to her and was stupid enough to reach for her too. "Do you think maybe we could go somewhere —*alone*— and talk about this rationally?"

"Hey—" I moved forward, but Isabelle's hand pressed in my chest to stop me from getting too close to her ex.

"Nick," she started again. "Caleb isn't leaving, but I think you should. There's nothing left to say and I'm really sorry you drove all the way here just to hear that, but—"

"I'm not going anywhere until you listen to what I have to say, Isabelle," Nick replied firmly.

"That's too bad," I retorted hotly. "Because it's time for you to go."

When Nick's eyes narrowed, taking on a grim, dangerous glint, and my body instinctively shifted so that I was standing directly between this pathetic asshole and my friend. Before all this started, I'd honestly been hoping I wouldn't have to get physical and now—well, I was sort of looking forward to it.

By this point, my mom poked her head out of the office, all narrowed eyes and annoyed glares. All I had to do was shake my head, signaling to her I had this situation locked down, and she got the hint.

Nick looked helplessly from Isabelle to me and then back to Isabelle again. He ran a hand through his hair and blew out a deep breath, like he was weighing his options.

"Look, Isabelle," he spread his hands out wide in front of him. "Just let me say what I need to say and then I'll go."

Isabelle glanced nervously at me, almost like she was asking for permission, and when I nodded curtly in the asshole's direction, his whole body relaxing with relief.

"Just answer me one question, okay?" Nick pleaded.

"What?"

"Are you happy here like this?" Before she could respond, he quickly held up a hand so he could clarify. "It's just a simple question. Are you happy? Do you like your life here?"

Well, I had to hand it to the prick.

I'd wondered that myself on numerous occasions and each time it crossed my mind, I always seemed to come to the same conclusion: how could she? After she'd told me the details of how and why she'd left school, I'd been able to wrap my head around her reasons for leaving. That made sense and it also fell in line with everything I knew about her.

What I couldn't reconcile was what she was doing back in town — while she claimed it was just a means to an end, that she was staying here and working at the shop just until she came up with a plan and some money, something about that just didn't add up. She didn't belong in Claremont, at least not for the long haul. Someone like her? She deserved more than what this town, and everyone in it, had to offer.

Isabelle was quiet for a few moments and I found myself anxiously holding my breath in anticipation.

"I don't know," she whispered finally. "But I do know that I wasn't happy at Duke and I wasn't happy with you either."

"You don't belong here, Isabelle. You never did and you know it. Don't sell yourself short — you're so goddamned smart and you could do anything you wanted to, so why waste yourself here in this place? You told me how much you couldn't wait to leave, how suffocated you felt here, so coming back just doesn't make any sense to me, not when there are so many better places for you to be."

After he'd said his peace, Nick took an exhausted, spent step backwards. If that was what he'd come here to do, then he'd accomplished it.

There was a small part of me, a part that wasn't quite tangible, that couldn't blame the guy for feeling this way. Why wouldn't he try to fight a little harder for Isabelle? Why wouldn't he refuse to give her up without a fight?

Isabelle was the kind of girl who was worth the fight.

Waiting for her to respond was like waiting for time to stand still — it just seemed to go on and on. Maybe she was delaying a response because she didn't want to hurt this guy's feelings anymore than she already had, but at this point, it felt like we both deserved some sort of resolution to this mess.

"Nick," she murmured, but her voice was steady and firm. "I appreciate that you care enough about me to drive all the way here to say that. I get where you're coming from. I really do. But it's not your responsibility to tell me where I belong and where I don't. You don't have that right and honestly, you never did. To tell you the truth, I have no idea where I should be or if Claremont is the right place for me, but I do know that I never belonged at Duke. I'm sorry you can't understand that, but where I go and what I do from here is my decision, not yours."

My eyes widened at her words. I'd half-expected her to yell at Nick, to demand he remove himself from the property and from her life, but I hadn't expected her to handle that like such an adult. I thought of all the times me and Ariel had screamed at each other, how she'd thrown anything at my head she could get her hands on, how I'd gotten so blinded with rage I'd almost physically lashed out at her more times than I was willing to admit, and neither of us had ever shown any kind of restraint, control, or clarity at the very end.

But now here was an example of how it should've gone — with maturity and consideration, not a blatant, selfish disregard for the other person's feelings and needs. The differences between Isabelle's situation and my own were staggering.

"Alright," Nick nodded slowly, seeming to recognize a lost cause when he saw one. "If that's really what you want and the way you feel then I guess I'll just go."

"Thanks," she reaffirmed, closing the short distance between them so she could wrap her arms around his neck. She released him just as fast and I had to swallow back a surge of pride that she was coming to stand next to *me* now and not him.

"I know you don't understand, but this is where I need to be right now. Bye, Nick."

"Bye, Isabelle," he smiled tightly, his hands sliding down to ball up into fists at his sides. Then, he abruptly turned towards me and extended his hand. There was nothing left to do but oblige him, so I silently shook it with a sharp nod.

"Take care of her," Nick pushed out with a hard edge.

"I will," I promised.

The funny thing was, I meant it too. Isabelle was my friend. Nobody forced me over here when Nick first showed up and nobody guilted me into staying for the whole non-showdown either. I stayed because I wanted to.

Then, Nick backpedalled for a few beats—probably for one last look and I couldn't fault him for that either—and then turned on his heel. When his car was down the street, I finally felt Isabelle relax next to me.

"Thank God that's over," she exhaled.

"Hey," I threw an arm over her shoulder and tucked her into my side. "It's done. He's gone and I gotta say, Iz, I'm impressed."

"Oh really?" she threw back at me. "And why's that?"

"Just the way you handled yourself," I shrugged easily, enjoying the fact that she was still nestled into my shoulder and hadn't enforced her no touching rule yet. "You didn't back down, Iz. I'm proud of ya."

"I don't know," she shrugged. "I think it was just the nail in the coffin he needed to see, you know?"

"Yeah, you're probably right..." I trailed off, searching for the right words here. "You okay?"

Her eyes were still on the car fading out into the distance. "Yeah, I'm okay."

"Good," I squeezed her shoulder and grinned down at her. "You think you can take your break now? I literally just sat down when what's-his-face showed up here like a bat outta hell and I'm hungry, Iz."

"Oh, come on, I see your sandwich over there on the table and it didn't melt in the sun. Promise."

"Hey," I pointed out. "My mom worked really hard on that this morning."

"Wow," she chuckled and for a moment, rested her head lightly against my shoulder. The second she realized what she was doing, her neck immediately snapped back up, lifting herself up and out of my grasp. "Maybe it's time you start making your own sandwiches, huh? You know, put on your big kid pants and make your own lunch for a change?"

"Over my dead body, Iz. Over. My. Dead. Body."

"How old are you again?"

I winked at her. "Same age as you."

She was still laughing all the way back to our picnic table and my fingers itched a little to touch her again. Thinking about how she smelled like flowery vanilla and spices or just how clear and how blue her eyes were wouldn't really be doing myself any favors right now. Or the fact that I couldn't tear my eyes away from her lips, the full, pillowy kind that made me want to know if they tasted as sweet as they looked.

Whoa...what the hell was that?

Just as I was trying and failing to come up with a way I could sit across from her on this picnic table and act like everything was normal, Isabelle solved that problem for me. Without a word, she pulled her sketchbook and a pencil from that huge purse, flipped it open, and then that pencil was scratching noisily across the paper.

I leaned forward to get a better look, but she playfully shifted so the sketch was a little too obscured for me to really see it.

"Nope," she told me with a grin. "Just wait a sec and then I'll show you when it's done, okay?"

So, I just leaned my elbows into the table and watched that pencil skim across the paper, completely in awe by her ability to sit down and do that like it was nothing. Finally, Isabelle flipped the sketchbook around and held it up. Squinting my eyes to get a clearer look, I didn't get it at first. The background sort of looked like the shop's parking lot and there was a skinny guy standing right in the middle of it with his hands straight up in the air while another bigger, burlier guy ran at him with a pitchfork.

Isabelle pointed her pencil at the skinny guy with a sly smile. "That's Nick."

I gestured with my head towards the other guy. "I take it that's me."

"You got it."

"Sorta," I leaned forward to swipe the pencil and sketchbook right out of her hands. With a few quick scratches, I fixed it up and held it back to her with a shit-eating grin.

"That," I pointed to the guy with the pitchfork again, but with huge, round arm muscles now, "is me."

118

Her shoulders were shaking now and she covered her mouth with one hand as she reached for her sketchbook.

"Wait, wait, wait, can I keep that? Please? That was a pretty proud moment for me back there. You know, standin' around and doin' nothing."

She promptly snapped the sketchbook shut and shoved it deep into her purse. "No. You can't have it. It's mine."

"Wow," I grinned. "How old are you again?"

Isabelle shot me that smile, the one that seemed to sear right through me, the one that reached all the way up to her bright blue eyes it made them shimmer, and I found myself leaning forward, eager to hang on every word.

"Seriously though, Caleb," she told me. "Thanks. I know you think you didn't do anything back there, but you really did. Just having a little back-up was nice for a change."

She had an edge in those last words and hell if I knew where that was coming from. It was right on the tip of my tongue to ask her what else was going on that I didn't know about, but the words died in my throat. She'd been pretty honest and open with me so far. If there was something else, she'd tell me about it if she wanted me to know, wouldn't she?

After that, we settled into our usual routine, laughing and joking around until our lunches and our breaks were over. Isabelle retreated back to her post in the office and I headed back to the shop, feeling like I was treading water again, just barely keeping my head above the surface.

My mind was elsewhere as I slid underneath the next car I had to work on and it never strayed too far from our break. At the end of the day, it didn't really matter that she hadn't needed my help. The point was that I'd been ready to give it to her. Ready to put Nick in his place. Ready to defend her. Ready to throw a punch for her if that's what I needed to do.

It felt good to be needed again and to be good for something other than pity. Maybe that was why it had been so easy, why it was so natural to just slide into that role. I'd almost forgotten what it that felt like and honestly, it felt good to *need* to protect someone again. To care enough about someone that I'd put myself directly in between her and whatever might potentially hurt her.

Whether Isabelle knew it or not, her little predicament had once again lifted me up and drawn me closer back to feeling human again. Every encounter, every conversation with her and I felt a little more like myself.

Life had a funny way of working itself out. Just when I thought things couldn't possibly be shittier, when I thought I couldn't possibly sink any lower, Isabelle shows up and teaches me how to put myself back together again.

CHAPTER FIFTEEN
Stuck In Reverse

A Few Weeks Later

Isabelle

When Brandon pulled into my driveway, I couldn't get out of his shiny new truck fast enough. I tried to tell myself it had more to do with the fact that he'd lit up a cigarette right in front of me—and in the confined space of his truck no less—than the date itself, but that was probably giving Brandon a little too much credit.

But the problem was that he'd just tried *so hard*.

Everything about our date went exactly as planned and exactly the way I'd anticipated. He'd picked me up on time, taken me to a nice restaurant for a nice meal, and that was probably just the most accurate way to describe the evening.

It was nice. *Fine*.

But as soon as my driveway came into view, relief was about the only thing I was feeling right now. This was the fourth time we'd been out together in the last few weeks and each date had been just like this. Nice. Fine. Reliable and predictable. Just like it used to be...*four* years ago.

His hands felt nice when they trailed up and down my body a few minutes ago and his warm breath kissing my neck made my skin tingle. I'd closed my eyes and enjoyed the feeling of a man's touch—it had been a while since I'd had any real contact like that and it was nice.

There was that awful, horribly vague adjective again. Nice. Fine.

I really needed to find a different way to describe how I was feeling. Those adjectives sucked with their general and ambiguous terms.

The problem was, I realized as Brandon followed me up to my front door, that I couldn't pinpoint exactly what my real emotions were.

After initially reconnecting with him, I hadn't realized how much I'd missed him until we sat down for a coffee on our first 'get-together' again. It was amazing how quickly I could forget all the little things, the things I used to think I'd always remember, especially after so much time had passed.

But then, it was like we just snapped right back into it, minus some initial awkward getting-to-know-you-again small talk. It was almost like we'd actually stayed in touch over those four years and that nothing had changed.

That was the part that probably bothered me the most.

The simplest answer was that I was over-analyzing, which was probably true, but that didn't make it any less difficult to swallow.

"So I'll see you tomorrow at Graffiti's, right?" Brandon's soft voice yanked me from my perpetually frustrating thoughts.

"What? Oh, right. Yeah. Tomorrow."

I'd almost forced myself to forget all about the inevitable intermingling of our very separate, very different group of friends. Any way you sliced it, this was probably the worst idea I'd ever had in my entire life. I'd just wanted my boyfriend to get along with my friends.

Talk about setting yourself up for epic, doom-ridden failure.

"You must kinda like me if you're letting me hang out with your friends, huh?" he grinned, wrapping an arm comfortably around my shoulders.

Something like that.

"Yeah, I guess so," I laughed tightly and prayed he didn't pick up on the anxiety that had to be evident in my voice.

Honestly, Brandon and his friends trying to hang out in the same bar as Caleb, Dominic, Eli, Lexie, and Becca was going to be...well, if the night ended without anyone storming off or getting smashed in the head with a broken beer bottle, then I guess it would sort of be a success.

Sort of.

In reality, I anticipated a disaster of tsunami proportions, but now that the plans were already made, I didn't know how to get myself out of it without looking like a complete bitch.

Caleb, Brandon, and beer was like the perfect storm.

Caleb and Brandon had steered clear of each other for most of high school, so it wasn't like there'd been this constant war between them or anything. It was more like a pattern of antagonism and underhanded disrespect. Whenever they passed each other in the hallway, it was just like one of those old Western movies I used to watch with my dad when I was a kid and he was still sober.

The gunslingers standing at attention when their opponent stepped within sight, fingers itching to draw at a split second's notice, waiting for the other to strike. While Brandon played easily on the cool jock vibe to get under his skin, Caleb was like a coiled snake, waiting for Brandon to step just far enough over the line so he could attack. Luckily for everyone involved, that line never got crossed while they were still in high school and after graduation, there was never another reason for Brandon and Caleb to ever interact.

Until tomorrow night.

In my attempt to keep the peace, I'd inadvertently put them on a collision course for that gun-slinging showdown anyways. All I could do was hope a public setting and some distance would be enough of a deterrent.

A girl could hope. And pray to sweet, little baby Jesus that the night wouldn't end in a bloodbath of swinging fists and smashing bottles.

"Is it alright if I call you later?" Brandon was asking me now, bringing me close enough to whisper in my ear.

That soft voice in my ear and that warm breath against my neck used to make my legs turn to jelly, but there was no point in focusing on things like "used to" or "nice" or "fine". Wasn't it enough that we were trying to get back what we'd lost? Wasn't it enough that he was doing everything I could possibly ask him to do to get back to what we used to be?

Everything was happening here on my terms and at my pace: when I wanted to be picked up, where I wanted to go, what I wanted to do, and how long I wanted to do it for. He really hadn't pushed me into anything I hadn't wanted to do and when he kissed me, his warm lips explored my mouth with a nice, easy pace.

There was that *word* again.

Then I registered what he'd just asked me and a fluttering of annoyance crept up into my stomach. We had literally just spent almost four hours together by the time we got to the restaurant, had a few drinks, had dinner, and then talked some more. What else did we really have to talk about tonight?

"Um, sure," I offered. "Well, I'm probably going to be working for a while tonight so..."

Please get it and please don't take it the wrong way.

A glimmer of understanding flickered across his chocolate eyes and he nodded. "Oh okay, you're gonna draw some pictures again tonight? Sure, no problem. I'll just call you tomorrow then, alright?"

I had to swallow back the sudden urge to lash out at him for calling my work, my *passion*, 'drawing some pictures'. He might as well have just called it doodling and been done with it. I never should've mentioned it. I should've just kept it on lockdown. No one needed to know anyways because it wasn't anybody else's business.

But, that snotty little voice whispered, *who else did you tell, hmm? What about him? You didn't show Brandon your sketches. But you showed him.* He *doesn't call it doodling.*

"Yeah, sure," I replied tightly. "That sounds good."

Brandon leaned forward and pressed a light kiss into my lips. "Can I come in for a little while?"

That sent a few shockwaves of panic right through me. The first thought that sliced through my mind was of my dad. Was he home? And if he was, what would we find? As soon as that passed, I found myself shaking off more irritation. The night was over, wasn't it? We'd said goodnight, he'd said he was going to call me again, so why did he have to push for more?

If I let him inside the house, he would expect to get *something*, at the very least. That was annoying too. And definitely not happening.

So I just politely shook my head no and he just grinned back at me, clearly unfazed by the rejection. He pulled me into a quick hug and I kinda wanted him to just leave already.

"Night, Brandon."

"Sweet dreams, Isabelle."

I smiled, a real, honest to goodness, genuine smile. That was something he always used to say before leaving my house and it was that breath of nostalgia that finally suppressed my budding agitation.

When the door was finally closed behind me, I leaned up against it and sighed, overwhelmed with relief. All I wanted to do was sit in my room, turn on some music, and work out whatever the hell I was feeling on paper.

I needed to rid myself of this restlessness and that was probably the only thing that would work.

I peeked in my dad's bedroom and closed my eyes. The empty bedroom was equally a source of relief and uneasiness. Sure, I had the house all to myself, but that was only until he called me, probably falling down drunk in some random bar, wallowing in grief and whiskey. That thought forced me to trudge into my own room to await the inevitable. No sense in wasting any time.

When I was sitting on my bed, notebook splayed out on the bedspread, music on, and pencil in hand, it was almost like there was too much going on in my head to focus. And when I glanced up, my room had somehow gotten smaller over the span of 30 seconds. My left leg jumped anxiously over the side of the bed and the pencil twitched in my hand.

Nothing but a clean, blank page stared back up at me.

During the last two months, all it took to get that creative spark going was shutting my door, turning on some music, and opening my notebook. Now, it was all I could do to just focus on the blank page, let alone feel even remotely focused enough to actually make the pencil dance across it.

"Crap, crap, crap," I muttered, running a hand over my face.

Nothing was going the way it was supposed to. Nothing about my life was working the way I wanted it to. And now, I couldn't even do the one thing I loved the most and the one thing was supposed to make me feel better.

I felt stunted, trapped in arrested development. My date with Brandon only highlighted what was wrong here. All the gains I'd been trying to make, but failing miserably at. All the changes I'd promised myself I'd make, but had yet to do anything about.

Moving back to Claremont seemed like an easy answer at the time. It was a solid, defensible solution to the escalating feeling that I was on the wrong path in life. I'd foolishly believed coming home would solve all my problems: I'd somehow figure out what I wanted to do with my life and help my dad see that he was ruining his.

The real problem was that I'd never really taken that extra step and thought about how I was *actually* going to make all that happen.

I'd been all talk and no follow-through.

And now here I was—completely stranded. Stuck in reverse. Alone in my room. All these grand plans to stop living my life for everyone else and nothing to show for it. Only now, I didn't have my mom to go running to for help. My mom wasn't here anymore to tell me everything was going to be alright or that everything had a way of working itself out or that she would always be there when I needed her.

My mom was gone. And my dad was on his way out too.

I knew what I needed. I just didn't know how to ask for it. Didn't know *who* to ask for it. Didn't know how to even begin to say the words.

The twitching and jumping got so bad that before long, I just gave up altogether. I hustled out of my room, grabbed my keys, and was down the driveway before I think I even fully understood what I was doing.

Calling Becca wasn't really an option. I didn't want to bother her with this or worse, worry her. Big girls should be able to take of themselves, right? And, my dad would be calling for a ride in a little while, so I might as well already be up and around town.

Yeah, whatever you have to tell yourself.

I briefly flirted with the idea of texting Lexie, my ally in the clubhouse and who I'd somehow, inexplicably struck up a friendship with, and then decided against it just as quickly.

Maybe I just needed to drive around, stop somewhere for coffee or something, anything to get my mind back to a more normal pace. So it wasn't necessarily by choice that I ended up in the parking lot of Aimee's Diner—my recent, embarrassing stint there as the most inept waitress in history made it the one place in Claremont I went completely out of my way to avoid, but it was also the only place around that was decent and still open at this hour.

On the bright side, the coffee was good and Aimee's homemade peanut butter pie was the best I'd ever had in my life.

At this point, I think I had to take whatever silver lining I could get.

CHAPTER SIXTEEN
Arrested Development

Caleb

Splashing some cold water on my face hadn't helped much. I rested both hands over the side of the sink and exhaled deeply. I was so tired my body just felt heavy and I wanted to sleep; I really did, but my mind just wouldn't let me rest. There wasn't one particular thing that nagged at me—it was more like *everything* nagged at me.

Marcus was on my ass about stepping up and all I'd been able to do was just swear everything was fine, that I was over "whatever bug crawled up my ass", as Marcus had so tactfully put it. There would be no heart to hearts, no therapy sessions with my club president, and I had no one to blame for that but myself.

Having anyone question my loyalty to the club was right at the top of the list of what I wanted to avoid like the plague and now I had to man up to prove my commitment. Which, unfortunately, meant I needed to quit hitting the bottle so hard. Which, unfortunately, also meant I couldn't drink myself into oblivion until I passed out anymore. It was the only thing that really helped me sleep and until now, I'd honestly thought it went unnoticed for the most part.

Funny how that worked itself out.

So I needed to be careful and I needed to show my brothers that I was turning a corner, that things were sliding back into place, and everything was normal again. The problem with that, though, was I wasn't turning myself around—at least not really.

While every day did get a little bit easier, that didn't mean I didn't wake up at night in a panic, drenched in sweat. That didn't mean the heaviness in my body was any lighter or that the open, gushing flesh wound was any closer to scarring over.

I wasn't better. I wasn't over it. And I just couldn't forget.

I hated it.

No amount of drunken nights with some random girl in my bed would ever get me there. I knew that. I just had to pretend like it was all water under the bridge, like I was glad to finally be rid of her, like I was better off without her.

Whenever things got hard, I tried repeating Isabelle's words in my head: *if she really wanted to be with me, she would've moved heaven and earth to make it happen*. That helped a little bit, but not enough. Maybe in a few more months, if I had a little more time, I'd be able to take that more to heart. But right now, the anguish in my chest just wouldn't dissipate.

In a brief moment of weakness, my fingers itched for a bottle of Jack. It would definitely take care of my sleep problem in a half hour, if not sooner. But even one pull from the bottle now would feel like a betrayal to the promise I'd made to my club. I briefly considered grabbing the first girl I could find in the clubhouse, but shook it from my mind. As soon as the deed was done, I would just be alone again and I'd probably just feel more alone after than before.

Well, I figured, if I wasn't going to sleep, I might as well ride.

The cool night air swept around me, clinging to my skin, pulsating into my pores, and re-energizing my senses. My Street Glide had never failed me before and she flew eagerly from street to street until I felt like I'd circled the entire landscape of Claremont two times over.

The haziness swallowing me up in the clubhouse was long gone and a clear focus, something that felt almost like calm, spread through my mind. Breath came in and out more easily than before.

I didn't want to think anymore. I didn't want to feel anymore. I just wanted to be present in the here and now.

But when my Glide rested at the stoplights right in front of Aimee's Diner, I almost fell right off my bike. My eyes landed on the lone black Trans Am parked off to the side first and then, scanning through the windows, rested on Isabelle, who was sitting in a booth, hunched over something on the table. A grin tugged at my lips and I had a pretty good idea what she was doing all hunched over like that.

Working.

Fascination didn't quite cover the emotion I felt whenever I watched her work.

It wasn't too often she'd sacrifice conversation at lunch in order to sketch in her notebook, but when it happened, I just sat back and watched in silent amazement. The fluid lines she produced and the stark, luminous images flitting across the page were nothing short of extraordinary. The level of raw talent it took to do something like that was something I would never be able to understand. So, for lack of being able to do anything remotely helpful, I just shut up and let her work.

But tonight was a different story. Tonight we were technically supposed to be sleeping because we both had to work the morning shift at the shop tomorrow. I couldn't imagine she made it a regular habit of working at Aimee's, especially since she'd basically been fired from there and especially since it was the middle of the night.

Something had to be up.

And what kind of guy would I be if I didn't go in and at least have a cup of coffee with her?

I was still grinning when I parked my bike right next to her car. As the door chimed behind me, my eyes flew right to the lone figure sitting a few booths away, lost in her own little world. The noise seemed to shake her out of wherever it was she went when she was working and she blinked in shock for a few seconds.

"What up, Iz," I called out to her as I approached her booth.

"What are you doing here?" she asked with a laugh.

"I could ask you the same question."

By now, I was hovering right in front of her table, but I didn't want to just assume I'd get an invitation to sit down. She seemed pretty settled here with her half-empty coffee cup, untouched piece of peanut butter pie, and her stuff spread out all over the table and I honestly didn't come in to bother her.

"Couldn't sleep," she shrugged easily. "I'm guessing you're in the same boat, huh?"

I just nodded, a touch of a smile lifting my lips. "Want some company?"

"Sure," she murmured softly, half-standing to clear some of her clutter from the table. As she grabbed her oversized purse from the table and set it over on her side, I slid in across from her.

"So," Isabelle started quietly. "Are you in the mood for some peanut butter pie? Once I got going here, I kinda forgot about it even though I *am* on my third cup of coffee."

I didn't need to be told twice and immediately reached for the plate. "Absolutely, Iz."

"Coffee?" she gestured towards the empty cup to my right. When I nodded, my mouth too full of peanut buttery awesomeness, she poured me a cup with a smirk.

"Do I want to know why you're out on the prowl tonight? Or...wait, if you just finished up with some girl at the clubhouse, I'm not sure I want to hear about it," she crinkled her nose a little as she spoke and if I didn't know her better, I would've thought her tone was a little harsh.

Good thing I *did* know her well enough to recognize sarcasm in her voice when I heard it.

"I'm trying this whole bein' sober thing," I grinned back at her. "Shocking, right?"

"Who knew you'd grow up to be so responsible?" she shot back and she bit her lip to keep from laughing.

"Gotta grow up sometime, I guess," I replied good-naturedly.

"Well," she smiled softly. "If it helps, I'm glad you're not face down in a gutter somewhere."

"I'd much rather be here with you, darlin'," I winked.

She just rolled her eyes and tossed an empty sugar packet at me. I gestured down to the open notebook and forced myself not to peek at, careful to respect her privacy and her space.

"Whatcha workin' on over there?"

She looked back at me sharply and then her expression shifted from surprised to confused to tired and finally rested on forlorn. I didn't have it in me tonight to even begin to understand what any of that meant or what my words had to do with anything. It was almost midnight and we should really be in bed.

Mind outta the gutter, Sawyer.

Separate. In different beds. Sleeping. Nothing else.

"Oh," she answered finally. "Nothing all that important really. I was trying to figure out some stuff, but that didn't work out too well."

"Alright, so when do I get to commission something?"

She frowned. "What do you mean?"

"Well," I shrugged as I shoveled another bite of pie into my mouth. "I figured you're gonna be rich and famous someday, so I better get an Isabelle Martin original while I can still afford it."

"Aw," she called out in a sing-song voice. "You called me Isabelle."

I wagged my fork at her. "Don't get used to it."

"Okay," she leaned forward a little more. "So, say you were to actually commission something. What would you want?"

That one was easy.

"My bike. Definitely. I can already see her..."

Isabelle's shoulders shook with laughter. "Wait a minute, wait a minute. Did you just refer to your motorcycle as a *she*?"

I blinked back her. "Uh. Yeah. That's what she is. She's beautiful and she's perfect and if you so much as say a bad word about her, I'm gonna get up from this table right now and I won't ever talk to you again."

Her hand covered her mouth to muffle her laughter. "Whoa, buddy. Simmer down. I promise," she made a cross sign over her heart, "I won't say anything bad about *her*."

All she got from me for that was an eye roll.

"I mean, you'll really do it, right?"

She was still laughing. "Well, sure."

"Do I still have to pay you?" I murmured in a low voice.

"Hmm...pay for the coffee and get me another piece of pie and I think we're square."

"Deal!" I thumped my fist on the table for good measure.

Isabelle just laughed with a wide grin on her face and for a moment, I felt frozen by how happy she looked. If I could just get a little of that, feel a little of what she was feeling right now, maybe I could get one step closer to actually feeling like a normal human being. But then again, every time I was with her, it was easy to forget everything else and just laugh and talk and just be *normal*.

"So," I cleared my throat. "What brings you here in the middle of the night other than the fact that you can't sleep?"

She was quiet for a moment and when her eyes flicked back up to mine, my chest tightened at the pain radiating in them.

"I guess I just...I just really missed my mom tonight," she murmured, staring into her coffee cup.

I nodded. That was a feeling I knew all too well. Something told me there was a little more going on, but didn't see the point in pushing her. I didn't want to overstep or make her any more upset than she already was, but this? Feeling the sting, the heart-wrenching loss of losing a parent...this was something I might actually be able to help her with.

"You know," I started cautiously. "It's still hard for me walk into the clubhouse everyday and not wonder where he'd be—where I'd be—if my dad was still alive and kicking. Sometimes, when I'm on the lot, I can almost see him in the shop, workin' on a truck or pickin' me up to take me for a ride. I guess it doesn't get any easier, but it helps to remember those things, you know? The little things, the good things, even if it sucks sometimes, because I guess that's all you have left, you know?"

Her eyes glimmered with something I couldn't quite put my finger on and I wondered if maybe I'd said too much or maybe not enough. It was always hard to tell with her. Sometimes, I felt like I knew exactly what she was thinking and other times...

"That's funny," she shook her head with a sad smile. "Because sometimes when I walk past our kitchen counter I have these flashbacks of when I was five and I remember racing home everyday after kindergarten to watch *Dirty Dancing*. I know, great parenting, right?"

A grin tugged at my lips as I chuckled with her. It was good to hear her talk this way, especially since the only time she'd really spoken of her mom was the night I'd completely lost my shit in front of her, and I knew, from firsthand experience, that she probably needed to talk about her mom more than she did.

"So, this one day," she continued softly. "I must have done something really bad—I mean *really* naughty—to make my mom this mad. I still have no idea what I did. Funny how that works, right? But I remember her being so mad she was just red all over—I mean furious with rage— and she takes my *Dirty Dancing* tape...you know the good ol' VHS ones? And she takes the tape, lifts it over her head all dramatic, and then smashes it into the counter right in front of me."

We were both shaking with laughter now.

"Oh, I cried and cried and cried. I couldn't believe she actually did it!

And I wouldn't come out of my room for the rest of the night because I was so mad at *her*. So then the next day, when I finally came down for breakfast, there was a brand new *Dirty Dancing* tape there waiting for me on the kitchen counter."

"Wow," I chuckled. "She must have felt pretty shitty to get you another copy like that."

"Yeah," she nodded with a grin. "Well, of course, I had to promise never to do whatever it was I did again in order to get it and she promised never to smash my stuff again."

I wiped my eyes from laughing so hard and shook my head. "I never pegged you for such a problem child."

"What can I say?" she shrugged. "I'm just full of surprises."

She didn't know the half of it.

"So..." I racked my brain for something else to talk about, sensing the need for a change in topic. "Tomorrow night, huh?"

The grin slid off her face and I knew I'd just made a huge mistake.

"Yeah. Tomorrow night. Can you promise me one thing though?" she pleaded quietly.

"What's that?"

"Can you please just *try* to be nice?"

I scoffed and rolled my eyes. "What makes you think I won't be nice?"

"Really?" she stared back at me pointedly. "Do I really need to explain it to you? Look, I would really, really appreciate it if you guys could *try* to get along."

"Alright, alright," I conceded, throwing my hands up in the air. "Fine. But only because you asked so nicely, Iz. Don't think I'm doing it for that dickhead."

"Nice, Caleb," she snorted. "Real nice."

"What?"

She just shook her head and poured a little more sugar into her coffee cup.

"So," I pressed on because this time, *I* needed the change in topic. "What do you have on the agenda for the rest of your night, huh?"

"Oh, I don't know. I'll probably just go home and have a movie marathon or something like that. That'll probably help me fall asleep."

My eyebrows shot up at this new piece of information—just another fascinating piece of the puzzle.

"Oh really? And what, exactly, does a movie marathon with you entail?"

"Probably *Star Wars*," she just shrugged. "I'm kinda in the mood for something that's gonna take me far, far away if you know what I mean."

"Seriously?" I shook my head in disbelief. "You like those movies?"

"Like them? Are you kidding? Who doesn't like them? I think I was Princess Leia for Halloween every year until I was like, 14."

I pointed to myself with a smirk. "You're lookin' at your Han Solo, darlin'. Well, actually, I switched between Han Solo and Indiana Jones, but I loved playing with that toy gun more than anything."

"Yeah, I could see that," she grinned, splaying her hands out on the table in excitement. "I can see you already with the belt and those high boots...wow, I can't wait to drill your mom for those pictures tomorrow at work."

My mouth dropped open. "You wouldn't."

"Wanna bet?"

"Shit. Okay, okay, forget I ever said anything. Jesus," my mind was scrambling now to her to forget about those incriminating pictures. "Favorite movie?"

Her eyes crinkled up in deep thought and I could practically see the wheels in her head turning.

"Hmm, I don't think I can choose just one. I mean, there are just so many..."

"Okay, fine. I'll make it easy. Top five?"

"Nah," she shook her head fiercely. "I don't think I could even do that, but if it helps, I think I could watch any Quentin Tarantino movie any day, any time."

"So you're a bad motherfucker, then, huh?" I grinned widely, wiggling my eyebrows at her suggestively.

"You know it, but I think I'd rather have a royale with cheese."

I barked out a laugh before shoveling in another huge forkful of pie into my mouth. "I think this pie might be better than that."

Isabelle's eyes lit up at the mention of her long-forgotten pie and she snatched up her unused fork and practically dove across the table to plough it into what was left of the pie. Still shaking my head, I motioned for the restaurant's lone waitress on duty and ordered another slice and another pot of coffee, making good on my earlier promise to her.

"So, Quentin Tarantino, huh?" I continued as I poured us both another cup of coffee. "I think my personal favorite will always be *Pulp Fiction* no matter what else he does."

"I think it's kinda tied for me with *Inglourious Basterds*," she replied between mouthfuls.

I nodded appreciatively. "Yeah, I think that's a close second for me to be honest. But if I'm not in the mood for some Tarantino—I'm not gonna lie, I could totally watch *Anchorman* any day. I mean, whenever it's on TV, I just stop what I'm doing and I watch it—it doesn't matter what part is on."

"For me, it's *Forrest Gump*. I think I've even caught it right at the end, you know the part where Forrest is talking to Jenny's grave...gets me every time."

She put a hand over her heart for extra emphasis and I found myself biting back a smile.

"How 'bout the *Die Hard* movies?" I threw out.

Her nose crinkled up a little and she frowned. "I've never seen them. Can't exactly say I've had a burning desire to."

"Aw, come on," I batted a hand out. "Those movies are awesome."

"Doesn't Bruce Willis play a cop trying to catch all the bad guys?" Her head tilted to the side as she spoke.

"What's that supposed to mean?"

"I don't know," she shrugged. "I guess I never pegged you as someone who would get all hot and bothered over a cop movie, given...you know."

She gestured to my cut with a sly grin.

My fork froze in mid-air as I tried to figure out whether or not she was messing with me. When her easy laughter rang in my ears, I was finally able to shake off how completely crazy it was that we were sitting here like this. Yet, here we were, sitting in a booth at midnight, drinking coffee, eating pie, and talking about movies.

For a moment, I wondered what it would be like to go back to her house and actually have that movie marathon with her. It would probably be just as much fun as this, if not more and thinking about it for too long would probably just set myself up for something I wouldn't like.

Thankfully, her phone buzzed in her purse and the spell was broken. She set her coffee cup down on the table and sheepishly held up a finger as her other hand dug for her phone. When she looked at the caller ID, it was like her entire body stilled in less than a second. Everything about her was tense, from the hushed way she answered, to the way her panicked eyes darted up to me for just a moment and then seemed to look anywhere but at me.

"Hello?" she answered.

I leaned forward to watch her more carefully as she listened to whoever was on the phone and my eyes narrowed when I saw her bite down hard on her bottom lip.

"Sure," she said into the phone. "Just give me a few minutes, alright? Stay there."

The second she tossed her phone back into her purse and smiled tightly as if to say everything was fine.

I knew everything wasn't fine.

"I have to get going," Isabelle murmured softly as she rummaged around in her purse, producing her wallet and motioning for the bill.

"Hey," I interjected quickly, digging into my back pocket for some money. "Don't worry about it. I told ya I'd get the next pot and another slice of pie anyways."

"No, you don't have to do that, Caleb. I was here first anyways," she glanced back up at me and the agitation and anxiousness swept off her in waves.

"You can get the next one. How 'bout that?" I offered, trying to be helpful, but I still felt like I was failing miserably. It wasn't like I expected her to tell me what was going on, but it would be a hell of a lot easier to help her if I knew.

She smiled tensely and then finally nodded. "Okay. Thanks, Caleb."

"Everything alright, Iz?"

The question hung in the air and she stilled again at those words. I had to ask it. If something was going on and she needed help, I had to let her know it was okay to tell me. A moment later, I watched her shake her head and put on a brave face.

"Everything's fine, Caleb. Seriously."

I knew what that really meant. It was written all over her face. I absolutely hated that word...*fine*.

As she slid out of the booth with a murmured goodbye and another thank you, I almost stopped her. I almost pulled her back so I could find out what the hell was really going on with her. But then again, if she wanted my help, wouldn't she have asked for it? I'd backed her up before. Wouldn't she know I'd do it again?

It wasn't until she'd pulled out of the parking lot that I finally finished my coffee and stood to leave, shaking off the uneasiness that almost had me sprinting out of the restaurant to chase after her.

Even as I swung my leg over my bike and started her engine, all I could think about was how in the hell Isabelle Martin had gotten so far under my skin.

CHAPTER SEVENTEEN
The Unlucky Spur

Isabelle

Standing by the bar with my friends by my side and my boyfriend's arm around my waist should have put me at ease. I should have been taking the drink Brandon handed me simply because it was a Friday night and because I wanted to have fun, not because I needed to calm my nerves instead.

It wasn't like anything had gone down between the two very separate groups on either side of me...yet.

The potential was there and that's all that really mattered.

Caleb and Brandon wisely kept their distance from each other, with each one on opposite sides of our disjointed group assembled around the bar at Graffiti's. Brandon's friends, and remnants of high school, kept to the right and the Horsemen stayed to the left. With each second that ticked by, I was seriously regretting ever agreeing to this. Who in the hell thought this was a good idea?

Oh right. Me.

Goddammit.

My eyes flicked to Becca, who was grinning like the cat that swallowed the canary. At some point, though, the other shoe was going to drop. It had to happen sometime. Lexie was warily eyeing Travis, Brandon's slightly overweight buddy who thought it was a good idea to jump the trashcan. Dominic and Eli looked bored out of their minds while Brandon and his friends laughed nonsensically over something I hadn't been paying attention to.

Because he'd done a pretty good job keeping himself carefully out of sight, Caleb was a bit of an enigma. And that was completely fine with me.

"Hey, babe!" Brandon practically yelled in my ear, despite the fact that he was standing right next to me. "Did you see that? That was awesome!"

"No, I didn't," I managed to push out through gritted teeth. I was too busy swallowing back a panic attack to give two shits about what was so funny.

Brandon slung an arm around my shoulders and drew me flush against him. "Don't worry about it, babe. It was so awesome though. Trav almost made it all the way over and..."

At that point, I wearily tuned him out. It wasn't so much out of disinterest, but more like self-preservation. Unfortunately, though, my eyes drifted over to my left and caught Lexie mirthlessly roll her eyes and Dominic shake his head, disgust curling his lips.

This was not going well.

Of course, it didn't help that I flinched when Brandon's fingers rested dangerously close to the space where my shirt ended and my jeans began. Maybe I shouldn't have worn something that skimmed the edge between sexy and flirty — so much for trying to look nice if he was going to get all handsy in public like this. Luckily, Brandon didn't seem to notice my agitation and kept his fingers splayed lazily across my skin.

The jury was still out on whether or not *that* was lucky. Probably not.

"Babe," Brandon whispered in my ear. "You alright?"

So scratch that about him not noticing.

"Everything's fine. Why wouldn't it be?" I replied a little too quickly.

A flicker of recognition passed through his eyes and I had a moment of panic. Any reaction, or overreaction, to my frustration was only going to make an already-deteriorating situation worse and my eyes, as if they had a mind of their own, flicked to my left only to find a particularly brooding biker glaring right in my direction.

Crap.

"You sure?" Brandon murmured, his breath tickling my ear and reeking of beer.

He leaned lower to press a sloppy kiss on my cheek without so much as a second's warning. Sheer willpower alone keep me from wiping it right off in response. I'd forgotten what he was like when he was this drunk and stupid. Many, many nights of high school nightmares past came flitting back to me and for a fleeting moment, I considered telling him that no, everything was not fine. I was close to freaking out—that's how *fine* I was.

So instead of doing what I wanted to do, I just nodded into his shoulder, purposefully avoiding his eyes and keeping my chin down. When his arm just pulled me in tighter, I knew I was in the clear for now.

When someone tugged on Brandon's collar to yank him away, I took a careful step back and threw a cautious glance to my left yet again, only to collide with the Caleb's eyes, which looked more like lethal bottomless pits than actual eyes. The sheer weight of it froze me in place until a hand shook me out of my trance.

"Hey, babe?" Again, Brandon didn't wait for me to answer. "Grant just called and said some people are going over to Shark's right now. You ready to go?"

It took me a moment to process what he was asking, or rather *telling* me.

"What? Um..." I glanced over to the other side of the bar and found Becca narrowing her eyes at the back of Brandon's head. "What's wrong with staying here for awhile?"

Brandon just shrugged. "Everyone's gonna go to Shark's anyways. We usually can get a booth and a pool table all to ourselves. Besides, this place is getting a little crowded if you know what I mean."

I knew exactly what he meant. Even though his reasons for wanting to leave weren't wholly unreasonable, that still didn't stop the uneasiness from creeping up the back of my neck at the prospect of leaving with him and leaving everyone to my left behind. Something told me it was time to finally listen to that intuition.

"I think I might stay here for awhile. At least until everyone else wants to leave and then I'll come meet up with you."

The words hung in the air for a moment too long and then Brandon just shrugged again.

"Alright, cool. If that's what you wanna do. Why don't you just give me a call when you leave here?"

"Okay."

He grinned down at me, having assessed the situation and found everything to be just *fine*. Then he leaned down and kissed me. But it wasn't a quick, see-ya-later-babe kiss. It was a hard, territorial kiss. He wrapped his arms around me in a goodbye hug, which, at least, gave me room to hide my eye roll, and then he headed for the door with his posse of annoying immaturity trailing behind him.

I didn't want to look to the left. I really didn't. But like stupid magnets, my eyes flicked there anyways and the expression in Caleb's eyes had shifted from dark to menacing. I swallowed nervously and edged back to my seat by the bar, hoping no one noticed how close I was to high-tailing it to the bathroom.

Becca was at my side in a matter of nanoseconds.

"Hey," she murmured lowly. "Brandon seriously just left? Is everything alright, Belle?"

Knee-jerk reaction, not to mention self-preservation, kicked in almost immediately.

"Yeah, all his friends just wanted to head somewhere else for awhile," I told her, even though part of me had no idea why I was defending Brandon. "I'll probably meet up with them later when you guys decide to head back to the clubhouse."

Right. Because there was nothing wrong with the fact that I was totally okay with my boyfriend leaving without me and going to another bar to do God knows what with his friends.

Yeah, that was normal.

Becca's eyes narrowed ever so slightly and then Lexie flanked the other side.

"I hate to say it," Lexie muttered under her breath. "But I'm kinda glad those guys are gone. No offense, Isabelle, but I'm not sure how much more of that I could take."

I just waved a hand. "Don't worry about it. It's not a big deal. I'll meet up with him later."

"Okay," Lexie replied, her voice hesitating a little with each syllable. "Should we hit up the jukebox or something? I kinda feel like dancing."

"Let's do it!" Becca called out over the escalating noise of the crowd and she grabbed for our arms to drag us over there.

"Hey, just hold on," I grunted. "I'll be right over. I think I need another drink."

When I finally had a little space to breathe by the bar, some of my tension uncoiled, slipping away with each inhale. And then I felt an elbow nudge me in the arm. I didn't even need to turn to know who was behind it.

"So."

Caleb was leaning an elbow lazily on the bar counter, his lips twisting in that cocky, confident smirk I knew so well.

And then a funny thing happened.

My heart fluttered, spiking with nervousness, but, at the exact same time, a rush of calm flushed right through me. How was it possible to be agitated and relaxed at the exact same time? I was pretty sure it wasn't physically possible, but yet...there it was. Rushing and twisting, bending and soothing all at the same time.

"So," I prompted, playfully lifting an eyebrow as I spoke. It was the only real defense mechanism I had left to play.

"Dickhead's gone," Caleb stated, his eyes sparkling conspiratorially.

"Uh huh."

"And you're still here."

"Very good, Caleb. I see you've been paying attention."

He grinned appreciatively and nodded. "Thanks, Iz. I'm glad someone noticed I'm not a complete idiot and no, you can't comment on that one. Anyways...where was I?" He tapped his chin in thought. "Oh right! Douchehole is currently MIA. You're still here."

"Your point?"

He wasn't fazed by my incisive tone.

"How 'bout a drink, Iz? You sure look like you could use one."

Caleb didn't wait for a response. Instead, he waved the bartender over with one hand and dug into his back pocket with the other. After we each gave our orders, a grin tugged up my face, the first genuine smile I'd felt all night.

He just draped an arm easily over my shoulder, like he'd been doing it for years and I practically shivered under his touch. There was seriously something wrong with the fact that the guy I *was* seeing and who definitely wasn't Caleb just had his hands on me literally minutes ago and I'd flinched at his touch, but yet I practically vibrated with electricity when Caleb just had his arm grazing my shoulders...again, *not* the guy I was seeing.

Our drinks arrived promptly; that kind of speedy service was one of the perks of being here with the Horsemen, and Caleb's arm slipped down from my shoulders to grab his drink. Some distance between us was probably for the best right now, but a part of me still mourned losing the warmth of his tattooed arm against my skin.

What the hell was my problem tonight?

Just as I was about to reach for my drink, my phone buzzed from deep within the folds of my purse. It was probably Brandon—either he was groveling or trying to convince me to head to that bar. Neither one of those options was really an appealing choice, but when an unknown number flashed across my screen, my mouth dipped into a frown.

"Everything alright, Iz?" Caleb's expression seemed to mirror mine.

"Yeah, I think so. I just don't recognize this number is all," I just shrugged as I swiped across the screen to answer.

"Hello?" I answered, acutely aware that Caleb's attention rested firmly on this impending conversation.

"Is this Isabelle? Sam's daughter?" An unfamiliar voice asked over the other line.

My eyes instinctively squeezed shut. "Yeah?"

"This is Jim down at The Lucky Spur. Yeah, uh, you gotta get down here and get your dad. He's passed out in the men's bathroom right now and I'm havin' troubles gettin' him up and outta my bar."

"What?" I couldn't hide the turmoil in my voice.

Getting a phone call saying my dad was at The Lucky Spur wasn't necessarily anything new, but getting a call from the *bartender* definitely was. A thousand possibilities, each of them equally horrific, flashed through my mind and it didn't matter that Caleb tensed next to me.

"Look," Jim continued pointedly. "The only reason I haven't called the cops yet is because I know he's going through some shit, but you gotta get him out of here. I'll give you 15 minutes, alright?"

"Sure," I nodded to no one in particular. "Thank you so much for calling. I'll be right over."

Before I even had a chance to slide off the barstool, Caleb's fingers closed around my wrist to stop me.

"Hey," Caleb's eyes brimmed with concern. "What's goin' on? And if you say everything's fine, I'm gonna tear my hair out or somethin'."

I wanted to laugh at that last part. How many times had I thought that exact same thing?

But this was no laughing matter and the narrowed eyes and clenched jaw signaled that Caleb wouldn't just let this go. There wasn't any time to weigh options or consequences, but still, I had to make a choice. When I glanced up at Caleb again, he was clearly on edge, but it was out of concern for *me* and that was enough to force my hand.

"That was the bartender at The Lucky Spur," I barely recognized the sound of my own voice. "He said I need to come pick up my dad."

Caleb didn't flinch at that revelation. His forehead creased almost imperceptibly, but that was the only moment anything like confusion flickered across his face. Instead, when he stared back at me now, the moment all the pieces clicked into place for him nearly had my knees buckling into the floor.

"Alright," he murmured hoarsely. "Let's go."

CHAPTER EIGHTEEN
Mirror

Caleb

When she started shaking her head, at first, I couldn't comprehend the motion, especially since I hadn't really asked her—I'd told her. It didn't matter that we were in a crowded bar with our friends. She couldn't just brush this off like it never happened and like I never heard it.

"Caleb," she started, her voice shaking and the sound just set me even more on edge. "You don't have to do that. I can handle it by myself."

"Maybe you can, but that doesn't mean you should," I pointed out. "I'm not gonna take no for an answer and let you go over there by yourself. You don't know what you're walkin' into if the bartender had to call you."

I paused for a second to gauge her reaction. The resolve and the steel behind her eyes confirmed this wasn't the first time she'd gotten a call like this, but when her chin dipped down in a nod, I figured that was probably as good as I was going to get. Her mysterious phone call the night before suddenly made sense and now, I just felt like the biggest asshole in all of North and South Carolina combined. I never should have let her walk out of the diner last night and I sure as shit wasn't about to make the same mistake twice.

"So, here's what we're gonna do," I pressed forward and hoped she'd actually let me take over from here. "You're gonna go tell Becca you're gonna meet Assface at that bar and I'm gonna tell Dom I'm headin' back to the clubhouse. Then you're gonna get on the back of my bike, whether you like it or not, and we're goin' over to The Lucky Spur to pick up your dad. He's got his car over there, right?"

She nodded. "Yeah."

"Okay, then we'll get him in his car. You'll drive it back to your house and I'll follow you."

Before she could protest, my hand reached out to her shoulder and gave it a reassuring squeeze. All I needed was for her to relent just enough so I could get her out of here. The longer we waited, the longer it would take to figure out what the hell was going on with Isabelle's dad and how long she'd been dealing with it on her own.

Isabelle seemed to register what I wanted her to do and even though it took longer than I would've liked, she nodded to affirm the plan. Whatever the reason she'd finally agreed, the crowd, the time constraints, or my instructions, I was just grateful for the quick turnaround.

"Alright," I kept my hand on her shoulder just for good measure. "Go talk to Becca. I'll talk to Dom and I'll meet you outside by my bike, okay?"

After she nodded blankly and pushed her way into the crowd in search of Becca, my eyes carefully followed her until I was sure she was actually talking to Becca. Dom wasn't hard to find at the bar because the people here seemed to innately know to give our cuts some space and I easily strode up to the counter, wasting no time.

It was a believable enough excuse anyways with little room for suspicion; it wasn't the first time I'd called it an early night and knew it wouldn't be the last, so Dom just shrugged, slapping me on the shoulder to send me on my way.

As I waited by my bike, my fingers twitched at my sides, practically begging for a cigarette, but I also knew the second I light one up, Isabelle would catch me right in the act and that was the last thing I needed right now. But Jesus, a hit of nicotine would really balance me out a little. I needed my head on straight because a million possibilities of what was waiting for us at The Lucky Spur ran on repeat in my head and that wasn't helping.

On cue, Isabelle pushed through the exit and the second her searching gaze found me waiting, she broke out into a jog to get herself there faster. Neither of us spoke as I hitched a leg over my bike and passed her my helmet. Her warm hands ghosted over my shoulders as she eased herself behind me.

The irony wasn't lost on me that this was the first time I'd had a girl on the back of my bike since Ariel, the only other girl who'd ever had the honor.

I didn't hold a lot of things sacred, but my brothers and my bike were right at the top of that list. Letting a girl ride on your bike signified that she meant something to you—a classification that most girls from the clubhouse and any other girl would never really qualify for. I'd relished every moment Ariel spent behind me on my bike, proudly parading my old lady around town for everyone to see that I'd claimed her, that she was mine.

But tonight with Isabelle? This was different. It might have been out of necessity, but a part of me knew that the circumstances didn't necessarily trump what Isabelle was to me either. She was...damn, I didn't know what she was.

She was friend, sure, but right now, it felt like that term didn't really accurately describe her either. She suddenly squeezed her arms around my stomach, making me painfully aware, despite my best efforts, that her thighs were clenching against the back of my hips.

The Lucky Spur was just down the street and I needed to get a handle on myself. I shouldn't have spent the whole ride there convincing myself that Isabelle's arms wrapped around my waist didn't make me need to adjust myself.

The whole thing was just so messed up it wasn't even funny...Isabelle probably spent the entire ride sick with worry and here I was so focused on the way her hands felt on me that I was lucky I got my bike parked without falling over.

Isabelle practically leapt off my bike the second I pulled into a parking space, giving me a quick opening to pull myself together. She was already right by the door and I had to scramble to get a hold of her before she burst through the door.

"Hey," I murmured and tugged on her arm to get her to turn around. "You gotta stay behind me, Iz. If it gets bad, you gotta let me take care of it, alright? No matter what happens?"

She nodded wordlessly, her eyes fixated on getting through that door and I obliged her, pushing it open and passing through first, my fingers wrapped gently around her wrist to tug her behind me.

The Lucky Spur wasn't necessarily the worst bar in Claremont, but it was definitely one of the grungiest and dirtiest, not to mention the second best place, next to The Sundown Saloon just down the block from here, where you could buy any assortment of narcotics anyone could ever ask for. It was a junkie's playground and not somewhere I typically made a habit of even being anywhere near if I could help it.

The Horsemen weren't stupid enough to touch that kind of hard shit, so the fact that Isabelle's dad was growing weeds under his ass here was particularly alarming. What did it say about a guy, who was supposed to be an upstanding, well-respected lawyer, who passed out face down drunk here if the Horsemen didn't even want to come within 10 miles of the place?

The bartender's expression shifted from relieved, probably when he recognized Isabelle, to pale and nervous, probably when he saw the Horsemen cut walking in with her.

"Bathroom's down the hall and to the right," the bartender gestured with his head towards the hallway.

Isabelle nodded robotically as I led her through the bar, weaving in and out around the stumbling patrons and beer-stained barstools. When the bathroom was just a few feet away, I cut her loose and she took off for the door, but I slammed right into her back when she skidded to complete stop at the bathroom's doorway.

Her shaky hands reached up to cover her mouth and her shoulders trembled. On reflex, my own hands shot out to her shoulders to steady her, to comfort her, but I had a feeling nothing was going to bring her much relief tonight.

Because Isabelle was frozen in place at the cracked, greasy doorway, I gently stepped around her, keeping my hands on her shoulders for as long as possible to help her stay calm. When I got a clearer look at the scene inside the bathroom, it was easy to see what kept her rooted right where she stood.

I could count on one hand the number of times I'd spoken to Samuel Martin. Each encounter was met with cold indifference and he'd always had a tendency to make me feel like I was no better than the dirt on the bottom of his leather shoes. Always dressed in the finest linens, tailored to perfection, with a haughty stare underneath his clean-shaven features, he commanded both your respect and your attention.

Seeing that same man lying face down on a grimy, beer-stained bathroom floor with only half its tiles was not an easy sight to swallow.

His once-crisp white shirt clung to his chest like he'd rolled around on this dirty floor and his mouth lobbed open like it was barely hanging on by its hinges. In that moment, it was like someone was shoving a mirror in my face, forcing me to see: was this what my family and my club brothers saw too? Was this what they saw when I got so wasted I couldn't even see straight? Was this what Isabelle saw the night she'd all but carried me back to my dorm?

Careful not to startle him, I knelt down to gain better access to his shoulders and with both hands firmly clasped underneath his armpits, heaved and pulled to drag Isabelle's dad to his feet. The unbalanced weight almost toppled us both over, but I got my bearings and shrugged down for a better grip so I could shuffle him out of the bathroom in an awkward dance.

Isabelle remained planted where she stood, gaping openly at the sight of me dragging her dad in my arms, but the second I gained some ground, the wall around her crumbled and she sprung to action. She swung one of her dad's limp arms around her shoulders, taking some of his weight onto herself, and together, we shuffled him out of the bathroom and into his car without a word to anyone still inside the bar.

As we situated her dad inside the backseat of his car, I shot Isabelle a careful glance. Her face was a blank mask, so expressionless and pale with shock it was scary, and my heart tore a little more at the sight of it. She was so goddamn strong—so resilient. How had I never seen this before? Why had I never stopped and seen her for everything that she was? How could I have been such a damned coward and let her deal with this by herself last night?

When she shut the car door, I wanted to reach for her, to do something, but for the life of me, I didn't even know how to begin to make this better for her.

Nothing was going to make this better.

All I could really do was be there and that just wasn't enough.

The drive to her house skidded by in a blur of darkness and shards of flashing lights and by the time we hoisted Isabelle's dad into the house, it was almost one in the morning.

I was starting to feel like I'd ridden a hundred miles tonight instead of ten and as I helped Isabelle lift her dad's legs into his bed, I knew I wasn't going to be leaving this house anytime soon either.

CHAPTER NINETEEN
A Good Man Is Hard To Find

Isabelle

It wasn't until I closed the door, leaving my dad slumped over in his bed, that the tightness in my throat devolved into a desperate suffocation. Needing to put some distance between myself and my dad's bedroom, I shuffled down the hall towards the staircase, my shoulders heaving with each step forward.

My eyes ghosted shut, unable to wipe away the image of my dad lying in that bathroom out of my head. Helplessness ran through my blood, covered my skin, ate away at my conscience, and almost knocked me off my feet. I stumbled from the wave, and then the barriers holding my emotions at bay crashed down...there was no more holding back.

And the worst part of all was I felt completely powerless. Utterly useless. Totally helpless. There was nothing I could do to help him, but pick him up and carry him home. I couldn't even do that without needing help.

Caleb knew everything now, every shameful, embarrassing detail, and there was nothing I could do about that either. One traitorous tear slipped down my cheek and then there was no stopping it. My hand flew to my mouth, muffling the sob ricocheting off the walls.

Warm hands suddenly slipped over my shoulders, turning me around until I was enveloped in a pair of strong arms. I inhaled leather, grease, gasoline, and musk and he squeezed his arms around me a little more tightly as one ringed hand worked its way through my hair with soothing strokes. With my head buried in his shoulder, my hands wound themselves around his neck, clinging desperately to something I wasn't sure he could give me.

"Hey, Iz," Caleb murmured in my hair. "Everything's gonna be alright. You're okay."

He gently lifted my head off his shoulder and tilted it so I could see him. When he brushed a stray tear from my cheek, it only made another slip down in its place.

"Why don't we head downstairs and then you can tell me what's been goin' on, alright?"

His voice was soft and calming and it cracked a little with concern for me. I couldn't have denied him even if I wanted to.

When we were sitting across from each other at the kitchen table, I didn't know what to say. I knew what he *wanted* me to say—I just didn't know how to put it all in words. How could I explain it to him if I didn't even understand it myself?

"When did this start, Iz?" Caleb's careful voice floated across the table.

For a moment, I wondered if I would even have a voice to answer him. "Right after my mom..."

He nodded quickly, not needing me to elaborate, his thumb running up and down on the water glass in front of him in thought. "Has it always been this bad?"

"Not like this," I shook my head and I bit down hard on my lip. "After the funeral, he was drunk for...I don't know, like a week straight. I told our family counselor and she told me to tell her if it got worse. And it definitely got worse, like he added another night to get wasted every week until he didn't have any left."

Caleb considered my words carefully and a few moments passed before I heard his voice again.

"Shit, Iz," he exhaled and leaned forward on his elbows. "I don't know how to ask this without sounding like a complete asshole, but...did you tell your counselor about it getting worse? I mean, we both know this is more than just a knee-jerk reaction to your mom. He needs to be in rehab or something."

"I know, I know," I ran a hand over my face. "I thought it would get better after some time passed, so I never said anything and I know I'm just making it worse now. I know that. And I've tried to get him to go back to family counseling with me, but the two times I got him to go, it ended with him screaming at both me and the counselor to stay the hell out of his life. I haven't been able to get him to talk to me about it since then."

He nodded again and blew out a deep breath. "And does he call you for rides like this a lot? Was that what that was last night when you left the diner?"

All I could do was just let my chin dip enough to give him his answer.

"Jesus Christ. Why can't he just call a cab or something? I don't get why it has to be—"

"Then I know he's home," I cut in quietly, hanging my head just a little and wincing as the words slipped out. "If I'm the one that picks him up, Caleb, then I know he's okay."

"So when you started workin' at the shop, all that shit about you needin' a job and money..."

"He told me he'd kick me out if I didn't have a job," I confirmed quietly, hanging my head again at my own stupidity. "If he kicked me out, how would I—well, I guess you already know now, don't you?"

"Shit," he sighed and fell back heavily in his chair, scrubbing his face with both hands. "You can't do this by yourself anymore, Iz."

I started to protest, but he just held up a hand.

"No, just listen to me, okay? I know you don't wanna hear this, but drinking like that, Iz, the kind that makes you black out—look, I know from experience that you do things you don't even realize you're doing because you're not really there. One of these nights, Iz, he could take all that out on you and it's just you and him here. Nothing would stop him from doing something he wouldn't even know he was doing."

It took everything in my power to strangle the sob in my throat at his words. They stung. It was like a slap in the face and it didn't matter that it was a truth I'd needed to hear since my mom's funeral.

"My dad wouldn't hurt me, Caleb."

"Maybe not, Iz," he just shrugged. "But who's to say what people are capable of when they're that far gone. And when he gets like that, you gotta call the cops or something."

My eyes widened and I shook my head from side to side furiously. "No, Caleb, I can't do that. He'll lose his job if he gets arrested."

"I don't—"

"If he loses his job...you don't understand. He's got nothing left."

I couldn't budge on this one and he would just have to accept it for what it was, even though it was still hard to reconcile why any of this really mattered to him in the first place.

"Yeah," Caleb muttered bitterly under his breath. "I guess you don't count, right? It doesn't matter that you're here dealin' with all this. You're just supposed to sit and take it?"

"Caleb..." I trailed off. I didn't know how to respond to that.

He shifted uncomfortably in his seat and swallowed, his eyes locked sheepishly on the glass in his hand. "I'm sorry, Iz."

"It's alright," I sighed.

"How does he even still have a job?"

"I don't know," I shrugged. "My guess is that he's doing a decent enough job keeping it out of work. He's gotta be going to work pretty hungover...I mean, he'd have to, but he's good at what he does. Always has been, sober or otherwise, and I guess people can look past everything else if you're getting the job done and not causing problems."

His eyebrows rose and then he blew out another weary breath. He looked exactly like I felt: tired, exhausted, and wanting to bang my head against a wall. My mouth opened and the words just came tumbling out before I could stop them.

"Caleb, I really appreciate you being here like this, but—"

"Look," he cut in, tugging a hand through his overly-long hair. "You gotta understand that I can't let you keep pickin' him up and bringin' him home like this by yourself, especially if it gets bad. I just can't let you do it, Iz."

My mouth clamped shut. The resolve in his eyes, let alone the fire, was something I wasn't used to seeing from him, at least, not since she-who-shall-not-be-named decided to take her indefinite leave of absence.

"You don't have do anything," I started quietly. "It's not your job to babysit me—"

"Are you kiddin' me?" Caleb shot back incredulously, his eyes widening. "Iz, I can't even imagine having to deal with this on a regular basis. I mean, I thought the clubhouse was bad, but this? This is different. This is your family. This is your dad. And it's just you here dealin' with all of this. You're so strong. You really are. And no, don't shake your head at me because it's true."

"I think you're overestimating me just a little bit," I countered quietly.

"Nah," Caleb shook his head dismissively. "You don't have a weak bone in your body, Iz. You're not runnin' from this shit, you know? You're here, you're taking what you've been given, and you're just dealing with it. I don't agree with it, but...if you're not gonna ship his ass to rehab, you need to at least let me help you because you can't do this by yourself. I'm not gonna let you."

Fresh tears sprung to my eyes and I swallowed hard as one slipped down my cheek.

"You can be pretty great when you wanna be. You know that, right?" I laughed in spite of myself as I brushed the tears away.

"Hey, I try," he shrugged and that cocky, crooked grin I knew so well slipped across his lips. "Anything for a friend though, right? And you and me, Iz, we're friends."

I nodded slowly, smiling back at him through me tears. This was the part of him I wished more people could see, the part that was kind and good. The part that I wanted to spend more time with.

"So, Iz," he was leaning forward now with his elbows on the table. "You gotta promise me that you won't take those calls by yourself anymore, okay? When you get a call like the one you got tonight, you need to tell me and I'll come with you. It doesn't matter where I am or what I'm doing. I'll be there. You just gotta trust me here."

There was no hesitation. No overanalyzing. No worry.

I knew instinctively that he was someone I could count on, someone who wouldn't let me down. The rationale might be a little murky, but that didn't make it any less true.

I trusted him.

I'd probably even trust him with my life.

So that was why I found myself nodding back to him, to agreeing to trust him, to letting him silently program his number in my phone because for the first time in way too long, I knew I didn't have to live in uncertainty anymore.

CHAPTER TWENTY
Rock Bottom

Isabelle

The next morning found me completely exhausted. When Caleb left my house, I'd paced around the living room for at least a good two hours before finally making an attempt at settling into bed. Sleep wouldn't come no matter how hard I tried, so I'd pulled out my sketchbook and spent the better part of the night working until the early morning light peeked in through the blinds.

In spite of three cups of coffee and counting, I still felt like a walking zombie. The second I walked into the office, Skyler narrowed her dark eyes and I knew I was screwed.

"Well," Skyler started easily as she leaned back in her chair. "Late night, huh?"

"I just had some trouble sleeping," I sighed.

I didn't need Skyler assuming I was hungover or something, but figured I knew the woman well enough to know she wasn't going to accept that as a sufficient answer.

"Yeah, looks like it," Skyler huffed. "Look, we've got a full schedule today and I'm gonna need you at as close to 100 percent as you can get, alright?"

I nodded and set my purse down in its usual spot, which held the product of my near-sleepless night, readying myself for work. When Skyler first hired me, the plan was for me to eventually handle office duties on my own, without Skyler's ever-watchful eyes, so she could free up some time to help her friend Celeste Bacall over at The Oval Office, the club's other sort of legit enterprise.

So far, Skyler had already left me alone for hours at a time, but never opening and closing and I got the feeling that everything, including today, was just one giant test.

I guess I'd better not fail today.

"Well," Skyler continued, gesturing to the garage window as she spoke. "If it makes you feel any better, Isabelle, it looks like Caleb is in the same boat as you today."

My head shot up at the mention of Caleb and my eyes found him out in the garage, clad in his blue Sawyer Auto Repair work shirt, and looking just as bleary-eyed and dead on his feet as I felt.

When he caught my gaze, he grinned sheepishly and waved. My heart leapt up into my throat at the simple gesture and I needed a moment to regain my bearings. It wasn't until I turned back towards my desk that I realized Skyler had observed the exchange with careful, if not slightly suspicious, curiosity.

I jumped on the stack of invoices on my desk and not on the fact that Skyler's eyes were still following me. The invoices, which my boss had so lovingly placed on my desk before my arrival, would definitely keep me busy until my lunch break.

Respite finally came when Skyler, satisfied with my performance, shooed me out of the office. As I shuffled towards outside, Caleb was already waiting for me at our picnic table and a flush of heat rushed to my cheeks.

This was so stupid. This anxiousness and nervousness...

This was just Caleb. He wasn't going to laugh at me or make fun of me, though up until recently, I wouldn't have put it past him. All I needed to do was woman up and pull the sketch out of my purse. It was the least I could do considering everything he'd done for me last night.

Simple as that.

Sure.

Caleb's head turned at the sound of my footsteps and an easy grin tugged across his face.

"Yo, Iz!" he called over to me with a wave. "Get your ass over here. I'm starvin'!"

"What?" I laughed as I swung my leg over the bench. "You think I brought you lunch or something? I'm not your mother, you know."

"And thank God for that," Caleb muttered under his breath.

"That's not very nice," I chided and wagged a finger at him. "Can you imagine what Skyler would do if she heard you say something like that? I think she'd have your balls in a vice faster than I could say hand over my Mountain Dew."

Caleb's shoulders shook with laughter and he shook his head, his fingers shooting down to the paper bag on the picnic table. In two seconds flat, his turkey sandwich was out of the plastic wrap and en route to his hungry mouth.

"Wow," I murmured, eyebrows raised. "You know you didn't have to wait for me, right? I'm pretty sure I would've gotten over it."

"Nah," he replied between bites with a shrug. "You know I can't eat without ya."

I huffed playfully. "God, what was I thinking last night making that present for you? I must have been out of my mind."

Caleb's eyes widened, mouth still full of turkey sandwich. "You made me a present?"

Suddenly, any nervousness or apprehension I felt going into this just slipped away.

Caleb seemed to just make everything easier and I should've known there was nothing to be worried about. He'd solidified his trustworthiness pretty well after last night anyways.

I knew there should be some part of me that was scared by that—the fact that I trusted Caleb Sawyer. But the more I thought about it, the more I realized it was one of the few things in my life I was absolutely certain of. I trusted him with my life. So why was I sitting here worrying I couldn't trust him with this?

Throwing all my remaining caution to the wind, I reached into my bag and handed over the folded piece of paper. "Yeah, ya jerk. I made you a present."

In a flash, the sandwich was left abandoned on the picnic table and he wiped his hands clean on his pants. His fingers nimbly unfolded the paper and it was then, as he stared silently at the sketch I'd made of his bike last night, that the nervousness swept back over me.

"I, um, I just wanted to thank you for last night. You really didn't have to do what you did and I know you said you wanted a sketch of your bike so..."

I didn't know what else to say and it definitely didn't help that he was just staring obsessively at the sketch in his hands.

"So, um," I tried again with the little courage I had left. "What do you think?"

Caleb's head shot up at my words, his brow creased in confusion. "What do I think? Iz, this is amazing. I wish I'd paid attention more in English class because I have no idea how to describe how cool this is."

"Oh," I bit my lip shyly. Another wave of heat rushed to my cheeks, but this time is wasn't from worry or embarrassment.

"I mean," he went on, his eyes sparkling with excitement. "You got everything about her perfect. Every line. Every curve. Just beautiful, Iz. She's beautiful."

With the way he was looking at me now, I sucked in a deep breath, a surge of...*something* rushing through me.

It was like he could see everything about me. Everything that I'd never really tried to show anyone else and here it all was, on a piece of paper in his hand. He just got it. He got all of it and he understood that it was just something I had to do. Not having to explain away every single thing to him or make any excuses for how I spent my time just felt so *good*.

"You know where this is goin'?" he was asking me now and he didn't give me a chance to answer. "Right next to my pillow, so I can see it when I roll my lazy ass out of bed every morning."

I laughed, chewing on the inside of my cheek to keep from showing too much emotion. I didn't really know how to describe what I was feeling right now either and I'd been the one actually paying attention in English class. These new emotions, just coiling around, wouldn't settle. They pulled and turned and bellyflopped all the way down to my stomach.

"I'm glad you like it. I had to basically do it from memory, so if I got anything a little off—"

"No," Caleb cut in. "It's perfect, Iz. You got everything exactly right. I told you already. It's amazing."

"Okay. When you put it like that..."

Caleb just shrugged and carefully folded the sketch back up, setting it gingerly next to his lunch bag. "You know, have you ever thought about going to some kind of art school or somethin'? I think those people would be kickin' down your door to get you to go to their school. Give you a scholarship or some shit like that."

"I don't know about that," I shifted a little in my seat. "I mean, that whole starving artist stereotype exists for a reason, you know? Besides, even if I *could* get into a school like that, what are the odds I'd actually be able to make any money off it?"

He shrugged like it was the most natural thing in the world. "I guess you'll never know if you never give it a shot. Maybe you wouldn't make tons of money, but who needs tons of money anyways, right? I guess what I'm trying to say is that whenever I see you sketching, you just look...totally and completely happy and you're sorta in your own little world when you're working. Like that's *exactly* what you were put on this earth to do and honestly, I think it is. It's not very often that people get a chance to go after something that makes them happy, Iz, and maybe this is your chance. I don't know. Somethin' to think about I guess."

No one had ever said anything like that to me before and I didn't know how to even begin sifting through everything he'd just told me. I'd gotten so used to believing I'd never be good enough at anything...hearing the opposite, from *him*, made tears prick my eyes.

"I think all the really good art schools are in New York or Chicago or something like that anyways," I allowed, especially since art school was never anything I'd even considered a legitimate possibility before.

"Well," Caleb shrugged again. "There's gotta be at least one good school somewhere around here, right?"

I spun my empty Mountain Dew can in my hand and figured it had to be true. It was just going to be a matter of mustering up the courage to research, let alone find the guts to apply. Ever since I'd found out my mom was sick, I'd been searching for something out of reach, something that felt so intangible at the time. And now, for whatever reason, I felt like Caleb had just thrust me on the path to finding out what that something was.

"Maybe I'll look into it."

Even if I still wasn't completely sold on the idea, it was still an idea. A place to start. A potential door to open.

Caleb grinned widely back at me like he'd just won some sort of undeclared battle between us. "That's what I like to hear, Iz. Well, at least I can say I finally have an Isabelle Martin original when you get all filthy rich and famous and forget about all the little people you had to step on to..."

He trailed off when Brandon's truck pulled into the shop's parking lot, rap music blaring from his rolled down windows. While the appropriate reaction to seeing my boyfriend pull up unexpectedly at my work should've been somewhere in between surprise and happiness, I found myself bristling with annoyance instead.

Then a glimmer of guilt popped right up next to it. None of this was really fair to Brandon. He really hadn't done anything wrong and he certainly hadn't done anything to deserve the way I felt towards him right now.

I glanced in Caleb's general direction and almost—*almost*—smiled when I realized his entire body had coiled, ready to pounce on Brandon at a moment's notice. Caleb's lips curled back into a barely visible sneer and his shoulders rose tensely, like he was waiting for Brandon to make one wrong move. His hands disappeared under the picnic table, probably so I wouldn't see how tightly his fists were clenched.

"Hey, Isabelle!" Brandon's deep voice called out.

When he broke out into a jog towards the picnic table, I kind of had to acknowledge his presence and so I shot him a weak wave and an even weaker smile.

When he reached our table, he bent down and pressed a hard, possessive kiss on my lips. It felt like I'd just been branded, right in front of Caleb, and I had a sinking feeling that was exactly what Brandon wanted to do. I was too shocked, too stunned to even bother looking for Caleb's reaction. I was pretty sure I knew what I would find anyways.

"Hey, Sawyer," Brandon rasped out quickly, barely glancing his way.

When I finally let my eyes find Caleb, I had to clench my teeth together to keep from reacting. It was like the Caleb I had been talking to only a few minutes before had vanished and a hard, impenetrable mask of cocky arrogance slipped into place instead.

"Davis," Caleb replied easily with a smirk and folded his arms across his chest.

"You mind if I have a minute with my girl here?"

Caleb's eyes flicked to me for a moment before leveling his gaze back on Brandon. "For you, Davis, 30 seconds."

He didn't wait for Brandon to reply and instead, swung his legs over the side of the bench and stalked off towards the garage. I watched him just long enough to see him dig into his back pocket for a cigarette. When I turned back to Brandon, he'd already slid in across the table, taking Caleb's place, and my heart lurched violently in my chest.

"Hey, Isabelle, I'm sorry for showing up here like this—"

"I really wish you'd called or something," I cut in abruptly. "If I wasn't already on break, you could've gotten me in a lot of trouble with Skyler."

Whether or not that was actually true, Brandon needed to know I wasn't exactly happy to see him right now.

"Okay, okay," he held his hands out in defense and then glanced over to the garage.

I followed his gaze and nearly jumped in my seat when I realized Caleb was standing at the edge of the garage's entrance, puffing away on a cigarette as he observed us with dark, hollow eyes. A moment later, he flicked the spent cherry to the cement at his feet and disappeared inside the garage.

"Look, Isabelle," Brandon continued quietly. "I just wanted to tell you how sorry I am about last night. I shouldn't have left with the guys. I know I should've stayed with you and I knew I'd really messed up when you didn't answer any of my calls. I just wanna make it up to you, okay?"

My eyes squeezed shut. I hadn't answered any of his calls last night because I'd been too busy taking care of my dad with Caleb to worry about what Brandon was or wasn't doing. Besides, if I had answered, it wasn't like I would've explained where I was and why anyways.

He never would've understood and I had a sneaking suspicion he wouldn't have offered his continued assistance either...unlike Caleb, who hadn't needed an explanation.

He just got it.

But it also wasn't fair to judge Brandon when I wasn't telling him the whole story. I hadn't really given him the chance to prove himself and here I was, comparing him to Caleb, someone he couldn't be more different from.

Another wave of guilt crashed against me and tears pricked at my eyes again. God, I hated feeling like I was always going to cry...

Brandon was trying to apologize for something he didn't do. All he'd wanted to do last night was hang out with his friends and that wasn't a crime. The worst part was, I wasn't even upset that he'd left—if anything, I'd just felt relief when he was gone. And that just made me feel even more like an asshole.

Here he was, trying to fix things between us and I couldn't care less.

I really was an asshole.

"Don't worry about it, Brandon," I replied with renewed determination.

He just shook his head, refusing to accept my indifference. "It wasn't okay for me to just leave you like that. I didn't even think about how you would feel."

A smile tugged at my lips. This was why I'd talked myself into seeing him again in the first place. He really was a good guy who cared about other people and he was trying so hard to make things work between us this time around. Didn't he deserve a little of that in return? I'd barely given him a chance here and now it was my turn to make up the difference, to put a little effort into it.

"I know," I whispered, barely recognizing the sound of my own voice. "I appreciate you coming here just to say that. It really means a lot."

His entire face brightened at that new admission and I couldn't help but feel a stab of guilt.

"So," he started and the hope creeping back into his voice kind of made me want to bang my head into the picnic table. "Does that mean you're gonna let me make it up to you tonight?"

"Depends on what you have in mind," I tossed back, trying to be playful, but it still felt forced.

"Oh, you'll just have to wait and see," he reached across the table to play with my fingers and I smiled at the sweet gesture.

"Okay," I grinned back.

My options were pretty limited here and I felt like I had to at least *try* to prove to him tonight that I was going to put just as much effort into this relationship as he was. This time around, things could be different. I could be different, if I just gave it a chance.

. . .

Later That Night

What the hell was I thinking?

When Brandon asked to come in, I'd known it was probably a bad idea, but couldn't turn him away after the night he'd planned so meticulously for us. He really had pulled out all the stops to 'make it up to me' and that just made me feel even more guilty.

I was trying. I really was. I wanted him to know this wasn't completely one-sided, or at least, I didn't think it was, and that I wanted to be with him.

I didn't know who I was trying to convince more—Brandon or myself.

The night was just about as perfect as he could've made it: reservations at my favorite restaurant, drinks at my favorite bar, and he'd even brought my favorite flowers when he picked me up. He'd done everything he thought he was supposed to do and yet, I still felt like something was missing.

The guilt followed me all the way up the stairs, when Brandon walked me up to my door and asked if he could come in. I couldn't say no, not after tonight and not after how hard he'd tried to make me happy.

And so I didn't say no when he started to kiss me and when he led me upstairs to my bedroom. I knew it was exactly what he expected and part of me really wanted to make him happy too; the other part of me just shut off completely.

Even when he was on top of me, moving against my body, I could tell he was trying to make it good for me. He was touching me in all the places he remembered, the ones he used to know so well. It felt good for a few moments, but was I wishing it was someone else's hands...someone else's mouth?

And then I just wanted it to be over.

"I'm so glad we're back together," he murmured into my hair. "I've never gotten over you, you know. All that time, all that distance, babe. I've always been thinking of you, wondering where you were, if I'd ever get to see you again."

All I could think about was how I needed to wash my sheets now and how I just wanted him out of my bed. I'm pretty sure those thoughts officially made me the worst person ever.

At least I could play this whole messed up situation with my dad to my advantage now. He'd be calling for a ride soon and there was no way Brandon could be in the house when that happened, if ever.

"Hey, um," I started, shifting away from him on the bed as much as I could without being too obvious about it. "My dad is going to be home soon and I know how much this sounds like old times, but..."

That was really all I'd needed to say and Brandon leapt off the bed, throwing his clothes back on with lightning speed. I almost wanted to laugh—how many years later and Brandon was still scared shitless of my dad, not like there was much left to be afraid of anyways. He was usually too drunk or hungover to bother with anything going on in my life, let alone care I'd gotten back together with the boy he'd once referred to as 'an idiot who would go nowhere'.

So when Brandon finally left, I found myself sitting restlessly at the kitchen table, waiting for that inevitable phone call. I just needed something to take my mind off how dirty I felt, how guilt had led me to make a such a stupid decision.

Sure, I was no virgin, but I'd also never had sex with anyone before and just felt *nothing*. There had always been some sort of feelings attached to the act, even if it was just drunken lust. But here, with Brandon, I'd just been plotting ways to get him out of my bed before he was even finished.

I had to end it.

I had to put him out of his misery. It wasn't fair to string him along like this and I couldn't keep up the charade that any of it mattered to me.

Rock bottom. That's what this was. And it felt like complete crap.

Brandon did nothing but try to take care of me and be a good boyfriend and I was a heartless bitch for going through the motions with him in return.

How did I let this happen? Since when did I let someone have sex with me because I felt I owed it to him, because I felt guilty? This wasn't me and this wasn't the kind of person I wanted to be.

This feeling...like I was stuck in reverse...it just was like when I first found out my mom wasn't going to get better. Everything was backwards and upended now and that was the opposite of the direction I wanted my life to be heading in. With the way things were going, I'd probably be better off back at Duke.

This wasn't what I wanted. This wasn't how I wanted to be. Repeating the past wasn't going to help anything. I was just backpedalling now and I just couldn't get myself to move forward.

It was only when a tear slipped down my cheek that I realized I was crying. Even that wet shakiness couldn't even bring me back from the brink. Wiping the tears away didn't help either because more just fell down in their place until I was hunched over on the kitchen table, sobbing into my hands.

My phone buzzed with a new text message, yanking me from my self-inflicted misery.

Pick me up at Sundown Saloon.

That was all I got from my dad. Simple, to the point, no time for a thank you. Either he was just too lazy or too drunk to physically make the call, but either way, it was probably better that we didn't talk right now. With my state of my mind, I didn't know what I would do or what I would say.

Ugh. The Sundown Saloon. Not a place I wanted to be anywhere near...ever, but at least he'd been smart enough not to go back to The Silver Spur.

And then my fingers rested over Caleb's number. Right now, I just wanted to hear his voice. Even if he was pissed about what had happened at lunch today, and even if he was probably too busy burying himself in whiskey and some random girl to even care that I was calling, I wanted to hear his voice. Even if all I got was his voicemail, I wanted to hear his voice. Even though he'd probably sense that something else was off tonight in about a second, I still needed to hear his voice.

Before I could stop myself, my fingers hit the send button and it was ringing. Sheer, irrational panic shot through my entire body and I scrambled to hit the end button before it was too late, but then I heard his smooth voice over the other end: "What's up, Iz?"

And just like that, everything instantly felt better.

CHAPTER TWENTY-ONE
Hey Jealousy

Earlier That Day

Caleb

All I wanted to do was lock myself in the clubhouse and down the first bottle of whiskey I could get my hands on. It didn't help matters that the garage was practically overflowing with customers all afternoon. The worst part was I'd thought I'd gotten past all this. But here my old habits were, rearing their ugly heads when the shit hit the fan.

When Davis finally left, Isabelle quietly returned to her post in the office without so much as a glance my way. The rest of my shift just dragged by while I came up with excuse after excuse to avoid having to go within 10 feet of the office. Which, honestly, was no easy task given that I was supposed to physically bring in the keys to let Isabelle know when I was finished with a customer.

I didn't mean to intentionally avoid her. I just couldn't face her.

Davis showing up out of the blue like that and ruining my lunch break had my blood simmering on a low boil, so seeing the two of them all cozied up on my picnic table pretty much upped my blood to scalding.

I really needed a drink. Or 10.

A relapse back down the rabbit hole wasn't going to convince Marcus or anyone else in the club that I'd turned a corner. With another run to Pittsburgh scheduled in a few weeks, Marcus had already given me the heads up that I was on the rotation. A run, especially dealing with the Warlords in Pittsburgh, was really just business as usual for the club, but it was a place to start.

That was good for me—a way to show the club I was committed and could keep a handle on everything long enough to get the job done. All I needed to do right now was keep my head in the game and drinking myself unconscious, even though I kinda needed it right now, was not the way to do it.

But by the time my shift was over and I was standing in front of the bar in the clubhouse, I couldn't stop my fingers from closing around the first bottle of Jack I could find.

I was allowed to have a good time and unwind every once in awhile, wasn't I?

This wasn't about numbing any sort of pain or taking my mind off things—this was about just letting loose. When I felt a pair of feminine hands wrap themselves around my neck, all I saw was blonde hair and then I closed my eyes and just let it happen.

But a few hours later, when the cloud cleared from my head and the blonde curled up next to me in my bed, slipping back into old habits wasn't the relief I'd been looking for.

This girl didn't mean anything to me and that just made me feel even worse than before.

Thankfully, the blonde, who I hadn't cared enough about to even ask her name, seemed to realize that our time together was over and she silently tip-toed around the room to find her discarded clothes.

I couldn't even really remember taking her clothes off in the first place, like I'd completely shut my mind off the moment she'd started leading me back to my room. Everything just went blank and the Jack I'd forced myself to swallow down wasn't completely to blame for that either.

Turning off my mind, just letting this just happen to me—the drinking and the women—it was all a dangerous, slippery slope. An occasional slip here and there wouldn't matter too much in the grand scheme of things, but that didn't make me feel any less like a damned failure.

When the blonde silently shut the door behind her, all the darkness left the room. Air was coming in and out more easily now and the heavy weight on my chest dissolved completely.

I almost called out to her, not to invite her back to bed, but I just had a sudden urge to apologize. If she didn't know what she was in for the second she stepped foot in the clubhouse, that was her problem. Odds were, she'd gotten exactly what she wanted from me, but there was still something about the whole thing that just made me feel like the scum of the earth.

My legs swung over the edge of the bed like they had a mind of their own and I swept my jeans off the floor, digging into my back pocket for Isabelle's sketch. I found myself tracing every line in pure fascination.

Short of sounding like a pathetic asshole, I'd almost told her no one had ever given me a gift like this before and I was still kicking myself for not being able to articulate what this meant to me.

It wasn't the same as getting a gift from my mom for Christmas or my birthday. She *had* to give me gifts, whether she wanted to or not. This was different. No obligations attached to it. No expectations behind it. She just did it...because. I couldn't wrap my head around that. In my world, you didn't give people presents just because and you definitely didn't give presents that were so incredibly personal and intimate.

Maybe that was what set me so off-balance. The intimacy. The time she'd spent working on it — I could practically see her hunched over, biting her bottom lip in thought as her pencil flowed expertly around the page, bringing my bike to life like I was sitting right next to her. The skill and the expertise she'd shared with me was something I didn't know how to reconcile.

Finally, I secured the sketch right where I'd told her I would: right next to my bed. Taking a slight step back, I surveyed the sketch and then quickly readjusted the tacks so the paper hung a little bit straighter. Part of me hated to puncture it at all, but I knew tape would potentially do more damage to it anyways and I wanted to preserve this for as long as possible.

A loud buzzing from across the room yanked me from my thoughts and I dove around to find my phone. One glance at the caller ID and I flipped it open immediately: "What's up, Iz?"

"Hey, Caleb."

My whole body tensed at the sound of that unmistakable hitch in her voice.

"Iz? Are you okay? What's wrong?"

"I'm okay. I am. I promise. My dad texted though and..." she trailed off, sniffling a little and the hairs on the back of my neck stood on end.

"Are you crying?" I practically barked and she just sniffed again. "Iz, you gotta tell me what's goin' on here."

"I was out with Brandon," she tried again, but I was way ahead of her and already jumping to conclusions that made my blood boil over.

"Did that asshole do somethin'?" I snarled. "I'll kill him if—"

"No!" she cut in quickly. "He didn't do anything and he's gone now. Look, Caleb, I called you because my dad texted me and *you* told me I had to let you know, so...that's what I'm doing."

I blew out a deep breath and tugged a hand through my hair, frustrated at this overwhelming feeling of helplessness.

"Okay, fine," I pushed out roughly and jerked on my jeans as I spoke. "Where is he?"

"The Sundown Saloon."

Jesus Christ. Of all the bars in town, why the hell did Isabelle's dad have to pick the worst one? What kind of a father called his daughter in the middle of the night to pick him up from a place like that?

"Please tell me you're not already there, Iz."

"I'm not. I promise."

"Good, 'cuz there's no way you're driving over there and sittin' in that parking lot by yourself. I'll be at your house as soon as I can, okay?"

I snapped my phone shut as soon as I was sure Isabelle would actually wait for me to get to her house and threw an old Horsemen T-shirt so I could get the hell out of the clubhouse.

Something was off with her and it had everything to do with that dipshit boyfriend.

So, when she threw open her front door, my mind was on constant alert, sniffing out the clues for whatever had gone down between them tonight. Her movements were stiffer, her eyes more hollow, her voice colder and detached like she was trying and failing miserably to hide from me.

It wasn't going to work.

I wasn't going to let her pretend that everything was *fine* when it clearly wasn't, especially when she seemed to lean in more and hold on tighter when she got on the back of my bike. She needed me for more than just an extra set of hands to help her with her dad tonight. And hell if I didn't need her just a little bit too.

171

Still, seeing her dad slumped over on a bar stool at The Sundown Saloon of all places, barely able to even hold his head up, let alone walk without leaning heavily on both Isabelle *and* me — I had a feeling this was never going to get any easier.

I never should've touched that bottle of Jack tonight. Now, seeing up close what it could do to you, what it could do to your family, what it could do to your body, the way Isabelle's dad couldn't even form a coherent sentence...I never wanted to touch it again.

That was over for me now. It had to be. The blackouts, the hangovers, the dirty hookups — I was done with all of it. I couldn't keep self-medicating with whiskey and hope that would magically solve all my problems. Because from where I was standing as I lifted Isabelle's dad into the backseat of his car, all whiskey did was make an already grim problem about a million times worse. I wasn't, however, in a position to let myself ruminate on why I'd suddenly switched to blondes instead of the brunettes I'd been prone to grab before.

Luckily for me, once Isabelle's dad was safely back in their house and in his bed, I could shift the focus away from my own shit, which was as uncomfortable as hell, to this new, detached and aloof Isabelle, which concerned the hell out of me. I trailed after her down the stairs until we were standing at the bottom of the staircase, staring back at each other awkwardly.

I shoved my hands into my pockets, rocking back on my heels a little and cleared my throat, fumbling for a way to stay here a little bit longer with her when she beat me to the punch.

"So, do you have anything going on for the rest of the night?" she asked.

"A whole lot of nothing," I shrugged and tilted my head to the side to shoot her a grin. Maybe that would ease the tension in the air a little. "Why?"

"You could stay if you wanted to. I mean, you don't have to leave yet. We could watch a movie or something?"

I chuckled. "Iz, I thought you would never ask."

.   .   .

I settled back against the couch cushions, waiting for Isabelle to come back with some popcorn. She'd run upstairs to change into some pajamas after I was officially sticking around tonight and when she came back down the stairs, my eyes just about popped out of my head.

The tiny tank top skimmed over her smooth, creamy skin, leaving just a little bit of her flat stomach peeking out underneath it. Just one look at the top half of that tank top pretty much screwed me. Barely any cleavage. Just a peak. But it was there. It was *there*.

Shit.

And the shorts she was wearing....Jesus, did that even count as a piece of clothing? They were practically nonexistent, just barely covering up more than underwear or a swimming suit would, and still left way too much room for my imagination to run wild. All that toned leg. I couldn't remember ever seeing so much of her before.

Shit.

I was *trying* to be a good friend here. I was *trying* to figure out what the hell was up with her tonight and she was making it real difficult.

"The movie's in the Blu-ray player already," she called from the kitchen. "You can start it up if you want."

There was that hitch in her voice again and it just wasn't like her. Something happened with Davis. While it probably wasn't as bad as I thought, that didn't mean the asshole was completely off the hook either. All I knew at this point was that he was over at her house tonight and she'd called me after crying. Someone needed to explain this to me pretty quick or I'd be banging down Davis' door in the morning and that probably wouldn't end well for either of us.

Even when she sat down next to me, careful to sit as far on the opposite side of the couch as possible, I didn't like this distance between us. I wanted her closer because I wanted to touch her just as badly as I wanted to know what happened with her tonight.

Shit.

After a few minutes of previews, the opening credits of *Die Hard* started and I let out a little whoop of excitement—my existing concern almost all but momentarily forgotten.

"You know, Iz," I threw an arm over the top of the couch so I could turn towards her more. "I had a feelin' you were gonna pick this one. It's like you read my mind."

"Well," she shrugged with an easy grin and popped a piece of popcorn in her mouth. "I figured I needed to see for myself if it was any good or not and who better to watch it with, right?"

"Absolutely, Iz," I grinned back.

Within two minutes of the movie, I found myself paying less attention to what was happening on the screen and more attention to what was happening with Isabelle. She kept shifting anxiously next to me and every time she moved, her shorts bunched up a little more by her hips. That was definitely not helping my concentration and I really, really didn't want to be *that* guy who could only think with that little head and completely lost my shit at the sight of just a little bit of skin.

Okay, it wasn't just a little bit of skin. She was showing *a lot* of skin.

That wasn't what this was about and my eyes searched anxiously for something to throw over her legs to cover her the hell up. When I realized my arm was resting over an afghan, I slapped it down over her legs until the offending material was completely covered.

Thank God. Her smooth legs looked so soft and if I let myself fantasize about them any longer, I'd be imagining what it would be like to feel those same legs wrapped around my waist.

Shit.

This wasn't helping me and it certainly wasn't helping me keep my head in the game here. What I needed to do was get her talking, but how exactly to go about making that happen was still a mystery.

"Hey, Caleb? Can I ask you a question?"

When I shifted my body to could face her, I nearly had a heart attack at the sight. She looked like she was ready to completely crumble in my lap and not in a good way. Her bloodshot eyes were brimming with fresh tears and I practically had to sit on my hands to keep them to myself.

"Sure, Iz. You can ask me anything."

My hoarse voice felt scratchy and foreign in my throat.

"How do you do it? I mean, how do you sleep with so many women and just...feel nothing for them? How do you make it look so easy?"

That was not what I was expecting. So I guess this was suddenly about me now...I was treading some seriously uncharted territory here and I didn't know the first thing about any of this.

"What makes you think it's easy?" I replied finally. I honestly had no idea what else to say.

"I don't know," she shrugged. "Because you seem to do it a lot. I don't mean to be rude or a bitch or anything. It's just that I wish there was a way I could be like that too. To just be able to turn it off and not feel like complete crap afterwards."

My eyes narrowed at her words, but I knew I couldn't push her too hard. If I did, she could shut down on me completely and then I'd never get the full story. And then I'd probably have to kill Davis.

"What do you mean?"

That seemed like as good a response as any.

She eyed me carefully, like she was weighing whether or not she could trust me with whatever she wanted to say. All I could do was pray she judged me and found me worthy. How was I supposed to help her, to be a good friend to her, if she didn't trust me?

"I think I need to break up with Brandon," she whispered.

"Okay," I exhaled. That wasn't what I expected to hear, as much as I'd wanted to hear it, but at least she was talking. "So, that's a good thing, right?"

"I just feel horrible," she sniffed, wiping a fresh tear from her cheek.

Seeing her cry, her face crumbling and blotchy with wet tears—that was probably the worst thing I'd ever seen and I'd seen an awful lot of shit in my life.

"Hey," I reached out and mindlessly brushed a stray strand of hair away from her eyes. "You didn't do anything wrong. It's not your fault if it's just not workin' out with him. You're perfectly entitled to do whatever makes you happy."

She laughed a little at that and I wiped away another tear from her cheek. After that, I couldn't stop myself from throwing an arm around her to tuck her under my shoulder.

"Tell me what's goin' on, Iz," I murmured into her hair. "I can't help you if I don't know what's goin' on."

She curled her legs underneath her and leaned all her weight into me like she was clinging to me for dear life. Maybe she actually was and I hated myself a little right now for enjoying the way her body fit against me, the way her cheek seemed to hit at just the right spot on my shoulder...

"I did something I shouldn't have," she whispered into my shoulder. "I feel like such an asshole for doing it and I never should've let it go that far."

I gently lifted her head away from my shoulder so I could get a better look at her. "What do you mean?"

"I..." Isabelle managed to choke out before burying her head into my shoulder again as a wave of sobs racked her entire body. I held her quietly as she cried, deciding it was best to just let her get it all out now. Maybe then, when it was all over with, maybe then she could finally tell me what was happening here.

Then I heard her hoarse voice again: "I slept with him tonight."

I blew out a breath to keep myself from reacting. Honestly, I'd suspected as much when she called me, but from what she'd just told me, it sounded like it was closer on the consensual side of things, unlike my overactive conclusions. Still, I hadn't prepared myself for how much actually hearing the words would affect me. Like a sucker punch to the gut. That's what it felt like. Knocked the fucking wind out of me.

And it was so hypocritical it wasn't funny because I'd been with someone else tonight too. Literally right before she'd called me. But the thing was, that girl I'd plucked from the clubhouse's main floor wasn't who I wanted.

I had a sinking feeling that the one I'd really wanted tonight was nestled under my arm right now and I had no clue what to do about it.

So, I did what I do best and deflected my attention elsewhere.

"Okay," I whispered into her hair. That was the best I could come up with and even that was a challenge.

"I don't know why I did it," she laughed and pushed some hair off her face as she spoke. "I guess I felt guilty for letting him try so hard."

"Try hard at what?"

"Being my boyfriend," she shrugged a little too easily. "I don't know why I started seeing him again in the first place. It was just..."

"Old habits die hard, huh?" I offered.

"Yeah," she nodded against my chest. "Something like that. He was just being so nice and he was putting so much effort into making it work this time around. I guess I thought maybe that was enough for the both of us. But now, I just feel, I don't know. I just feel dirty, like I need to take a shower or something. Being with Brandon was easy...it was comfortable, but now I know I'm just going backwards with him and that's not what I wanna do."

I was completely out of my element here. Then she forced another laugh again and abruptly pulled herself out of my arms to wipe her face. She curled her legs underneath her, but still leaned against my arm. I didn't realize how grateful I was for that warmth until it was almost gone.

"Look, Caleb," she started again, more firmly this time. "I'm not a..."

"A prude?" I offered and Isabelle smacked me on the arm.

"Fine, I'm not a prude," she laughed. "And it's not like I was exactly a virgin either. It's just that I can't do the no-strings thing, you know what I mean? Don't laugh at me, but I guess I'm not the kind of girl that can just hook up with someone and be okay with it not meaning anything. I need the emotional attachment. I need it to mean *something*. And it wasn't there with Brandon tonight and I did it anyways because...I'm not really sure why. And I feel like crap now for doing it."

I wrapped an arm around her and pulled her closer. "I get it, Iz. There's no shame in that. In fact, there's absolutely zero shame in that. You haven't done anything wrong here. You know that, right?"

It took her a little too long to find the words to respond. "Then why do I feel so awful right now?"

I smiled and fought the urge to press my lips into her hair. "Because you're a good person. That's why it feels bad now. But I can tell you this much, I wish I had half the conscience that you do. I'm not kidding. I think you might be on to somethin' about being with somebody you actually care about. It just feels a little empty when it's not. Trust me, I know exactly how you feel."

"Then why do we do it?"

"Well," I grinned. "I can tell you from experience that I think I kept hopin' it would make me feel number than alcohol ever could. Maybe not so much physically but emotionally, if that makes any sense. And if it makes you feel any better, it used to be pretty easy for me, but not so much anymore."

"No?"

"I guess I just realized that it's not fixing any of my shit any faster. I'm still pretty messed up in the head and all the mountains of Jack and one-night stands in the world aren't gonna make that better any time soon. And I know I need to quit all that. I just...I'm not gonna do that anymore, okay?"

I needed her to understand that. I needed her to know I was done with all that. And when she smiled and leaned her head against my chest, I felt like I could breathe again. Maybe I didn't deserve to have that as my reward, but I was gonna take it anyways.

"I figured you'd get there eventually, but thank you for telling me," she whispered. "And you're not messed up, Caleb. No more than me or anyone else."

"Thanks."

"No problem."

When she laid her head on my shoulder again, I quickly shifted my focus back on the TV to keep my fingers from exploring the bare skin in between her shorts and her tank top.

"You feelin' better?" I asked her.

"Yeah," she nodded. "I'm sorry you had to deal with all this. I feel like I've been a complete train wreck the last couple of times I've seen you and I'm sure this wasn't exactly on your list of things to do tonight."

"Hey," I told her. "I'm glad you called, Iz. You know I got your back, right? If it's your dad, if you need to talk, all you gotta do is call me and I'll be there."

This time, there was no hesitation, no doubt, and no regret in her eyes as she nodded back to me. I just pulled her closer against my chest, knowing I wouldn't always get to feel this, that I wouldn't always get to spend my nights on a couch, watching a movie with my arm wrapped around a beautiful girl.

In the morning, she would just be my friend again, but for tonight, maybe I could get away with letting myself wonder what it would be like if I was lucky enough to have this all the time.

"Everything's gonna be alright now, Iz," I murmured into her hair. "Everything will work itself out and you'll be exactly where you're supposed to be, doing exactly what you should be doing. You can't beat yourself up over things you can't change."

I only wished I could say the same for myself.

CHAPTER TWENTY-TWO
One Step Forward

Isabelle

It didn't matter that I'd done everything in my power to make this as easy on Brandon as possible. I'd waited until we were alone, until we could really sit down and have a real conversation. All I wanted to do at this point was let him down as gently and as painlessly as possible.

Brandon, unfortunately, had other ideas. In fact, he was doing everything in *his* power to make this as difficult on *me* as possible.

"So...what?" Brandon was staring at me like he hadn't heard me literally just say we needed to break up.

"What do you mean?"

Maybe if I clarified one more time that this was permanent and that no, it wasn't him...

Brandon just shrugged and frowned down at me. "I mean, if you need some time, I get it. I just don't see why it needs to be like this, Isabelle. This is our chance to get things right this time around. Don't you want things to be just like they used to be?"

Where was the nearest wall? I needed to bang my head into something hard. Preferably concrete.

"That's what I've been trying to say," I couldn't stop myself from gritting my teeth. "Everything is *exactly* like it used to be. That's not what I want right now."

Oh no...why did I have to say *right now*? He was going to read too much into that and pretty soon, getting him to face reality and really listen to me was going to be like pulling teeth, one bloody incisor at a time.

"Well, you just need some time, right?" he asked hopefully, shifting from one foot to the other.

"No," I shook my head. "That's not what I meant."

"Okay."

"This," I gestured between us, "is exactly the same as it used to be. At least, I guess it is on your end, but it's not what I want anymore. We're 21 and I don't want to be doing the *exact* same things I did in high school with the *exact* same people. I'd like to try to grow up a little and I can't do that if I'm still stuck like this. Please don't take that the wrong way because this really has nothing to do with you and everything to do with me."

Brandon's coffee-colored eyes melted into a burnt amber as he seemed to finally absorb what I was telling him. Any hope of a reconciliation seemed to dissipate in his expression and a pang of guilt stabbed at me. This was what I'd wanted since the night we slept together, with disastrous results on my end, but now that he was finally listening, the aftermath wasn't going to be pretty.

"Is this about Sawyer?"

I blinked.

"What?"

Brandon licked his lips, glaring at me with a menace I'd never seen before, at least not directed at me. "I guess that means you think I'm an idiot then."

Was this some kind of sick joke?

"I honestly have no idea what you're talking about."

"Right," he folded his arms across his chest and the air between us shifted. "You think I haven't seen the way he looks at you? That I haven't seen him *touch* you for shit's sake?"

"Caleb and I are friends."

He threw his head back to laugh, but it just came out bitter and spiteful. "My ass you're friends."

"Brandon, this has nothing to do with him. This is about *us* and about us not working. I've tried to be nice about this because, honestly, this isn't really about you, but you don't have to be such a fucking jerk about it."

The minute the words came flying out, I wanted to clamp my hand around my mouth. I knew him well enough to know that the it had pretty much just hit the fan.

"*I'm* the jerk? *I'm* the asshole?" His face had flushed a scary shade of crimson. "Why did you even start this with me again? Why did you even go through with it?"

I deserved that. I really did. What I did not deserve, however, was being spoken to like I was some kind of heartless and conniving bitch. Maybe I *had* used him as a placeholder for something, but it wasn't like I'd done it with malicious intentions. So much for trying to end things quietly and respectfully.

"How the hell was I supposed to know I would end up feeling this way? I have nothing but good memories of us together when we were in high school, but you know what? We're not in high school anymore, Brandon, and it's time to grow the hell up. That goes for both of us."

"Oh right," he threw his hands up in the air. "The way I see it, you've just traded one for the other here, Isabelle. You think I'm just doing the same shit I was doing in high school with the same people? What about Sawyer, huh? What the hell is *he* doing? This is complete bullshit. You know that, right? Just one excuse after the other."

"I told you before—this has nothing to do with Caleb or anyone else," I clamped my teeth down on my bottom lip in unbridled frustration. This whole thing just escalated out of my control and now I was done trying to play nice.

I needed this to be over. *Now.*

"So this is it, Isabelle? This is how you wanna end it?"

I folded my arms across my chest and refused to budge. "Yeah. It is. I think you should leave now."

"What a waste of time," he spat as he shoved past me and stalked towards his car.

It wasn't until that stupid, pretentious, asshole Tundra was all the way down the street that I felt like I could finally exhale. All the weight just disappeared from my shoulders and relief seemed to seep into every pore.

Finally.

Moving forward didn't seem so far out of reach now. Maybe this was the push I'd needed to snap the hell out of it. Maybe now I could finally figure out a way to fill the void that had just deepened since my mom died.

That final thought propelled me back into the house and sprinting up the stairs. Since I had the whole house to myself until whenever my dad decided to call for a ride, I would have more than enough time to do some research and figure out where the hell to go from here. It was time to finally put myself in the driver's seat and take control for once.

What had Caleb said?

"You'll never know if you don't try, Iz."

It was time to figure out if I could try.

After an hour of scouring my Google search for art schools in North Carolina and beyond, I had a solid list of programs that seemed to be everything I was looking for. Each one had similar course requirements, and from what I could tell, all my gen eds at Duke would transfer, so I'd only be looking at two years for each program instead of four.

There were three in particular that caught my eye: the School of the Art Institute of Chicago, the University of North Carolina School of the Arts, and the Virginia Commonwealth University. Duke, of course, had something to offer in the way of fine arts, but I couldn't even stomach the idea. If getting back together with Brandon was a step backwards, returning to Duke would be jumping back a mile.

The Art Institute of Chicago was ranked number three in the entire country for drawing and painting, which was probably where I'd land, in terms of my major.

Chicago.

God, that would be so cool. That would be freaking awesome...the number three school in the country. The number three school in the country that was also 10 hours away from Claremont, North Carolina.

I just couldn't see myself ending up that far away from home. The distance wasn't something I was comfortable with for reasons I also wasn't quite sure I could articulate.

The program at the Virginia Commonwealth University, or VCU, had the best reputation within a five hour range in terms of productivity and quality. It also had the advantage of working within the Washington, D.C. art scene, which helped make the program more nationally recognized too. Maybe settling for the number seven art school in the country wasn't really settling anyways.

The program here in North Carolina honestly didn't look that different from the one at VCU and it was ranked as the best in the state; in fact, from what I could tell, it seemed like I'd have more control over developing my own coursework and projects, which definitely had its advantages.

The biggest factor that stuck out to me, though, was location. VCU was in Richmond, Virginia which was a big, progressive city with tons of history and even potentially the type of change I was looking for but...it was also five hours away from Claremont. Winston-Salem, where the UNC school was located, was less than an hour away and I could easily commute if I really wanted to.

The only thing I could really do was start filling out an application for both. All I could do was try. I probably wouldn't get into either one anyways. Schools like that needed some sort of professional portfolio and all I had was a sketchbook. But, if I wanted to potentially get accepted for the spring semester of this school year, I couldn't waste much time.

After a whole night of filling out over fifteen pages of applications, writing a personal statement that didn't sound too pathetic—how did one explain a semester-long break from Duke anyways?—and somehow keeping all the details straight, I needed a break. And a drink.

I leaned into the wooden chair, my back stiff from sitting for so long, and stretched my arms over my head. I compulsively snatched my phone off the computer desk and scrolled through my contacts until I found Caleb's number and then my fingers flew across the keys to stomp out a text.

Guess what I'm doing right now.

A few moments later, my phone vibrated with his response and I bit back the wide smile that slipped across my face.

What's that Iz?

Applying for art schools.

Less than a second later, his response flashed across the screen and I laughed out loud.

No shit!! Thats awesome Iz!!

I found 2 that look pretty amazing so I'm doing it.

What do u have to lose rite?

I smiled at his response—it was like he could read my mind.

That's exactly what I was thinking.

Ur applyin too the best 1s rite?

I wasn't sure what I was smiling at now: his reply or his grammar. He really wasn't kidding about not paying attention in English class.

Yep, not sure which 1 is the right 1 tho.

U'll figure it out Iz.

Thx, Caleb.

Anytime Iz. Lunch tmrw?

Sounds good. C u tmrw.

Can't wait. Bye, Iz.

Bye.

I set my phone down on the desk, a small smile creeping across my face, and I was ready to get back to work now.

That was all the motivation I needed.

CHAPTER TWENTY-THREE
Like I Need Air

Caleb

Marcus hammered the gavel to call church to start. All the deep, gruff voices immediately hushed at the sound and I settled back into my chair next to Dom. In the three years I'd been able to sit at the table, it still felt a little surreal to really be here. Since I could walk, this was all I'd ever wanted: a cut, a bike, and a seat at this table. No matter what else was going down, *this* was home.

Looking around the table, at all the faces I'd known for the better part of my life, *this* was my family. Heath, Dom's dad and the club's VP, nodded to Marcus from his spot to the Prez's left, signaling that he was ready to just get this over with already. Everyone else waited patiently and respectfully for their club president to move forward with church, and each body in a seat was my brother.

Casey, the club's sergeant at arms, sat at Marcus's right, followed by Eli, our intel officer, Tiny, our secretary who was also anything *but* tiny, ZZ, a recent transfer from our charter in San Antonio, Doc, the name speaks for itself—every single one would take a bullet for me if they had to and I'd do the same for them.

Dom and I were always side by side at the table and that symbolism hinted at both our legacy and our shared futures in the club. Heath's health was slipping, his heart was getting weaker and his lungs couldn't quite keep up with all the smoke he inhaled on a daily basis. Someday, probably sooner rather than later, he was going to have to step down from a ranked position at the table, leaving me to slide into his place. When the time came for Marcus to step down, he'd hand the club over to me with Dom as my VP. It had practically been written on our birth certificates the moment Dom and I came out of the womb.

Outlaw was what I was born into, but it was also what I was born for. There just weren't any other options for me because this was everything I'd ever wanted. My legacy was at this table and there was no way I'd ever do anything to jeopardize that.

"Alright," Marcus began, calling attention to order. "We got a few items on the agenda that need dealin' with. First things first, got the call from Ortega, so it looks like the Lobos are gonna move forward with patchin' over the Cobras. He wants to give them a little test run, if you will, to make sure Padilla will perform up to par. We got this run for the Warlords coming up and Ortega thinks this would be a good opportunity. Padilla and his boys make the exchange with us, everything's good, and they patch in the Cobras."

A low murmur cascaded around the table as that marinated and it was clear the club might have a divided vote on this one.

"So...what?" Heath huffed from his seat next to Marcus. "We just let ourselves be guinea pigs for those assholes? If the Cobras are as untested as Ortega makes it sound, why the hell are we responsible for tryin' out the new merchandise?"

"He's got a point," Dom chimed in. "I know it's just a run, but there's a helluva lot that could go wrong, especially if Padilla isn't up to par. Could cause us some problems with the Warlords if they're not happy with the delivery."

I chewed on my bottom lip in thought and flicked my cigarette in the ashtray next to me. "Gotta keep the Lobos happy though, bro. If this is something they need to stay happy, then maybe we need to give it to them. Besides, things work out with the Cobras, we stand to benefit from that patch-over too. More muscle for the Lobos means more muscle for us. Everybody wins."

The impressed expressions on Marcus and Tiny's faces weren't lost on me and this was just yet again another golden opportunity to prove myself. It wasn't a secret that my motivation and my dedication had been called into question enough times in the last few months to make me squirm under the pressure. Here was a chance to show any naysayers I was all in.

At this point, all this shit with the Lobos and their potential patch-over was really a blessing in disguise for me, even if the Cobras just ended up being a thorn in the club's side.

I was smart enough to take care of this. I had to be.

"Anybody else got somethin' to say?" Marcus motioned to the table with his cigarette.

"I think it would be a good show of faith on our part," Casey shrugged. "This run should be a piece of cake. Same old, same old."

Doc nodded emphatically from his side of the table. "If the Cobras somehow screw this up, it's better Ortega and his boys know now rather than later."

"Well," I started again, seizing the opportunity to have the last word. "As far as I can tell, we're not gonna talk the Lobos outta this patch-over even if we wanted to. And we kick up some issues with the Lobos by pissin' them off with this...could attract some unwanted attention. Whatever keeps the ATF outta North Carolina is what we need to do."

"I agree," Marcus nodded as he clamped his teeth down on his cigarette. He paused for a few short moments to gauge the mood of the table. "Vote?"

After the nods signaled everyone was ready, the votes went around, with all swayed but Heath, which wasn't much of a shocker. It was the little bit of validation I needed to know that my opinion was worth something at the table and to know that when I spoke, my brothers would actually listen.

The plans were simple enough: the Lobos would route our normal order to a specific pickup point for the Cobras, who would make the exchange with us, and we would, in turn, pass the shipment to the Warlords, our contacts in Pittsburgh. That shipment was exchanging hands more times than I was comfortable with, but at the end of the day, we really couldn't make it any simpler for Padilla. Now it was just a matter of seeing this thing through to the end.

The club had a long history of business with the Los Lobos MC in Raleigh and they were pretty much our main suppliers for all the cargo we sent up north. If we lost the Lobos as an ally, we also lost most of our Northern business too, which we couldn't afford to do. And even though everything I'd heard about Diego Padilla and the Cobras was that they were stubborn and hot-headed...well, I figured that wasn't really my problem as long as they did the work and came through as the muscle.

As soon as church adjourned, I shot a glance at the clock, knowing if I hurried, I could still meet Isabelle at our picnic table for lunch. It was my day off at the shop, but I was here and it felt a little weird to eat lunch without her now.

The few times that had happened I almost didn't know what to do with myself. The last time we'd worked separate shifts, I'd spent more time glancing around for her, even though I knew she wasn't working, than actually eating my lunch. Besides, I was chomping at the bit to hear all the details about those applications she'd filled out last night. It didn't matter that I already knew she and Becca were coming out with us tonight—why not just hear about everything now?

My mouth dipped into a low frown when I didn't see her at our picnic table right away, so I turned on my heel and headed straight for the office, trying to shake the feeling that something was wrong. Hell, it wasn't like I was her babysitter or anything and she didn't necessarily need anyone keeping tabs on her either. Still, I could barely keep myself from sprinting into the office to make sure she was there and that today was just a normal day.

I nudged the door open with an elbow and my lips tugged upwards when I saw my mom and Isabelle huddled up together by the printer.

"I was sure if we just hit this button, the damn thing would work, but..." my mom trailed off as her dark eyes flew up to me. "Hey, baby. Church just get out?"

"Yeah, just a minute ago," I tilted my chin towards the printer. "What're you ladies doin' over there?"

"Well," my mom jutted a hand on her hip. "We're trying to scan some of Isabelle's sketches, and I don't know if our wireless is down or what, but neither of us can get the damn thing to actually work."

I shifted my attention to the other beautiful woman in the room, cocking a playful eyebrow at her and pushing away the way my heartbeat spiked at her shy smile.

"You're scannin' sketches now, Iz?"

"I need to put a digital portfolio together and Skyler said I could use the scanner," she just shrugged.

I nodded slowly, painfully aware that my mom's ever-watchful dark eyes were currently darting between Isabelle and me with a curiosity that made me a little nervous. It took a deep breath and a loud exhale for me to realize that Isabelle was watching me now too. At least she was still smiling at me.

Just as I was about to open my mouth to say something, anything to break this awkward spell, my mom stepped away from the printer, her lips twitching with amusement.

"Well," she started softly. "I suppose I should go find Eli and see if he can fix the scanner. I'll leave you two kids alone."

Thankfully, she didn't linger too long and was out the door a half a second later because I wasn't sure I could take that prying gaze right now. With Isabelle in the room, I didn't know what it was. I tended to lose focus on anything but her and the last thing I needed right now was for my mom to ask me some obsolete, mindless question I wouldn't be able to answer just because I was too busy looking at Isabelle to even hear what she said.

"So..." Isabelle started slowly, her eyes sparkling like a deep ocean in the sunlight.

"So, I wanna hear all about those applications. You take your lunch break yet?"

"Nope," she smiled and gestured with her head towards the door. "Let's go."

.　.　.

When we were sitting at our picnic table, I felt like I could finally breathe. And focus. Sometimes, I wasn't sure if it was just her presence that calmed me or if it was all in my head because being so close to her tended to make me *lose* focus sometimes too. Either way, all I knew was I was starting to need these quiet moments with her like I needed air and I had no idea what to do with that.

"So, you're making a digital portfolio," I prompted her as she unwrapped her granola bar and took a bite.

"Yep," she nodded in between bites. "All the websites I looked at last night said you need that to at least be considered. It just sucks though. I mean, I don't have any letters of recommendation, no transcripts that really matter. All my gen eds will transfer, so I'd only have two years of school left instead of another four, but it's not like anything else I did at Duke really counts now anyways. I just don't know if this portfolio is going to be enough."

"It will," I nodded, needing her to see just how firmly I believed in this and in her abilities. "Maybe it's better this way, ya know?"

"What do you mean?" she frowned.

I just shrugged and leaned over to grab some of her Gardetto's. "This way you can just let your work speak for itself. It's enough, Iz. It really is. So, when do you think you're gonna apply?"

When she chewed on her lip, her head leaning downward, my heart lurched in my chest—what did I do? What did I say?

"As soon as I have my portfolio ready, hopefully by the end of this week. Skyler told me I could use the shop as my home address just because I don't know what my dad will do if he sees anything in the mail," she murmured softly, still unable to meet my eyes. "Thanks, Caleb."

Something tugged at the edges of my heart, making it twist and compress deep in my chest. Would this feeling only intensify when she finally brought her eyes back up to me? I didn't really need to think about it. The answer was obvious.

"It's not a big deal, Iz," I shrugged, which was just my lame attempt at grasping for something to shove me back into reality.

"No, Caleb," Isabelle shook her head and just that slight movement made my heart ache. "It is a big deal. You have no idea."

I waited as she struggled to find the words she was searching for and tried not to reach out to her. Every instinct sparking through me was screaming to touch her—just once, to comfort her, to help her find what she was looking for, to do whatever she needed right now. I just wanted to be there, to be what she needed, and I knew I should be nothing but eternally grateful she was even letting me sit across from her right now.

"It's just that," she whispered, gesturing between us. "I've never had this before. I've never had anyone tell me that...ugh, I know what I'm trying to say but I—anyways, what I mean is, thank you for everything. Your support, your encouragement, that's what I've never had before. You're the only who's really seen my sketches and you're also the only one who's ever told me that I'm good at it. I don't know that I would've even *thought* of applying to art school if it wasn't for you. I guess I just didn't think of it as an option for me until you suggested it. I have no idea if I'll even get in, but at least it's something, right? At least I'm trying. *Finally*."

I figured it was going to take some serious introspection before I could even begin to wrap my head around everything she'd just said and what it meant. So, instead of trying to think of something profound or meaningful, I just leaned into my elbows and shrugged.

"You're welcome, Iz," I shot her a soft grin and then, I slapped my hands on the table. "So, tell me about these schools, huh? I wanna know everything. Don't leave anything out."

I resisted the urge to lean my head on my elbow to listen as she went into animated detail about each school, the location, programs, cost, student loan options, professors, reputations—she really didn't seem to leave anything out.

The obvious choice, at least to me, was VCU. It would probably be the perfect place for her to hone her artistic abilities and most importantly, to provide that fresh start she seemed to crave. Besides that, it was the best art school in this whole region of the country. She deserved the best and I was just so damned proud of her for reaching for it.

If our roles were reversed, I doubted I'd have the balls to pull myself together and actually try to accomplish something worthwhile with my life. She was doing something real, something that would take her places, and if it led her out of Claremont, I knew I needed to prepare myself for that exit too.

Something stabbed at me from the inside out just at the thought of Isabelle ending up five hours away from Claremont. It was the best thing for her. It really was. The cold hard truth was that, deep down, I knew I wouldn't want her to leave whenever that time came.

"Hey," Isabelle threw a pretzel at me, drawing me out of my thoughts. "You're coming out with us tonight, right?"

"What? Uh. Yeah, I don't see why not."

"Good," she exhaled. "I really need a drink."

"Why's that, Iz?" I frowned.

Her blue eyes sparked with realization. "Oh crap, I didn't even get a chance to tell you! I ended things with Brandon last night, right before I started filling out those applications actually, and needless to say, he did not take it well."

I leaned forward, eyebrows raised and instincts engaged. "Really? Everything alright?"

"Yeah," she dismissed my concern with a wave of her hand. "He probably said some things he shouldn't have said, but I guess it could've gone worse."

"But you're okay?"

"I'm fine, Caleb," she grinned back at me and that calmed my nerves a little bit. "Better than I've been in a while, actually. I just feel like a giant weight has been lifted, you know? But, I still need a drink."

"Well," my lips curled into a smirk. "I guess I better help you out with that then, huh?"

CHAPTER TWENTY-FOUR
Brawl

Isabelle

I couldn't imagine being anywhere but at this table, surrounded by the people who'd become such an integral part of my life. Becca and Eli were directly across from me with Dominic and Lexie to my right and Caleb to my left. Finally, after a rough couple of days, unwinding a little felt really good. This, right here at Graffiti's, was exactly what I needed.

"I don't care what anyone says," Dominic was goading Eli. "You can't tell me the Eagles are better than the Panthers. I won't listen to a damn word you have to say."

"No, that's blasphemy and you know it!" Eli practically stomped his foot in response and Caleb just barked out a laugh.

Even though the two had been going back and forth, with arguments ranging between most Super Bowl showings to rushing yards, I wasn't putting too much effort into following along. The song, "Follow Your Arrow" by Kacey Musgraves, was playing in the background, so completely fitting for my life right now, and kept me rocking my shoulders to the beat until Caleb playfully hip-checked me right into Lexie.

"Hey, asshole," Lexie pointed her index finger at Caleb with faux sternness and hooked her finger towards her swollen belly. "There's a baby bump here. Did you forget that, buddy?"

Caleb's hands immediately flew up in defense. "Hey, sorry if I forget sometimes, Lex. It feels like you've been knocked up forever."

"Jerk. I'm *really* glad you're gonna be my baby god-daddy," Lexie smirked back at him, carefully sneaking a glance at me as she spoke.

"Listen, Lex," Caleb threw back at her with a cocky grin. "All you gotta do is admit how much you love me and we can stop pretending."

Lexie just rolled her eyes as Dominic tossed a handful of popcorn at Caleb. "Right, tell me again why I'm gonna miss you when you're gone?"

Although I was literally right in the middle of them, that last comment caught my full attention. Gone? The immediate frown that crossed my lips couldn't be stopped and my heart thudded in my chest as my mind spiraled into a whirlwind of questions. Where was he going? How long was he going to be gone? Why didn't I know this happening?

I didn't want to sound like a clingy, desperate *something*, but I couldn't stop myself from turning to face Caleb. "Where're you going?"

Caleb just shrugged and draped an arm around my shoulders. "Just a run, Iz. No big deal."

"Oh, okay," I nodded slowly, painfully aware that all eyes at our table were fixated on us.

It didn't matter that I didn't entirely understand what a run all entailed. Someone, probably Lexie, could explain it to me later. All I could really put together through my hazy grasp of the situation was that Caleb was going to be leaving and the idea of him leaving, even for a few days, just did not compute.

Something shifted in Caleb's ocean blue eyes and I felt myself suck in a sharp inhale...it was like he could read my mind and knew exactly what was running through it. I really hated that about him right about now.

"You alright, Iz?" he murmured into my ear.

I pressed on a fake smile, but it quickly faded when I realized he was just going to see right through it. No, I wasn't alright and I couldn't pinpoint exactly what it was that bothered me so much: the fact that Caleb was going to be putting himself in a potentially dangerous situation or the fact that he was leaving for an undetermined amount of time.

Realizing that both of those things were troubling me, especially since I had no real reason for it, was probably what upset me the most.

"Aw," Caleb was murmuring in my ear again and this time, I shivered. "You're gonna be lonesome when I'm gone, aren't ya?"

His teasing eased a little of the tension and my lips twisted into a grin. I elbowed him in the side, making him scoot back with a yelp.

"Nah," I threw back. "Miss you? Are you kidding me?"

Caleb's hand covered his heart and he pretended to wince. "Ouch.

That hurts me, Iz. That really hurts."

"Whatever," I just shrugged.

It was then that my eyes slid to my right and caught Lexie's curious smile. I quickly averted my gaze straight ahead only to collide right into Becca's sly smirk. Wasn't the emotional confusion enough tonight?

"Well," Becca started, the knowing smile never quite leaving her eyes. "You guys are only gonna be gone for a few days, right? I mean, it's not like it's gonna be weeks or anything like that."

"Nah," Caleb shook his head. "We're headed to Pittsburgh. Should just be a few days to get everything squared away. Same old shit as usual."

"Oh, so that's not..." Becca trailed off, her eyes wide.

Everyone at the table turned their heads to follow her gaze and I almost choked on my drink. Crowding into a corner across from us was Brandon and his band of assholes. He was teetering unsteadily on his feet and if that wasn't enough proof he was half in the bag, I could spot the glassy eyes a mile away.

After how everything played out last night, it was only fair we both had the same idea to unwind with friends and a few beers, but Brandon wobbled like he'd had about 15.

"Shit," I heard Caleb exhale next to me.

Becca's face quickly crumbled. "Hey, Belle, we don't have to stay here. We could go somewhere else, right?"

She looked frantically to everyone else at the table for confirmation. When a round of nods passed around, she visibly relaxed, but still kept her wide, almost desperate eyes fixed firmly on me. Becca was just trying to help, but seriously, her overblown reaction was definitely not helping the situation.

"Nah," I swatted out a hand with a shrug. "We don't have to leave because we were here first. Besides, if we leave now, then the terrorists win, right?"

After that last comment, Caleb's eyebrows lifted up deep into his forehead. Then the warmth of his hand grazed my back and his breath tickled my ear.

"You sure, Iz?"

I just nodded. There was no point in making a bigger deal out of this than it already was and ruining everyone's night.

"Well," he continued softly. "I don't care about that asshole over there, but if you change your mind, just say the word, a'ight?"

I could only nod in response, still reeling from all the turmoil flooding around me. The one-two-punch of Caleb leaving to Brandon's arrival sent me flying completely off-balance and so, I did the only thing I could do: I just took another drink from my glass and tried to pretend like none of this was happening.

And for about 10 minutes, it worked. Conversations went back to normal and the situation seemed to be contained. Everyone was staying on their respective sides of the bar, even if Caleb's gaze flitted back and forth from me to Brandon for the better part of our peaceful quiet.

Everything was, for the most part, back to the way it'd been before our interruption until Brandon decided to saunter towards our table, swirling beer in hand.

Caleb swiveled his body to put himself directly in front of me and the second Brandon skidded to a stop three feet from our table, all three Horsemen cuts stood a little straighter, ready to strike if necessary.

"Hey everybody," Brandon slurred, waving his beer around as he spoke. "Just wanted to come over and say hello. Thanks, Isabelle, for doin' the same."

Caleb tensed next to me and made a move towards him, but my hand shot out to his bicep to stop him.

"Caleb, don't. It's not worth it."

Even though Caleb backed down and was leaning towards me now, Brandon just snorted and took a step closer to our table with an unstable sway that had Caleb shifting uncomfortably next to me.

"Right," Brandon laughed mirthlessly, gesturing towards us with the neck of his beer bottle. "Slummin' it just like I knew you would, Isabelle. I don't think Mommy would be too happy to know her precious little princess ditched Duke to come back here and play biker whore for this asshole—"

He didn't get a chance to finish because Caleb was already shoving past Eli, knocking over some glasses and nearly our entire table, and slammed his fist squarely into Brandon's already slack jaw. Within seconds, Caleb had Brandon flat on his back and landed a few more furious punches before Dominic and Eli pulled him off Brandon's limp body.

"Jesus Christ!" Dominic yelled. "What the hell are you thinkin'?"

Caleb yanked himself free just as the bartender jumped over the bar, screaming at us to get the hell out. Everything was a blur as Becca dragged me towards the door. I didn't even realize I was outside until the cool breeze picked up the edges of my hair and blew it around my face.

Caleb stumbled out next to me with Dominic, Eli, and Lexie right on his heels and he was digging into his back pocket before he was even completely out the door. But by the time he'd lit the cigarette and taken a few unhealthy drags, his cloudy eyes lifted from the cement and slammed right into mine.

He blinked once, his eyes widening, and as his cigarette sailed to the cement, he muttered, "Shit."

"Let's get the hell outta here before this gets worse," Dominic barked out, his eyes trained furiously on Caleb. "Lex, follow us back to the clubhouse, alright?"

Lexie nodded quickly and I quietly slid into the backseat of Lexie's Oldsmobile as Becca got into the front seat. Motorcycle engines roared to life next to us and I could see Caleb's shoulders rising and falling violently through the dim parking lot lights. As Lexie pulled onto the street to follow the three bikes ahead of us, I had no idea how to process what had just happened and *why* it happened.

I was still trying to make sense of the bitter, cruel things Brandon had said to me—let alone Caleb's response to it. Everything seemed to happen in slow motion and in a blur at the same time. All I saw was a flash of black leather and then there was just a crescendo of breaking glass and shouting.

Even though I was grateful for the complete silence on the way to the clubhouse, it still wasn't enough to wrap my head around the last 20 minutes.

But the most frightening moment of the night came as I passed Caleb on the way inside.

He was hunched over on his bike with one hand in his hair, the other resting on the handlebars as Dominic approached him. As if he sensed my presence, he tugged his sullen gaze up from the pavement and met me head-on. The pull of his eyes, of his presence, almost had my knees buckling from the pressure. I wanted to leap into his arms and wrap every limb around his body and that was absolutely terrifying.

Completely paralyzing.

Out of self-preservation or fear, maybe even both, I just kept my head down and continued towards the clubhouse, shaking off the fact that Caleb's eyes never left me.

CHAPTER TWENTY-FIVE
Denial

Caleb

I blew out a shaky breath as Isabelle headed inside the clubhouse. Well, at least I could finally have that damned cigarette now. I shifted on my seat to dig for my pack again, and my mind grasping at straws to figure out how everything spun so disastrously out of control tonight. Everything was going fine. Same old, same old for a Friday night.

And it wasn't until that dickhead decided to show his face and spout his mouth off at the one person who didn't deserve it that I completely lost my shit. It would be easy to blame everything that had gone down solely on Davis, but I knew better.

That was the key here. I knew better.

But it felt so good to finally give that asshole what was coming to him —a couple of times. I clenched my sore knuckles...at least I hadn't broken anything. Still, the payoff of finally getting to pummel the hell out of Davis wasn't high enough to counter the disappointment. I was just so damned disappointed in myself for letting this happen in front of Isabelle.

I didn't wanted this and I certainly didn't want her to have to take the verbal abuse Davis dished out at her. As far as I was concerned, it was a no-win situation. At least I'd gotten to sucker punch Davis right in the jaw for being such a goddamned insensitive prick. I wasn't entirely sure which comment pissed me off more: the one about Isabelle slumming it as my biker whore or the one about her being her mom's precious little princess. Both were equally callous and mean as hell, especially considering the target.

"Bro," Dom was murmuring lowly to jerk me out of my thoughts. "What the hell happened back there?"

I just shook my head with a shrug. "I don't know, Dom."

"What do you mean you don't know? That's bullshit and you know it," he shot back, his forehead creasing with concern.

"I don't know, bro," I sighed heavily and pushed back on my bike. "You know me and him have always had a beef."

Dom's eyebrows rose. "That wasn't about some old high school beef back there."

I lit a cigarette and took a few healthy drags before feeling like I could finally answer my best friend. "I guess I just couldn't sit there and let him say all that shit to her."

Dom nodded slowly and ran a hand over his face. "So that's what this is about then?"

"Maybe."

Dom pushed out half a laugh and a smile tugged at his bearded lips. "You know, I've been meaning to ask you about that. Everything with Lexie and the baby's got me side-tracked a little but..."

"What's your question, Dom?"

Or better yet, just spit it the hell out already.

"I don't know," he scratched the back of his head. "It just seems like you and her are always together at the clubhouse. Some people think you guys are hooking up or something."

I frowned. I definitely didn't like where this was heading. "Who's *some people*?"

"Does that mean you are?" Dom's lips twisted into a knowing grin and I had the sudden urge to bitch slap it right off.

"Damn gossip around this place is worse than a bunch of women," I spat back.

"So," he mused, crinkling his forehead like he just didn't understand. "You're not hooking up with Isabelle then."

"No, I'm not," I shot back, spiking the spent cherry between my fingers down to the pavement in frustration.

Dom paused for a moment, like he was trying to think of the best way to word his next comment.

"Do you want to?"

"Jesus Christ," I shook my head.

"Okay, okay," he held up his hands in defense. "You don't have to get so pissy, bro. I'm just tryin' to figure out what the hell is goin' on with you and her because...well, *something* is."

"She's my friend," I pushed out curtly.

When Dom's eyebrows flew into his forehead, I cursed under my breath.

"Yes," I clarified. "I said, *friend*."

"Just wanted to be sure. I feel like I don't know what's goin' on with you half the time anymore," Dom shrugged. "So, what, you guys talk during your shifts or somethin'?"

"Yeah, somethin' like that. I don't know, Dom. I guess I can't explain it."

He nodded soberly and shoved his hands into his front pockets. "You and her aren't entirely out of the realm of possibility though, you know? And you're different when you're around her too—you're a little calmer...happier, kinda like how you used to be before...ah, it's shot to hell now, considering what you pulled tonight. But, I mean, you guys have left the bar and the clubhouse together before and you're together at work all the time. You've really never thought about it? Not even once?"

"It's complicated, Dom."

"So un-complicate it."

He said it so simply like that was the only possible answer when Dom didn't even know the half of it. Even though the timing of this conversation really sucked, it was one I'd been meaning to have with him anyways.

"Look," I started hoarsely. "I'm only tellin' you this because I need you to know in case somethin' happens when I'm gone on the run. And you can't say a word to Iz or anyone else about this unless somethin' happens, alright?"

"Okay," Dom nodded, mirroring the serious turn this conversation had taken.

I sighed and tugged a hand roughly through my hair. It was now or never and even though Isabelle would probably kill me for this, I needed some sort of provision in place while I was gone in case she needed help. If I couldn't be the one to help her, Dom was the only other person I trusted with the job.

"I've been helpin' Isabelle with her dad. That's where we go whenever we leave together. Her dad usually calls her from some dive around town, drunk off his ass, and then we go pick him up and bring him back to their house. I usually stay until I'm sure she'll be alright there by herself with him."

"Damn," Dom exhaled.

"Yeah," I nodded tightly. "Look, I'm gonna give her your number so she can call you if she needs some help when I'm gone, alright? But don't say anything to her about it. She's probably gonna try to smother me in my sleep for tellin' you all this and the last thing I need is for her to freeze me out now."

"Alright," Dom nodded in understanding and I could see the wheels in my best friend's head turning. "Yeah, I can do that. No problem."

"Thanks, bro."

Dom's forehead creased again in thought. "Can I just ask—and you can punch me later—but are you sure there's nothing else there? I mean, this isn't the kind of thing you just do for a friend. And I don't wanna sound like a chick or anything, but I don't know, brother, I don't see too many guys throwin' punches over a girl that doesn't mean anything to them."

I bristled a little at that and shifted to the defensive, tugging another hand through my hair. "She's just a friend, alright? I guess if I'm being completely honest, aside from you? She's probably the best friend I've ever had."

"Come on," Dom pressed, gesturing to himself. "You're not lumpin' her in with me, right? We're not really comparing apples to apples here."

"Fine," I conceded. "Maybe it's not the same, but that doesn't mean I'd try anything stupid with her though. I've got too much shit to straighten out right now to do anything but mess her up too and I'm not gonna do that to her. Someone like her, Dom? She deserves better than what I have to offer her right now."

My best friend was silent for a few moments, turning to look towards the clubhouse in thought. When he finally spoke, his simple, quiet words pretty much guaranteed me a sleepless night:

"Maybe not now, bro, but when you do pull yourself together, I think you're gonna need to revisit that."

CHAPTER TWENTY-SIX
here is the deepest secret no one knows

Isabelle

I trudged down the stairs, with Caleb right behind me, and headed back down to the living room. My dad was stone-cold in his bed, which was probably the best I could hope for when it came to him. About an hour after the gunslinging showdown at the bar tonight, I'd gotten the call. It was almost like clockwork at this point.

All it had taken was a quick, inconspicuous text to Caleb and we were headed out to the fine Claremont establishment, The Sundown Saloon. There'd been no resistance from my dad tonight either, which just made things as easy as they could possibly be. After the night Caleb and I had both had, it was a relief to just plop down on the couch and completely zone out.

"You don't have to leave, you know," I murmured over my shoulder. I jumped a little when his hands grazed over my shoulders, but I still couldn't turn to face him.

"Alright," he replied gently.

"Movie?"

"Sure. You pick."

He followed me into the living room and I heard him drop down heavily on the couch. He probably looked as tired as he sounded, but I just couldn't bring myself to turn around and look. Facing him now meant facing everything that might be better left unsaid and I wasn't ready to do that until I absolutely had to.

So, like the coward I was, I sat down cross-legged on the carpet with my back to him. Grateful for the welcome distraction, my weary eyes scanned the rows of DVDs and blurays until my lips curled up in a smile.

Yep, that one was the perfect choice, especially given the current company, and I shifted a little so I could hold up the DVD box for him to see.

"What about this one?"

Caleb, who was lounging on the couch now with one arm strewn over the top edge, frowned as he tried to place the title.

"You don't remember this movie, do you?" I continued, biting back a smile.

His forehead crinkled and his lips curled back into a deeper, more confused frown. "No. Should I?"

"We watched it in American Lit class our senior year," I chuckled and chucked the copy of *The Crucible* at him for a closer look.

I had to smother a laugh as he examined the cover with escalating, albeit comical, bewilderment.

"Uh, I guess that chick looks sorta familiar," he finally exhaled.

That only made this all the more entertaining.

"You really don't remember this movie? Well, actually, I think we read the play first, then we watched the movie. We had to write a big paper on it and everything," I grinned back at him.

"Yeah, uh, I think I probably slept through the whole thing," he admitted sheepishly.

I cocked an eyebrow at him. "What do you mean probably?"

"Okay, fine. I *absolutely* slept through the whole thing."

"Yeah, I figured that, but I think it's fair to say you slept through the whole *semester*," I laughed. "Why were you even in that class anyways?"

"What, you callin' me stupid?"

"No," I batted a hand his way with a laugh. "You know what I mean. I figured your schedule would've been a little full with all those shop and gym classes, you know?"

"Oh, wow. First you insult my intelligence and *then* you insult the only classes I actually liked and yes, I realize study hall doesn't count as a class. That wounds me, you know that, Iz? That really wounds me."

"You never answered my question," I grinned. "Why take a class you were just going to sleep through anyways?"

He sighed and tugged a hand through his hair. "I needed the English credit and that was the only class that fit into my schedule, okay?"

My eyebrows raised smugly, already knowing the answer to this next question, "Why did you need the credit so bad, hmm?"

His hand muffled the answer, but I still caught the gist: "'Cuz I failed English junior year."

No words needed to be said. He knew I'd won.

"Oh, come on, Iz," Caleb rolled his eyes dramatically from the couch. "It was *English* class. And you know what? Ds get diplomas, Iz. That's what counts here."

"Hey," I nudged an elbow on my hip, rising to my knees. "I actually liked that class. Don't knock it just because you didn't get anything out of it."

Caleb held up his hands with a smirk. "Jesus, settle down, will ya? That was, like, what? Four years ago? Can I just ask one thing?" he gestured down to the movie as he spoke, "why do you even *have* that?"

"It's a good movie," I just shrugged. "And I found it in the $5 bin at Wal-Mart a long time ago. So what?"

"Okay, okay," he held his hands up again, the movie still in his left hand. "Chill out, Iz. I guess you were a little more into that class than I was."

"Right," I stated simply. "That's why you cheated off me on the final."

Caleb's mouth opened and then clamped shut as he bit down hard on his bottom lip with a wince. "Shit."

"You did a pretty terrible job of hiding it too," I shot back victoriously. "I still can't believe Mrs. Anderson didn't realize what you were doing."

"That's just because she didn't want me showin' up for summer school," he smirked. "I think she was secretly in love with me, but you know, I guess she didn't wanna end up in jail either."

"Oh God," I shook my head, lifting my eyes to the ceiling. "You probably think everyone's secretly in love with you."

A smile curled up on his lips, but it didn't quite reach his eyes. That was about when the full realization of what I'd just said hit me.

Cue the awkward silence.

With nothing better to do than play anxiously with my fingers and saw on my bottom lip with my teeth, I fumbled frantically for something that would make this awkwardness fade away.

"Hey," I pushed out suddenly. "Wanna see something? Maybe you'll remember this."

I waved for him to follow me, even though I had no idea where this was coming from or why I was doing it in the first place. This was just as heavy as what had happened outside the clubhouse tonight, but this time, there was no safety net to fall back on. No friends or bar tables here as a buffer, nowhere to retreat to when and if things got too complicated. It was just Caleb and me here—in my bedroom.

As I pushed through the door, cold panic gripped my throat. Did I leave dirty underwear on the floor? My bed wasn't made and yesterday's work outfit was strewn across the carpet and there was a plate next to my bed with days-old pizza crust left carelessly to mold. He would think I was gross and messy and—but there was no going back now because Caleb Sawyer was standing in the middle of my bedroom, waiting for me to do something about it.

Finally, my mind cleared just enough to remember why I'd brought him up here in the first place. It only took me a couple of minutes to dig my sketchbook out from under my bed, but I still needed a minute to flip through it until my fingers skimmed across the one I was looking for. Then, like they had a will of their own, my arms extended the sketchbook towards him.

"You remember this one?"

I gestured down to the sketch, a winding, thick tree with long, expansive roots with buds of hearts, all overlooked by an intertwined sun and moon. I'd be the first to admit it was a pretty literal interpretation of the text, but I was also only 17 when I'd stayed up late one night to work this image out of my head. At least I'd had the foresight to scribble specific lines next to the visuals.

Caleb's forehead creased in deep concentration as he studied the lines and shades on the paper, trying to make sense of it. From the perplexed expression on his face, it was clear he was trying to place where he knew those words.

"It's "i carry your heart" by ee cummings," I offered quietly. "We read it in class that semester. I don't know, for some reason, that one's always stuck with me. The words are just beautiful."

He nodded, craning his neck to see what I'd written next to the intertwined sun and moon, and read the words in a quiet voice, "*Whatever a moon has always meant and whatever a sun will always sing is you.*"

"It's just..." I exhaled. "The most perfect explanation of what love is supposed to be. What it's supposed to mean. That whatever is going on in the world and in your life, everything's going to be okay because you've got this person who's tipped your whole world on its axis, even if you can't be with them the way you want to. Everything's okay because this person is in the world and you know them and you love them."

His cloudy gaze leapt up from the page, sparkling with something I couldn't quite place, and he nodded soberly. "You're right. It is beautiful."

I tilted my head a little with a smile. "You don't remember reading this, do you?"

One side of his lips pulled aside in a grimace and he shrugged helplessly. "Kind of. Maybe if I'd seen it like this the first time, I'd have remembered it a little easier."

"Well," I chuckled. "I remembered it, as you can see. A couple years ago, I saw one of his poetry books at Barnes and Noble and I had to buy it."

I grabbed it from the bottom shelf of my nightstand and held it up. "See?"

The book was even dog-eared to the poem's exact page. I guess I just hadn't been able to help myself.

Caleb's eyes widened in surprise. "You bought the whole book? Just for one poem?"

"So what?" I shrugged. "I had a gift card."

"Sure you did," he smirked knowingly. "Couldn't you have just ripped out the page or something?"

"What?" I shrieked in horror. "No! You can*not* deface a book like that! Please tell me you've never done that before."

"Whoa," he held up a hand. "Simmer down. I promise I've never *defaced a book* and I can't remember the last time I even *read* a book, so just relax, Iz. Jesus."

I winced a little as my words replayed in my head. "Okay, sorry. I guess I did freak out just a little there."

"Nah," he shrugged. "Don't worry about it. Would've saved you that

208

gift card though."

"Shut up."

He grinned back at me as he carefully closed the sketchbook. He rolled back a little on his heels, shoving his hands deep in his pockets and then we stared at each other for a few long moments because neither of us seemed to know what to do or say next.

"Hey, Caleb?"

"Yeah, Iz?"

I swallowed tightly, unsure of exactly how to say this, but knowing I needed to do it all the same. "Thanks for...you know, tonight."

Caleb's eyes widened and one of his hands fell out of his pocket to tug through his hair. "I'm just sorry you had to see it. That shouldn't have happened and he shouldn't have—you know what? It's done and you never have to see him again if you don't want to."

"Yeah," I sighed. "Thank God for that, right? Still, you didn't have to do it, but thank you."

It wasn't so much the fight itself I was grateful for, that I could've done without, but more so the way he'd defended me, jumping to put Brandon in his place for saying such awful things about me—and my mom.

No one had ever done anything like that for me before and I guess if there would ever be a situation where someone had to throw a punch for me, it wasn't really a surprise that it was Caleb who did it, that it was Caleb who was defending my honor.

"Don't worry about it, Iz," he was telling me now. "Trust me, it was a long time coming."

I laughed. "Yeah, I guess."

Caleb's lips twisted into a sly smirk and then he tugged a hand through his hair again, a nervous gesture I'd picked up on a long time ago. His eyes burned a deep sapphire and I couldn't help but be drawn in, wanting to somehow get closer.

"Hey, Iz?"

"Yeah, Caleb?"

"We don't really have to watch that shitty movie, do we?"

I just laughed again and shook my head, gesturing towards the door. "No, we don't."

CHAPTER TWENTY-SEVEN
Lonesome When I'm Gone

Caleb

I checked the time on my phone for the tenth time in the last five minutes. That idiot Padilla had kept us waiting for almost a half hour now and with every second that ticked by, my patience depleted infinitesimally.

Talk about an epic fail.

There was nothing complicated about what was supposed to happen here: Padilla and his boys had to pick up five barrels of cargo from the Lobos's normal supplier on the coast, and then all they had to do was bring it to us on time and all in one piece to our rendezvous point just outside of Claremont, so we could take it the rest of the way to Pittsburgh and the Warlords. Ortega couldn't have made it any easier on them and what were they doing? Just screwing up left and right.

I lit up another cigarette and ignored the sideways glance Tiny tossed me. My agitation was clearly showing and I needed to dial it back. This was my test run just as much as it was Padilla's and I'd be damned if I let the incompetent asshole Ortega wanted to patch in screw this chance up for me. An opportunity like this one might never come again, at least not anytime soon, and there was no way I could prove both my dedication and my ability to lead if I couldn't keep my head in the game.

Of course, it didn't help that I'd spent the better part of my night lying on a stiff hotel bed, trying to talk myself out of calling Isabelle. Calling her, I'd reasoned, might be a little too much and would make me feel a little too pathetic. But *texting* her? A little friendly back and forth to help me sleep wouldn't hurt anything.

I was worried about her. That was it. And I needed to make sure she was okay and that she hadn't needed to use her Dom calling card yet.

It started with just a simple: *Hey, Iz, made it to the hotel in 1 piece.*

Then she'd responded back with: *Good. Now I can sleep tonite ;)*

I hadn't been able to just let that go and quickly pounded out: *Glad to know ur thinkin bout me in bed, darlin.*

She'd almost immediately called me an asshole back with another smiley face and then it was all over with from there. We'd texted back and forth for a good hour and when she finally told me she was starting to fall asleep, I'd tossed and turned for the rest of the night as I tried to push the images of her out of my head.

The second I closed my eyes—there she was. Her bright, warm smile that seemed to light up the entire room and those eyes that seemed to freeze me in place and cut me in half at the same time. I even missed the sound of her voice, her laugh, everything. I missed her.

Just that realization alone was enough to keep me up the rest of the night.

I *missed* her.

And even though I was going to be back in Claremont in less than two days, it didn't seem like it could come fast enough. My lips tugged up into a grin as our slightly awkward goodbye played over again in my head. She'd pulled me in for a quick hug and whispered in my ear to be safe. It was all I could do to keep my hands locked around her waist and nowhere else. The scent of her hair, flowers and musky vanilla, surrounded me again and I'd even felt a little dazed from the impact.

"Jesus Christ," Doc swore under his breath. "When are these assholes gonna git here already, huh? I'm sick a-waitin'."

"It's hot as hell out here, too," I added, stomping out the spent bud as I spoke. "You'd think they would be a little more punctual, you know?"

"Punctual?" Tiny huffed. "I'm not sure those assholes would know how to be on time if it bit them in the ass. Punctual?" he narrowed his eyes at me a little with a sly grin, "isn't that a kinda big word for ya, Caleb?"

"Hey, shut it," I tossed back.

"Nah," Doc shrugged. "I think our boy's just been spendin' too time with that pretty blonde thing in the office."

"Ah, yes," Tiny nodded. "Always chasin' that tail, huh, Caleb? You sure lunch is all you're doin' with her at that picnic table every day?"

Seeing as how this simple, fool-proof opportunity for me to prove myself had eroded into nothing but an opportunity to rag on me, I figured I was better off just keeping my mouth shut on this one.

Anything I said here was just going to be more fodder to give me shit about anyways. I needed to focus on the matter at hand and that matter, as it happened, was finally riding up to our rendezvous point—a half hour late.

"Finally," Tiny exhaled. "I wasn't sure how much longer I was gonna be able to stand it out here. I'm roastin' like a pig on a stick."

"Yeah, well, let's just hope they didn't screw anything else up," I nodded, keeping my voice as level and as calm as humanly possible.

"Heard ya on that one," Doc nodded.

We watched warily as Padilla, three other guys on bikes, and a truck pulled up to us from the gravel back road. Ever since the club learned Ortega was going to patch over the Cobras, I hadn't been able to place the uneasy feeling that crept through every one of my instincts.

There was something about this whole situation that didn't feel right and from my experience, usually when something didn't feel right, it *wasn't* right. That feeling intensified when Padilla swung his leg over his bike and sauntered over to us with a misplaced smugness and an air of superiority.

Ah. There it was.

Being untested and unproven, Padilla had nothing backing up his attitude but smoke and mirrors. Time to put the new patches in their rightful place.

"You're late," I called out to him and tapped the invisible watch on my wrist to drive the point home.

"Yeah...'bout that," Padilla slurred and I narrowed my eyes right back at him. "We just lost track of time for a little bit. We're here now and that's all that matters, right? Let's get to business."

I cast a quick look at Tiny, who rose his eyebrows at me in silent reply. If my initial guess was right, this was a whole lot more messed up than I'd originally thought. I took a small step forward, eyes still narrowed, to see if my suspicions were correct. Padilla's eyes were red and glassy and the idiot reeked of weed and booze.

I couldn't believe what I was seeing.

"Are you drunk?"

Padilla just shrugged like this was no big deal and didn't seem fazed by the question. "Nah, man. The party just went a little late last night is all. No problems, *ese*, okay?"

"No problems?" I rose my eyebrows in disbelief, my voice becoming deadly calm. "No problems? You don't party *before* you make the drop-off, asshole. You party *after* everything's said and done. When you know there were *actually* no problems."

"Hey," Padilla threw his hands up in defense. "We're here. The cargo's here. Shit got a little carried away last night because we were celebratin', but it'll never happen again. We good now?"

My eyes narrowed at the defensive, condescending tone. At this point, I was grateful Tiny and Doc were taking a backseat on this one. This was my show here and this little dumbass needed to be put in his place immediately. The scary part was that Padilla actually believed this wasn't really an issue, that he could just show up late to a drop-off because he felt like it with no repercussions. Besides, how the hell could he be stupid enough to celebrate before his club was even completely patched in? What kind of idiot did something like that?

"Listen, asshole," I jabbed a gloved finger at him. "If you wanna get yourself patched in with the Lobos, you'd better clean up your shit. This can't happen again and it never should've happened in the first place. We need to know you're reliable and right now, I ain't seein' it, bro."

Padilla shuffled a little in the gravel, taken aback by the shift in conversation. "Back off, alright? You got your cargo. I made a mistake, okay? Do you wanna take a look at the cargo or not?"

"I'd watch your tone if I were you, *ese*," I folded my arms across my chest and shot him a hard glare. "I'm lookin' forward to givin' your new Prez a full report though."

Padilla's upper lip curled back in a snarl as he turned on his heel, his arms flailing out to somehow signal to his guys to open the back of their truck. Luckily for Padilla, the entire shipment was there, all five barrels filled with our livelihood.

Part of me almost wished we were missing one because then I could've beaten the hell out of that whiny tool. But, given our first go-round, I figured this wouldn't be the last time a careless douchebag like

Padilla was going to screw up. There would be plenty of opportunities to grind Padilla down into dust and now, I was planning on savoring every single second.

Once the barrels were loaded into the club's truck, it was time to get the hell out of there. The sun was mercilessly beating down on us and the longer I was forced to stand in it, the more pissed off I felt. This was supposed to be simple. This was supposed to be fool-proof. And it was too bad it turned out Ortega and the Lobos had decided to align themselves with idiots.

"Let's git the hell outta here," Doc muttered.

"Got that right," I nodded.

I jutted my chin out to Padilla and lit up one last cigarette for the road. "Next time, you better be on time, understand?"

Padilla just nodded grimly, his eyes glazing over with something that looked a lot like resentment and animosity. Shaking my head in disbelief, I just couldn't understand how someone, who seemed to have everything just handed to him on a platter, could be this indifferent about such a glaringly obvious mistake. Sooner or later, all that was bound to catch up with him.

"Let's go home," I muttered to Doc, who was already half-way into our truck.

Right about now, home never looked so good.

.　　.　　.

The clubhouse was already booming when church let out. We'd only been back in town for about an hour and already, I just wanted to find somewhere dark and quiet to crash.

Tiny and Doc took a backseat during church and allowed me to relate the details of the drop-off to the rest of the club. There'd been no questions or concerns, other than the obvious misgivings about Ortega's judgment, and I'd been met with simple nods of approval all around the table, even from Heath.

While I knew this in itself wasn't enough to completely shake off any lingering doubt about my commitment, at the very least, I was on the right track to proving I could lead the club.

The clubhouse was filled with all the usual suspects and within less than 10 minutes, Casey was already trying to shove tequila shots down my throat. A pair of hands wrapped themselves around my waist, but I just jerked away and sidestepped around the three girls looking to warm themselves in my bed. My tired eyes scanned the smoke-filled room and I frowned when I didn't see who I was looking for.

Dom and Lexie were already here, right next to Eli and Becca. If Becca was here, wouldn't she be here too? They usually came together, even if I did end up leaving with her to pick up her dad. But if she wasn't at the clubhouse tonight, my mind immediately ticked off all the different possible explanations: something was up with her dad, she was with some new guy, she'd forgotten I was coming home completely—I wasn't exactly happy with any of those scenarios.

It took me a little longer than I would've liked to get to the pool table where the two couples were currently camping out. Jesus, it was like all the girls in the clubhouse latched on to me and I was dragging every single one of them along the way.

"Hey, Caleb!" Lexie called out to me as she wrapped her arms around my neck. I grinned at the ever-growing baby bump that nudged into me.

"Hey, Lex," I leaned down to her. "How's my god-kid doin', huh?"

"Just fine, Caleb. I'm glad you're back."

I squeezed her shoulder before slapping Dom on the back in greeting. Then, I wasted no time to get to the heart of the matter and called out to the person most likely able to get me an answer.

"Hey, Becca, where's Iz tonight? She sick or somethin'?"

I carefully avoided Dom and Lexie next to me and chose instead to focus on Becca's answer.

"Uh, I don't know, actually," she yelled out over the music. "I told her to come, but she said she was tired or something like that."

"Sure, right," I nodded quickly.

Suddenly, I didn't really feel like mingling here in the clubhouse any longer than I had to. A little small talk here and there, make an appearance...I had three long days behind me, including the longest trip back from Pittsburgh of my life, and I honestly didn't see anything

215

wrong with just wanting to crash somewhere for a while and tune all this
other white noise out.

About 10 minutes later, I found an opening to sneak off to my dorm
room and collapsed onto my bed, but not before shaking off another girl
in my wake. They were relentless. How did I put up with that shit for so
long? I was starting to wonder why I'd ever thought that was a good
idea in the first place.

I punched my pillow in a vain attempt at getting more comfortable
and tossed around in my sheets before finally throwing them off
altogether. The music, combined with all the yelling and clanging around
—it was all just too loud right now. I couldn't hear myself think even if I
wanted to.

With a frustrated huff, I snatched my phone off the end table and
flipped it open. It was only 10:30 and here I was, lying in bed alone with
the party going on without me. Even stranger yet, I was sort of okay
with that.

But if I was being completely honest with myself, I knew what was
really bothering me. If she was out in the clubhouse right now, I knew
I'd be out there right next to her. But she wasn't, so I was here instead.

So, instead of really deliberating about what all that meant, I hit send
over her number.

"Hello?"

The second I heard her voice, all my agitation and frustration slipped
away.

"Hey, Iz."

"Hi, Caleb. Everything okay?"

I could hear the smile in her voice and felt my own tugging across my
face.

"Yeah, why wouldn't it be?"

"I don't know," she replied a little too easily. "Lexie told me you guys
usually throw a big party when you come back from runs, so I don't
know, I just figured you'd be doing something like that."

The fact that she expected me to be partying tonight kind of made
me want to punch myself, but then again, my past behavior had taught
her to expect nothing less. Even despite that, just the sound of her voice
calmed the nerves playing hopscotch on my stomach and waiting until

our shared shift at the shop tomorrow morning was too long to have to wait to see her.

"So," I started. "Why aren't you here at the clubhouse?"

"I wasn't sure I was invited."

"You're always invited, Iz," I frowned. "Why would you think you weren't?"

"I don't know. It just kinda seemed like a club thing."

"Okay," I exhaled and scrubbed a hand over my face. "What's up with your dad tonight?"

"He didn't go out. Actually, he's already in bed."

That was new. Still, I was glad we wouldn't have to deal with him tonight because right now, I just wanted her all to myself.

"Huh."

"Yeah, I know," Isabelle laughed. "Kinda weird, right? Maybe he's finally realized he has to slow down. So..."

"It's loud as hell over here," I jumped right into it. You don't ask, you don't get, right? "I'd kinda like just a low-key thing tonight, so would it be alright if I stopped over by your place? I don't know, watch a movie or somethin'?"

I waited, chewing anxiously on the inside of my cheek, and waited as she seemed to mull over my request.

"Okay, sure. Come on over. I'll get some popcorn going and I'll even let you pick the movie this time."

"Awesome, Iz. See ya soon."

I snapped my phone shut and all but leapt off my bed, shoving my wallet and phone in my pocket. I couldn't get out of here fast enough because for the first time in a very long time, the clubhouse just wasn't where I wanted to be.

CHAPTER TWENTY-EIGHT
Lonesome When You're Gone

Isabelle

Popcorn and a few cans of Mountain Dew already waited patiently on the coffee table and I had our movie selection narrowed down, so now all there was left to do was pace nervously around the living room as I listened for the tell-tale roar of a motorcycle engine.

Texting him last night just made everything worse. My fingers itched by my phone ever since he left and just that small, fleeting contact with him wasn't really enough. While the initial worry for his well-being was still there—Lexie had informed me that runs usually weren't all that dangerous and were also usually followed by rollicking, sex and booze-filled welcome home parties—I'd just felt off-balance the second he'd pulled away from the clubhouse on his bike.

The last few days I'd walked around like a zombie, lost and wandering around aimlessly. I just had no idea what to do with myself without him.

It was crazy—I hadn't realized just how much I depended on him for, well, everything, until he wasn't around. Dependence wasn't exactly the right word. Okay, maybe it was, but I think it had more to do with wanting than anything. I didn't necessarily need him to sit by me at lunch, but I wanted him to. I didn't necessarily need him around when I was bored or watching a movie at home by myself, but I wanted him there.

I missed him.

He'd only been gone for three days, but it felt like three *weeks*.

The actual act of missing him was just as complicated as trying to reconcile why missing him affected me so much.

Lunch, especially, the last few days was pretty much unbearable.

Eating alone just compounded an already hopeless and pathetic situation. Sure, Dominic had taken pity on me today and dutifully ate with me, but the picnic table just felt colossally empty without Caleb sitting across from me.

At a certain point though, I was just grateful for the company and Dominic was Caleb's stand-in, after all—as he'd so eloquently joked. At first, I was horrified when Caleb told me Dominic knew exactly what was going on whenever we had our 'late night getaways' and I was even more horrified to learn that, through the office grapevine gossip, pretty much everyone in the clubhouse assumed we were secretly hooking up.

It was as embarrassing as it was untrue. In fact, that couldn't have been further from the actual truth.

In between small talk about Lexie's baby/bridal shower three weeks from this Friday, followed by their wedding that same weekend—Lexie, apparently, wanted to get it all over with in one shot and I couldn't really blame her—I realized that this happy occasion would also bring Ariel back to town. As far as I knew, Lexie's maid of honor plans hadn't changed, which also might have been part of the reason for this trifecta of baby shower, bridal shower, and wedding all in the same weekend.

No need to freak out. No need to have a panic attack over nothing. Everything was perfectly fine.

Caleb's ex, the same one whose abandonment had driven him to drown himself in whiskey, women, and weed, was coming back to town in three weeks. No big deal, right?

After that, focusing on Dominic was about the only thing that kept me from bolting right from the table. We rarely got the chance to actually have a conversation, especially since our interactions usually just amounted to some small talk. With his quiet, observant demeanor and behemoth height, it would be easy to feel a little intimidated by him, but I was quickly learning there was nothing to be afraid of.

Besides, I'd needed to call him the night before for help with my dad. Other than the fact that I knew Caleb would crap a brick if he knew I didn't call for help, I also knew how stupid it was to have gone solo for as long as I did when it came to those late-night runs to the seediest parts of Claremont.

Dominic hadn't said a word; he'd just swung one of my dad's arms around his shoulder and carried him out of The Sundown Saloon, put him in the car, and helped me get him into bed with as much quiet respect as I would've expected from Caleb's best friend and confidante.

If that didn't bond us, then I didn't know what would.

And then, as we quietly ate lunch together earlier today, Dominic had not-so-discreetly dropped a few items of intel that I still didn't know how to process.

"Thanks for your help last night," I'd told him quietly.

Dominic just batted a hand at me. *"It wasn't a problem. Besides, Caleb would kill me if I hadn't, so there's that."*

"Yeah."

"But at least he'll be back tonight, so if somethin' happens..." he'd trailed off, clearly sensing that this was a pretty sensitive topic. *"He really cares about you, you know."*

My head had snapped up and my heart stuttered and spiked in my chest. Dominic had laughed softly, his shoulders shaking a little as he shook his head.

"Trust me, it's true. He wouldn't have told me any of..." he'd trailed off again and gestured with his hands to convey what he was really trying to say. *"Look, I'm just sayin' that Caleb isn't the type of guy to just go spillin' other people's business without good reason. It was just about him tryin' to take care of you. I hope you know that."*

"Yeah, I do," I'd nodded slowly. *"He's a good friend."*

Dominic's eyebrows had lifted up high into his forehead. *"Right."*

Even as he'd chuckled across from me, it was like he knew something I didn't or maybe...couldn't. And despite my valiant efforts, there was no stopping the hot blush that seeped into my cheeks.

So, in between wringing my hands over all these feelings, I couldn't exactly distract myself either from waiting around for those art school applications I'd sent in a few weeks ago. If Caleb was here, he would've told that me that it didn't mean anything, that the letters were coming with good news, that I didn't have to worry, that I just needed to wait a little longer—but he wasn't here, and so I'd been driving myself crazy dissecting the possible realities that awaited me when those letters finally arrived.

Then, because I'd gone crazy, I did something drastic. Well, not exactly drastic as in chopped-off-all-my-hair-and-dyed-it-purple-drastic, but still.

With my mom's birthday just two weeks away, I figured this was as good a time as any. And since my dad was in no state of mind to help me, the task of sorting out of her closet would've fallen to me eventually anyways. At first, just stepping inside the closet was a trial in itself. The air inside the modest-size walk-in closet still lingered with faint traces of Chanel No. 5, which, not going to lie, I'd absolutely hated when she was alive.

Old lady powder. Or better yet, old lady vaginal powder. That's exactly what that perfume smelled like. And I'd never been afraid to tell her as much either.

But now?

Now, I'd douse my pillow in that stinky perfume and inhale it for the rest of my life if it isn't just so goddamn painful.

In just a few hours, I went through the entire thing, making careful piles of what I wanted to keep and what I wanted to donate. There were some items that were just too personal, like a half-empty bottle of that gross perfume, some of her beautiful cocktail dresses and matching high heels...items I'd probably never wear, but items I also couldn't bear to part with either.

The dresses and heels I tucked away in a far corner of my own closet for safe-keeping. Someday, I might want to revisit those dresses, but I just wasn't quite there yet. I'd put the perfume on my vanity in the bathroom mainly because just seeing it there made me feel a little better, not that I had any plans on actually using it.

However, in a closet full of shoes, clothes, jewelry, old photo albums, a few dusty boxes of my old baby clothes, and a fraying quilt my grandma made years ago, I'd stumbled across a hidden treasure. Well, at least I thought it was. It was the kind of thing I really had no use for, regardless of its actual or sentimental value, and it was also the kind of thing I didn't necessarily feel comfortable having in the same house where my dad went on nightly benders.

Said hidden treasure was currently waiting patiently on the coffee table in the living room for its new owner to arrive.

I really hadn't expected to hear anything from Caleb at all tonight—

maybe a text, if I was lucky—and I already had my pajamas on and everything. Both Becca and Lexie told me I could and should be at the clubhouse tonight for the homecoming party, but uneasiness kept me home tonight.

There was really nothing I'd rather do than see Caleb, especially since I'd missed him more than I was ready to admit, but I also didn't want to seem too eager either. And, given what I'd already seen during parties at the clubhouse, I didn't think I could stomach seeing some random girl all over him tonight, let alone see him and said random girl stumble into his dorm room.

Finally, the roar of Caleb's motorcycle ripped through the walls and even though I thought I'd feel relieved, my heartbeat just spiked in anxious anticipation. It felt like my entire body was on fire as I flung open the door to greet him.

His hair hung down past his ears, still a little wet from a recent showering, and he was wearing his typical white T-shirt with his Horsemen cut over the top. Nothing out of the ordinary yet seeing him, finally, with that sexy smirk, made my chest wind so tight I thought it might burst.

He was leaning into the doorframe, waiting expectantly for me to invite him in. That smirk curved, stretching up the side of his handsome face and I just about lost my grip on the door handle.

"You gonna stare at me all night?" he grinned. "Or are you gonna get over here and gimme a hug?"

I huffed out a laugh and then I closed the distance between us, wrapping my arms around his neck. His hands slid around my waist and I couldn't help but shiver a little at finally feeling this again. Leaning into him, I allowed myself one inhale of musk, leather, and grease and just leaned in ever deeper when I realized his nose was practically burrowed in my hair. I just wished I didn't feel so cold when his hands left my waist and I had to reluctantly unwind my arms from around his neck.

"Come on in," I gestured towards the hallway softly.

Suddenly, Caleb pulled me to him again and practically lifted me off the ground as his biceps squeezed my waist, making me yelp a little from surprise. His hands were in my hair, on my back, all over my waist, and I felt a little light-headed from all of these feelings rushing around me at once. When he finally set me back down, our cheeks collided and my head spun at the feel of his stubble scratching my skin.

Then I caught the way he was looking at me, with dark, hooded eyes that focused on my lips, and my breath hitched in my throat.

His hot breath grazed my neck and this time, there was no way to stop the shiver that shuddered through my entire body. Every sense was heightened; every touch felt like it would set me aflame. Caleb exhaled against my neck and then lifted his head as he gently brushed some hair out of my face with his fingertips. For a moment, I could have sworn he leaned forward.

And then just like that, the spell was broken.

His arms dropped to his sides and he took a small step backwards, coughing lightly as he slipped off his leather cut and tossed it onto the armchair next to him.

Awkwardness had taken over the room and I could only try to beat it back.

"So, um, how was the run?"

Caleb ran a hand through his hair and shrugged. "It was...interesting, I guess. Things didn't exactly go the way we planned, but it all worked out."

"That's good," I nodded and shot him a weak smile.

There was obviously more to the story, but he clearly wasn't going to share those details either. I wasn't entirely sure I needed them anyways —that was one aspect of his life I could honestly say I really didn't know much about and, sometimes, I figured I was better off not knowing.

Caleb blew out a deep breath before settling down on the couch. He reached forward and cracked open the Mountain Dew can I'd set out for him, gesturing towards the case on the coffee table with his free hand.

"What's that, Iz?"

My eyes widened in excitement. I hadn't actually been waiting that long to give this to him in the grand scheme of things, but it felt like I had. I literally couldn't wait any longer and swept my hand out towards the case.

"So, I was going through my mom's closet and..." I trailed off when Caleb's eyes widened the size of baseballs and his soda can froze in mid-air.

It was like he thought he was suddenly sitting next to one of those dinosaurs from Jurassic Park and if he didn't make any sudden movements, I wouldn't see him and therefore, wouldn't eat him. Wow. Melodramatic much, Caleb?

Instead of acknowledging his reaction, I just carried on like it wasn't really that big a deal, even though both of us were woefully aware it kind of was.

"Her birthday's in two weeks," I tried again and forced my voice to stay steady. "And I don't know, it's been almost 10 months. The stuff is just sitting there and it's not like she needs it anymore anyways."

Caleb swallowed tightly as he set the can back down on the coffee table and faced me again with somber blue eyes swimming with empathy.

"So anyways, I went through everything while you were gone and cleaned it all out."

He cleared his throat. "You're keeping some stuff too, right? I mean, more than just..." he gestured with his head towards the case on the table.

"Oh yeah," I smiled. "I found some pretty cool stuff I forgot she had like these gorgeous cocktail dresses she used to wear whenever her and my dad would go out. I'm definitely keeping those and her perfume too. Oh, and I found these kickass tan suede boots. I can't wait to wear those."

Caleb's lips curved up, relief filling his eyes, and he nodded, a little more at ease now that he could tell I probably wasn't going to break down crying anytime soon.

"That's great, Iz. I know how rough that is—we had to do the same thing with all my dad's stuff in our shed. It's not easy, but you gotta do it sometime. Part of livin' is packin' up the ones who checked out already, you know?"

"Yeah," I smiled softly and reached for the case. "I know. So, I did manage to find something pretty cool that I think you're really gonna like."

I held the case out to him, a rush of anticipation washing through me. My body practically buzzed with excitement and I couldn't wait for him to just open the thing already. He frowned back at me, like he couldn't piece together why I was giving him something that came from my mom's closet of all places, which, to be fair, was a little weird at first glance.

"Seriously, Caleb," I extended my arms out a little more to get him to take it. "Come on! Open it!"

His fingers gingerly took the case from me and after casting me yet another confused, cautious glance, he nimbly snapped open the clasps holding the case together. As he lifted it open, Caleb's eyes widened in disbelief and they just grew wider and wider the longer he stared at the case's contents.

"Holy shit," Caleb exhaled and lifted his eyes back up to me. "This is...this was just sittin' in her closet?"

"Yeah," I just shrugged. "It was on the top shelf all the way back against the wall. It had to be my grandpa's or something because there's no way that ever belonged to my dad."

He shook his head in disbelief as he slid the ancient-looking pistol out of the case and gripped the handle in his fist. There was some brown rust around where the metal met the handle and on the safety, so my mom obviously never sat around and cleaned it or even took very good care of it, but it was something.

"So, do you know what it is?" I asked sheepishly. I felt a little stupid now that I'd given him something like this and didn't even really know the official name of it.

Caleb shot me a wide grin and lifted the pistol up a little higher so I could see it. "It's a Luger. These babies were all over the place in World War Two. Definitely German. I mean, we'd have to get it checked out by someone who knows a little more about this than me, but they can tell the year and the make pretty easily from the markings so you'll know what it's worth."

I leaned forward a little. "It's pretty cool, isn't it?"

"Very cool, Iz," he nodded, that wide grin still plastered across his face. "Man, you know who woulda loved this? My dad...he would've went crazy playin' with this thing and figurin' it all out."

He snapped one of the pieces back and held it up to his eye level to line it up as he spoke.

"So that means you're gonna take it off my hands, right?"

Caleb tensed, almost instantly blanching at the suggestion and he shook his head, swiftly putting the pistol back in the case.

"I can't take this. You could probably get a lot of money for this thing. No way, Iz."

"Yeah, well, it doesn't feel right to sell it, so I think it should be with someone who can appreciate it and let's face it, that isn't me."

He chuckled, but he was still shaking his head. "This was your grandpa's. Your mom's. You should keep it."

Well, it looked like it was time to bring out the big guns.

I leaned into his shoulder, batting my eyelashes and everything. "So, maybe you can just hold on to it for me? Besides, I'm not sure I really feel comfortable having it in the house right now anyways."

Caleb eyed me warily and even though my motives were as about as transparent as plastic wrap, I knew he wasn't going to say no to me now either. I'd hoped I wouldn't have to play that card, but it worked just like I knew it would.

He already had the case flipped back open, casting me a glance with just a little bit of annoyance probably because he knew he'd just been played, but his lips were still curving up in that sexy, crooked grin I loved so much.

"Besides," I pressed on. Time to do my victory lap. "You can add it to your collection, you know? Put it in with all your other little treasures and see how it feels?"

He lifted an eyebrow at me. "My *collection?*"

"Yep."

Caleb shook his head, but this time, he was looking at me with nothing but warmth and something else that made my stomach flip-flop. He snapped the case shut and dragged a hand over the top.

"Well, I can't say I'll be bringing it on a run or strapping it to my holster anytime soon," he smiled at me softly and I couldn't stop myself from reaching out to let my fingers graze his tattooed forearm.

His eyes flitted shut for just a moment and when they flicked back open, they burned bright blue.

"But, Iz, I would be honored. Honestly, you don't have to do this, but I know I'm not gonna win this argument, so, I'm just gonna add it to my *collection* like you said. I promise I'll take care of it, okay?"

I smiled back at him, letting my fingers brush his bare skin one more time before pulling them back. "I know you will. And if anyone should have it, it should be you."

Just as Caleb opened his mouth to reply, an upstairs door creaked open and faint shuffling echoed all the way down the stairs until my dad appeared, rumpled and hungover, at the bottom of the staircase. My body might have been rooted to the couch, but Caleb jumped into action, ready to pounce at a moment's notice as he shifted his entire body to put himself between my dad and me.

My dad stared back at him like a deer caught in the headlights and Caleb didn't move, watching my dad's every movement and holding his ground beside me. A moment later, the standoff ended and my dad continued shuffling into the kitchen.

Even as I listened for the refrigerator door to open and close, I found myself inching closer and closer to Caleb until he swung an arm around my shoulders.

Always knowing what I needed. Always knowing what to give and how much.

I leaned into his shoulder, inhaling leather and musk, and squeezed my eyes shut. When I opened them again, my dad was standing at the bottom of the staircase again with a glass in his hand and openly gaping at us huddled on the couch together. At least he was smart enough to know better than to say anything, especially given the way Caleb repeatedly dropped everything to pick his sorry drunk ass up on a regular basis. When he disappeared back up the stairs, all the air finally rushed from my lungs in one fell swoop.

"You know," Caleb murmured into my hair. "I hate to break it to ya, Iz, but I don't think your dad likes me very much. In fact, I'm pretty sure he hates me. No, he definitely hates me. And he *definitely* doesn't like me hangin' out here like this."

"Oh well," I burrowed myself a little deeper into his shoulder. "I like you hanging out here, so my dad can suck it."

He chuckled and I thought I felt his lips in my hair, but that was probably just wishful thinking on my part.

"I don't like you being here by yourself with him movin' around like this," he murmured quietly above me. "I'd say you could come back to the clubhouse with me, but things were already pretty much fallin' apart when I left. So, I think I'm just gonna crash here on the couch tonight instead."

He'd just stated it like it was already fact, already a done deal and set in stone with no room for argument or negotiation. Like spending the night on the couch here was no big deal when it was...everything.

"It's only fair, Iz," he went on. "You know after you all but tied my hands behind my back with that Luger. Compromise, Iz. Compromise."

"If you say so," I laughed into his shoulder, reveling in the way his strong arms wrapped all the way around me, pulling me in deeper. "Thanks, Caleb."

"Anytime, Iz. So, how 'bout that movie, huh? I feel like I've been waitin' forever for you to start the damn thing already."

All I could do was laugh, grab the remote, and hit play. With the thought of sleeping under the same roof as Caleb, who had somehow become so ingrained in the very fiber of my life, bouncing around in my head, that was about all I could focus on.

CHAPTER TWENTY-NINE
Accepted

Two Weeks Later

Isabelle

I stared at the clock, nervously tapping my pen against the desk and glanced out the office window again.

Nothing.

My eyes fell back to the pile of paperwork in front of me, but that was the least of my worries. Anytime now...the mail should be coming at any time, but still, no stupid mail truck. Didn't the postal service know I was sitting here, going crazy over their inability to be punctual *ever*?

To be fair, this had pretty much been my routine for the last two weeks around this time. As soon as 11:00 rolled around, my palms got sweaty and my whole body twitched in nervous anticipation. Sooner or later, that mail truck would have those letters and I wanted to throw up just thinking about it.

"You know," Skyler called out from her end of the office. "You keep tappin' that pen like that, you're gonna wear a hole in the desk."

I looked up to find her watching me with an amused grin and she raised an eyebrow as her dark eyes flicked to the clock over the door.

"Mail should be here soon," Skyler shrugged. "You could go drag Caleb outta bed while you're waiting. I don't know what I was thinkin' scheduling him this late. That boy thinks he can sleep the whole day away—what?"

Crap. She must've caught the not-so-discreet stink eye I shot her out of the corner of my eye.

"You have to do something while you wait for the mail to get here," she told me pointedly, barely biting back a grin. "Might as well be productive since that paperwork sure isn't gettin' done anytime soon. Besides, I'm sure he'd much rather get a wakeup call from you instead of me anyways."

My eyes lifted to the ceiling and held my hands up in defense. "Okay, okay, got it. I'll get back to work. Geez."

Skyler just shrugged a shoulder. "I still think you should go drag my son's ass outta bed. He'd appreciate wakin' up with you at the door, I'm sure."

"Wow," I shook my head. She was really on a roll now. "Why don't you just come out and say what you really mean, huh?"

"Oh honey," she laughed, her lips twitching with amusement. "You know what I mean. Everyone knows what I mean. If you two don't —"

The loud, rickety engine of the mail truck echoed down the parking lot, cutting Skyler off mid-sentence. We both stilled and stared at each other from across the office, then we shot off our seats at the same time in a mad dash for the door, meeting the long-suffering mail lady, Gina, in the lot.

"Hello there, Isabelle. Mrs. Sawyer. Sorry I'm a little late today," Gina called out to us as she hopped out of the truck with a few packages in her hands. She handed them over to Skyler as she spoke, "Here you go. Don't need a signature. Oh, and before I forget," she leaned across the truck through the window and pulled out a stack of envelopes, thrusting them out to us from behind her. "There you go. Hopefully there's something in there you'll like."

Gina waved goodbye and hopped back in the truck to get on her way, but I barely noticed. My entire focus rested solely on the stack of envelopes in my hand and my shaky fingers began sifting through them before I could stop myself. And when my fingers brushed across the VCU and UNC insignias resting on two large manila envelopes, I just about had a heart attack.

It was easy enough to just hit send on those applications a month ago because once they disappeared into the Cloud, the rest was out of my hands. But now, reality stared at me right in the face. If they'd judged me and deemed me unworthy, I didn't have a plan B; hell, I barely even had a plan A.

Suddenly, I just wanted to shove those letters into the deepest depths of my oversized purse and forget about them. My future was in those letters and that scared the ever-loving crap out of me.

With my fingers still trembling against my will, I shoved the rest of the mail to Skyler, not caring about the rest of it. Now, I just held those two manila envelopes in my hands. They didn't feel nearly as heavy as they looked. And now that they were finally in my grasp, all I wanted was my mom. And Caleb.

"Are you gonna open them, Isabelle? Or are you gonna wait 'til..." Skyler trailed off, her eyes drifting towards the clubhouse as she spoke.

I knew what she was asking, but I didn't know how to answer her.

Skyler jerked her head towards the parking lot. "Go."

"What?"

"You heard me," she laughed and gently pushed me towards the clubhouse. "Go. Take your break now and if you don't get back right away, I won't mind. Promise."

My feet were glued to the pavement and Skyler laughed again, nudging me on my way. It wasn't until I was already halfway in between the office and the clubhouse that I realized what Skyler already seemed to know: yes, I missed my mom and I wished she could be here with me when I finally did face what was in those letters. But even if my mom was still here, even if she could be right next to me when I ripped them open, I would have waited for Caleb anyways.

It just didn't feel right to open them without the person who'd encouraged me to apply in the first place. Without his support, I doubt I would've ever had the guts to do this on my own and he needed to be here when I got the news, whether it was good or otherwise.

As I stepped through the clubhouse's threshold, it was so quiet it was eerie. Bikers partied late and slept late, but this place was like a ghost town and it was already almost noon. Of course, Caleb was still asleep. That was no big surprise. I'm sure he'd sleep until three or four if he didn't have to be at work in an hour.

What I wasn't prepared for, though, was the greeting I received from the sole patron parked at the bar. Casey, the club's sergeant at arms, was perched on a stool with a beer bottle in one hand and a cigarette in the other. His crazy eyes lit up when they zeroed in on me and his lips spread into a wide grin.

"Hey there," Casey called out to me, lifting his beer bottle in greeting. "You lookin' for your boy?"

I shifted uncomfortably under the weight of Casey's insinuation. It wasn't a secret that just about everyone affiliated with the Horsemen and Sawyer Auto Repair thought Caleb and I were together, or, at the very least, hooking up. But being confronted with that idea and not having a buffer in between myself and the truth underneath it—handling *that* in addition to the two envelopes in my hands all in the span of 10 minutes was a little much.

"Uh," I answered finally, staring down at the envelopes in my hands and wishing I was back in the office where I had a safety net. And now, a panicked, abrupt thought—one I was kicking myself for not considering until now—gripped hold of my throat and squeezed tight.

"Caleb isn't with anyone in his dorm by any chance, is he?" I asked, wincing as the words fell from my lips.

Part of me almost couldn't bear to hear the answer. Granted, I couldn't remember the last time I'd had to witness him lead his flavor of the night back to his dorm, but if he had a girl in there with him right now, I just couldn't handle that. If I was being completely honest with myself, I'd never really been able to handle that.

The idea of seeing another girl in his bed when I had these letters in my hand, when I wanted to share this with him...luckily, Casey's voice yanked me out of that terrible reality only to push me into a different one.

"Well," he lifted an amused eyebrow at me. "Seein' as how you're standin' right here, I'd say your boy's in there all by his lonesome."

Momentarily stunned, it took me awhile to find the ability to speak again. This time, it was Casey gesturing towards the hallway to push me towards Caleb instead of Skyler.

"Go on then," he grinned. "Wake his ass up."

For lack of a better response, I just smiled tightly and hightailed it down the hallway, eager to get away from Casey with his crazed eyes that leered a little too closely at the skirt hugging my hips and the tiny bit of cleavage peeking out from the top of my shirt.

Yeah, time to get moving.

By the time I was standing in front of Caleb's door, my hands were trembling and I was feeling all itchy again, but I swallowed it down. With a deep breath, I knocked on the door, holding the letters in a vice-grip in my free hand.

Silence was all I could hear from the other end of the door and I just stood there, not sure if I should be laughing or freaking out right now. He was sleeping, so of course he wasn't able to just fling the door open and invite me in. So, I knocked again. And again. And again.

The door suddenly flew open to reveal Caleb, clad in only a pair of striped boxers with a cigarette dangling from his lips.

"Hey, Iz," he drawled, one hand curling around the doorframe and those lips curving into that crooked grin.

Talk about sensory overload.

My eyes just didn't know where to focus first...the smooth, muscular planes of his chest, the rippled eight-pack that I had the sudden urge to run my tongue down, the black ink tattooed all the way up both taut forearms, the strong, broad set of shoulders...not to mention whatever was tucked away inside those boxers. I think my eyes might've rolled back into my head.

Luckily for me, Caleb was too busy eradicating both the cigarette and the smoke from the room to notice the way my drool pooled into his carpet and he scrambled around the room, frantically mashing his cigarette into a nearby ashtray and waving his arms around to waft away the smoke.

"Sorry 'bout that," Caleb called from across the room as he tossed a pile of clothes into a corner. "Aren't you supposed to be at the office right now?"

To my dismay, he pulled a pair of black Nike shorts on as he spoke. Somewhere, an angel was sobbing. Good thing he didn't see the need to pull on a T-shirt. That really would've been a tragedy.

"Actually..." I trailed off, holding up the over-sized letters for him to see.

His eyebrows rose as he realized what I was holding, his eyes glimmering with excitement.

"So big envelopes are good, right?" he murmured.

"I hope so."

After a moment's pause, Caleb blew out a breath and ran a nervous hand through his hair. "I take it they just came in the mail?"

"Uh huh," I nodded. "Your mom let me take my break a little early so I could open them with you."

His crystal-clear blue eyes widened in surprise. "Really? You haven't opened them yet?"

"I guess it didn't feel right to open them up without you," I shrugged. "I mean, I don't think I even would've applied if you hadn't brought it up in the first place."

Something clouded over Caleb's eyes that I couldn't quite place. If he stared at me like that any longer...I didn't know what I would do. Probably something embarrassing and humiliating.

"Well, Jesus, Iz," Caleb called out and tugged another anxious hand through his messy hair. "Are you gonna open those or what?"

I laughed nervously, tucking one of the envelopes underneath my arm and clutched the other in between my shaking hands. God, I felt like I was going to puke. Panic had my throat in a chokehold and now, I couldn't do it. I think I really *was* going to puke.

Before I could stop myself, I shoved the letters into Caleb's chest. "I can't...I don't think I can do it. You open them. Please?"

His fingers curled around my hand, which was still pressed into his chest, and he gently pulled it away from his skin as he slid the letters from underneath my grip. Then, his fingertips caught my hand before it fell away and he brought it up to his mouth, brushing his lips across my knuckles. As he let my fingers slip from his grasp, my heart thundered in my chest now, but not because of the impending reveal. Now, all I could think about was the heady feel of his lips on my skin.

"Alright, Iz," he winked. "Let's see what's in these damned things, huh?"

Taking the top letter in one hand and holding the other envelope out for me to take, he held it up for me to see. "This one's the UNC letter."

"Okay, okay," I swallowed and blew out a deep breath as he tore it open.

My heart stopped as I watched his eyes skim over the words and slam back up to me. His lips curled up and I knew it before I heard it: "You got in."

I covered my mouth with a hand, a surge of frenzied disbelief rushing through me. Caleb gestured for the VCU letter in my hand with a wide smile and as I held it out to him, his hand curled around my wrist to pull me closer to him like he didn't want that much distance between us.

A beat later, his index finger flicked underneath the envelope flap to rip it open and his eyes scanned the contents before both his arms shot up into the air in victory.

"You're in, Iz!"

My mouth dropped open. Everything froze and then, before I knew what I was doing, my hands shoved Caleb right in the chest.

"Shut up!"

His broad shoulders shook with laughter as his arms crossed over himself in self-defense when I just shoved him again.

"Watch it!" he laughed. "Don't shoot the messenger, Iz. Come on."

Both hands covered my mouth now and I just couldn't believe it. I couldn't believe it. I got into *both* schools.

Both schools wanted me.

Both schools thought I was good enough.

I didn't know whether to laugh or cry just from the sheer impact of that truth. It was almost too much. Too many feels...all rushing and twisting and rolling around me at once. My knees buckled and would've sent me tumbling to the ground if not for Caleb's palms closing over my shoulders to steady me.

"Hey," Caleb laughed. He crouched down to get a better look at me and gave my shoulders a little shake. "You alright, Iz?"

"Yeah," I murmured. "I just can't believe I got in."

He grinned. "I can."

He pulled me into his chest and I leaned into his bare skin, reveling in the way it felt underneath my cheek. Feeling his strong arms enveloping and surrounding me just lifted me up and carried me away. My chin tilted just enough as I stood up on my toes to brush my lips against Caleb's. It happened so fast my mind could barely keep up and then I was on solid ground again, staring up at him as he blinked back at me in surprise.

"I'm sorry. I didn't—"

His touch stilled my words as both calloused hands closed around my face and his thumb brushed my cheek and then he leaned forward to press his lips into mine. It started out soft and sweet as his mouth moved over me, tasting and exploring with his hands in my hair, pulling me into him and I wrapped my arms around his neck to somehow draw him in deeper. When my lips parted, his tongue slipped through, and sent me flying into outer space.

Everything seemed to be happening in slow motion now. The taste of his lips, mint and cigarettes, something I never thought I'd ever actually enjoy—I couldn't get enough. I just wanted more. And I took it, melding my body against his firm chest, tangling my hands in his hair, and slipping down to feel his smooth skin underneath my fingertips. I was barely aware of the fact that he was slowly but surely shuffling us backwards and right towards his bed.

When the backs of my legs hit the edge of his bed, one of his arms wound around my waist as the other reached out to lower us down to the mattress. He groaned into my mouth and his hands were everywhere, drifting through my hair, down my back, sliding over my waist. As his body settled over me, just feeling him pressing against my thigh, so close to being where I really wanted him, but still so far away, my eyes nearly rolled back into my head.

That's when I knew it was time to pump the brakes.

If we kept this up, I was never getting out of this room, which might have been perfectly fine if I also didn't have to go back to the office at some point today.

"Caleb," I murmured breathlessly, pressing my palms gently into his chest.

He was leaving a trail of light kisses against my neck and the longer he did that, the more light-headed I felt. It would be a miracle if I'd be able to get up from this bed and not immediately fall back down from dizziness. Caleb had stolen my equilibrium right out from under me.

"Sorry," he hummed into my skin and lifted his head. "Too fast?"

His chest muffled my laugh.

"No, I have to get back to work. Your mom's gonna kill me if I don't go back soon."

He pushed himself off me and pulled me up with him. His hands trailed down my hips to rearrange my skirt and when he winked at me, I felt it right in between my legs.

"Can't have that," Caleb smirked. "Just gimme a second to get changed and I'll go with ya."

My eyes narrowed. "You don't have to be at work for another hour."

"Ah," he just batted a hand in the air as he sifted through a pile of clothes with the other. "You still gotta eat lunch, don't you? Least I can do is eat with you today, seein' as how we're celebratin' and all."

Celebrating what, exactly, still remained to be seen, but I was all about the celebration today.

I watched with careful fascination as he slipped a white T-shirt over his head, kicked off his shorts right in front of me, and pulled on a pair of semi-clean work pants. After he buttoned up a blue work shirt, he reached for my hand with one arm and scooped up my art school acceptance letters with the other.

He led me down the hallway and through the clubhouse's main floor, right past Casey, who lifted his beer bottle up to us in a silent toast with a knowing wink. If I wasn't already so off-kilter, that exchange might have made me uncomfortable, but I was too preoccupied by the feeling of my hand tucked firmly inside Caleb's much larger one to care.

As we stepped outside into the warm, breezy sunlight, he wrapped an arm around my shoulders and tucked me into his side. His lips found the side of my head and when I tilted my head up, his eyes were glittering down at me with all the happiness and excitement I was feeling too.

We'd barely made it halfway through the parking lot when the office door slapped open to reveal Skyler, watching us with hawk-like dark eyes and just a hint of a smile crossing her face.

"So?" she called out to us. "Are you in or what?"

Caleb glanced down at me happily and then lifted my acceptance letters high in the air. "She's in, Ma!"

Skyler's lips parted in elated surprise. "To both?"

"Both!" Caleb answered for me and just tucked me in deeper underneath his shoulder.

Pretty soon I found myself sandwiched between the two Sawyers and honestly, mosh-pit style hugging never felt so good.

. . .

"So, which one do you think you're gonna go to?" Caleb asked me as he swung his leg over the side of our picnic table.

After the initial celebration, Skyler had shooed us away to finish out my lunch break, giving me a whole extra 15 minutes to boot just because she was feeling generous. So now, as I settled onto my bench, preparing to eat, I also hadn't prepared myself for how to answer that question.

It was an inevitable one, but one I also hadn't really let myself think about for too long. And in light of what had just transpired in Caleb's dorm, my head was still strapped to that roller coaster, rolling and twisting, lucky to somehow still be on the tracks.

"Well," I sighed. "The programs aren't all that different. I could commute to Winston-Salem no problem and still live here in Claremont, but I'd have to move to Richmond for VCU."

He nodded carefully, like he'd weighed both statements but hadn't found them as heavy as I did. "So which one is the best?"

"VCU is the number seven school in the country for drawing and painting programs."

Caleb nodded again, this time a little more tightly. "What about UNC?"

"It's the best art school in the state, definitely, but I don't think it even ranks in the top 20 in the country."

He just lifted a shoulder, clearly having heard everything he needed to hear. "So VCU has gotta be the one then, right?"

"But it's in Richmond, Virginia, Caleb. That's, like, five hours away from Claremont..." I trailed off, immediately struck by the weight of what that statement meant for me and maybe for us, too.

Caleb seemed to waver for just a moment as he rubbed a hand across his mouth. Pain flashed across his face—if I blinked, I would've missed it —and then a mask not unlike the one I'd seen for the last four months slipped right back into place.

"But it's the best one?"

. I nodded, wishing there was a way I could somehow transplant VCU to Claremont, or, at the very least, to North Carolina.

"I mean, you deserve to go to the best school, don't you?" he went on. "Number seven in the entire country? Iz, that's a once in a lifetime opportunity you might never get again."

"I don't know," I shrugged. "Best in the state isn't exactly anything to sniff at either."

"Maybe not," Caleb pointed out, leaning forward on his elbows now as if that would somehow reiterate his point. "But after everything...you deserve the best, Iz. You've earned it. And there's no stoppin' you now, babe, 'cuz you made it. You're in and you can do anything. I know you can. You gotta go to VCU because you deserve to have the best of everything."

Just because it's the best school doesn't mean it's the right school.

Aren't you what's best for me too?

I just can't be that far away from you.

My thoughts raged in my head, bouncing from one side to the other, and I just couldn't make sense of all this. And I also couldn't make a rash decision based off one hot make-out session in Caleb Sawyer's dorm room at the clubhouse that might not mean anything anyways.

I wouldn't be the girl that made this kind of life-altering decision because of a boy.

I would be the girl that made this kind of life-altering decision because it was the right decision for *me*.

I just didn't know what that decision was yet.

So because I didn't know what else to say, I smiled softly and told him: "Thanks, Caleb."

He grinned right back and took a healthy bite from his sandwich, but after a few chews, his expression turned more thoughtful, more somber.

"Hey, uh, not tryin' to be a killjoy or anything, but I think we should talk about tomorrow."

Oh right. That.

My mom's birthday.

Just like that, my good mood flushed down the toilet.

"Yeah," I blew out a deep breath.

Caleb wiped his hands on his work pants and shot me a quick smile. "I got it all worked out, okay, Iz? You don't have to do anything. I already talked to my mom and she said she could just switch your shift to

Monday—"

"No," I shook my head. "That's not gonna work. I'm the only one in the office tomorrow and you know your mom hasn't left me alone all day very often yet. I'm not switching shifts. If I wanted to be off tomorrow, I would've asked off."

He winced and his hands jerked up in defense. "Okay, okay. Got it. Sorry, I'm just tryin' to help, Iz."

I ran a hand over my face, wanting to punch myself. All Caleb was guilty of was having my best interest in mind as usual. Biting his head off wasn't called for.

"I'm sorry...I know you're trying to help. It's just that if I don't work tomorrow, I'm just gonna sit in that big house all day and drive myself insane."

He nodded slowly and chewed thoughtfully on his inside of his cheek. Even though I'd clearly thwarted his initial plans, I could already see the wheels in his head forming a new one.

"So you go to work tomorrow," Caleb tried again, a little more hesitantly this time. "I'll be there too. When you're done at four, you just go straight to Becca's. Bring whatever you need for the night with you to work, but just go right to Becca's. You two can hang out, do whatever girls do, and then when you get that call from your dad, all you gotta do is call me. You don't have do anything else. Me and Dom got it covered tomorrow night."

My throat tightened again for what seemed like the tenth time today, but this time, it wasn't from panic. This time, it was to keep the tears that pricked my eyes at bay. This time, it was because Caleb's words and his thoughtfulness and just the way he always seemed to know how to take care of me was too much to take.

So, I just nodded and whispered hoarsely, "Okay."

This boy meant more to me than I could even begin to comprehend and sooner or later, I was going to have to reconcile what that meant for the course of my life.

CHAPTER THIRTY
Birthday

Isabelle

I blew out a deep breath as I stared down at the pile of paperwork. With three hours left to go on my shift, it was more than likely that the pile would be sorted, signed, and dated before four, but then again, I was also moving a little slower today.

This morning went smoothly enough and I'd been able to keep it together during lunch because Caleb dutifully distracted me, but right now, it was getting harder and harder not to think about my mom today, which would have been her birthday. Thankfully, I had the office all to myself, so, at the very least, if I was going to wallow, I could wallow without an audience.

Every time I closed my eyes, all the images I'd suppressed for the last 10 months came flooding back to me. Every cherished memory, every moment in the hospital I'd tried to forget—there was no stopping it now.

My mom had never made a big deal out of her birthdays, so it was always been up to my dad and me to figure out a way to make it special. We'd surprised her on her 40th birthday by taking her on a trip to New York and other years, it was as simple as making sure we had her favorite cake and went to her favorite restaurant.

My mom always feigned surprise, but it wasn't a secret she'd come to expect something, if not because my dad refused to let her birthday be just another day.

But as my mind wandered to that last birthday, the one we'd had to spend in the oncology wing, my eyes fluttered shut to trap in any tears that threatened to splatter right onto my long-forgotten paperwork.

My mom's frail, pale body had barely been able to stay upright long enough to eat the food we'd brought in and since her stomach couldn't handle much more, we'd had to take the small piece of chocolate cake back home.

"*Forget this one,*" my mom had whispered into my ear as I leaned down to hug her goodbye. "*Just remember the good ones, okay?*"

I wanted to. I really did. But it was just so hard, as painful as it was, to not think about that last one. I couldn't close my eyes and not see my mom, bald from chemo and forcing a pained brave smile on her hollow face, trying so hard not to let us see how exhausted she was and how much of a struggle it was to even breathe.

And now she was gone. No more birthdays. No more hellos. No more goodbyes.

It was then that those stupid, traitorous tears slipped down my cheeks. I knew it wouldn't do me any good to sit here, when I was supposed to be working, and ruminate over everything my mom would miss, but I just couldn't help it. Birthdays, Christmases, gallery openings, my wedding someday, babies....and because I just couldn't do anything else, I whirled around in my chair to face the wall as my shoulders heaved with sobs.

I didn't know how long I sat there like that, quietly sobbing into my hands until I felt my chair swiveling around and rough fingertips pulling my hands away from my face. Those same fingers gently brushed some hair away from my eyes and then curved around my jaw to bring my face up.

"Hey, Iz," Caleb's quiet voice floated around me and just like that, the tension walling up inside me began to crumble. "Just breathe, okay?"

I inhaled shakily and when my body seemed to falter, his hand reached out to rub my back.

"Just breathe."

My eyes travelled up from the carpet to find Caleb level with me, crouching down so he could get a better look at me, his forehead creased with palpable worry.

"I'm...I'm fine," I sputtered unconvincingly.

To his credit, a quick smile crossed his lips before sliding right back into concern. He blew out a deep exhale and anxiously rubbed his hands on his denim work pants.

"I know, Iz. I just wanted to make sure you were alright in here."

"How did you know?"

He shrugged as his lips twisted into a sheepish grin. "When your chair turned around, I figured somethin' was up."

Of course he'd been keeping an eye on me. I really shouldn't have expected anything less.

"Look, don't hit me for sayin' this, but maybe you should just take off now and head to Becca's right away. You don't have to stay here if..."

I didn't need him to finish; it was clear what he was about to say. If it was too much. If it was too hard.

What was I going to do if I went to Becca's right now anyways? I'd be alone until Becca got home from work and being alone right now was not a position I wanted to put myself in.

When I started shaking my head, Caleb just exhaled exasperatedly, like he'd already expected that response.

"I'll be okay," I tried to reassure us both with faltering confidence. "Really. I just had a bad 10 minutes here where it was hard to forget, but look, if I leave now, what am I gonna do?"

We'd hashed this out already. I needed the normalcy today or as normal as today could be. And I *absolutely* needed to be around people, especially people that knew what today meant and would understand.

"And anyways," I continued softly. "If I leave now, Skyler's going to have to come in early to close up the office and I don't want to have to deal with that today either."

"Don't worry about my mom," Caleb shot back sharply. "I can handle it. But if you need to—"

"I'm fine," I cut in. My fingers rested around his cheek to reassure him even further and then I quickly let my hand fall to his shoulder.

He scrubbed a hand over his face and blew out a deep breath. "Alright, if that's what you want."

"I've got a huge pile of paperwork here to distract me that has to be finished before I leave. It'll be fine, promise."

He didn't look anymore confident in my words than before, but let it go. While I knew all this concern and worry was coming from a good place, bringing Caleb down with me today wasn't going to help either of us. He leaned forward and pressed a quick, tender kiss on my forehead, letting his lips linger there for a moment as his fingers tucked some hair behind my ear.

When he finally rose back to his feet, still rubbing his hands anxiously on his pants, I was suddenly struck by the loss of that closeness. He always seemed to know exactly what to do and exactly what I needed —always able to read me so well.

The rest of my afternoon was much more productive than my morning. With that pile of paperwork beckoning to me, I settled in and whipped through it, probably a little too quickly, but the distraction was a God-send. Once I got into work-mode, it was easier to let everything else slip away. And in about two hours, I'd completely exhausted my workload.

That was a problem for a number of reasons, mainly that I'd probably done a half-assed job and now, I had nothing to distract me.

So, in an effort to seek out that necessary distraction, I took a bathroom break. On my way, I squeezed past a long row of cars with various mechanics under the hoods and all the way underneath the engines and as I brushed past the Honda Caleb's head was ducked under, a greasy hand shot out to stop me.

I'd mentally prepared myself to just pass through the garage on my way to the bathroom. We were both working and this wasn't the time or the place for...whatever this was. But when Caleb pulled me closer to him, I couldn't exactly ignore him either.

"You okay, Iz?"

My reassuring grin sure had gotten a lot of practice today and this time, I hoped it actually worked.

"I'm alright. I'm just going to the bathroom. Promise," I laughed nervously, acutely aware that there were a few sets of eyes on us now.

Great. Just what I needed today: more attention on myself.

His thumb smoothed over my cheek and those same lips I'd just kissed yesterday curled up into a lopsided grin.

"Okay," he grinned. "Just wanted to check."

He winked at me as he let my hand slip through his fingers. The catcalls and whistles started just as I snuck away and closed the bathroom door behind me. Leaning back against the door, I squeezed my eyes shut and when they flicked open again, my gaze flew up to the mirror.

The smudge was barely visible from this distance away, but it was still there. Just a tiny streak of grease across my cheek and Caleb put it there. My hand reached up to wipe it away, lingering a little too long over the skin he'd touched.

It was official. I was pathetic.

Last night, after we picked my dad up and got him into bed, Caleb crashed on the couch again, but that was pretty much it. We'd watched a movie, but I'd barely paid attention to any of it. Instead, I'd spent the better part of the night waiting for...something. He'd swung an arm over my shoulder and tucked me into his side, just like he'd done countless times before, his lips brushed my forehead a few times, and he'd kissed me goodnight before I went up to my bedroom.

Part of me had wanted to pull him into my room and at the very least, spend the night curled up in my bed with him. As far as I was concerned, that seemed like a pretty good night. The other part of me was scared shitless.

And for better or worse, that was the part that won out in the end.

Something was happening between us.

If I was being completely honest with myself, that something had been happening for a long time, I'd just been too scared and too stubborn to do anything about it.

When we sat next to each other in American Lit class, the one thing I'd always been able to count on like clockwork was his low whistle and some sort of double entendre whenever I sat down. I think I'd always known that, deep down, those comments infuriated me because, even though I knew I shouldn't, I'd always secretly liked the attention from him.

It was like I was always hyper-aware of him when he was in the room, like I could feel his presence before even making eye contact with him and there'd always been an electric charge between us. In reality, we'd been circling each other ever since I started working at the shop. Up until the moment I kissed him in his dorm yesterday, I'd always just chosen to ignore it.

I couldn't ignore it anymore and I *knew* he felt it too.

All my preconceived notions about him got tossed out the window a long time ago. Sure, he was cocky, more than a little self-absorbed, and it was no secret he'd had more than his fair share of conquests. All those girls...all that history...but if he felt the same way I felt about him...

Whatever this was, it wasn't him rebounding. It wasn't about a whiskey-fueled hook-up in the dark.

He was more than the cocky, panty-chasing, rough-around-the-edges biker persona he wore so well because he'd come through for me more than anyone else in my life combined. He'd stepped into the tornado that was my life and shrugged off the debris like it was nothing. He'd shouldered the burden of my dad with me and had literally forced me into realizing I'd needed help. He'd defended me and protected me. Hell, he'd even gotten into a bar brawl for me.

And in the process, he'd become the one person in my life I couldn't live without and the best friend I'd ever had. I needed all of him because somehow, he'd become my partner in all this. Somehow, he made me whole.

That last thought had me skidding to a stop.

My mom told me once, long before she'd ever gotten sick and before I'd left for college, that love was like a puzzle. While the individual pieces themselves might not seem like part of the puzzle, it was about making all the pieces fit. It was about what made you feel like your best self. It was about what made you feel whole.

This gut-wrenching, all-encompassing feeling like I might combust right now if he didn't feel the same way...that was love?

As I looked at myself in the mirror now, looking for some sign of change in me, I knew, without having to look that far, that the answer was simple.

That was absolutely what this was.

This was love.

I was in love with Caleb Sawyer.

I think a part of me had always been in love with him.

Even when he annoyed the hell out of me...maybe even *because* he annoyed the hell out of me. Even when we weren't friends. Even when I had to watch him drink and screw his way through a breakup because of another girl.

I'd always loved him.

With this truth came an overwhelming sense of peace. There were so many unknowns that *should* scare me, starting with his life in the club. I didn't know the first thing about how to really live in that lifestyle, how to wear it and feel comfortable in it, but I could try. With Skyler and Lexie's help, I could learn.

Everything had changed now.

We'd kissed. We'd gotten tangled up on his bed. He looked at me like I hung the moon and the stars. He touched me like someone might handle a rare and precious painting. His eyes lit up whenever I came into the room like it was Christmas morning, his birthday, and the day he'd take over the Horsemen all rolled into one.

For all intents and purposes, we were already acting like a couple. The problem was that we had no boundaries, no parameters, and no conversations about what this actually was. If he wanted to continue touching me and kissing me, we needed to talk about where we stood. It was only fair.

Given the way his last relationship ended, I couldn't blame him for being a little gunshy about starting something new. Ariel had really messed with his head and...today was Friday...which meant that in a week, Caleb's ex, the one who'd ripped his heart out and stomped on it all the way to California, was going to be back in Claremont for Dominic and Lexie's wedding weekend.

Suddenly, as I gripped the bathroom counter, I could see with sharp clarity what I needed to do. If there was even a chance that Caleb felt even a little of what I was feeling right now, I needed to know before this Friday. I needed to know if a relationship with him was even possible before Ariel came back into town.

All the kissing, hugging, touching...none of it mattered if Caleb didn't feel the same way and I needed to know that there was something worth fighting for. I needed to know that if it came down to it, there was a possibility he could still choose me when he faced Ariel for the first time since she left him.

After a quick glance in the mirror to check my hair and my makeup, I pulled myself together and headed back to the office. As I weaved around the cars, my eyes scanned the room for the one person I was looking for and when I saw him, his chin lifted and his eyes sparkled.

Yeah.

I was totally in love with him.

So now, as I made my way back to the office, I knew I could just sit on my hands and watch Ariel sink her claws back into Caleb or I could be proactive. There was no doubt in my mind that the second Ariel saw Caleb again, she would realize the epic mistake she'd made, if she didn't already. And I'd be an idiot to think he wouldn't at least consider it if Ariel threw herself at him at any point this upcoming weekend.

The only way I'd even have a shot with Caleb was if I talked to him first and asked him point blank if he was serious about me. Because if I didn't sit him down and talk this out, odds were I would lose him next weekend anyways, regardless if we were still friends or not.

I didn't have the time to ruminate over what losing him would mean for my life.

. . .

At 4:00 on the dot, Skyler arrived to handle the closing paperwork, unceremoniously relieving me of duty. Seeing as how she was all about micro-managing, I couldn't really blame her for not completely trusting me yet to close up shop on my own.

With my work for the day done, I pushed through the office doors to head out into the garage. Caleb materialized at my side almost immediately and threw an arm around me, tucking me in under his shoulder.

"Ya made it," he leaned down to whisper in my ear. "Now get outta here and go watch some movies or eat ice cream or whatever you ladies do together."

"Oh, okay," I laughed. "I think we're having a *Project Runway* marathon tonight, but sure."

"And you're gonna call me when you get there, right?"

He was still smirking down at me, but that familiar worry crept back into his eyes.

"Yes, Caleb," I tried to toss back. "I promise."

He was practically pushing me towards the parking lot and I couldn't help but laugh as he playfully nudged me with his elbow. His hand rested on the small of my back as he walked me to my car, careful not to linger too long, but long enough to let me know he was still there, right by my side, giving me whatever I needed.

As he pulled the Trans Am's driver side door open, his fingers brushed my arm, like they itched to pull me into his arms.

I really wished he would.

"Maybe Eli and me will stop by Becca's later?" Caleb was asking me now, a hopeful grin sliding up his lips. "I don't know if I can handle *Project Runway*, but maybe we'll order a pizza. Eli and me can play poker or somethin' while you ladies are gettin' your fix in, I guess. And then when you get that call, I'll already be right there. You won't even have to call me."

I didn't know how to tell him that spending time with him tonight would be the one thing that would make me happier than anything. Time with him always seemed to do that and the more time I spent with him, the more I felt like as long as he was there, everything would always be okay.

"I'd like that," I allowed with a soft smile and I swallowed down a flurry of butterflies when Caleb rested a hand against the door, all but boxing me in against my car. The proximity made my head spin and all I could concentrate on was that intoxicating concoction of musky shampoo and gasoline filling my senses.

That crooked, sexy grin I loved so much curled up his mouth and I found myself wishing I could somehow get closer to him. So I did.

"And," I reached out to take a fistful of his work shirt to bring him closer. "I think we should talk tonight."

Might as well get the conversation started while we had the time.

Surprise with just a hint of confusion flashed across his ocean-blue eyes and his eyebrows bent into a frown. "Talk about what?"

Typical guy.

Whatever would we have to talk about?

I reached up to pat his scratchy cheek, which was in desperate need of a shave. "Oh," I laughed, arching a coy eyebrow at him and I leaned up on my tiptoes to press a light kiss into his lips. "I'm sure you can figure it out."

Caleb's eyebrows flew into his forehead as my heels hit the pavement again, but he bounced back impressively, sliding his free hand around my waist to draw me flush against him. He wasn't fighting fair, not with his hands burning into my skin and the way he leaned in to brush his nose across my cheek.

"Okay, babe," he grinned, his breath tickling my skin. "Let's talk tonight."

Just as he was leaning forward again, aiming right for my lips, a voice cut through our detour into La La Land.

"Would you two get a room already? I'm tryin' to run a professional business here, you know," Skyler called out. She was perched on the office's stoop with her hands lodged into her hips, but I still caught the amused grin on her face even from this distance away.

"Oh yeah?" Caleb called over his shoulder, barely sparing his mom a glance. "And yelling across the parking lot like a banshee is *real* professional, Ma."

Skyler just batted a hand into the air, but she still shot me a sly wink as she turned back to the office.

When Caleb turned his attention my way again, he grinned down at me as the hand at my waist gently nudged me into the car. "Better get on the road, babe. I'm not outta here for another hour, but I'll get my ass over to Becca's as soon as I can, a'ight?"

I grinned back to him, feeling like I was surfing on cloud nine and riding the wave of this crazy, stupid love. That wave took me all the way out of the parking lot and straight for Becca's apartment on the other side of town. But the further I got from Caleb, the more a sick sense of dread seeped through my stomach. Even if it *might* have had something to do with the growing physical distance between Caleb and me, it ran deeper than that.

With a fun night in ahead of me, I really should've just been focusing on distracting myself from the hole in my own heart, rather than anyone else's. Caleb made sure of that today.

It stung just as much as it made my heart stutter and skip. The reality that I couldn't spend this day with my dad, that I couldn't mourn with him, cry with him, share memories with him all because Caleb just didn't trust him today—that ache throbbed almost as much as the rest of it. The other side of that, the side that illuminated just how embedded

Caleb had become in my life, was more than him just not wanting me to have to see the state my dad would be in today. It was him wanting to protect me from it that flung my heart into new heights.

It just reaffirmed what I already knew.

The problem was that the closer I drew to Becca's apartment, the more my guilt multiplied exponentially. There were people who cared enough about me to make sure I'd be looked after today, but who was looking out for my dad? Who was going to be there for him?

When I'd left the house this morning, I'd known I wouldn't be coming back, at least not for a few days, mainly because Caleb wanted us to keep our distance from each other for awhile to let the dust from this day settle. And while I understood where he was coming from and what he was trying to do, there was something about it that just felt wrong.

It wasn't right for my dad to be completely alone today. It wasn't right for us not to see each other at all, even if it was only for a few minutes. We were the only people in the world who truly understood the depth of the loss we felt today and guilt gnawed away at me for not even bothering to check in on him once.

At the end of the day, he was still the only real family I had left.

Caleb's first priority was about shielding me from my dad and distracting me from my memories, but there were no provisions in that plan to make sure my dad would be taken care of too other than to pick him up from whatever bar he landed at tonight.

A surge of protectiveness and stupid impulsivity shoved everything else away and I abruptly swerved to my left to pull a U-turn, sending my car in the opposite direction from Becca's apartment. Ten, fifteen minutes tops, and I'd be heading back this way.

I just needed to make sure my dad was still breathing first.

.   .   .

When I pulled into my driveway, dread rooted me to the driver's seat.

Part of me wanted to just shift the car in reverse and hightail it to

Becca's. Right about now, the weight of Caleb's misgivings about today hovered dangerously in the air.

There was no telling what I would find if I went inside, but maybe he wasn't even there. Maybe he hadn't been able to stick around any longer than me and was sucking back whiskey after whiskey at some bar. At least he'd be around people then.

Besides, Caleb would skin me alive if he knew what I was doing. All I'd have to do was call. That was it. One phone call and maybe I'd have to wait here in the driveway a little longer, but I knew Caleb would get to me the first chance he got so I didn't have to do this alone.

But there was another side to this coin, too. For my dad, Caleb was the opposite of family. The *last* person my dad probably wanted to see today was the person, who, at least to him, represented everything he hated and despised more than anything. It just didn't feel right to invite him in to see my dad at the very bottom of his despair, even though Caleb had already been witness to more drunken nights than I could count.

If the way he'd looked at Caleb after he came home from the run was any indication, loathing probably didn't even begin to round the corner of what my dad felt for him.

Then a terrifying thought gripped me. What if he hadn't left? What if he'd been in the house all day? All by himself...no one around to keep an eye on him...no one around to stop him from...

And then I grabbed my phone from my purse, shoved it into my back pocket, threw the car door open, and sprinted up the walkway as fast as my feet could carry me. When I was finally inside the house, my steps skidded to a halt.

It was just too quiet in here.

Nothing but the ticking grandfather clock in the living room filled the vast space in front of me and the house just felt so massive and empty.

My blood ran cold and my body wouldn't budge, paralyzed to the ceramic tile cemented to my feet. When the spell broke, I almost turned on my heel and fled the house altogether. Whatever I was about to find, I had a feeling it would haunt me for the rest of my life and yet, I couldn't bring myself to do it.

As if my feet had a will of their own, they carried me from the living room and then to the kitchen, only to find both rooms empty. So, when I stood in front of my dad's office, there was little doubt in my mind this was where I would finally find him.

What was waiting for me on the other side of that door was a different story.

When I pushed open the door and my dad's slumped over figure came into view, two thoughts simultaneously ran through my mind: *I need to call Caleb...is Dad even breathing?*

The latter thought propelled me into the office as everything else numbed to the stuttered thumping in my chest. It was like I was hovering over my body, watching myself reach out to check his pulse, trying and failing miserably to trick myself into believing any of this was just a bad dream.

And as much as I knew I should turn back and run, there was no stopping my body from its current path.

Because slumped over in his chair, with broken glass littered across the desk, was my dad.

All the moments when he'd actually been a true father washed over my mind and I had a clear vision of myself sitting on his lap at this very same desk so many years ago, watching him type away as he explained each case, line by line, even though I hadn't understood a word of it.

I couldn't walk away. I couldn't leave him now. Not when he needed me the most, even if he wasn't sober enough to realize it.

He jerked underneath my touch and when his head turned, his eyes glazed over, squinting at me like he was trying to place who I was.

"Dad?" I whispered.

Something muffled rumbled from his chest as he pushed himself up by the elbows and somehow groped for the half-empty bottle of whiskey in front of him.

"Dad," I called after him, my arms reaching out, but unable to grasp him.

He grunted half-audibly in response and my breath choked in my throat as his shaking hands grasped the whiskey bottle to top off his glass.

"Dad, please, don't."

The glass slipped from his hands and tumbled to the desk, bouncing as it fell and spewing shards of glass on the surface, on the floor, everywhere.

"I tried so hard," he whispered hoarsely. "All I wanted to do was make her happy. I tried so hard to make her happy..."

"She was, Dad. She was," I tried desperately to reassure him and I barely felt the hot tears slipping down my cheeks.

He just shook his head, his eyes boring a hole into the desk in front of him. "No, she wasn't. I did everything I could, anything I could think of...it wasn't enough. It wasn't goddamn enough for her."

"You were enough, Dad. I know you were."

I was reaching out to him again, but this time, he just shrugged me off.

"No, I wasn't," his knuckles turned white from gripping the edge of the desk so tightly. "I don't know why she stayed so long. After you left for college, she didn't have to anymore...you look just like her, you know that? I *hate* how much you look like her."

My hand flew over my mouth to mask the sob that erupted from my throat. I couldn't let him see how much this was shattering me, how much I needed him too, not when he was so weak. There was nothing harder.

"Dad, I..." I trailed off, all words failing me. There was nothing I could possibly say that would ever make this better for him.

He was shaking his head now as his fingers closed over a large shard of glass.

"There's no point in trying anymore, Isabelle," he muttered, bringing the shard closer to his wrist. "I'm no good to anyone. No one at work trusts me anymore, no one even looks at me anymore. You're ashamed of me. There's no point."

As soon as I realized what he was about to do, I lunged forward, strangling a cry, arms outstretched and flailing towards their destination. My left hand flung out to snatch the shard from him just as he brought it down to attack his wrist. The glass sliced through my skin, but there was no pain—I was submerged underwater and everything around me was hazy.

My dad slumped over again as I stumbled back, finally looking down

at the red droplets of blood sprinkling the carpet beneath me. Was that
—was that *my* blood?

My uninjured hand dug into my back pocket, fumbling for my
phone. But as my fingers swiped across the screen, scrolling until I found
Caleb's number and hit dial, my dad suddenly sprung to life, charging up
from the desk and straight for me just as Caleb's smooth voice picked up.

"Hey, Iz."

"Ca—"

That was as far as I got.

My dad's hand launched out to slap the phone away, sending it
plummeting to the carpet.

"Who was that? Sawyer?" he spat. Suddenly, he lurched down,
swept my phone up in one hand and smashed it into the wall behind me.
"You'd bring that...that *felon* over here? What the hell is wrong with
you?"

I'd been scared of my dad before. Scared of bringing home a B.
Scared of what would happen if I didn't become a lawyer. Scared of
disappointing him. Scared of not living up to his sky-high expectations.
But I'd never been scared of him *physically* hurting me before—until
now.

"I'm sorry," I whispered.

"Always your first instinct to run to the criminal, huh?" he shook his
head, disgust oozing from his pores, right next to the stench of whiskey.

"I just thought..." I swallowed tightly, edging closer to the wall.
Anything to put more distance in between us. "I thought he could help."

He bit out a bitter laugh and shook his head, wavering unsteadily on
his feet. "Help from Caleb Sawyer. Help from the Horsemen. Jesus,
what is the world coming to?"

"Dad," I whispered, a fat tear trailing down my cheek. "He's—"

"Lemme tell you something about Caleb Sawyer, Isabelle," he cut in.
"Caleb Sawyer won't do anything but get you pregnant and leave you. Is
that what you want?"

I shook my head furiously. "Dad, you don't know him like I do—"

"Don't play dumb with me, Isabelle. Boy's got a one-track mind and
he's not hangin' around you the way he does outta the goodness of his
heart."

I winced at his words, which seemed to slur and run together the more he stumbled and staggered around his office.

"Don't let him degrade you the way he has every other girl in this town. Your mother and I raised you to be smarter than that."

My emotions shifted in a flash and suddenly, all the bitterness I'd pushed down underneath the guilt and obligation crashed over me in waves. I didn't have to listen to this. I didn't have to listen to him talk crap about the person I loved. And suddenly, the dull ache in my left hand and the blood dripping into the carpet didn't matter anymore.

"Stop it, Dad," I whispered angrily, wiping a stray tear from my cheek as I spoke. "You have no idea what you're talking about. And you wanna know something else? This..." I waved my hands in front of me, gesturing towards the broken glass, "this has to stop. We can't live like this anymore, Dad. You need help."

"Help?" he snarled, teetering dangerously closer to me. "We've had this conversation already before, but let me remind you again: you don't tell me what to do. You don't give me orders. *I* am the parent. *You* are the child!"

A fresh wave of tears streamed down my cheeks, but now my body trembled with resentment and animosity.

"Yeah?" I shot back. "And you're drunk. You're always drunk. And you stopped being a parent the day Mom died, so I'm pretty sure your opinion doesn't mean shit."

"You watch your language," he pushed a pointed finger into my chest, knocking me back towards the wall.

"Oh, fuck you, Dad."

I felt it before I heard it.

The sting burned through the side of my face and I stumbled backwards, my uninjured hand flying to my throbbing cheek. And as I regained my bearings against the wall now, I just didn't care anymore.

"I hate you," I murmured. I didn't even care if he could hear me. "I hate that I never wanna come home anymore. I hate that we can't even be in the same room anymore. I hate that you're not my dad anymore. The only time we ever talk is when you call me to pick your drunk ass up from a bar. What kind of parent does that? What the hell is *wrong* with you? Don't you care about me at all? Don't you care what this is doing to me...to see you like this? You know what Mom would say? She'd say you're a monster. You know that? You're a monster!"

His hands shot out, shoving me viciously backwards and my head bounced against the wall with a sick smack as my shoulders collided with the drywall.

Everything went blank and maybe that was a good thing.

Then I couldn't really feel when his hand slapped me across the cheek again or when his hand curled into a fist, slamming me backwards into the wall until I slid down in a daze.

With my sliced-open hand throbbing and dripping with blood, the pounding in the back of my skull, and the burning across my entire face, it was all I could do to get back on two feet. My dad stumbled backwards, staring down at his fists in disbelief, but all that mattered was that there was a good three feet in between us and now I had an opening to get as far away as possible.

Even when I managed to shakily hoist myself up, dizziness nearly knocked me right back down.

Somehow, I stumbled out of the office and scrambled up the stairs, tripping just once as adrenaline pushed me all the way up and into my bedroom. When I was safely behind the door, my good hand flipped the lock and I shuffled backwards.

The tears tumbling down my cheeks stung the open cut underneath my left eye, but that didn't stop them from coming.

Self-preservation was about all my instincts could manage without completely short-circuiting and I scrambled across the room and into my walk-in closet. But once the door was shut behind me, and I knew another locked door stood between me and the monster downstairs, reality set in.

I tucked my knees into my chest, buried my battered face in my arms, and let my body shake with sobs.

CHAPTER THIRTY-ONE
I Got You

Caleb

Thirty minutes.

Isabelle had been gone for thirty minutes.

She should've been at Becca's apartment by now, which meant she also should've called me by now too. Or, at the very least, texted. There was no way Isabelle would forget to let me know she'd made it there. That just wasn't something she would do.

This was all but driving me out of my mind. My fingers twitched at my sides, just itching to dig into my back pocket for my phone, but indecision kept me from going through with it.

By all rights, it had only been a half hour, which, even I had to admit wasn't *really* that much time.

There were plenty of plausible reasons to explain why she hadn't called yet: she could've stopped for gas or at an ATM or maybe she was already at Becca's and had just lost track of time.

Something wasn't right here and I just didn't know how to beat back this craziness.

Because I couldn't wait anymore, I tried to flag Eli down and when I couldn't get the douchebag's attention, I jogged through the shop to get to him, sidestepping wayward tools and grease-stained rags along the way.

"Yo, Eli!" I called out sharply, annoyed that I still couldn't seem to get the dickhead's attention. When Eli's dark, buzzed head finally popped up, I fired off my demand. "Hey, can you get Becca on the phone for me?"

Eli's eyebrows flew up into his forehead. "What? Whaddaya need to call her—"

"Just do it, bro," I snapped.

Eli blinked back in surprise and then hastily dug into his back pocket, quickly making the call.

"Ask her if Isabelle's there yet," I directed, shoving my hands deep into my pockets to mask my nervousness.

Eli nodded silently and it was all I could do to not rip the phone away to talk to her myself. Instead, I just stood there like a helpless asshole.

"Hey, Becs," Eli was saying into the phone now. "Hey, is Isabelle at your place yet?"

I waited, practically leaning forward in anticipation as I listened for what I needed to hear. Eli's frustrated expression told me everything I needed to know: Isabelle was still unaccounted for. Still, Eli shook his head for quick confirmation as he listened to Becca on the other end.

"She says she hasn't heard from Isabelle yet either," he relayed. "When did she leave?"

I blew out an exasperated breath, resisting the urge to slam my fist into something. That wouldn't help me right now. I just needed to—the vibrations in my back pocket caught me off guard, but I dug it out of my pocket in a frenzy to see the caller ID.

"Nevermind, bro," I swatted out a hand as I stepped away, bringing the phone to my ear. "She's calling me right now. Everything's good."

"Hey, Iz," I answered.

Everything was fine now. She was going to tell me she'd just pulled into Becca's apartment complex or something like that. No big deal. Relief shot through me just knowing she was on the phone, knowing I'd be able to hear her tell me herself that everything was really okay.

Because I'd literally just talked myself into believing that all my initial worries about today and everything that could go wrong with it were just smoke and mirrors, I wasn't prepared to hear the sounds coming from the other end of the phone.

"Ca—"

Isabelle's voice cut out abruptly and then I heard her dad's bitter voice: "Who was that? Sawyer?"

Static hummed over the line and then...nothing.

My heart crashed into my stomach and everything churned around me at once: the sound of her panicked voice, her dad's furious words, the static. Immediately, my instincts kicked into high gear and the paralyzing fear snaking down my spine would just have to wait. Everything could be dealt with later. I just had to get to Isabelle first.

I was already flying out the garage and sprinting towards my bike when Dom and Eli caught up to me.

"What's goin' on?" Dom called out.

I barely looked over my shoulder because there just wasn't enough damn time to slow down. "Iz called me. Somethin's wrong, Dom."

"Do you know where she is?" Dom yelled back as both he and Eli swung their legs over their bikes next to mine.

"Her dad was there, so she's gotta be at her house."

Dom and Eli just nodded, ready to follow my lead. The office door swung open and my mom stalked towards us, one hand shielding her eyes from the sun. Even from across the parking lot, Skyler obviously hadn't left her post to bitch me out for deserting my shift. She'd sensed the danger just as much as I did.

"Caleb? What's going on?"

"I gotta get to Isabelle's," I yelled back to her, frustrated to have to waste another second in this parking lot. "I'll call you when I can."

Not willing to spare another moment waiting for a response, I blasted through the parking lot with Dom and Eli right behind me. The entire ride to Isabelle's house flew by in a blur—and, honestly, a miracle that one of us didn't get our asses pulled over—but we made it to the other side of town in a record 10 minutes.

When her house finally came into view and I saw Isabelle's Trans Am parked out in the driveway, my adrenaline spiked, raging furiously and coiling through my veins as my fears took on a more tangible shape. Dread and lethal fury raged through me for control and neither one was really an option for me right now. I had to stay calm. I had to get to Isabelle.

I leapt off my bike, sprinting up the walkway and banging my way through the front door, but my steps skidded in the entryway.

This house was just too quiet. It was eerie. It felt cold and barren, despite the fact that it was almost 70 degrees outside.

Cold panic spiked in my chest, tightening and choking me, but I had to push through it. With Dom and Eli right on my heels, we broke off through the house, each systematically scouring the abandoned space for signs of life as quickly as possible.

Between the living room, the kitchen, and all the hallways in between, we found jackshit. But as I pivoted down yet another darkened hallway, the edge of another door came into view, opened just a crack, but enough to see Isabelle's dad slumped over against a wall. Fury lurched me forward and I slammed through the door, darting over to Samuel Martin's limp body.

Gripping him by his shirt collar, I hauled him up only to slam him against the wall to force that asshole to open his eyes.

"What did you do, you son of a bitch?" I spat in his face. "Where is she?"

Samuel Martin's face crumbled and a low groan vibrated from his throat, mumbling something so inaudibly that I had to lean forward just to make it out.

"I'm sorry," Samuel sobbed into his hands. "I'm so sorry."

I shoved him away, too disgusted with the man to even look at him, and that was when I saw it.

Droplets of blood sprinkled the carpet where we stood and my heart backflipped all the way down into my stomach. Forgetting all about the man curled up into the fetal position at my feet, my eyes followed the tiny beads of crimson past the door's threshold. I was up on my feet, rushing out the door just as Dom skidded to a stop in front of me.

"Stay with him," I barked over my shoulder and I took off for the staircase, bounding up the steps two by two to get to Isabelle's bedroom.

"Iz?" I pounded on her door with one fist and shook the locked door knob with the other. "Iz, it's me. Come on, open up."

I waited two more seconds, then took a step back before ramming my shoulder into the door. When the door creaked and groaned, but still didn't open, I reared back again, slamming my shoulder through her bedroom door. My eyes frantically scanned the bedroom and all the air left the room when I finally found her.

I couldn't move. I couldn't think.

She was crawling out of her closet on her hands and knees with a blood-soaked rag wrapped around one hand, but that wasn't what rooted me to the carpet. My heart sliced in half at the sight of her bruised, blood-smeared, tear-stained face, her disheveled blonde hair, and those frantic, desperate blue eyes.

My feet jerked to life, sliding across the carpet until I fell on my knees in front of her and tugged her to me. I had to give her whatever she needed right now. Anything to erase that haunted look in her eyes. Anything to make it so this never happened.

"I got you, Iz," I murmured into her hair, wrapping her even more tightly against my chest. "You're okay, babe. You're gonna be okay. I got you."

Her shoulders shook violently and her tears soaked the front of my work shirt. All I could do was just hold her and swallow the lump in my throat threatening to topple the rest of my emotions. My fingers found her chin and I gently brushed the tears from her eyes. I needed her to look at me, to really *see* me, so she knew I was really there, but I also needed to take a quick inventory of her face.

There was a cut across her left cheek and a smattering of purple dots right underneath her eye, which would probably be a nasty shiner in the morning. Another stray tear trailed down her cheek, but I caught it with my thumb. My lips brushed against hers, just needing to give her some kind of comfort.

That was the best I could do right now and I'd never felt so helpless in my entire life.

"Hey, babe," I said hoarsely, gesturing down at her injured hand. "Can I take a look?"

She nodded and I took her tiny left hand to gingerly unwind the fabric, which was probably torn from the first shirt she found in her closet.

Swallowing tightly, I pressed the fabric back into the slash across her palm. The smaller, less threatening scrapes across her fingers would probably be fine but the long, jagged slice down the length of her palm might be another story. I'd seen a lot of bad situations through my involvement with the Horsemen over the years and none of the danger and none of the potential blowback had ever really seemed that tangible, but this? This wasn't something that could just be tossed aside and forgotten.

This was a nightmare.

Tossing the soiled piece of fabric aside, I lifted up the edge of my own shirt, tearing a piece of it off with my teeth. After wrapping the cloth back around the cut, I reached up to brush the tears from her eyes. I just wanted to make this go away, to make everything better, and it killed me that all I could do was kiss her forehead, her cheeks, and her lips. This was the best I could do? Wipe away her tears and give her a kiss?

With one hand tangled in her hair, I wound the other around her back to pull her even closer. Her tears wet my face, but I just leaned back to wipe the ones that still streamed down her cheeks. Cupping both hands around her face, the distraught, haunted expression swimming in her eyes ripped what was left of my heart right out of my chest.

"This can be fixed, Iz," I murmured into her hair. "You're alright. You're gonna be fine. I got you."

She turned her head to bury her face into my work shirt that was already splattered with her tears. Her whole body was trembling and the only thing I could do was just hold her tighter.

"I got you," I promised, kissing her hair. "I got you."

Some movement and a little shuffling from the doorway caught my attention and I turned my head to see Dom behind me, staring back at the scene in front of him with an appropriately grim expression.

"Hey, Iz?" I murmured to her, nodding to Dom as he crouched down next to us. "You gotta tell me what you want us to do."

"What do you mean?" her voice came out in hushed, hoarse whispers and her eyes darted between Dom and me.

"We can take you to the hospital," I told her gently. "But they're gonna take one look at you and have a shit-ton of questions. If that's what you want, I'll do it. You just gotta say the word, babe, and I'll do it."

Isabelle swallowed tightly. "What's my other option?"

"We take you to the clubhouse. Get you patched up. Anything else you need. And then you can decide what you wanna do about your dad."

Even mentioning that piece of shit in passing made me want to shove my fist through a wall. Luckily, Isabelle was already shaking her head and I could refocus my attention back where it needed to be.

"I don't wanna go to the hospital," she whispered and leaned into my chest, her eyes desperate. "I don't wanna answer any questions. He'd get arrested then, right?"

Hell, yes he'd get arrested and right now, that seemed like a pretty good option, seeing as how beating the living hell out of him wouldn't solve any problems either. Asshole deserved to sit his ass in jail after what he did.

And if jail wasn't an option, there was nothing I'd love more than to take my Ka-Bar knife and bury it right in Samuel Martin's chest, but Isabelle didn't need to know that.

So I just nodded.

"No hospitals," she blew out a haggard sigh. "But I don't wanna go to the clubhouse either. I just—I don't want anyone to see me like this."

"What're you talkin' about?" I grinned down at her and ran my thumb over her cheek. "You're beautiful, Iz."

She huffed out a laugh, wincing a little from the movement. "Yeah. Whatever you say. But...not the clubhouse, okay?"

"Okay," I agreed, my eyes flicking to Dom in silent communication. "How about my mom's?"

"Just for now?"

"Just for now."

Her chin dipped down in a nod and Dom was up on his feet a moment later with his phone pressed to his ear to make the call. Once the arrangements were made, I gingerly pulled Isabelle to her feet, tucking her safely underneath my shoulder to help her down the stairs, careful to steer her as far away from her dad's office as possible. Eli already had the door shut and was stationed in front of it to stand guard until further notice.

Grateful I finally had something to do that would actually help her, I loaded Isabelle into her car, slid into the driver's seat, and backed us out of the driveway to head towards my mom's house with Dom right behind us.

. . .

By the time I pulled Isabelle's Trans Am into the driveway with Dom coming in right next to me, my mom already had us beat. She was rushing to the passenger side door before I even had a chance to reach over and unbuckle Isabelle's seatbelt. She flung the door open and gathered Isabelle into her arms like any good mother would.

"Come on, sweetie," she told Isabelle. "Let's get you in the house, okay?"

Just as she was moving to help Isabelle out of the car, I slid out of the driver's side, jogged around the car and shot my mom a hard glare to get her the hell out of my way. Her dark eyes widened, but she got the hint, dutifully stepping aside so I could lean down to wrap my arm around Isabelle's shoulders and help her out of the car.

As we moved through the garage and into the house, Isabelle leaned into me, gripping my free hand with her good one. My mom was already ahead of us and held the door open so we could step into the kitchen.

Once I eased Isabelle into a chair at the table, my hands ghosted over her shoulders as I dropped into the chair next to her. Even though we were seated just inches away from each other, that minuscule bit of distance had my nerves jumping up through my throat and my fingers compulsively reached out until I found her skin, just needing to touch her, just needing to feel that she was still here.

My mom moved over to the other side of Isabelle, setting a first aid kit down on the table while Dom fell into a chair on the opposite side of the table. No one said a word as my mom appraised Isabelle's injuries, quickly bandaging the bloodied slice across her left hand before moving on to dabbing at the cut on her cheek and securing a few tiny band-aids over the wound. When she rose from the table to get an ice pack and some meds, I took that opportunity to wrap my arm around Isabelle's shoulder again and kissed her hair.

When Isabelle had an ice pack to her cheek and downed some Tylenol, my mom cleared her throat, melodramatically addressing the giant elephant in the room.

Isabelle needed to rest, but first, she needed to tell me what the hell went down inside that house.

"Iz," I started carefully and shifted in my chair so my body completely faced her. "You gotta tell us what happened."

With my arm still glued around her, I squeezed her shoulder to give her a gentle nudge in the right direction, to let her know it was okay to tell us whatever she needed to say.

Her bloodshot eyes flicked to me and if my heart wasn't already torn in two before, it was completely shredded now.

"I went to the house because I wanted to check on him. I know that's not what I was supposed to do, but I just wanted to make sure he was okay. I was only gonna stay for a couple minutes and then I was gonna go to Becca's," Isabelle whispered and she was looking at me now like she expected me to start yelling at her or something.

I leaned forward to make sure she heard this: "None of this is your fault, Iz. You weren't the one that did anything wrong today."

She nodded and inhaled sharply. A tear slipped down her cheek, but she brushed it away. God, she was so strong. Even now, bloody and bruised, having survived something so goddamned horrific and she was still sitting here, standing tall and held together.

My mom reached over and squeezed Isabelle's hand to prompt her to keep going. "What happened when you got to the house, sweetie?"

"I found him in his office," Isabelle started again and I winced at how hoarse she sounded. "He was...I've never seen him that bad before. It was like he just gave up, you know? He dropped a glass and grabbed one of the pieces, but I stopped him before he could hurt himself."

She held up her bandaged hand with a sad smile and swallowed tightly.

"What happened after that, babe?" I asked as gently as possible because I knew this would be the hardest part for her to tell, but the part I needed to hear the most.

"I don't know," she shook her head, wincing a little in pain from the effort. "I think I just snapped. I was just so sick of always having to deal with him drunk and taking all his crap every single day. I just couldn't do it anymore and I said a lot of things I shouldn't have said and then he started hitting me."

My jaw tightened and I had to clamp my teeth down on my bottom lip to keep from physically reacting. I wanted to kill him. I wanted to murder the bastard for even thinking about laying a hand on her, but my main priority was sitting right next to me and I had to take care of her first.

Isabelle's gaze sought me out and I wasn't going anywhere.

"I called him a monster, Caleb," she whispered as fresh tears trailed down her cheek. "And I told him my mom would think he's a monster too."

As far as I was concerned, she didn't tell the asshole anything that wasn't true, but that wasn't going to help her right now.

"Hey," I drew her into my shoulder so I could kiss her hair. "He had no right to do what he did to you. Don't make excuses for him, okay?"

She nodded and squeezed her eyes shut. "I know."

My mom reached out to brush away a stray piece of hair on Isabelle's face and gave her a reassuring smile. "I know this is hard, Isabelle, but you really need to tell us what you want us to do about your dad."

Isabelle swallowed hard and sawed her bottom lip with her teeth. "Do I have to decide now? I mean...can't we wait a little while?"

My mom shot me a glance over Isabelle's head and I shook my head.

"The longer we wait, babe, the worse it's gonna be for you and for him," I told her gently. "I know it doesn't seem like it right now, but the faster you get him wherever you want him to be, the better it'll be for both of you."

"I don't...what are my choices?"

I lifted a shoulder. "Well, I'll happily drop him off at the station for Chief Kelly to deal with if that's what you wanna do."

She laughed, but I didn't hear much humor in her voice. "No, I don't want him to go to jail, Caleb. I don't think that's the right place for him. I just want him to get help. I just want him to at least *try* to get better."

Well, if that's what she wanted, then who was I to deny her? Deep down, I knew I'd do anything this girl asked without hesitation.

So...time to get that asshole to rehab.

CHAPTER THIRTY-TWO
All I Want Is You

Caleb

Hard silence permeated the air between us and I knew if I looked at the man sitting next to me, I just might pull Isabelle's Trans Am over and completely lose my shit. Up until now, I'd done a pretty good job of keeping it together for Isabelle's sake, but that was about it.

As far as I was concerned, the man sitting next to me might as well have been dead.

In hindsight, insisting that *I* be the one to drive Samuel Martin to the hospital probably wasn't the smartest idea I'd ever had. I could barely stand to be in the same room with him before and now, here I was, driving the man to rehab and quietly fantasizing about strangling him.

My hands twisted around the steering wheel, imagining it was his neck instead and it was all I could do to shift my focus elsewhere to something that didn't involve killing him, or at the very least, causing him serious bodily harm.

I just couldn't make sense of what happened tonight. Couldn't wrap my head around how someone could do something like that to someone he was supposed to love and take care of. To his *daughter*. To actually *hit* her?

Thinking about this right now just got me one second closer to pulling the car over.

I glanced at Isabelle's dad anyways, just to make sure he was still somewhat coherent, and found him boring holes into his hands like he couldn't believe what he'd used them for tonight.

Good.

Try to sleep on that for the rest of your life, asshole.

Luckily for me, Claremont was about as small town as it gets and the

268

hospital was only a quick drive from Isabelle's house. My mom had taken care of making all the calls and getting all the information and then she'd slipped into that mother role for Isabelle again, making sure she had something to eat, checking her bandages, and putting her into my old bed at the house for some rest.

My job wasn't quite done yet. I just had to get this worthless sack of shit into the hospital, sign a few forms, talk to a doctor, and then I was leaving his ass here where he belonged, where he couldn't hurt his daughter anymore.

When I shifted the Trans Am into park, I hesitated, waiting to see if he'd even be able to get out of the passenger seat on his own. He'd sobered up a little since we'd found him and Isabelle in their house, but I didn't exactly trust that he was in any position to do just about anything right now either.

"I bet you're really enjoying this right now, aren't you?"

My neck snapped to the passenger side of the truck at the sound of his cold voice and my fists pressed into the sides of my legs to keep myself from throwing a punch.

If he wanted to talk, fine.

We could talk.

"Yeah, you would think that," I told him, but I didn't bother looking at him. He just wasn't worth it. "But seein' as how you don't know anything about me, you also don't know jackshit about how I'm feelin' right now either."

Samuel's shoulders shook with bitter laughter. "I know exactly who you are and what you are."

"Oh, yeah?" my eyes stayed locked on the hospital's main entrance as I spoke. "And what's that?"

"You're not better than me. Just because you're here, driving me to this place, doesn't mean you won."

"I didn't realize we were competing," I shot back dryly.

"And you're not as smart as you think you are either. I can see right through you, Sawyer. I see the way you look at my daughter and the way you've been sniffing around her and you're not fooling me. You're not the good guy you pretend to be whenever you're around her," he paused and shook his head angrily. "You know what you are? You're just a street thug dressed up in leather on a Harley. That's it. And you're not worth the dust on her feet or the dirt on her doorstep. You don't even deserve to come within 100 miles of her."

His words simmered and twisted, hooking themselves around me until all I could do was growl back: "Neither do you."

Even from the corner of my eye, I could still see Isabelle's dad nodding the affirmative. At least he was sober enough to admit when I was right.

"I hurt my daughter tonight," his hoarse voice sliced through the heavy air between us. "I never thought I'd ever be the kind of man that could lay hands on his own *child*. I lost my mind. I took everything out on her and...I didn't even know I was doing it. I made her suffer because of my shortcomings, because of my failures and I'll never forgive myself for that. I don't expect her to either."

He paused after that and when I finally allowed myself to turn his way, he was staring out the passenger side window with his shaking hands folded into a white-knuckled knot on his lap.

"I know I've forfeited the right to be part of her life now and that I don't deserve to have any say in anything she does anymore," he went on, his voice growing firmer with each syllable. "But at the end of the day, I'm still her father, and so I'm going to say this anyways: I want you to stay the hell away from my daughter."

My shoulders shook with humorless laughter and my eyes flicked to the car's ceiling.

"I would say with all due respect, but seein' as how I don't have any respect for you, I'll just say this," I kept my focus firmly in front of me because if I let myself look at him now, the results wouldn't be pretty for either of us. "I get why you wouldn't want her anywhere near me, but you need to understand that I care about your daughter more than I care about myself. And I'm well aware I haven't done anything in my life to justify getting to have someone like her, but just so you know, I'm a better man when she's around. She makes me better just by standing next to me. And I would rather cut off my own arm than hurt her, which is a helluva lot more than I can say for you."

And I'm pretty sure I'm in love with her. No, I'm 100 percent sure I'm in love with her.

Because those thoughts needed to be shelved for the time being, I focused on the matter at hand, this time turning in my seat to face the man who'd just used his fists on the girl I loved.

Time to lay down the law.

"So here's what's gonna happen: you and me are gonna head into that hospital and sign all that paperwork to get your ass into rehab. Then you're gonna follow every instruction, every requirement, everything to the damned T. Maybe Isabelle will wanna see you when you're in there, maybe she won't, but that's up to her. We both know she'll reach out to you when she's ready, whenever that is, so you better pull your shit together. You better sober up and figure out how to be a father to her, if that's what she wants. If I had my way, you'd either be sittin' your ass in one of Kelly's cells at the station right now or you'd be six feet under in some hole outside of town. The only reason we're sittin' here is because this was what Isabelle wanted. This is a gift. This is mercy. So, the way I see it, you get one chance. Don't fuck it up."

Samuel Martin blinked at me. Then he blinked again. And then he nodded.

Good enough for me.

· · ·

By the time I parked Isabelle's car back in my mom's driveway, exhaustion pretty much weighed down my entire body. I needed a stiff drink. And a cigarette because a hit of nicotine would feel like heaven right now.

When I pushed inside the house and threw Isabelle's keys on the counter, my mom was already sitting at the kitchen table with a mug in one hand and a cigarette in the other. She was up on her feet before I had a chance to do much else and gestured with her head for me to sit at the table while she rummaged through a cabinet to get me a mug.

"Where's Iz?"

She turned and pointed down the hallway. "Resting in your old room. Doc stopped by while you were gone. Said he didn't think she needs any stitches, so I guess that's finally some good news, huh?"

I dropped down into a chair at the table with a nod and finally blew out the breath I felt like I'd been holding since I woke up this morning. This day was always going to be rough. I'd known it the second Isabelle got that misty look in her eye when she'd mentioned her mom's birthday a few weeks ago. But in all my plans, all my provisions, and all my worries about this day, I'd still never anticipated it would be *this* rough.

"How did everything go?" my mom called out softly from behind me. She set a steaming mug of black coffee on the table and slid into the chair next to mine.

"About as good as could be expected," I lifted a shoulder and reached for the mug. "He pretty much called me a piece of shit. I dropped him off, made sure he signed everything he needed to sign, and then I left his ass there."

"He's always been a hypocrite, so I can't say I'm surprised," she shook her head. "Don't take any stock in what that man says, baby. He's not worth it."

She slid me a pack cigarettes and I gratefully slipped one out of the pack. We puffed away in silence and those few moments were enough to let all the emotions simmering inside me finally shove their way under the surface again.

My mom's voice broke through the quiet as she laid a hand on my arm. "How you doin' with all this?"

I blew out a hard breath and tapped my cigarette into the glass ashtray in front of us. "I don't know."

She nodded, shooting me a sad smile. "It's hard watchin' the person you love go through somethin' like that, isn't it?"

My eyes widened when her words finally grabbed hold of everything else swimming around in my mind, but my mom just laughed and gave my hand a quick squeeze.

"Come on," she chuckled and shook her head. "You really think I didn't know? Why do you think I always scheduled your breaks together, hmm? And all that will-they-or-won't-they bullshit was really startin' to get on my nerves, by the way."

Jesus, what was I supposed to say to that? I didn't even get much of a chance to react because as she tilted her head to get a better look at me, her dark eyes glimmered with something I'd seen many, many times throughout my life.

"So, I was thinking I'd ask Isabelle if she wanted to help me out with Lexie's party next Friday. How do you feel about that?"

My eyes narrowed a little. Not so much because of the question itself, but more so *why* she was asking it in the first place.

"I think that's a good idea. If she's feeling up to it, of course."

"Of course," she nodded. A sly grin crossed her face and I didn't like it one bit. "Yeah, I figured she could help put up decorations or help me in the kitchen. You know, with all the other old ladies."

If she was throwing out a line, I wasn't stupid enough to take the bait.

"Right," I nodded, shooting her a wary glance. I had a feeling I knew where she was going with this and I'd yet to work out if this line of questioning was good or bad for me.

"I'm glad we're on the same page because I don't think Isabelle belongs workin' clean-up duty with all the other girls like Becca and Ariel."

Ah. There it was. Shoulda known.

"You don't consider Becca an old lady?" I asked, determined to beat her at her own game. "Her and Eli have been hookin' up for awhile."

"I think the answer's in the question. *Hookin' up*," she made air quotes with her hands as she spoke, "doesn't mean anything and you know it. Besides, I don't trust that girl as far as I can throw her. She seems nice enough to your face, but there's just something about her that seems a little, I don't know—shifty."

"Huh."

I'd never thought about Becca like that before, but then again, whenever we were in the same room together, I was always too focused on her best friend to really give two shits about her.

"And Ariel?" she arched an eyebrow and it was clear she was enjoying this a little too much. "Never an old lady in the first place, so I don't see the need to give her any kind of status on Friday. She's weak. Always been selfish. And she walked around the clubhouse like her shit didn't stink. Someone who's got all those book smarts, but no common sense doesn't hold much value as far as I'm concerned. That's not the kind of old lady you need."

"Oh yeah?" I shot back playfully. "You got someone in mind?"

"Yeah, I do, actually," she grinned back at me slyly, turning in her chair to face me. "Blonde hair. Blue eyes. About, I don't know, 5'6, maybe. Real pretty. Gorgeous."

"You mean smokin' hot," I cut in with a smirk.

"Okay, fine," she threw up her hands dramatically. "Smokin' hot. But that's not the point, baby."

"I know, Ma."

"She's strong. Resilient. Unbreakable, even. Look at what's happened in her life and you'd never even know it 'cuz she's not the kinda girl who wears her problems for everyone else to see. She's held herself together in a situation where most people would either be curled up in the fetal position or knee-deep in a bottle. You wanna know what she said to me when I told her before that you were takin' her dad to the hospital? She said she wished she could do it so that you didn't have to. That girl—she rolls with the punches and then keeps on swingin'. And she loves you unconditionally, baby. That girl is more than just an old lady for you. That girl is your partner. But I think you already knew that."

Yeah, I did know that already.

"Now, she's gonna need some help navigating through everything that comes with the club, but that's what she's got you, me, and Lexie for."

I nodded silently.

"I guess I just needed to see where your head's at before this weekend."

"What's that supposed to mean?" I frowned.

"You know exactly what I mean. You're gonna see Ariel this weekend. You know, the girl who up and left you, the girl who made you miserable, the girl who made you see the bottom of more bottles than I really wanna know about, the girl who—"

"Okay, Ma. I get it. Jesus Christ."

Hearing it all listed out loud like that hit a little too close to home. I didn't want to think about that part of my life anymore, especially since it was over long before Ariel ever split town. Man, I hadn't thought about her in—when *was* the last time I thought about her?

"All I'm saying, Caleb," she went on, that hard glare I hated was simmering in her eyes again, "is that you gotta make sure you know what's gonna happen when you see Ariel again. If you think, even for a second, that seeing her again might make you change your mind, you gotta figure that out now before you take things any further with Isabelle. She doesn't deserve you hurting her that way and you know it."

This wasn't something I even needed to waste a second thinking about. I'd known my answer a long time ago.

"Ma," I made sure my voice mirrored just how serious I was. "You don't have anything to worry about. I honestly haven't even thought about Ariel in — I don't even know how long. I really don't see it as making a choice because from my end, Isabelle *is* the only choice. She's...she's *it*."

"Good," she smiled. "I'm glad you finally got your head outta your ass. Because from *my* end, watching you with her...the way you look at her...Caleb, that's all I've ever wanted to see. She's good for you and she's gonna help you become the man I know you can be. And whether you believe it or not, I think you're good for her too. And even if you haven't spent much time thinkin' about your ex bein' back in town, I can tell you that Isabelle most definitely has."

Wow, Mom, way to rain on my parade.

I scrubbed a hand over my face and shot her an exasperated glare.

"What?" she shrugged. "If you're as serious about her as you say you are, you gotta make sure she knows how this weekend's really gonna go. Don't leave any room for interpretation. Even if you're not quite ready to have the I-love-you conversation yet, you still gotta give her something. Let her know she doesn't have to worry, alright, baby?"

That last part was a little harder to wrap my head around and just as I was trying to figure how to give Isabelle the reassurance she needed, she shuffled into the kitchen with her long hair in a messy knot on top of her head. Her face wasn't quite as flushed red as before, but the bruising around her eye was more defined now, and she was wearing an old pair of sweatpants and one of my old T-shirts.

My cigarette was in the ashtray a half a second later and I jerked my hand downwards, signaling for my mom to do the same. She obliged just as quickly, but not without that stupid, sly grin on her face.

As soon as that business was taken care of, I slid off my chair and scrambled over to her.

"Hey," she smiled. "I heard voices and thought you might be back now."

My arm wrapped around her shoulders to tuck her against me and my lips found the side of her head immediately. Even though I'd only been away from her for less than two hours, her presence was like a balm to all my raging anxieties and I instantly felt calmer, more relaxed just at the feel of her warm body pressed against me.

"Hey babe," I murmured into her hair. "You need somethin'?"

"That coffee you guys have looks pretty good."

"Coffee it is," I gestured with my head towards the kitchen. "Let's get ya some."

Just as I led her over to the counter where the still steaming pot of coffee sat, my mom's voice called out to us: "So, I think I'm gonna head over to the clubhouse tonight. Check in with Marcus, you know. Looks like you two kids have it all handled here and don't need me hangin' around you anyways."

"Yeah, Ma," I nodded, shooting her a wide grin over the top of Isabelle's head.

"You kids have fun," she called over her shoulder.

Once my mom was safely out of sight, out of mind, Isabelle turned to me with a wary glance. "*Checking in*, huh?"

"Yeah," I laughed and poured her a cup of coffee as I spoke. "I guess that's what the old people are callin' it these days. Oh, and just so we're clear, when my mom says she's *checking in* with the club Prez, she really means she's *hooking up* with the club Prez. Just so you know."

Isabelle laughed. "I kinda figured that, but thanks for the clarification."

"Yeah, I made peace with it a long time ago. Better than the alternative, you know?"

"I guess that's one way of looking at it."

I handed her a coffee mug with a wink. "Babe, that's the *only* way of lookin' at it."

She took the mug from me, which was probably too hot for her anyways, and set it back down on the counter next to me. Then I felt her warm hands wrap around my waist as she leaned deep into my chest and my arms folded around her shoulders, hugging her to me as tightly as I could.

My lips found her hair again and I wished we could just stay here like this, with our arms wrapped around each other, for the rest of the night, the rest of the week. Letting the real world back in, especially after the day we'd had, didn't really appeal to me right now.

"How you feelin', Iz?"

"Like I got punched in the face," she chuckled into my chest, but for the life of me, I just couldn't see the humor in this.

There was nothing funny to me about the cut across her cheek, the bruising underneath her eye, or the nasty cut sliced across her palm. I lifted her head off my shoulder so I could gauge what she was really feeling.

"Seriously, babe, you feelin' okay?"

She just lifted a shoulder and leaned back into my chest. "My head hurts. My hand's throbbing. It hurts to move my face. Is that what you wanted to hear?"

"I just want you to be honest with me. I can't help you if I don't know what's goin' on."

"I know," she sighed against my chest. "I know. Sorry."

"Nothin' to be sorry about, Iz."

I kissed the top of her head and pulled her tight against my chest, wishing I could get her closer somehow.

"You're really great, you know that?" Isabelle murmured.

She tilted her head back so her chin rested on the top of my chest, letting her look directly at me and giving me direct access to her lips. Never one to miss an opportunity, I tilted my neck down just enough to brush my lips against hers.

"How did everything go with my dad?"

I sighed into her hair and leaned back against the counter, pulling her along with me. "There weren't any problems, Iz."

She nodded into my chest and burrowed herself a little deeper into me. "Good. Honestly, I was a little worried about you two being alone in the same car together...you and my dad are never gonna get along now, are you?"

I really wished I could tell her otherwise, that I could say with at least some certainty that we might be able to set aside our obvious differences and animosities at some point, but in light of everything he'd done to her today, I just didn't see that ever happening. I couldn't imagine a scenario where I would ever feel comfortable with the two of them being alone in the same room together, so imagining *myself* in the same room as her dad, let alone tolerating him, wasn't even in the realm of possibility.

Because I couldn't give her the answer she wanted, I opted to just kiss her forehead and hoped that was enough.

"He said some really shitty things," she sighed and all I could do was just hold on to her so she could get it all out. "He just kept going on about how my mom was never happy with him and how he didn't understand why she stayed after I left for college. I never knew any of that. I never knew they had those kind of problems."

"All couples have problems, Iz," I shrugged. "And I think your dad's memory might be a little sketchy anyways, you know?"

Her neck tilted back and when I got a good look at those beautiful blue eyes, my heart felt like it got swallowed by my stomach.

"He said he hated how much I look like her. Do you...do you think I look like her?"

My thumb brushed a fresh tear from her cheek and then my hand moved to her face in an attempt to give her the comfort she needed right now. An image of Katherine Martin flashed through my mind and as I looked down at her daughter now...yeah, they did look alike. Same beautiful blue eyes, same shiny blonde hair, same kind smile. Like mother, like daughter for sure.

"Yeah, you do," I told her, my voice hoarser than I'd intended. "It's a good thing, Iz. Don't ever think that it's not—it's like you're carrying her with you, you know? Don't let him ruin that for you."

"Thanks..." Isabelle trailed off and rested her head back into my chest. "He said some really shitty things about you too."

"Yeah," I chuckled. "I think I have a pretty good idea."

"No, you don't. And it was all just so off-base, so *cold-hearted*. Don't ask me to tell you because I really don't want to."

"Okay, babe."

She sighed again and I felt her leaning into me, like she needed me to just support her entire weight right now, something I was happy to do.

"After he said all that about you, I just sorta lost it. I couldn't stop myself from saying everything I think I'd needed to say to him for awhile. I even told him to fuck himself too."

"Good for you, babe."

"He should've been in rehab a long time ago."

"Yeah."

I could feel her swallow tightly and she hesitated, wrapping herself even deeper around me, if that was even possible.

"I wish I'd done everything differently. I should've put my foot down. I should've made him listen to me."

"Hey," I lifted her head off my chest again to force her to look at me. "You did the best you could. All you're guilty of is caring about your dad."

She was quiet for a little while after that and we stood there in the kitchen, with me leaning against the counter and her arms wrapped around my waist. If this was what she needed tonight to find some peace, then I couldn't be more grateful I was the lucky bastard she'd chosen.

It was still difficult to wrap my head around—what I felt for her and what I knew she felt for me.

There wasn't anything in my past, present, and probably foreseeable future to make me attractive to someone like her, someone whose life was the exact opposite of mine and someone who had a beautiful future outside of this town to look forward to.

I had no business loving her. No leg to stand on when it came down to whether or not there was someone else out there that made more sense for her. There were always going to be parts of my life she wouldn't completely understand, even if she tried to, and those parts could rear their ugly heads at any moment. Samuel Martin had been right about at least one thing tonight: I really didn't deserve to come within 100 miles of her.

Even if I couldn't reconcile the idea of actually being good enough for her, she was the best thing in existence for me.

I wanted to try. I wanted to be the kind of man she needed me to be. I just hoped it would be enough.

Isabelle's soft voice called out to me: "Hey, Caleb?"

"Yeah, Iz?"

"You know how I said today before I left the lot that I thought we should talk?"

"Yeah."

"Can we still have that talk tonight?"

I swallowed tightly, weighing the pros and cons of whether or not this was a good idea. This conversation, which I was pretty sure was the are-we-in-a-relationship-or-what conversation, was one we needed to have soon, but it definitely didn't have to be now or even tonight. But judging by the hopeful, expectant look on Isabelle's face, this was an argument I probably wouldn't win and the last thing I wanted to do with her tonight was anything that looked even remotely like arguing.

Might as well give it a shot anyways.

"Aren't we talkin' right now?" I shot her the best cocky smirk I could muster.

"You know what I mean."

Well, I tried.

"Okay, Iz," I exhaled and tilted my head back so I could get a better look at her. "Let's talk."

She smiled softly up at me with just a flash of shyness and maybe even a tiny bit of insecurity too and now I just needed to replace that with something else.

"Okay," she started, chewing on her bottom lip a little. "So, you and I..."

"Are you sure this is what you want, Iz?"

My throat seized a little, but I had to do it. I had to give her an out because she deserved to have one, but when her eyes flashed with that determination I loved so much, my worries felt a little premature now.

"Don't try to talk me out of the way I feel about you, Caleb. It's not gonna work," Isabelle told me, her eyes hard.

I think I kinda liked when she was all angry and bossy with me. It was scary and hot as hell all at the same time.

"I'm serious, Caleb," her hands fisted in the front of my shirt now to force me to hear what she was telling me. "I know what I want and what I want is you. I've wanted you for longer than I'm really willing to admit, but I think you knew that already."

My lips tugged up my mouth and my heart felt like a sledgehammer pounding away in my chest. This was everything I'd never let myself even hope for—everything I always knew I needed from her. She stood up on her tiptoes to kiss me and both my hands closed around her face to hold her there a little longer.

"I did know that," I murmured against her lips.

It was funny how I knew exactly what I wanted to say to her, but the actual act of pushing the words out was way scarier than I thought it would be.

"I think you might be the best thing that's ever happened to me," she went on and I think I just about fell out of my skin at those words.

I didn't deserve this. I didn't deserve her standing here, looking at me like I was some sort of hero with her sweet body pressed up against me. Maybe I didn't deserve it yet, but that wasn't going to stop me from taking it either.

"I kinda feel like we've been gravitating towards each other ever since I came home, you know?" Isabelle told me, her eyes just as soft as her voice. "I just don't know where I'd be if I didn't have you. I don't know how I'd even be standing here right now without you next to me."

"I don't know about that, Iz. You're plenty strong on your own without needin' any help from me."

She lifted a shoulder, beaming that gorgeous smile back up at me. "Maybe not, but I feel stronger when you're standing next to me."

It was right on the tip of my tongue to tell her, to say the words I'd known were true way too damned long ago, but my throat was heavy with cement.

Because I couldn't figure out how to tell her, the best I could do was show her instead. My hands closed around her face again and kissed her with all these overwhelming and scary emotions raging through me. I just hoped she could feel it.

Even if the words I *really* wanted to say were still stuck to my thick throat, I think I was still at least a little capable of articulating something she needed to hear.

"Just so we're clear," I affirmed with a nod. "You and I are together now."

Her entire face lit up at those simple words, which, for all my issues, were honestly the easiest ones I've ever said in my life.

"Oh really?" her eyebrows rose and I quickly caught her smirk with my lips.

"Really."

"Okay," Isabelle laughed and fisted her uninjured hand in my shirt to bring my neck down to her level so she could kiss me. "We still have some things to talk about though."

"Okay."

"I have some questions."

I just lifted a shoulder. "Okay."

"Well, maybe it's not really a question, but I'm just not sure how all this," she waved her uninjured hand towards the cut on my chest, "works, you know? I mean, I know you've been arrested before, but I don't really understand everything else and I don't expect you to explain it all to me right now either, but..."

She obviously knew about the time Dom and I got taken in for disorderly conduct when we were 16 and stupid. I guess that meant she had no idea about the *other* two times I'd been arrested though.

My throat was starting to close up again and I swallowed hard with a tight nod. "It's not gonna be easy, Iz. I mean, I know my life seems pretty tame right now, but it's not always gonna be this quiet. I'm not tryin' to scare ya, trust me, that's the last thing I wanna do. Sometime, we'll sit down and I'll answer any questions you wanna ask me."

She bit down on her bottom lip and nodded. "Okay. I'm good with waiting a little bit for that. I have no idea where to even start."

Yeah, me either.

"And..." she trailed off, still gnawing on her bottom lip and boring a hole into the front of my chest. "I think I should probably let you know right now that there can't be any other girls, Caleb."

I opened my mouth to put in my two cents about *that*, but she didn't give me much of a shot.

"I'm not asking you to make me any promises right now," Isabelle pressed on, this time looking me right in the eye with every word. "*Except* when it comes to other girls. If you say I can trust you, I'll believe you. I just need to hear you say it. This can't go any further between us if you can't at least give me that."

Fair enough.

I could give her that and raise her one too.

My hands closed around her face and I pressed our foreheads together. "Babe, I don't want anyone but you. As far as I'm concerned, any other girl might as well not even exist, okay? You never have to worry about that."

That seemed to be enough for her and she stood up on her toes—I loved it when she did that—and gave me a light kiss on the lips. Then she pushed back against my chest, putting too much space between us and just as I was getting ready to protest the loss, Isabelle tugged on my hand, gesturing with her head towards the hallway.

"Let's go to bed," she murmured.

"You tired, babe?"

Isabelle glanced at me over her shoulder, a soft smile playing across her lips as she pulled me down the hallway and into my old bedroom. "Nope."

My feet somehow managed to move in front of the other until she pushed open the bedroom door. For the first time in my life, I was being led to a bedroom by a girl and I didn't know what I wanted.

Obviously, I wanted Isabelle naked underneath me or on top of me or in front of me, but now? Like this? My thoughts were like a deck of unshuffled cards, disorganized and helter-skelter, and my only option was to just keep taking one off the top until I found one that felt right.

I didn't get much of a chance to feel out those cards because as Isabelle stepped in front of me, heading right for the twin bed in the center of the room, that pair of sweatpants she was wearing fell to the floor.

My mouth dried up like I'd just swallowed a handful of sand.

I watched, completely rooted into the carpet, as her hands dipped underneath my old T-shirt and slipped it over her head. Now she was standing in front of me in a pink bra and matching panties like a living, breathing fantasy.

My eyes squeezed shut. I couldn't believe I was about to do this...

"Iz."

"Hmm?"

"We don't have to..."

Her head tilted to the side and she shot me that beautiful smile that hit me in all the right places. "You mean you don't want to?"

I grimaced and scrubbed a hand over my eyes. "I just think that maybe...maybe we should take this slow. Do this right."

My heart just about skyrocketed into my throat as she glided across the carpet, striding towards me with a confidence that, despite everything I knew about her, shocked the hell out of me. Her hands slipped underneath my shirt, skimming up my stomach and leaving little trails of fire in their wake.

"What if I don't want slow?" she murmured, her voice husky in a way I'd never heard before.

Isabelle was always sexy to me. She was always the most gorgeous thing in the room. But this...this was a whole other level of hotness that pretty much short-circuited my brain.

I was trying so hard to do this right, to do right by *her* because I needed her to understand that she was different. She wasn't just one in a long line of many for me. She was *it*.

I needed this to show her everything I couldn't get myself to say and I definitely didn't want the first time I finally got her naked to be on the same day her dad punched her in the face, but I wasn't stupid enough to say that out loud.

"Babe," I tried instead. "The first time I finally get you naked is not gonna be in my old room at my mom's house."

Her eyebrows rose, but her hands still continued their torture on my skin. "Should we go to the clubhouse instead?"

Oh, hell no. There was no way I was gonna see her all spread out on that bed, on the same mattress, on the same sheets that had seen more shady decisions than I was willing to own up to. I'd give anything to rewind the last few months and handle myself better, so all that history would barely be a blip on our radar now. Instead, I had a feeling those demons would trail after me every time we were in the clubhouse and I didn't want to put either one of us through that if I could help it.

She deserved better. She deserved more. I think I needed to just burn the whole bed and start from scratch.

"No, Iz," I shook my head. "I can't take you there. I don't want you in that bed after...and I don't want you to have to think about it either."

Isabelle's lips curved with understanding and I needed to touch her so bad. I needed to taste her. I needed to be inside her. I needed to wait. I needed to do this right.

Her hands slipped around my waist and she leaned forward, ghosting her lips over mine as her fingers fell to my belt buckle. She tugged on the buckle, jerking my hips towards her with a playful smile curving her pillowy lips and those hooded, sweetly beckoning eyes I always knew would be my undoing.

"I'm not gonna break, baby," she whispered against my lips. "And you can't tell me you don't want me as much as I want you."

My head shook from side to side because I'd lost the ability to speak. Her fingers nimbly unbuckled my belt and tugged my jeans to the carpet, watching me expectantly. With a grin, I obliged her and kicked off my jeans. Then her hands slid underneath my shirt again until she slipped it over my head. My hands finally got what they wanted as they curved around her waist, feeling nothing but smooth, soft skin.

I leaned in to catch her mouth, tasting those sweet lips and slipping my tongue in between them when they parted for me. We were slowly edging towards the bed, still entangled, still consumed, until I eased Isabelle back onto the bed. Then I scooped up my jeans to dig into the back pocket for my wallet, slipped out what I needed, threw the wallet over my shoulder, and playfully tossed the condom onto the bed right next to her.

She laughed and it was the most beautiful thing I'd ever seen. Her eyes followed my every move, waiting for me to finally join her on the bed, and now I just wanted to take that lip she was chewing on in between my teeth.

But as I lowered down to the bed on my knees and hovered over her, I had to take a moment to let all this in. Here, spread out in front of me, for *me*, was everything I'd never let myself even begin to hope I could have. I'd wanted all of this with her since longer than I really knew and now here it was, laid out on my bed with her tight body, beautiful eyes, and gorgeous smile.

I loved this girl. I *loved* her.

The girl of my dreams was in my life and in my bed.

I didn't deserve it, but hell.
I was gonna take it.

CHAPTER THIRTY-THREE
Old Lady

Isabelle

Caleb's eyes flared dangerously, sending pricks of anticipation from my chest all the way down to my toes. My chest was heaving, my mind was swimming, and I needed him lower, preferably in between my legs.

Like he could read my thoughts, he sank onto the bed, hovering over me until I thought I might explode from the torture. My hands skimmed around the sides of his waist to press into his taut back and he buried his face into my neck with a low groan. His lips left a blazing trail of kisses up the side of my neck and curved over my jaw, singeing my skin and setting me aflame.

When his lips finally captured my mouth, the world lit up before my eyes, casting a bright spotlight over this boy who'd tilted the very axis my life rested on.

I loved him.

God, I loved him.

He was reaching around me, snapping the clasp on my bra with more skill than I was ready to think about yet. His thumbs brushed over the tops of my nipples and my back arched off the bed when his mouth closed over one and then the other. Everything else fell away as his hand drifted down my stomach, stopping long enough to hook his fingers around my panties and glide them down my legs.

Breathing wasn't exactly a priority when his thumb brushed in between my legs in tiny circles, shooting sparks through me and little moans escaped my lips. I didn't know it was possible to feel this way...just everything all at once and all over me, rushing around me in hot tendrils of things I'd never felt with anyone else before.

"Caleb," I whispered, burying the back of my head into his pillow.

"Please, I can't..."

He murmured something into my neck, reaching with his free hand for the foil packet on the mattress next to me while I tugged impatiently on his boxers. Once he was ready, I could feel the heat between us, the electricity coursing in the air around us, and then he pushed himself inside me with his mouth flattened against my neck to stifle his groan.

He stiffened on top of me, completely unmoving with his forehead buried in my neck, and I could feel his chest heaving against my skin like he was fighting some sort of internal battle.

I needed him to move. I needed that burn, that friction. I couldn't take it if he didn't move and my fingertips pressed into his sinewy back to give him permission, loving and hating the feel of his stunted, hot breath against my ear because I needed him to move *now*.

Suddenly, his head jerked up from its burrow in my neck and he sucked in a sharp breath. I didn't understand what was happening here and I was too drunk on him right now to even know where to start. His eyes were cobalt blue, glazed over with a heat that ran deeper than where he was buried right now.

"Iz," his eyes flashed and his breath was haggard.

"Baby, please," I arched my back up and off the bed, desperate to convince him to move.

"Iz," Caleb exhaled again, but this time, the hitch in his voice gave me pause. His eyes sought me out and everything stilled when his lips parted and he murmured, "I love you."

I stared back at him, eyes wide, my body completely rooted underneath him, and a rush of heat surged up my chest.

"I love you," he repeated just as softly as before, this time closing his mouth over mine in an impatient kiss.

Somehow, beneath the hurricane of emotions churning through me, I found my voice.

"You love me?" I whispered hoarsely.

His eyes blazed down at me. "Yeah."

All the breath dove out of my lungs and my lips curled up into a hesitant smile. "I love you too."

A slow smile spread across his gorgeous face. "Yeah?"

"Yeah."

That must've been all he needed to hear because the moment that word fell from my lips, his hips started sinking into me until I thought I might split in two. Every movement of his hips seemed to bury himself even deeper, like he was planting the connection between us as far as he could possibly go and I couldn't get enough. The sensation just kept building and my fingers dug into his back to steady myself as his mouth found my lips again and his tongue danced inside my mouth, mimicking the movement of his hips.

A low groan rumbled in his throat, catching me off-guard, and his hands slipped underneath my hips to pull me into him as close as our bodies would let us. My breath was coming in and out in sharp gasps, my hands clung to him to hold on, and I felt him everywhere.

Every inch of me — he was there. Branding himself onto my skin with every touch, every kiss, every rock of his hips.

This was connection. This was the intimacy I'd always craved in my life.

I was tipped sideways, upended, and carried away.

Everything else fell away as I floated along with the movement of his body, lifting my hips to somehow get closer. It was right there, coiling, flaming out, and enveloping my entire body and that fluttering pressure sent me flying over the edge, rippling little explosions through my entire body.

I shattered under his hands; the tremors practically lifted me off the bed and my head pressed back into the pillow, desperate for something to hold onto as the intense tidal wave crashed against me, shooting stars all the way down to my toes.

I cried out at the impact, barely aware through this hazy fog that Caleb had gone rigid above me, his forehead pressed into my neck and he muffled a groan into my skin. I was on fire and all the tension finally snapped as cascades of dizziness echoed around me until it lulled into tingling in between my thighs.

As we came down, he kissed me, grinning lazily against my lips, and pressed our foreheads together as our breathing slowed to a more normal, less chaotic pace. He was still hovering above me and I wished we could stay like this all the time, intertwined as completely as possible.

I never thought I'd be the kind of girl that would enjoy being claimed like this—totally and completely owned. Possessed. His. Because that's what I was now. I was his.

When he finally settled back against the pillow next to me, careful to keep one arm leisurely around my neck, I nestled against his shoulder with a deep, satisfied sigh and completely wrapped around him.

"Wow," I exhaled. "That was..."

Caleb nodded and kissed my hair. "Yeah, it was."

My head tilted back into the pillow so I could get a better look at him. "I think we should sleep for a little bit and then do that again."

His mouth twisted into that sexy crooked grin I loved so much and his lips found mine again, kissing me thoroughly despite how spent we were.

"Babe, I think that's the best idea I've ever heard."

. . .

I woke up several hours later surrounded by Caleb. There was no part of me that wasn't touching some part of him and since we'd ended up on the floor at some point during the night, our limbs were happily tangled up in skin and blankets.

It was the most beautiful way to wake up.

And it was too bad that the second consciousness seeped back in, the dull ache in the back of my head, the sharp pain underneath my eye, and the throbbing on my left hand stuttered through my blissful peace. I winced and tried to stretch out the stiffness plaguing my entire body, but one tiny, uncomfortable groan slipped out, which unfortunately, also stirred the hot piece of man-meat currently using my right boob as a pillow.

He nuzzled into me a little and then his head lifted, his bleary blue eyes searching for me.

"You okay, babe?" he murmured sleepily.

I wanted to respond with actual words, but the best I could do was grimace as my body tried to adjust into the carpet. Alerted by my obvious pain, Caleb's head shot off my chest and started awkwardly untangling himself from me.

"No," I pouted, tugging on his bicep to try to keep him with me for as long as humanly possible. "Don't get up yet, baby. Come on."

He tossed aside the blanket we'd knotted ourselves up in with a laugh. "Don't worry, Iz. I won't leave you hangin' for long," he winked, "I'm just gonna grab you some meds and then I'll be right back."

After he stood up and ambled across the room to pull on his boxers, he puckered his lips up into an air-kiss over his shoulder as he headed for the door. I don't know what I was expecting, but the rear view I got shocked a jolt of reality through this Caleb-love-haze.

Bare-chested Caleb wasn't just drool-worthy, but award-worthy too. Barebacked Caleb was something else entirely.

I'd only seen flashes of his full-back tattoo the day I'd forced him to open those art school acceptance letters for me, but never the full view I had now. With the emblem of the Iron Horsemen MC, a furious black horse with blazing-red devil eyes, staring back at me, my throat tightened just a little. It was the exact same emblem on the back of the leather cut Caleb wore whenever he wasn't working at the shop. I'd known he had a back tattoo like that and I knew what it meant, but seeing it full-blown like this was a shock I hadn't anticipated.

I loved Caleb. There was no doubt in my mind about that.

But everything else? I didn't know how to make sense of it and that scared me more than I could probably comprehend right now. The Iron Horsemen was widely known as an outlaw MC according to more people in town than just my alcoholic father. I'd never seen any evidence of it myself, but that didn't mean it wasn't true. Wasn't there always some tiny kernel of truth to every rumor?

What I saw at the clubhouse was only a small fraction of what the club was really about and by Caleb's own admission, things weren't always this calm and uneventful. Because nothing of note had really happened since I'd started coming there with Becca, at least in legal terms, it was easy to forget that the clubhouse was meant for anything other than rowdy, raunchy, and, most of the time, wild parties.

Those thoughts weren't able to gain much traction because Caleb materialized in the room again with a glass of water in one hand, a bottle of painkillers in the other, and I could see the corner of a tell-tale foil package curling around the glass in his hand.

Hmm, it looks like someone had some other errands to run in his little escapade out of the room.

He held up the bottle with a smirk and gave it a little shake.

"I wasn't sure how many you'd want, so I brought the whole thing."

"I think I'll start with two and go from there," I laughed.

He glided back over to the spot where we'd camped out on the floor in all his glory, kneeling next to me to hand over what I needed. I swallowed the pills with a long gulp and set the glass on the nightstand directly above my head, turning back around to find Caleb already hovering in my space with his tattooed forearms settling on either side of me. The foil packet fell to the floor next to the pillow and I had to bite back a laugh.

Looks like he's wide awake and ready to go.

"You're lucky I knew where my mom's stash was 'cuz I only had one of those in my wallet," Caleb informed with a cocky grin.

I slapped my good hand over my face. "Oh my God, you did not just steal a condom from your mom."

"You got any better ideas, babe?"

"I *am* on the pill, just so you know, and we don't have anything to worry about on my end."

He swallowed hard and all the light in his face seemed to dim right before my eyes.

"Caleb," I jumped into damage control mode and pressed both my hands into his chest to force him to focus on me. "I didn't mean—"

His lips found my neck, halting the words in my throat, and I didn't know what I could do to fix this.

"I don't want there to be anything in between us either, but just gimme a little time, okay?" he murmured and I knew what that meant.

He was the one, out of the two of us, that potentially had something to worry about and he'd have to take a trip to the doctor before we could get what we wanted. Just the thought of it, the very *idea* alone, slapped some reality back into me. And now, with reality seeping through the door I'd slammed in blissful ignorance, those questions I'd been too scared to even consider asking bubbled to the surface.

"Can I ask you a question?" I ventured cautiously, sitting up a little so I could meet his eye level more.

"Sure, babe."

I sucked in a hard breath and went for it. "How many have you...?"

God, I couldn't even finish the sentence and the second the words left my mouth, pain and something a lot like humiliation flashed across Caleb's face and he quickly scrubbed it away.

He blew out a deep breath, settling back on his knees and rubbing his thighs anxiously. "I'm not really sure. I wish I could give you a number, but I can't."

That wasn't really going to cut it.

"Try, Caleb."

He rubbed the back of his neck with a grimace and I could practically see the wheels in his head turning, sifting through all his whiskey-clouded memories. After a few silent moments, he scrubbed his face with both hands.

"If I had to guess," he told me, but his voice was still muffled by his hands. "Forty. Maybe more. I don't really know."

I don't know what I was expecting, but I hadn't mentally prepared myself for an estimate like that. Most of that was probably racked up in the last few months alone. My breath blew out in a slow, long exhale and when I glanced up again, I found Caleb leaning forward with both hands scrubbing over his eyes.

Maybe if I just ripped off the band-aid for him, we could move past this already.

"I've been with five people, including you," I blurted.

Judging by the sullen look glowing in his ocean-blue eyes, that little confession hadn't had the effect I'd intended. But I had a point to make and goddammit, he was going to listen.

"Brandon was my fir—"

"Don't," he cut me off, his voice hard and his eyes stared black holes into my bare thighs. "I don't think I can handle hearin' you say it."

I slid forward, slipping my hands over his shoulders and wrapping my legs around his waist as I eased myself onto his lap. With all my limbs wrapped around him, hearing me now would really be his only option unless he threw me off his lap, which I knew he wouldn't do.

"Brandon was my first," I finished. "I was 16. I thought I loved him. He thought he loved me. We were both wrong. Then there was Ben. I met him at a frat party my freshman year, got drunk, and I think you know what happened from there. We actually tried dating for a few weeks, but I just couldn't compete with *Call of Duty*, you know? After that, there was Lucas. He lived in the same dorm as me and I dated him for a couple months. The next one was Nick. You remember Nick, right?"

A hint of a smile curved up one side of his face and that's how I knew I was finally getting somewhere.

"Nick and I had a comparative law class together my sophomore year...trust me, it was exactly as boring as it sounds. We were friends for awhile and then we dated for two years before everything happened with my mom and I guess I stayed with him as long as I did because—I don't know. He was pre-law, just like I was, my dad loved him. It just sort of fit the plan, you know? I was wrong about him too. And then, there's you."

Caleb swallowed hard and his chest was heaving a little too much for my liking.

"Does it matter, Caleb? Does it change the way you feel about me? Now that you know?"

He shook his head and I rested my uninjured hand on top of his cheek.

"It doesn't matter who's come before you," I whispered. "Because out of all the things in my life and all the people in it, you're the only one that feels right, you're the one that feels like *home*. You're the only one that I've ever...what happened last night between us...I've never felt that before. I've never felt so connected before, so loved before and that's because I'm finally with the person I was always supposed to be with. All that matters is us, Caleb. Please tell me you see that."

He nodded tightly as my fingers slipped up his neck and cupped both sides of his face.

"I don't know if I can handle seein' you in my bed at the clubhouse because I don't want you thinkin' about..." he murmured hoarsely and squeezed his eyes shut.

"I'm not saying it doesn't matter at all, baby," I told him gently. "We both know that's not true. I'm not gonna lie to your face and tell you just thinking about it doesn't make me wanna bitchslap every single one of them. I hate it just as much as you do."

"I doubt that," he huffed.

"Okay, maybe not as much as you, but it doesn't change the way I feel about you, Caleb. It doesn't change how much I want you or how much I love you. It's just..." I trailed off, searching for the words I wanted and now I wasn't sure who I was trying to convince more, me or him. "It's just a piece of the past. Something we can live with. That's it, baby."

I brushed my lips across his mouth, hoping this would be enough for both of us. This entire conversation was equal parts a balm to my insecurities and a match to the gasoline and I had no one to blame for that but myself. I'd started this, so now I had to finish it.

So, I leaned back all the way until my elbows hit the carpet, my legs still somehow wrapped around his waist and slipped my panties down to my ankles with my good hand. His eyes flashed, pooling with hungry need, and he lifted my ankles to free them of my panties, tossing them over his shoulder. He held out a hand to me and I took it, letting him pull me back up to his chest, and watched me with hooded eyes as I grabbed the condom packet and tore it open.

I rolled it over him and tilted my hips down, sliding him inside me and our mouths crashed together as rough fingertips dug into my waist to press me even deeper into his lap. My arms enveloped his neck and our chests clamped together as my hips rocked against him.

It was different this time. The first time we'd been connected this way, it felt momentous, heavy with newly-expressed declarations of love and I felt like he'd been consuming every inch of me. This time, I was the one consuming him. I was the one doing the branding and mixing myself into the black ink tattooed across his tanned skin.

Every slow back and forth rock of my hips let me take a little more of him. Let me own another piece of him.

I had to believe that he was mine now. Lingering doubts wouldn't get us anywhere, even if they still existed and even if those same insecurities were justified, I had to believe he loved me enough to make those doubts disappear. It wouldn't be today. It probably wouldn't even be next month, but if we kept talking like this, if we kept connecting this way, I had to believe we'd be able to withstand anything life threw at us, whether it was his life or mine.

We had to figure out how to meld the two together, how to make his life in the club and my life outside of it work as one.

And when I broke apart underneath his fingertips and he pushed his forehead into my chest, his entire body trembling because of me and what my body was doing to him, I knew we *would* figure it out.

We just had to.

Now that I'd had him, I wasn't so sure I would know what to do without him.

.   .   .

His fingertips trailed down my shoulder and I shivered a little under that light touch. I felt his lips in my hair and I burrowed my face in his chest, desperate to get even closer.

"I love you," Caleb murmured into my hair.

My mouth spread apart into a dreamy smile and I had to bite down on my bottom lip to keep myself in check. "I love you too."

His lips moved to my forehead. "You feelin' better now?"

"I feel like I just slept for a whole week."

"Can't imagine why."

His skin muffled my laugh and I was really starting to love the way that felt. "Yeah, I guess not."

There were more questions bubbling up to the surface again, but this time, I had a feeling these questions would be received a little better than my last ones.

"So..." I tilted my head up to him, suddenly feeling a little shy about what I wanted to ask him and I found myself tracing a finger around the intricate lines of the black skull tattoo on his right forearm as I geared myself up for this conversation.

"So..." he prompted.

"I'm not sure what I'm supposed to call you. I mean, I know boyfriend isn't the right term and I think this is a little more than dating, right?"

Caleb nodded, his eyes glittering deep blue. "Right. So, my old lady wants a little clarification, huh? I guess I can manage that."

My eyebrows rose at that term. "Old lady?"

"Yeah, that's what you are to me, babe."

I chewed on my bottom lip in thought. I'd heard that term before at the clubhouse in reference to Lexie, but no one had ever really explained exactly what that meant.

"So what's the difference then?"

"What do you mean, Iz?"

"If I'm your old lady and what we're doing is more than dating, then what's the difference between being your old lady and just dating?"

He nodded his understanding and his lips curled up like he was looking forward to having this conversation with me. "I guess the best way I can explain it is that being an old lady is kind of like being a wife."

My eyes must have flashed with the panic I was feeling because he chuckled and just pulled me back into his chest.

"Okay, maybe that wasn't the best way to explain it. It's about the commitment, babe. It means we're exclusive and monogamous and everything that goes with it."

Now my head was spinning a little with all this new information.

"So," I ventured hesitantly. "Is it like that with everyone in the clubhouse?"

"For Dom and Lex, yeah. For my mom and my dad, absolutely. Her and Marcus — I don't know, I think they have an arrangement that works for them and it's honestly something I choose to just not think about, you know? Don't get me wrong, Iz, not everyone in the club has an old lady or even wants one. Some of them just aren't one-woman kinda guys and that's what works for them."

"But you are," my eyebrows rose as I spoke and it wasn't really a question. I already knew the answer anyways.

"Yeah," he grinned down at me. "I am. You being my old lady means I will love you and protect you and you'll love me and support me back. And the club will respect that. I know it might not seem like it, but it's something we all take really seriously. Old ladies are looked at as part of the club's family, like an extension of the patch she belongs to. If anything were to happen to an old lady, especially if it was because of club business or something like that, none of us would hesitate to go to battle for her. That would be more out of respect to the club brother responsible for her, but you get the idea."

"Yeah," I smiled back. "I get it. So, if I'm your old lady, what does that make you then?"

He shrugged. "Traditionally in the club I'd be your old man."

I crinkled my nose at that term. That just didn't fit him.

"I don't know if I want to refer to you as my old man. It kinda makes you seem like you're my dad or a pedophile or something, doesn't it?"

A low chuckle rumbled in his throat and his shoulders shook with laughter. The arm around my shoulder clenched to lift me up across his body so he could murmur huskily into my hair: "Then I'm just your man, babe."

"I think that sounds about right."

I arched my neck up to get better access to his mouth and brushed my swollen lips across his.

"At some point," his fingertips trailed down my back as he spoke and I shivered under his touch. "Old ladies get their man's ink too. I was thinkin'...when we're ready, you could get mine right here."

His fingertips brushed my lower back and I lifted a wary eyebrow up at him. All this talk about property and ownership was making me a little itchy.

"You mean like a brand?"

"Aw, come on, Iz. It's not like that."

"So putting it right there isn't like a tramp stamp either?" I countered lightly, but I still needed him to understand that I wasn't totally down with the whole *ownership* part of this.

To his credit, he chuckled and kissed me. "It's not like that, babe. Lex has Dom's. My mom still has my dad's. It's like a promise, you know? It means that you're mine."

I narrowed my eyes at him. "So what would it say, huh? Property of Caleb Sawyer?"

"No," he laughed. "We'd figure out the design together. ZZ would do it. He does all the club's ink. But my initials would be somewhere on the design. I don't know, I was thinkin' a pair of angel wings would look pretty good on you right there."

His fingers traced the space on my lower back and in spite of my reservations, I still shivered under his touch. His explanation was logical enough and there was something about the way his eyes pleaded with me to understand and to accept this tradition for what it was, that it was something important to him—needless to say, for better or worse, I was starting to warm up to the idea.

Still, it did seem a little one-sided.

"Would you get one too?" I asked him warily. "I seem to remember seeing Lexie's name tattooed on Dominic's neck, you know."

His mouth crinkled up on one side and I could tell he wasn't exactly surprised by this new line of questioning. "If that's something you wanted, I would."

"I think it might be. It's only fair."

He laughed, pressing his lips into the side of my head. "True."

It was right on the tip of my tongue to ask him if he'd had this very same conversation with his other old lady and that was the first time I also realized what that meant. Maybe I was his old lady now, but I wasn't the only one he'd ever had. I wasn't the first. And if he wanted me to get his ink now, I could only imagine that he'd wanted the same thing with Ariel too.

I was faltering again. Swept away in hesitancy and self-doubt already and we hadn't even been together for a full 12 hours yet. I hated it, but I couldn't help it either.

"Hey, babe?" Caleb's soft voice called out to me. "You okay?"

Swallowing back my doubts for now, I forced a smile across my face and hoped he wouldn't notice.

"Yeah."

He grinned back at me, oblivious to the way I'd frozen in fear in his arms. "So, Dom and Lex are gettin' married on Saturday."

Hmm, maybe he *had* caught on after all.

"They are."

"Well, I was hopin' it would already be a given since you're my old lady and all, but I think you should be my date."

My lips spread into a smile before he even finished his sentence. "I think that's a good idea."

"I thought so. But you should know right now that I'm game for the slow dances and that's about it."

299

Carry Your Heart

"I can live with that," I laughed.
I just hoped I'd be able to live with everything else.

CHAPTER THIRTY-FOUR
Status Update

Isabelle

I spooned some more potato salad into one of the many large bowls in the kitchen and carried it out onto the main floor to set it on the bar. The clubhouse was already filled with women who'd arrived for the shower: old ladies from other charters, friends of the club, Lexie's mom and sisters, Dominic's mom, and an assortment of girls Skyler had recruited for clean-up duty.

With Lexie scheduled to open her presents soon and food served immediately after, it was only then that the men would officially be allowed back inside their clubhouse. Even though I'd been around the clubhouse for the last four months or so, I was still trying to get a hang of the order of things here.

Any psychologist or sociologist would have a field day studying this hierarchy where the men essentially regarded women as property, but could just as easily relinquish their *lair* for a bridal/baby shower. It was a patriarchy that was as archaic as it was misogynistic and yet, I'd willingly attached myself to it.

I was still working out how I felt about that.

Everything Caleb had told me, everything that had happened between us, the fact that I was here in the clubhouse at a club-sponsored event as his old lady and that his mom had me setting up for the party with all the other old ladies—I knew it meant I was in this world now and I also knew it meant I had to find my place in it as well.

I just had no idea where to start because despite the fact that Lexie's shower was about as tame as it would probably ever get in the clubhouse, my head still felt like it might explode.

A flash of red from across the room caught my eye and I blew out a deep exhale. I'd been trying to avoid Ariel like the plague, purposefully staying on the opposite side of the room and dodging small talk at any cost. Skyler had graciously saved me twice already, but sooner or later, I'd have to look the demon in the eye.

Ariel had had the balls to breeze into the clubhouse with her arms full of presents and dressed in a skintight red dress that hugged all the curves I'd forgotten she had and showed more leg and cleavage than necessary for a shower like this. Showing up late, over-dressed and over-enthusiastic hadn't sat well with the majority of the party guests, Lexie and Skyler included, and I wished I'd been able to take some consolation in that. But if Ariel had gotten the memo that there weren't too many people here happy to see her, she sure as hell didn't show it.

I glanced down at my own attire on reflex, just a black maxi skirt with a white tank tucked into it, and shook my head.

Ariel wasn't fooling anyone and the endgame was obvious. Everyone in the room seemed to already know Ariel was pulling out all the stops today for one reason, and one reason alone: she knew the guys would be showing up right after the present opening for food and cake.

"Hey, Isabelle?"

I turned my head at the unfamiliar voice and found an exoticly beautiful girl looking back at me with a hesitant smile. My lips dipped into a frown as I tried to place where I'd seen her before because I *knew* I'd...and then it hit me. About three months ago, this very same exoticly beautiful girl with her long, curly chestnut hair and olive skin had wrapped herself around Caleb, walked down the hallway just feet away from where we stood now, and disappeared inside his dorm room with him.

Don't panic. This is fine. No big deal.

"Yeah?"

Daring a glance at this reminder of Caleb's past, I didn't see anything other than courtesy and even a little politeness from her.

"Hi, um, I don't think I've gotten a chance to...um, I'm Elena, by the way."

There was a small part of me that briefly considering holding my hand out for her to shake, but no...there was a line to what I could tolerate and this would be stepping over that line in a big way.

"Hi," I told her instead and pressed a fake smile onto my face.

"So, um, Skyler told me to ask you if you needed anything."

I blinked back at her and looked down at the spread on the bar. "There're just a few things left to bring out from the kitchen and I think I can handle that no problem."

Elena shifted uncomfortably, making her legs flex in those sky-high heels and my throat tightened at the idea that Caleb had seen those same legs up close and personal not so long ago.

"Actually, that's not, um, that's not what I meant. I'm not supposed to work in the kitchen..." she trailed off awkwardly, glancing down at her shoes and my eyes instantly darted across the room to find Skyler surveying our interaction like a hawk.

She tipped her chin in the air and winked with a sly smile. I didn't understand much about this culture I'd found myself thrust into, but I liked to believe I had enough common sense to understand what was happening here: the queen bee was giving me status and helping me claim my place.

"So, do you need something?"

I hesitated, mainly because I wasn't used to doing this. I could say no and send Elena on her way, but then, everyone else watching this right now would wonder...I wasn't really sure what they would wonder and because of that, I also couldn't really leave it to chance. This was an opportunity and although I knew Skyler would make sure I had more, it seemed like bad form to let it go to waste.

"Uh, yeah," I told Elena finally with a bright smile. "I would love a beer."

Elena's face lit up, probably grateful I was going to give her something to do and being polite about it too.

"Okay, I'll be right back with that."

I nodded with a smile that probably looked more like an uncomfortable grimace. "Okay then."

My eyes followed Elena as she stepped around the bar to get me that beer and then my gaze snapped back to Skyler, who was already nodding to me with approval. But when Skyler's dark eyes widened, locked onto something coming up next to me, I had no time to prepare myself.

"Hey, Isabelle," Ariel's voice called out to me with enough sugar in it to pass as friendly.

As if on reflex, my eyes darted around the room, searching for someone, *anyone* to act as some sort of buffer between me and Caleb's ex-old lady, but unfortunately for me, Skyler was way on the other side of the room, Lexie was busy enjoying her shower, Becca was in the bathroom, and that just about covered everyone I knew in the clubhouse right now.

So, with no other options in front of me, I had to deal with it head-on, and forced a smile onto my face. "Hi, Ariel."

Ariel's eyes widened when she got a good look at me. "Oh my God. Isabelle, what happened to your face?"

I blew out a deep breath and instinctively folded my hands in front of me so she couldn't see the wide bandage in the center of my left palm. Sure, a little tact would've been nice, but there was also no way she could've possibly known that the fading yellow bruise underneath my eye was a sensitive topic around here.

"Uh, you know, it's a long story."

And it was one I also had no interest in sharing with her.

She seemed to sense as much and quickly shifted topics. "You're still working at the shop, right?"

I nodded, eager to get this obligatory conversation over with already. "Yeah, I am."

Skyler had conspiratorially let me know before the party got rolling that she'd informed Ariel this morning, probably with great pleasure, that her son had officially moved on and had another old lady in his life now...me. I should have been grateful the cat was just out of the bag and out in the open because I had nothing to hide, but if anything, it also made having this conversation a million times more difficult to fake.

We both knew this was for appearances only and I wanted to get this over with as quickly and as painlessly as possible. When Elena materialized next to me and handed me a beer, Ariel's bright smile quickly contorted into a pained expression of confusion.

"Thanks," I told her and Elena shot me a quick, respectful smile before stepping away from us.

Ariel was chewing nervously on the inside of her cheek now and I stared back at her, not wanting to draw attention to the giant elephant in the clubhouse.

"So, uh, how's school? How's California? It must be really great this time of year. I mean, it's December and you still have what? Seventies and all those palm trees, right?"

It was all bullshit, but I needed to say something to curb the awkward silence between us.

Whatever fog was surrounding Ariel, she quickly shook herself out of it and plastered a cool smile on her face. "It's great, actually. I have a great apartment and I'm going to a great school. Everything's just great."

I nodded slowly. The sadness and insincerity in Ariel's voice was unmistakable and I felt myself bristling a little in response. It wasn't so much that Ariel was obviously unhappy in California—it was what that meant for me that just about sent me into a tailspin.

Before coming face to face with Caleb's ex, I'd been able to talk myself into feeling confident in our relationship. He'd already told me he loved me—many, many times in the span of one week—we'd spent every night together, he'd told me I was his old lady. What more did I really need? What else could I really expect from him that he hadn't already given me?

It should've been enough to smother my insecurities about this weekend, but I just couldn't help it.

And now, standing literally toe to toe with the girl whose abandonment had sent Caleb into such a severe downward spiral he'd had to self-medicate with whiskey, weed, and sex, I found myself battling to keep a crippling panic attack at bay.

"So, um, Skyler told me you got into a couple art schools?" Ariel was asking me now.

"Yeah, I did."

Ariel smiled softly and it *almost* seemed genuine. "Congratulations. That must be really exciting. Yeah, she told me you got into, like, the number seven school in the country. Is that where you're gonna end up?"

"Yeah," I nodded carefully. That was the first time I think I'd ever acknowledged it out loud to someone other than Caleb and I really hated that it was to *her*, of all people.

For Caleb, it was already a foregone conclusion, but there were still so many unknowns that made going to a school five hours away yet another factor into my panic.

"Skyler just kept going on and on about how talented you are and how successful you're going to be. You know, if I didn't know her any better, I'd say she was bragging about you a little."

Her tone made it difficult to tell whether she'd meant that as an underhanded compliment or an actual one, but it was probably best to just shrug it off, especially since starting a catfight with a so-called romantic rival was also pretty bad form.

"Yeah, well," I just sighed. "Skyler and I get along pretty well, so maybe she was."

I *almost* didn't catch the way Ariel's eyes narrowed for just a split second and that was pretty much the end of this conversation. I was trying to be civil; I really was, but Ariel was making it really difficult probably without even trying that hard.

"Okay, well, I'd better let you finish up here before the herd of hungry men show up," Ariel chuckled as she started to back away. "It was nice seeing you again, Isabelle."

"Yeah, you too, Ariel."

I blew out a deep sigh of relief when Ariel finally backed away and retreated to the other side of the clubhouse, clearly needing distance between us just as much as I did. I weaved in and out through the main floor until I dropped into one of the folding chairs and took a long pull from my beer. This little bit of space allowed me some breathing room and while I normally wouldn't drink a beer, I was grateful I had one now. Suddenly, Lexie, with her round baby belly, eased down into the seat next to me with a plate of food in her hands.

"Hey, hun," Lexie started cheerily.

"Hey, Lex. How you liking your party so far?"

"Oh, you know, it's kinda nice being the guest of honor. Everyone waits on me hand and foot and I always have some barbeque in my hand. It's pretty great actually."

"Sounds like you've got it made today," I laughed.

"Exactly," Lexie nodded with a wide smile. "Hey, thanks for all your help by the way. It really means a lot."

"Don't worry about it," I just swatted out a hand dismissively. "I was happy to do it. Besides, it's not like you don't have anything else going on this weekend, right?"

"What you mean like a wedding?" Lexie laughed. "Oh right, that. Yeah."

"No big deal or anything. So, are you nervous or do you just wanna get it over with?"

Lexie just shrugged. "A little bit of both, I guess. I can tell you I'm definitely more than ready to get rid of this though," she pointed down to her protruding belly, "I am uncomfortable as hell and I still have a month left. Right about now, I'm really hating myself for holding off on the wedding so Dom and I could save some money. We really should've just gone to City Hall or something and been done with it."

"Or even better yet, why not just do it at the clubhouse? You coulda just turned this party into a wedding."

Lexie smacked her thigh and shook her head. "Now, why didn't I think of that? That sounds like the best idea ever."

"Oh well," I laughed. "At least you got a pretty great party out of the deal."

Lexie beamed back at me. "Yeah, there's that."

Just as I was about to respond, Becca appeared from the bathroom, with Elena right behind her, and she was staring down at her phone as she walked towards our chairs, a deep frown etched across her face.

Lexie and I exchanged a confused glance as Becca flopped down on the other side of me.

"Hey, Becs," I started hesitantly, glancing back at Lexie over my shoulder. "What's up?"

As it turned out, Becca didn't really need to say a word. Instead, she held her phone up for me to see and I squinted to get a better look. It took me a couple moments to understand what I was seeing, but when my brain finally caught up, my heart had already lodged itself in my throat.

Because staring back at me from Becca's screen was a picture of Ariel and Caleb, probably taken a few years ago. They were smiling happily into the camera from what could only be his bed here in the clubhouse, judging by the wide black flag with the Iron Horsemen MC emblem pinned right above the headboard. The caption read, *"This weekend is going to be the best! Can't wait to see the person I've been missing more than anything in the entire world."*

Lexie was leaning around me to squint at Becca's screen and her eyes widened before shooting right to where Ariel was chatting up one of the guests.

"And then," Becca related grimly as she flicked her thumb to scroll up the page. "She literally just posted this two minutes ago."

Two minutes ago—which probably would've been right after she and I had our awkward, albeit tense, conversation. This was probably going to suck, but I had to look. I couldn't force myself not to. It was yet another picture, but the only thing that was visible was Ariel's bare back and an intricate rose tattoo with the initials CS etched into one of the petals right in between her shoulder blades. No caption needed. The picture said everything Ariel wanted to say. I couldn't even take comfort in the fact that the tattoo itself, minus the initials, was about as generic and impersonal as it gets.

And just like that, all my resolve, all my forced confidence, and everything I thought I knew about my relationship with Caleb vanished into thin air.

"You don't think Caleb's seen this, right?" Becca asked in a hushed whisper.

Lexie and I shook our heads at the same time.

"No," I answered for the both of us. "He's not on Facebook."

And even if he was, he definitely wouldn't be sitting by the computer refreshing the screen, especially for someone that still carried a flip phone.

But *Becca* was on Facebook and apparently, was friends with Ariel, who Ariel also knew would see those suspiciously-timed updates. It didn't take a genius to figure out who those updates were really meant for.

"When is she gonna grow up?" Lexie muttered under her breath. "Hey, look, Isabelle, I'll talk to her, okay?"

"No," I shook my head firmly. "Don't do that. This is your party. Your wedding is tomorrow. That's all you should be concerned about right now."

Besides, Ariel was doing this for attention and to stir up drama during her supposed best friend's shower, which was a really shitty thing to do any way you looked at it. Why give her what she wanted?

"You okay, Isabelle?" Lexie asked and rested a hand on my shoulder.

All I could muster was a quick nod. I wasn't so sure I could do anything else convincingly.

From across the clubhouse, Skyler started waving her arms, signaling that it was time for Lexie to open all her presents.

"Well," Lexie laughed. "I better head over there before Skyler gets all over my pregnant ass."

I waved a little as Lexie stepped back into the crowd of guests and I settled back into my chair next to Becca, and a careful distance away from Ariel, who'd positioned herself right in between Skyler and Lexie. Annoyed didn't even begin to describe the emotion I felt as I watched Ariel throw her head back and laugh at something Lexie said.

"I really hate that bitch," Becca whispered.

Heinous bitch is more like it.

It was right on the tip of my tongue to ask her why she was even friends with Ariel on Facebook if she hated her so much, but then, connecting online didn't really mean anything anyways. Killing the messenger wasn't really fair to Becca when all she'd done was be a good *actual* friend.

"I mean, who seriously does that?" Becca went on in a loud whisper. "Who posts a goddamn selfie with their ex-boyfriend in bed like that? When you know the new girlfriend will see it?"

Someone who wants the ex-boyfriend back. That's who does that.

"Are you gonna say anything to her, Belle?"

"No. Absolutely not," I shook my head furiously. "She's obviously delusional about how this weekend is gonna go. Why add fuel to the fire?"

Becca nodded carefully and I knew I was starting to crack under the pressure.

"If that's what you want...I don't know, Belle. If I were you, I'd get in her face, claim my man, and put that bitch in her place."

I shot her a wary glance. "I'm not gonna get in her face. If I do that, then the terrorist with her immature psychological warfare wins."

"Yeah, you're right. Sorry," Becca shrugged sheepishly. "I guess I'm still just a little pissed I got stuck with garbage duty again. Hey, how did you get out of it? I've been slaving over dirty dishes and sticky floors for the past six months and you and Caleb are together for what, a week, and all of a sudden you're helping in the kitchen? That sucks."

Skyler had her reasons for setting things up the way she did and I knew better than to question why I was with the other old ladies in the kitchen and Becca was picking up garbage.

When Lexie unwrapped her last present, the clubhouse doors burst open to let in a stream of black leather cuts herding through the hallway and right for the food. Becca got up to meet Eli, leaving me alone among a sea of people, some familiar and some completely foreign to me.

With a familiar blonde head still MIA, I couldn't stop myself from watching Ariel out of the corner of my eye and my heart thudded unsteadily as she smoothed down her hair and her dress before scanning the flood of leather anxiously.

She even stood up on her heels to look for Caleb as if no one else was in the room, as if she couldn't care less who was watching. My teeth sawed on my bottom lip when Caleb, who had a tattooed arm wrapped around Dominic's shoulders, finally came into view. I almost stood to go to him before Ariel had a chance, but right now, the better choice was just staying put.

Because of the crowd and because I was still sitting on the opposite end of the room, Caleb would see Ariel before he'd ever see me, regardless of which one of us he was actually looking for. And because the masochist in me reared its ugly head, I decided to hang back and see how this whole sorry show played out.

From my vantage point across the room, it seemed like everything was happening in slow motion. Dominic and Caleb strode into the clubhouse's main floor together and from where I sat, it looked like Dominic caught sight of Ariel first. He bent down to mutter something in Caleb's ear and Caleb's head snapped to Ariel's direction.

With a shaky breath, I watched, practically wringing my hands helplessly, as Caleb and Ariel saw each other for the first time in four months. It was Caleb's face I was fixated on. That was the reaction I needed to see.

He stood locked to the floor, blinking back at Ariel and from what I could tell, seemed genuinely startled, if not bewildered, to see her standing less than 10 feet away. Then an indecipherable mask slipped on over his face as he and Dominic walked the short distance separating them from the girl who'd thrown him into a pit of whiskey-fueled despair. Dominic reached down to pull her into a quick embrace and then stepped away to find Lexie, leaving Caleb and Ariel alone.

They both seemed to reach for each other at the same time. Seeing Caleb putting his arms around his ex...I hadn't anticipated the knife in my heart would twist this brutally. Their arms seemed to linger around each other a little too long, even though I was, admittedly, biased, and then Caleb gently pulled away from Ariel.

He was speaking to her now with a small smile spreading on his face and then he nodded to her. My stomach churned when Ariel beamed back up at him, her entire face brightened just by this fleeting moment they'd just shared together, confirming all my suspicions and her motivation for those stupid, pot-stirring Facebook posts.

Just as my chest was beginning to heave from a panic attack, Caleb turned on his heel and started to backpedal away from Ariel. He was weaving around the crowd now, sidestepping the throngs pushing up to the food table, his eyes anxiously scanning the crowd.

He was looking for *me*.

His face broke out into a wide grin when he finally found me and I held myself back, letting him come to me. Then I felt his warm, rough hands slide around my waist to pull me into his arms as he leaned down to give me a quick kiss.

"Hey, babe," he murmured into my ear. "Havin' fun?"

I barely had a chance to nod before he was leaning down to kiss me again. He gestured with his head to the beer in my hand and arched a curious eyebrow at me.

"Beer, huh?"

It wasn't my usual vodka and soda, but well, if I was going to be in this world, I wasn't going to do it half-assed. Go big or go home. Or more accurately, when in Rome...

"Yeah," I shrugged. Because I was already a little off-balance, the words fell out of my mouth before I could really think about the

311

implication of them. "Elena got it for me."

Confusion flickered across his face like he couldn't quite place the name or what significance that might have, but when he followed my gaze to the pretty, petite brunette, who was stuffing some leftover wrapping paper into a garbage bag by a nearby table, his Adam's apple bobbed violently. His eyes darted back to me, laced with some apology, a little bit of embarrassment, and mountains of uncertainty.

"You okay?" Caleb asked finally, frowning his eyebrows down at me to give me his full attention and focus.

That was probably the only one of all my awkward interactions today I was the most comfortable with, at least where his past was concerned, so it was easy to let my lips curl up into a smile and stand up on my toes to kiss him.

"She was...respectful, I guess?"

He nodded tightly. "Good. You eat yet?"

"No, I haven't gotten a chance."

"Figures," he muttered, pulling me with him to the long and winding food line.

Keeping both hands gripped on my waist, he walked me to the end of the line and just that light touch pretty much set my body aflame. I'd only been away from him for a few hours for the party and that time apart seemed like a few days, rather than hours.

"By the way," he whispered behind me as we waited our turn for the barbeque. "You look smokin' today, babe."

I laughed, grinning widely as his hand slid around my stomach to pull me closer to him.

Glancing over my shoulder, I rose an eyebrow. "I think you just might be saying that because you're gonna miss me tonight."

His eyebrows flew into his forehead and I shivered at the sensation of his hot breath next to my ear. "I don't have to stay at the clubhouse tonight, you know. Screw Dom. He can have his last stag night without me."

My shoulders shook with laughter and I turned around so I could wrap my arms around his neck. "Your best friend is getting married tomorrow. You're staying here tonight. Besides, I'm pretty sure I'll find a way to survive without you for one night."

"You wish, babe."

He wrapped his arms around me a little more tightly now that I was facing him and took the opportunity to kiss me again. It was that moment when my eyes wandered over Caleb's shoulder, only to collide with Ariel, who was standing like a statue about 10 feet away.

She was gaping back at us with wide, pained eyes, her face pale and twisted with grief. I quickly turned myself back around in Caleb's arms and he slid his hands around my waist again, none the wiser that his ex had just witnessed our entire exchange.

Part of me wanted to fist pump in victory, or at the very least, post a picture of this moment on Facebook just to rub her nose in it.

The other part of me knew it wasn't that simple.

Regardless of the terse encounter we'd had before, I didn't want to play these games with her. As far as I was concerned, no good could come from engaging Ariel in any way. This was Lexie and Dom's weekend and the last thing I needed right now was to find myself in an all-out brawl with Ariel and put Caleb in the middle of it, mainly because I didn't see the point in testing fate if I could help it.

After we'd eaten together and Caleb gave me a quick kiss goodbye, he and the rest of the club high-tailed it out of there before the last plate was cleared. Since all the girls, Becca included, were already at work cleaning up the dirty dishes and assorted garbage, all I could really do now was sit back and hope this weekend wouldn't end in a tragedy.

. . .

With the clamoring and whoops echoing through the reception hall, it was just that much more difficult to pretend like something, or rather someone, wasn't grinding a million nails into my heart. Somehow, I had to figure out how to make it through the rest of this night in one piece, and I resolved to do just that as I stepped through the hall's threshold with Becca at my side.

The wedding itself went off without a hitch. Lexie looked radiant in her form-fitting white dress as she strode up the aisle, proudly displaying her baby bump for all to see. And when the opening notes of Aerosmith's "I Don't Wanna Miss A Thing" started playing as Lexie floated up the aisle, I couldn't keep from smiling along with the rest of the wedding guests. I probably shouldn't have expected anything less from a biker wedding.

But after the ceremony, the sight of Dominic and Lexie's respective best man and maid of honor walking down the aisle together arm in arm almost sent me teetering over the edge. I'd had to fist my fingernails into my hands just to keep from screaming.

Up until that moment, I think I'd held myself together pretty well.

Caleb, making good on his promise to bring me as his date, stopped by Becca's apartment with Eli that morning to bring us to the wedding. Becca had spent way too much time on the loose waves in my hair, but she claimed it was because she wanted me to look dynamite and because the hair went with my dress, which was just a strapless, knee-length LBD with some fullness in the skirt.

I'd purposefully kept everything simple because I didn't want to look like I was trying too hard, so I'd felt a stuttering glimmer of hope when Caleb whispered in my ear that I looked beautiful. I'd been able to fan that hope all throughout the morning and the entire ceremony up until its last moments.

That glimmer of hope was on its last legs when I saw the look on Ariel's face as she walked down the aisle with her arm secured underneath Caleb's. It was a look that read triumph. Excitement. Hope. Vindication. Like she had the world at her feet and was about to regain her place in this confusing, overwhelming world. It had taken all of my remaining willpower not to stand up in the middle of all Dominic and Lexie's wedding guests and scream.

Instead, I sucked in a breath and prayed that image wouldn't be forever seared into my memory. Of course, it didn't help that Caleb's duties as best man had made him basically absent from the pre-ceremony to the start of the reception. It wasn't necessarily his fault. This was one of the biggest days of his best friend's life, but his absence wasn't doing anything to curb the dread settling at the pit of my stomach.

As Becca and I settled into our seats a few tables away from the wedding party, she absentmindedly scrolled through her phone and I had half a mind to rip the stupid thing out of her hands and throw it across the room.

There was no *good* reason to feel that way and I knew that by feeling this way, I really was letting the terrorist win, not to mention basically ruining what should be a fun night for myself. I just couldn't help it.

He'd already told me loved me. We'd spent every night together for the last week, wrapped around the sheets in my bedroom. He'd officially made me his old lady. We'd discussed what getting his ink meant, even if it was still a ways away. He'd been attentive, affectionate, loving, and everything else I could have ever wanted from him.

So it wasn't fair to him or to myself that I had these doubts. There was nothing more he could do, nothing more he could possibly say to prove to me that this was real, that he was serious, except tackling the one subject we'd purposely skirted around.

Ariel.

If I was being completely honest with myself, I'm not entirely sure talking about her would even have helped. I think I'd still feel this crazy with self-doubt and unfounded jealousy and I knew if I did anything, I would just end up looking as crazy as I felt. I knew he loved me and I believed him every time he said it, but he'd loved Ariel too.

At some point tonight, Ariel would try to get him alone. I was about as certain of that as I was that the sky was blue. What happened after that was on Caleb.

I hated feeling like I *had* to be this passive, like I *had* to leave it alone, but all my hands were already played out. I'd gotten all the confirmation I could possibly get from him, told him I loved him back, and slept with him as many times as physically possible in the span of seven days.

All I could do now was let the chips fall and see how it played out. Regardless of the outcome, I knew that if I eliminated the choice for him, what would I really have? On some level, wouldn't it mean more if Caleb had the opportunity to get back together with Ariel, but chose me instead? And if there was a chance that he would choose Ariel even after everything we'd been through together, and there was most definitely a chance, wouldn't it be easier if I just knew now?

I was setting myself up for heartbreak tonight. This passive-aggressive strategy wouldn't get me anywhere in the long run, but I felt like it was the only real place I could go without making a scene and without forcing Caleb's hand.

I didn't need him staying with me out of obligation. I needed him staying with me because he legitimately and whole-heartedly wanted to be with me.

"Hey, Belle?" Becca's worried voice called out to me. "Are you okay?"

It would be easy to confide in Becca because she was the one who'd stumbled across the evidence in the first place. But that would mean having to say the words out loud, to admit what I was really feeling, and I just couldn't stomach that either.

I shook myself out of my stupor and forced a fake smile across my face. "Everything's fine."

Then, with a quick sigh of resignation, I gave in...just a little bit.

"Hey, Becs? Has Ariel, you know, posted anything else online since yesterday?"

Becca frowned back at me and I almost wished she would decide not to be my number one enabler right now. Almost. Since my best friend loved drama and obviously wanted to help me, it probably wasn't a difficult decision to make. The phone was in her hand again and she was scrolling through it without so much as a warning that I might not like what she found.

Oh well.

She held the phone out to me a few moments later with that familiar grim line crossing her face. This was probably the worst idea I'd ever had in my entire life, but I did it anyways. This time, Ariel had uploaded a picture taken on the bar inside the clubhouse. It was just two bare arms side by side without a caption, but I immediately recognized the intricate black skull tattoo on the obviously male forearm.

"You want me to cut that bitch?" Becca muttered lethally. "'Cuz I totally will."

I just shook my head as Becca kept scrolling to the update Ariel just posted a minute ago like she could literally see what we were doing right now and maybe she could. Bitch.

"Best weekend ever with Lex, Dom, and CS!"

If she'd wanted me twitching with rage, all she'd have to do was look under the table right now to see my heels digging into the floor to keep myself from charging right for her skinny little throat.

At the very least, I could rest assured that all this drama would be resolved at some point tonight because there was no way Ariel would miss her chance. I was just going to have to figure out a way to reconcile whatever happened next.

Becca exhaled loudly. "Seriously, Belle, how are you not knocking over tables right now and beating the hell out of her?"

"Because she's doing this to get a rise out of me," I pushed out through gritted teeth. "Besides, anyone named after a Disney character just isn't worth the effort."

Becca shot me a sympathetic glance and chewed on the inside of her cheek, quickly setting her phone back on the table. My eyes scanned the crowd, searching for that familiar blonde head and leather cut, and even with all these people, I found him almost instantly. It was like I could just sense where he was.

His back was to me and his head was bent low to hear something Lexie was telling him. As he brought his beer bottle to his lips, the bottle suddenly froze in mid-air. His head snapped to the side and then he put his hand on Lexie's back just as quickly to give her a quick kiss on the side of her head.

I lost all train of thought when Caleb turned on his heel and headed right for our table. His steps were purposeful, weaving in and out around the tables and I found myself mesmerized...the way he walked with so much confidence, so much swagger, it was hard not to swoon. I'd like to believe I was part of the reason why he walked with so much cool, easy self-possession, but now everything I knew about us felt twisted.

"'Sup, babe?" Caleb hovered over me to murmur in my ear as his warm hands settled over my shoulders and I curled into the welcome sensation. He glanced over at Becca and tipped his chin to her in greeting.

My senses were just going into overdrive today; everything was heightened, everything more intense and his touch wasn't enough to scare away all the doubt and anxiety lingering in my stomach.

"Hey, baby," I shifted a little to turn my cheek and he gave me a quick kiss.

"Sorry I've kinda been a shitty date. Duty calls, you know?" he chuckled and dropped down into the chair next to me. He reached forward to tangle our fingers together, and he was observing me carefully now, worry etched across his gorgeous face and part of me just wanted to throw my napkin down and run into the bathroom until this night was finally over. The other part of me was very aware that doing something like that would cause the scene I was trying to avoid.

There had to be a part, buried somewhere underneath all this anxiety and craziness, that knew I had to be strong enough to see this through to the end. I just had to find the strength to make that a reality and hold my head up.

"Don't worry about it, baby. It's not a big deal," I answered and put on the most convincingly brave face I could muster for him.

His eyes narrowed for just a moment and then he rubbed my fingers with his free hand before brushing his lips across my knuckles. The sweet gesture was something he'd done before, something I should be used to at this point. I wanted to take that as a sign of reassurance, of him wordlessly communicating that everything was going to be okay, but I also couldn't afford to fall into a trap of false hope.

"I've been kinda MIA for you during this thing and it feels like this is the first chance we've gotten to really talk since I saw you at the shower yesterday. I'm sorry about that, babe," he told me, still holding onto my knuckles. "Look, Iz, Lex told me —"

He never got a chance to finish because Ariel suddenly materialized next to us, positioning herself directly above where we sat. Caleb glanced up at her with exasperation creeping across his face and he sighed heavily.

"Hey, Caleb?" Ariel asked in a voice so syrupy-sweet I wondered if I'd get diabetes just from hearing it.

Caleb's eyes flicked back to me for a second before turning to her. "Yeah."

"Do you think we could talk?"

That bitch must've had balls of steel to start this right in front of me. But then Caleb's eyes shifted back to me. "Is that alright, babe?"

Because of all the thoughts poisoning my mind already, I didn't immediately understand what was really happening here. I think I'd almost talked myself out of believing this night could actually end well for me and now I found the love of my life watching me with that beautiful, crooked smirk twisting his lips.

"Yeah, I think that'd be okay, baby."

That smile across his lips just widened and he leaned forward to press a quick, meaningful kiss into my lips, lingering there for a few extra moments to make his point.

I got it.

As it turned out, I hadn't needed to be worried about this weekend at all.

Ariel gaped down at us, dumbstruck as Caleb nodded to her and then he pushed out of his chair, gesturing with his head for her to follow him. As they weaved around the tables, he glanced over his shoulder and shot me a quick wink. It didn't matter where they were going or when they got back. I knew how that conversation would end now.

Becca's elbow nudged my side and she leaned in to whisper, "He loves you."

My eyes followed that leather cut all the way out of the reception hall and a slow, confident smile spread across my face.

Yeah.

He loved me.

CHAPTER THIRTY-FIVE
Somebody That I Used To Know

Caleb

I led Ariel out one of the side doors to the reception hall, hoping we weren't bringing too much attention to ourselves, and only took a few strides into the hallway because I wasn't going any further if I could help it.

"Alright, let's make this quick," I cut right to the chase. "What's up?"

After all this time and in spite of all our history, it was still strange to be standing like this in front of her now. I didn't feel the way I thought I would feel. She didn't look the way I thought she would look. And that was okay because things were different now.

Ariel's eyes darted around nervously and she folded her arms around herself. "Caleb, can we go somewhere...I don't know, more private? I have some things I really need to say to you and I don't really want to do it like this."

I just shrugged. "Nah. I'm not gonna do that. Maybe we should just start with all that shit you posted online, huh? You know to try to mess with my old lady?"

Her eyes bounced up from the floor in shock.

"Yeah," I shrugged again. "Lex told me what you were doin'. Even for you, that was some real petty, immature bullshit, don't you think?"

Her dark eyes narrowed, even though she knew she'd been caught. Now, her voice took on a sharper edge, a tone I knew well from all our screaming matches before she left. Jesus, what had I ever really seen in her in the first place? Why the hell did I stay with someone so selfish and heartless for as long as I did?

"So, that's how it's gonna be then?" she snapped. "This is really gonna all revolve around *her?*"

This time, I didn't want to fight.

"Ariel?"

She shook her head before shifting her gaze back up to me. "Yeah?"

I didn't miss a beat. "Isabelle is my old lady. You know that. It's not new information. I don't have to be out here with you right now and she didn't have to agree to it either. So, say whatever you gotta say, but watch yourself."

Her arms wrapped around her middle, a defense mechanism I'd seen her do a thousand times, and that's how I knew the shit was really about to hit the fan.

"Why her, Caleb? Why did it have to be *her?*"

"Because I love her," I shrugged simply. "That's why."

Ariel shook her head violently like the swaying motion would somehow jerk that reality from her consciousness.

"I don't believe that," she told me, her voice firm but quiet. "You've always known how much I don't like her. How Little Miss Perfect always drove me absolutely crazy. I know that's why you're doing this— you knew how much it would kill me to see you with her. That's why you chose her, right? You wanted to hurt me in the worst possible way by picking the one person you knew I wouldn't be able to stomach seeing with you?"

Some things finally clicked into place for me now. The way Ariel's eyes always seemed to narrow whenever we passed Isabelle in the hallway. The way Ariel never missed an opportunity to demean just about everything she could about Isabelle from her overachieving grades to the way she wore her hair—and making sure I was in earshot for all of it. Suddenly, that punch to the head I'd suffered in high school for watching Isabelle's high kicks a little too closely made a hell of a lot of sense now. Ariel felt about Isabelle the exact same way I'd always felt about Brandon Davis.

Still, she was way off-base in her twisted logic to make sense of my relationship with Isabelle.

"Trust me, Ariel, your feelings about Isabelle have nothing to do with why I'm with her."

Unfortunately, Ariel still just heard what she wanted to hear.

"So she's just a rebound then, right?" Ariel asked, hope creeping into her voice in a way that set me on edge. "That's it? She's just a rebound?"

I shook my head. "Isabelle's no rebound. I told you already. She's my old lady. I'm *with* her. Sooner or later, you gotta figure out how to make peace with that."

Her chest was heaving now and her fists twisted up into tight white balls at the sides of her bridesmaid's dress. "I never should have left. I should've stayed here in Claremont with you."

I scrubbed a hand over my face before letting myself look at her again.

"Little late for that, Ariel," I told her hoarsely.

Four months ago, I would've given anything to hear those words come out of her mouth. And now, I just wanted to turn around and head back into the reception so I could dance with my old lady.

"I don't believe that," she shook her head furiously, her entire body literally shaking.

"Well, I don't know what to tell you then."

It was as simple and as complicated as that.

"You don't have to say anything, Caleb, because I have so much I need to say. So much I need to tell you. These last four months have been absolute torture for me. I hate California, I hate my school, I hate my life there and every day I wake up, wishing that I was waking up with you in your bed."

I just shrugged, folding my arms across my chest and staring a hole into the carpet at my feet.

"There were so many times I wanted to call you," she went on, her voice shaking with each syllable. "I just wanted to hear your voice, to tell you...but I thought you'd hang up on me."

"Yeah, well, you were right," I shot back darkly.

Her eyes widened and then she launched herself across the carpet, quickly closing the space between us. I didn't have much choice but to backpedal until she'd literally backed me into the wall right behind me.

"I never should've left because I still love you, Caleb," Ariel whispered into the still air. "I wanna come back home for good. I need to be with you again."

Ariel was reaching for me now and just as her hands were about to come in contact with my chest, I roughly batted them down. I was trying to be civil—I really was, but the longer we stood here, the more difficult this was becoming. The more difficult *she* was becoming.

"Caleb, don't," she sobbed, desperately groping for me, but I just shoved off the wall to put some space between us. "I know I hurt you. I didn't mean to. I was just trying to do something for myself. I never meant to hurt you and I'm so sorry, Caleb. I'll never forgive myself for that."

She was trembling now and furiously wiped away the fresh set of tears that streamed down her cheeks. Seeing her cry had always been one of my weaknesses and it looked like that hadn't changed because I just couldn't bring myself to walk away from her now. She must have read my silence as an opportunity because that just spurred her forward.

"I'll move back to Claremont," Ariel sputtered desperately. "I know it'll take some time, but we can fix this. We can go back to being us again. I know you still love me, Caleb. Even if you really do have feelings for her, you can't tell me you don't feel anything for me at all because I won't believe you."

I just shook my head and scrubbed both hands over my face. "It's been four months, Ariel. A lot of shit has gone down and you...you destroyed me. I'm not gonna lie to you and tell you otherwise. All I did for a month was guzzle whiskey, smoke weed, and screw any girl who was willing, but I'm not that guy anymore, Ariel, and that's because of her. And the fact of the matter is that if you really wanted to be with me, like you just told me, you never would've left. You would've turned your ass around in that cab and come back. You never would've gotten all the way to California and stayed there for four months if you really wanted us to be together."

Ariel flinched violently at those words and reached for me again, but I shrugged out of her grasp.

"It took me awhile to see it, but it's always been her," I spread my hands out in front of me to reiterate my point. "I think we've both known that for a long time. Neither of us just knew what to do about it."

She just pretended not to hear me. "She'll get over it and go to art school or wherever and you and I can go back to the way things used to be."

"You and me were never gonna work, Ariel. You gotta see that."

Ariel's lips parted slowly, like she was trying to find the words to respond, but was coming up empty. A few moments of silence passed as she just sniffled across from me, unable to bring herself to make eye contact with me. So I just pressed forward. She'd said everything she needed to say and it was time I did the same.

"Look, Ariel," I started hoarsely. "We were never good for each other. You and I both know that there weren't many days when we weren't fighting, and Jesus, that shit's just not normal. Everything was always a battle, everything was always a screaming match. We made each other miserable and you know it. Even before everything started this summer about you leaving, there was always something we were pissed at each other for, always someone lookin' for a fight."

"I don't remember it that way," Ariel called out softly.

"That's because you're not thinking clearly right now. But in a few days, maybe even a few weeks, you'll know I'm right."

"So you're saying it's my fault?" she demanded, her hands perched angrily on her hips and her face flushed red. "It's my fault because I did *one* thing for myself?"

"No, that's not what I'm saying," I shook my head. "But you did all that behind my back. How do you think that made me feel? There were plenty of schools you could've went to here and we might've been able to find a way to make it work, but you had to choose the one that was just about as far away from Claremont as you could go. Ask yourself why you did that, Ariel. Ask yourself why you chose California, why you chose UCLA, and then look me in the eye and tell me you still wanna be with me."

Ariel's eyes widened and I knew I'd finally struck a chord. Her hand flew back to cover her mouth and her eyes squeezed shut, her shoulders drooping down in defeat.

"We were never gonna make it," I went on softly. "Even in high school, we were always just trying to force each other to fit into something that never really had a chance and we should've let each other go a long time ago. But being with Isabelle isn't like that. She's taken all the bad, she's seen me at my worst, and for the first time, Ariel, I feel like everything fits. And I—" I shook my head suddenly. "You know what? I don't have to explain this to you. All you need to know is that I've never been more sure of anything in my life."

Something shifted in Ariel's eyes and then she was charging right for me. Her hands reached for my face to kiss me and I just shrugged her off, gently brushing her hands back down. But when she reached for my face again, I wasn't so gentle.

"Ariel, stop," I held her wrists down at her hips so she couldn't move any closer to me. I didn't understand why she didn't get it yet, why she was making this so damned difficult, and now, I just needed this to be over. "There's nothing more to say here. I said I'd talk to you because...I don't know, maybe because we were together for so long and I'm tryin' to be respectful here and I really don't wanna hurt your feelings, but this needs to stop."

She shoved out of my grip, stumbling back on her heel as she fumbled for something to support her.

I just shook my head. "We're done here, Ariel. And I'm sorry you came into this thinking it was gonna end differently, but this can't really be a surprise. You saw me with her before at the table, at the clubhouse —didn't you see the way I feel about her?"

Ariel's face crumbled and she whispered hoarsely: "I didn't want to."

I folded my arms across my cut as I appraised her, hoping she was finally starting to get it.

"You really love her?"

I felt myself nodding before I could even verbally confirm it. "Yeah, I really do."

"And you're happy?"

"Yeah, I really am."

She inhaled shakily before brushing another fresh set of tears from her cheeks. Then she pressed a pained smile across her face, murmuring, "Okay."

I shot her a sad smile before reaching forward to pull her into one last hug. Now that I knew she was on the same page with where things stood between us, it felt like it was safe to touch her without room for misinterpretation. She clung to the edges of my cut and buried her face in my chest, probably because she knew this was the last time I would ever hold her like this. When I gently pulled away from her, she sighed desperately, letting her hands slip down at her sides.

"You're gonna be okay, Ariel," I smiled down at her, my hands giving her shoulders a reassuring shake. "You're gonna go back to California and be a kickass social worker who helps people all the time."

She laughed in spite of her tears, quickly wiping another one away. I looked up just in time to see Isabelle rounding the corner of the hallway and she stopped short, her eyes widening as they locked in on the sight of my hands on Ariel's shoulders. On reflex, my hands immediately fell away and reached out for my old lady.

Isabelle pressed a quick smile on her face and just waved a hand. "Sorry. I didn't mean to interrupt. Really. I was just looking for the bathroom and I didn't think you guys would..."

She trailed off, but Ariel was already shaking her head and she looked back at me with sad brown eyes that used to tug and tear at me. Now, I felt bad that she was hurting and sorry that I was the one who'd hurt her, but I was more concerned about the blonde behind her. I was more concerned about *her* feelings, just as I should be.

"Hey, Iz," I called out as she started backpedalling away from us. "Wait up, okay? We're done here anyways."

I glanced down carefully at Ariel, who just nodded and brushed away one more stray tear. Isabelle hadn't moved yet, her high heels rooted into the carpet like she couldn't take a step forward if she tried.

"Hey, Isabelle," Ariel took a step towards her and quickly angled herself towards the nearest exit. "I just wanted to say that I'm sorry about...you know. I was trying to..."

Ariel trailed off, looking down at her shoes and chewing nervously on the inside of her cheek. All three of us knew exactly what Ariel had been trying to do this weekend and now, all three of us also knew Ariel hadn't had a snowball's chance in hell of succeeding. In hindsight, I probably should've anticipated she was going to try *something*, but seeing as how I didn't give two shits about social media or anything revolving around it, I also hadn't really anticipated she'd play that card either.

To her credit, Isabelle smiled graciously, looking to me for some direction out of this awkwardness. Ariel got the hint, waving to us with pain and something else that looked a lot like acceptance in her eyes and she stepped away, heading right for the parking lot.

Once she was out of sight, I blew out a deep breath. That whole conversation was heavier than I'd thought it was going to be, but at the end of the day, the closure was good for both of us, even if it took Ariel awhile to come around. Isabelle was walking towards me now and her soft hands flitted up my shoulders until they curved around my neck.

"Hey, baby," she smiled softly.

"Hi, babe," I grinned back and leaned down to kiss her.

"How did your talk with Ariel go?"

I just shrugged. "We both had some things we needed to get off our chests and now it's done. Thanks for letting me talk to her, by the way."

Her eyes narrowed, amusement creeping across her face. "You didn't need my permission, you know."

"Sure I did," I tucked some stray blonde hair behind her ear as I spoke. "I wasn't gonna leave the reception with her unless you were okay with it."

"So," her eyebrows rose. "If I'd said no..."

I lifted a shoulder. "Ariel just would've had to deal with it."

"She probably would've made a scene."

"Yeah, that's probably what she wanted."

Isabelle blew out a deep breath and leaned into me a little more. "That's what I was trying to avoid."

My lips curled into a smile. "Yeah, Lex told me what she was doin'. You did the right thing just lettin' her make a fool of herself."

"That's not really what I wanted," she sighed again. "And I'm sorry I let her get to me. I shouldn't have given her a second thought, but I just couldn't help it. I wanted to believe her being back here this weekend wouldn't matter, but I couldn't stop myself from..."

She trailed off like saying the words out loud was too ridiculous and she was probably right about that too.

"Hey," I tilted her chin up to force her to look at me. "I get it, Iz, I really do. I don't blame you for wondering, but next time something like this happens, next time you're not sure about something, you gotta talk to me, okay? Pull me aside, shoot me a text, whatever you gotta do to get my attention, but don't let yourself just sit there, like you did this weekend, and wonder. I'll always tell you the truth, babe, and I'll always tell you whatever you wanna know."

"I know, I know," she nodded into my hands. "I'm sorry. I just didn't want to cause any drama this weekend."

And that right there was one of the key differences between Isabelle and Ariel. Where Ariel wanted to do everything in her power to push Isabelle over the edge, to get Isabelle to react and get in her face, which, if I knew Ariel, would've ended up with the two of them rolling around on the floor, hands flying and pulling each other's hair...Isabelle just stayed calm. She stayed cool and level-headed and the only reason I even knew all that was happening under my nose was because Lexie stepped in and had Isabelle's back.

"That's because you're classy," I told her with a smirk. "And you're not all about the drama, unlike some people we know."

"Knew," she corrected softly.

"Knew," I agreed.

"I shouldn't have doubted you," Isabelle went on, her eyes drifting down to our feet. "I think it just had everything to do with the fact that we've only really been together a week and I just didn't know if I could compete with all the history you have with her."

I walked her backward until her back rested against the wall behind us and both my arms boxed her in, forcing her to hear me.

"You gotta understand something, Iz," I started, leaning in so our faces were almost touching. "When she left, I thought that was it. I thought I'd never be happy again. I thought I'd always be living in my own personal hell. Even smiling hurt. I was so lost...and had no idea how to dig myself out of it. But then you came along and you saw all the stupid shit I was doin' to myself. You forced me to see what I was doin' to myself without judging me and without making me feel even worse. I was drowning and you didn't just throw me a life preserver, but you jumped in after me and pulled my sorry ass out. How could I not love you after that?"

I paused to brush a tear away from her cheek with my thumb.

"Four months ago, I would've told you to just let me drown. Four months ago, I couldn't even see straight, let alone see what was standing right in front of me. I can see you now, Iz, and everything I need is right here. There was never a choice, Iz. It was always gonna be you."

Both my hands closed around her face now and I leaned forward to kiss her, to show her everything I was trying to tell her, but wasn't sure if I'd said the right way. I always found myself fumbling for the right words to articulate everything swimming around my head, but given the tears in her beautiful blue eyes and the happy smile curving up those lips I loved so much, I felt like I'd finally gotten it right.

"Baby?" she was asking me now, her eyes shining with unshed tears. "What are we gonna do when I go to VCU in January?"

I pushed out a rough breath and tugged a hand through my hair. We hadn't really talked about her going to art school yet, at least not like this, and so, we might as well put it all on the table now.

"We'll see each other every weekend," I shrugged. "I know you're worried about being that far away, but I'm not. You gotta do what's right for you and babe, going to VCU is the right thing. That's where you need to be and a semester's what? Four months long? Then you'll have summer or winter break and be home for awhile and then before you know it, those two years will just fly by and you'll be done. We can do it, Iz, because that's what we need to do. It's just something we can live with, you know? Everything's gonna be okay."

She nodded wordlessly and my lips captured her mouth again. There was nothing else either of us needed to say because thinking about it and talking about it would only burst this little bubble of happiness. My focus now was on the taste of her mouth instead.

I loved the way her hands slipped around my neck and her thighs parted just enough so I could press myself between them. Everything just fit with her. There was no awkwardness, no indecision; it all just worked. All the times I'd let myself fantasize about what her skin would feel and taste like...it was all mine now. I could live in it, own it, and do what I wanted with it. I knew she'd let me.

And that gave me a beautiful idea.

"Hey," I murmured into her lips. "Weren't you headin' somewhere before?"

"Uh huh," she sighed back. "The bathroom I think. I don't know. You're making me forget."

I chuckled and pushed us off the wall, gesturing with my head down the hallway, where the bathrooms were. Our fingers tangled up together as I led her where she needed to go and she stood up on her toes to give me a quick kiss before disappearing inside. With my back leaning up against the wall again, now I just needed to bide my time and listen for those telltale noises that she was finished up in there. Then I got to make my move.

When I heard the faucet running inside, that was my cue. I pushed off the wall and was through the door to the women's bathroom a second later, quickly reaching over my shoulder to flip the lock on the door.

Isabelle was standing by the sink, gaping back at me like I'd just sprouted a second head...well, that was sorta true.

"What are you doing?" she half-laughed, still shaking her head at me in confusion as I stalked towards her.

My hands ghosted over her shoulders, turning her around until her back was leaning against my chest and I pressed a gentle kiss into the bare skin on her shoulder.

"Love you," I murmured into her neck as my hands drifted down past her shoulders, curving around her waist until they finally settled at her hips. My eyes flicked up to the mirror to find her hooded, sexy blue eyes watching my every move. "Hands on the counter, babe."

She obeyed immediately, splaying her hands out in front of her as I pressed in as close as I could go.

Yeah, she knew where this was going.

"You know," I hummed into her skin, savoring the way she shivered under my touch. "I've always had this fantasy about you in a skirt."

One side of her lips curved up into a knowing smirk. "Oh, really? I wonder how that came about."

I chuckled, letting my hands slide all the way past the edge of her dress so they could creep up her thighs, and I buried my nose in her hair. "Well, you know, this isn't a cheerleading skirt, but it'll have to work."

"Poor baby."

I shot her a wolfish grin through the mirror as my fingers glided over her bare skin until I felt the thin strip of lacy material I was looking for and my forehead slammed into her shoulder at the contact. "Jesus, babe. Are you tryin' to kill me or what?"

"That's kinda the idea. I'm not wearing a thong for my health, you know."

I wanted to laugh, but I was too busy concentrating on moving that thin lacy strip aside and covering as many inches of her neck with my lips as possible. We had to be quick now and as much as I hated to do it, I slipped a hand out from underneath her skirt so I could unzip my fly. Her eyes widened back at me, reflected in the mirror, and I recognized the question in them right away.

"We're all good, babe," I smirked at her before pressing my lips to her neck again. "All good."

I'd planned on surprising her, so to speak, with this news when we made it back to her bedroom after the reception, but as it turned out, I just couldn't wait until the end of the night. She sighed under my hands, tilting her neck to the side to give my lips better access as I slipped inside her, wrapping myself up in her warmth and that sweet tightness I wanted to take over and over again.

I planned on doing it for the rest of my life.

.   .   .

The reception was still in full swing when I led Isabelle back inside the hall. As far as anyone knew, we really hadn't disappeared for that long, but she still leaned into my shoulder, flushed pink with embarrassment.

"Just you wait, babe," I whispered into her ear. "That back there was just a warm-up for tonight 'cuz I plan on burying myself inside you until the sun comes up."

That only deepened her blush and her cheek cemented to my shoulder as she shyly chewed on her bottom lip. When we made it out onto the dance floor, nothing else mattered other than the fact that I just wanted to feel her in my arms and breathe in her sweet, flowery perfume.

As I wrapped an arm around her waist, I locked our hands together, brushing my lips against her knuckles before pulling her hand into my chest. She rested her head against my chest with a sigh, giving me ample room to just hold her closer as Paul McCartney's scratchy voice hummed "Maybe I'm Amazed" through the loudspeakers.

Good ol' Sir McCartney understood exactly what I was feeling. Everything was different for me now and it was like all the pieces of my life had fallen right into place, whether I could believe it or not. As long as this girl was in my arms, I was invincible. Nothing could touch me. Nothing could touch us. And I knew I needed to hang onto that feeling for as long as possible.

The outlaw life was all I'd ever known. It was my legacy and my birthright and while I knew Isabelle inherently understood that like she understood everything else about me, I knew that eventually, the life would catch up to us.

My mom had always told me there was no in between with old ladies: it was either all or nothing. Full disclosure or nothing but murky, vague answers.

She was right about that. Dom didn't sugarcoat anything with Lexie and even though that probably caused more fights between them than he probably cared to admit, he'd always told me that he wouldn't have it any other way with her. Old ladies needed to be informed, Dom had said, so that they could make an informed decision when they needed to.

It really worked both ways: we had to be forthcoming and give each other all the facts so the other could do what was best for both us and for the club. That was the only way we would be able to make it through the long haul.

My ink was already going on that beautiful body sometime in the near future. A ring and babies wouldn't be that far behind. Part of me just wanted to laugh at myself—a week ago, I'd been trying to pump the brakes with her, to take things slow and here I was thinking about rings and babies and a future with her. My lifestyle didn't exactly afford many certainties, but I still found myself praying I'd be able to keep her, even with her leaving for art school looming over us like a beacon of doom.

The only way we'd be able to stay strong and united was if we gave each other the hard truths, without omission and without fear that the other person would run. I knew I'd need to remember that when things got hard. And with the club, at some point, it was going to get hard. That was just the nature of this life—it ebbed and flowed, sometimes it was down, sometimes it was up and those twists and turns happened at breakneck speed.

When the song was over, a Black Keys song started up in its place and that was my cue to exit the dance floor. Slow dancing was easy.

Anything other than that wasn't exactly my thing. So, when I kissed my old lady on the forehead and stepped away, her best friend swooped in and dragged Isabelle further out onto the dance floor.

As much as I didn't really like being separated from her, that still gave me a little room to catch up with the rest of my club brothers, apologize to Dom and Lex for being MIA, and finally face down my mom's ever-watchful glare to let her know everything was fine. I was careful never to let my eyes stray from Isabelle for too long and that effort earned me a big smile whenever I winked at her. It wasn't until Marcus pulled me aside that reality brought everything to a screeching halt.

"So, you and the office girl," Marcus questioned in his low, gravelly voice. "You official now?"

I wasn't entirely sure where the club Prez was going with this, but figured I might as well just play along. There was something in Marcus' tone and the fact that he'd referred to Isabelle as 'the office girl' that had me on edge.

"Yeah, it's official."

"Old lady and everything?"

"Old lady and everything," I confirmed with a nod.

Marcus appraised me with a cool, level stare and the hairs on the back of my neck stood on end. "You trust her?"

"Of course I trust her," I frowned. "She wouldn't be my old lady if I didn't."

My club Prez held his hands up in defense. "Alright, son, alright. I just wanted to make sure. Old ladies are privy to a lot of inside club shit, probably more than any of us would really like to know. You just gotta be sure that anything you tell your old lady, you tell her because you know you can trust her. The right person comes around at the wrong time...might try to exploit that and use it against the club."

My eyes narrowed. "Why are you tellin' me this now? Ariel was my old lady for five years and we never had this conversation."

"You were a kid," Marcus waved off. "To be honest, I'm surprised you kept her around as long as you did and you're not some 16-year-old with a hard-on anymore. Your mom tells me this one," he gestured with his beer bottle towards Isabelle on the dance floor, "is the real thing. The way you're lookin' at that girl right now tells me as much. You and I both know Heath's on his last legs as my VP and everybody and their mother knows you're next in line. I just gotta know that my future VP is all in, 100 percent, and that your old lady's gonna be able to get behind anything you might have to do for the sake of the club. And if she can't, maybe you need to rethink who you're investin' your time in. You and Dom are the future of this club, Caleb, and I just gotta make sure it's being taken care of."

I folded my arms tightly across my chest, not at all comfortable with the direction this conversation was heading in. "So you're saying *you* don't trust her."

"I didn't say that, son," Marcus backpedalled quickly. "She's a good girl. Everybody knows that. No one's sayin' she isn't. But she's an outsider, Caleb. She may know about all that pussy and Jack you've been takin' on the last few months, but she don't know shit about what you do for the club or how you really make the cash that's gonna set her up in a nice house someday. Problems at home and problems with your old lady because of what you need to do for your club will screw with your priorities, son. You gotta figure out if she's gonna be an asset or a weakness because she can't be both."

I bristled at his words. "I trust her. It doesn't matter that she's an outsider. I'll get her on the same page with everything. It's not an issue."

"Well," he shrugged. "We got that patch-over party comin' up. Should be a good test for her, huh?"

All I could do was nod tightly and tell him what he needed to hear: "She'll be fine."

It would be a major culture shock for her, that was for sure, but as long as I stayed close to her, she really would be just fine.

"Alright," Marcus clapped me on the shoulder. "Just wanted to be sure *we* were on the same page. I'm happy for ya, Caleb. I really am. You've been in a pretty dark place lately and I'm glad to see you finally on the other side of it. If she's the reason you've got your head back in the game now, then so be it."

My club Prez's words were like a sandpit I'd sunken into and I had to crawl my way out of it even as he clapped me on the shoulder. He stalked off to mingle with the other MCs who'd shown up for support, all the while playing the part of the cool, level-headed leader, despite that last warning glance he shot over his shoulder at me.

What the hell was that? The inquisition, followed by the abrupt turnaround, was just as surprising as it was unsettling, not to mention completely uncalled for.

While I knew Marcus was only technically doing his job as club president and pointing out that Isabelle was an outsider was well within his rights, it pissed me off that Marcus wouldn't trust *me* enough to make the right choice here.

My eyes scanned the dance floor and my mouth curved up into a smile when I found her shaking her hips with Becca. Isabelle was absolutely the right choice.

Sure, she was going to need some guidance, but she could do it. Marcus didn't know even half of what Isabelle had already dealt with in her life and I knew that when the time came, and Isabelle once and for all proved herself to be the strong, iron-willed old lady she needed to be, Marcus would eat his words.

And as another slow song started and I weaved in and out through the crowd to find her, I couldn't have been more confident in my relationship with her, even though it was still so new. I'd dove in headfirst with her and there was nothing about it that scared me.

My hands slid around her waist to bring her hips closer and I could feel her sigh as her arms wound around my neck. This was where I was supposed to be.

I'd been lost and I'd found myself again in this girl's arms.

"Hey, babe," I whispered into her ear, loving that it was enough to make her shiver. "Couple more slow songs and then let's get outta here, okay?"

She bit down on her bottom lip and nodded back shyly. "Okay."

CHAPTER THIRTY-SIX
Initiation

Isabelle

Culture shock.

That's about all I could think right now. Caleb warned me—he'd told me it would be wild, he'd told me it would be rowdier than all the times I'd been at the clubhouse combined, but that still hadn't mentally prepared me for the patch-over.

It was literally impossible to move anywhere on the clubhouse's main floor without rubbing up against someone. People of all shapes, sizes, and beard-lengths packed the floor from wall to wall and the music blared that much louder from the speakers overhead just to even be heard. In between Def Leppard and Metallica, which I wasn't crazy about, someone was also blasting Tom Petty, Rush, and The Doors too, which was totally fine.

Lexie had wisely decided to sit this one out and I couldn't blame her one bit because if I was eight and a half months pregnant, there's no way I'd be anywhere near this place right now either. Becca, on the other hand, *was* in attendance, but I could count on one hand the number of minutes I'd actually spent next to her tonight even though the patch-over party had officially gotten off and rolling well over an hour ago.

When my supposed best friend wasn't sucking the lips off Eli, she was holed up in the bathroom. Her and Elena always came out one right after the other and at this point, I was pretty sick of the disappearing act.

Despite all that, I was never really alone during this thing because Caleb had yet to leave my side even once. His arm was just casually draped over my shoulder, but that constant contact was exactly what I needed to keep my head in this game. I was here, at this Horsemen-sponsored patch-over celebration, as his old lady and he'd taken every opportunity to make that very clear to anyone not directly connected to his club.

Since they were hosting two other clubs in their clubhouse, I figured this constant contact was as much about claiming his property as it was easing my nerves and even if the term *property* grated on every feminist instinct in my body, for this occasion, I just had to grin and bear it.

This time was different than all the other times I'd been here. Before, it'd been strictly about the party. This time, there was as much business happening here as there was celebration.

"That's Cesar Ortega," Caleb murmured lowly in my ear, gesturing with his beer bottle towards a burly Latino with a thick black goatee and a leather cut with a Los Lobos emblem stitched into the back. "He's the Lobos' Prez."

He'd been discreetly keeping me in the loop like this since the two clubs arrived and just as I was about to ask Caleb why the Horsemen were even involved in all this patch-over business in the first place, I felt him stiffen beside me as another Latino, a short man with days-old dark stubble covering his cheeks, sidled up in front of us with his arm wrapped around a tiny, gorgeous girl. They were probably a good 10 years older than us, but between the glassy, red-rimmed eyes and smug expressions, they definitely weren't acting that way.

Caleb tucked me in even tighter under his arm, angling his body to put himself between me and the sneering couple, who looked like they were absolutely perfect for each other.

As they approached, the man's eyes crawled up and down the length of my body and my skin recoiled even though he hadn't actually touched me. In these 10 seconds alone, I suddenly felt like I needed to take a shower. The man's lips widened into an arrogant, knowing smirk, not unlike the Grinch, as he leered back at me, but when I glanced at Caleb, I saw exactly where the source of this evil grin really lied.

Caleb gone completely rigid next to me and his lips had ever so slightly curled up into a furious snarl. This whole exchange, even though no one had actually said anything yet, suddenly reeked of danger and hostility and all I could do was lean into Caleb even deeper for protection.

"Classy broad you got there, *ese,*" the man goaded, taking the opportunity to let his dark eyes trail from my chest down to my toes and all the way back up again.

Desperate for a distraction, I glanced down at my own attire versus the woman sneering across from me. I'd taken great care tonight to make sure I looked like I belonged here, but also that I looked like I was *with* someone here too. My black, stretchy skirt flared out a little at my thighs and was short enough to draw attention to my legs, but long enough to still leave something to the imagination. I'd tucked a silky teal tank top into my skirt that showed just a teeny bit of cleavage and completed the look with spiky studded high heels, loose, beachy waves, and a few gold bangles around my wrist.

Compared to the other woman, with her midriff-baring tube top, barely-there jean skirt, and heavy-handed makeup—yeah, I really did look classy. So, basically, I got the reaction I wanted.

Caleb sagely chose to ignore the comment and instead tilted the neck of his beer bottle towards the couple. "Iz, this is Diego Padilla. He's with the Cobras."

"Club president of the Cobras," Diego corrected, his mouth matching Caleb's snarled sneer.

Caleb just huffed out a laugh, his lips twisting into that cocky grin I knew well. "Sure. Whatever you say."

Their standoff went on for a few more long moments as both Caleb and Diego seemed to circle each other without even moving. Finally, Diego nodded to me.

"I take it she's your old lady, huh?"

The arm draped around my shoulders stiffened. "That's right."

Diego lifted a shoulder. "Looks like you did well for yourself, Sawyer," he jutted his chin out towards the woman under his arm, "Luz is my girl."

Caleb afforded the woman one courteous nod, but all the goodwill and civility was sucked right out of this exchange the second Diego brought his glowing cigarette to his lips and blew the smoke right into my face.

Caleb swung his arm out from around my shoulders and charged towards Diego until he gripped him by his leather cut with both white-knuckled fists, hoisting Diego up to his eye level.

"You wanna show a little fuckin' respect?" Caleb practically spat in his face, fury singeing off him in hot fumes.

Diego jerked away from Caleb's grip and shoved him in the chest, his hard face twisted with rage. I was frozen to the sticky floor, helpless to do anything but watch as Caleb stumbled back a half step and then sprung forward again, violently pounding Diego right back in the chest. Before either had a chance to make another move, Dominic had Caleb by the shoulders and someone else with a Cobra cut tugged Diego away from the scene to separate the two.

I dared a careful step forward, but a hand closed around my wrist to yank me back. Skyler was already shaking her head, silently telling me that I should know better than to try to get involved. That wasn't really what I was trying to do. I didn't want to get in the middle of anything, but my first instinct was just to get to Caleb.

Skyler kept her grip on my wrist as we observed from the sidelines. Marcus, with his bulky arms and gruff orders, was in between the two sides in a matter of seconds, calmly jerking his thumb over his shoulder towards the main entrance, but even from where I stood, the cold menace in the club president's eyes was unmistakable.

When the smoke cleared, Skyler gingerly released her hold on me, gesturing with her head towards her son to let me know it was safe now. We approached the three Horsemen cuts together and Marcus' eyes flashed darkly at me from over Caleb's shoulder.

"Take your woman and step outside," Marcus was murmuring to Caleb as we got closer. "Have a smoke, get some head, whatever you gotta do, but don't come back inside my clubhouse until you've cooled your ass off, got it?"

Caleb nodded tightly, his jaw still clenched and his shoulders still rigid. Even I knew it would've been disastrous for all parties involved if any punches had actually gotten thrown and all for some smoke blown in my face. Whatever issues existed between Caleb and Diego ran deeper than what had just happened and I had a feeling we were all really lucky it hadn't escalated any further.

From the corner of my eye, I could see Cesar Ortega reading Diego the same riot act and then the Lobos' club president shoved his new patch away and out of his sight. Caleb was already draping his arm around my shoulder again to lead me outside and his warm breath in my ear was about all I could focus on despite the commotion.

"You okay, Iz?"

I nodded, locking my hands around his waist to support him just as much as he was supporting me and then Caleb pushed us out through the main doors with his free hand. There were still hordes of leather cuts and barely-dressed women packed outside the grounds, but unlike inside the stuffy and smoky clubhouse, I felt like I could actually breathe a little bit now.

"Are *you* okay?" I asked as he led me past the crowd and through the parking lot, headed right for our picnic table next to the shop.

"Don't worry about me," Caleb just shrugged. "Nothin' happened anyways, you know?"

For all his protests, his chest was still heaving and his eyes were still glazed over a dark animosity I'd never seen before. I frowned back at him as he dropped onto the bench and gestured for me to do the same. As I settled onto the bench, cozying up to him as close as possible, his arm found my shoulder again and his left leg jumped manically underneath the table.

"Baby, it's fine. Just do what Marcus told you to do and have a cigarette. I'm not gonna do the other thing he said, at least not out here, so I guess that's your only option," I told him diplomatically.

Caleb arched an amused eyebrow at me. "What other thing?"

When he slipped his fingers underneath my skirt and trailed them up my thigh, I smacked him on the shoulder.

"Shut up."

He gestured with his head towards the clubhouse with a wolfish grin, his hand still planted under my skirt. "We could sneak in through the back and go in my dorm. No one would ever know."

I shot him a wary glance. "What about your complex with me and the bed in your dorm, huh?"

"Desperate times call for desperate measures, babe," he shrugged a little too easily. "Besides, who said anything about using the bed? There's the floor, my bathroom, my dresser...we could get creative."

My eyebrows rose. "You done?"

His lips twisted a little. "Sure."

"Just have the cigarette, Caleb. It's really okay."

He shook his head and squeezed my shoulder. "I'm not gonna do that with you right next to me and I'm not gonna leave this table with you sittin' here by yourself either."

"Wow," I shook my head at him in disbelief, but he just shrugged. "You can have a cigarette. *One* cigarette is not gonna kill me, you know."

Caleb's face dipped down in a somber grimace and he tucked me even deeper underneath his shoulder to press his lips into my hair. "That's not funny, Iz."

"I know. Sorry. But seriously, just do it. You and I both know that other than sex, which isn't happening right now, that's the only thing that's gonna calm you down."

With one more exasperated glance in my direction, he shifted on the bench to dig his cigarette pack and a lighter out of his back pocket. Once it was lit, he purposely angled his head away from me so he could blow his smoke in the opposite direction. The second he took the first pull from the cigarette, all the tension seemed to roll right off him.

Part of me wasn't sure how much I'd be overstepping my new role as old lady by asking questions, but then again, Caleb had told me he'd answer any question I had. Even if he could only give me vague responses, it would still be better than the next to no information I had right now.

"What happened back there, baby?"

He lifted a shoulder and turned his head to blow out some more smoke again. "Padilla's a dickhead. That's what happened. He and I haven't gotten along pretty much since day one."

"Why?"

"I can't really explain it, but there's just somethin' about him that I don't trust. Somethin' that just doesn't feel right, you know?"

I nodded. "Yeah, I kinda got that feeling about him and his girlfriend too."

"Take this last run," Caleb went on and he obviously wasn't shying away from the details I wanted. "Everything's planned to the T, right down to the last second because it has to be. And what does the asshole do but ride in a half hour late, still drunk and high from the night before, and acts like it's no big deal. All because the dumbshit decided partying before the drop-off was a better idea than partying after, which is what anyone with half a brain knows is what you really do. That was his club's test run and it was like bein' on time wasn't even a consideration."

"Sounds like his ego is the only big thing about him."

"Right," he huffed out a laugh. "But you know, I think the part that pissed me off the most was that he could've screwed that whole run up for me too."

"Why?"

I felt like that word was on continual replay on my tongue, but this was the only way I'd ever start to make sense of this chaotic world. Even though I'd been doing my best to pay attention to the structure of the club as much as I could, there was still so much I didn't know and still so much I didn't quite understand.

"I gotta prove I can lead, babe," Caleb told me, leaning his shoulder down into mine with a soft smile playing on his lips. "Someday soon, when I get that VP patch, I need the club to be behind me, especially since VP leads to Prez."

"Isn't Dominic's dad the VP already though?"

"Yeah," Caleb told me with a grin. Clearly, he was proud I'd been doing my homework. "But Heath's gone downhill pretty quick over the last few years. His heart's seen better days and his lungs are next, I think. Pretty soon, he won't be able to ride, and if you can't ride, you can't rank. He could still sit at the table and everything, but he couldn't hold an office."

"So, the next in line is you?"

"Yeah."

"Because of your dad?"

Caleb scrubbed a hand over his face and flicked his spent cherry into the night air. "Maybe that's my foot in the door, but I like to think I'm qualified for the job 'cuz of more than that. This is what I was born to do. I don't know how to do anything else anyways, but I want the gavel because I earned it, not just because of my last name. And this club, these guys, they've been my family since I was born, had my back, dealt with all my shit. The least I can do is step up and have their back just as much as they've always had mine."

That made sense, especially given what I knew about his family's history within the ranks of the club. Of course he'd be heading in that direction, or at least, wanted to be.

"Well, if it's any consolation, I think you're gonna be a great leader someday."

He leaned forward to brush his lips against the side of my head. "Thanks, babe."

Now, that we were rolling with all this club business, I figured we might as well keep the train going.

"I have some more questions, if that's okay."

Caleb's eyes flicked ahead of us, probably to gauge whether or not we had enough privacy to be having a conversation like this out in the open and then nodded as he looked back to me. "Ask me whatever you want, Iz."

"I'm still trying to work out how all this...hierarchy works. I don't know if that's the right word, but I feel like I'm at least starting to wrap my head around the ranking with the women here in the clubhouse. I mean, your mom is way up here," I raised my hand high above my head to emphasize my point, "and Lex is about here," I lowered my hand down about six inches, "I think I'm about here," I lowered my hand down another six inches.

"Actually, babe," Caleb interjected softly and his fingers closed around my hand to lift it up a few inches higher. "I'd say you're about here."

"Really?"

"Absolutely," he nodded. "Everyone knows we're serious. Like I told you before, that's not something we take lightly around here and it's not something I'd push you into if I didn't really feel that way about you. I know this is a lot to take in all at once, but you gotta know that because you're standin' next to me, you've got status in the clubhouse. The only reason you've got Lex that far up above you is because she's been around a lot longer than you. Your status as my old lady follows my patch, so when I'm VP, that'll move you ahead of Lex. And you gotta own that too, Iz."

The idea of having that kind of status in this world and knowing what to do with it on top of that...I didn't know where to begin even considering it, let alone have it be my reality.

I blew out a deep breath. "I'm not really sure how to do any of that."

He just lifted a shoulder like he hadn't really thought about it before and that's probably because he'd never really needed to. "You'll figure it out. You know my mom and Lex will help you with whatever you need. Show you the ropes, you know?"

"Yeah, I know. So, I guess that means if I'm here," I gestured with my hand in the air again, "then Becca's here too, right?"

Caleb shook his head and chewed on the inside of his cheek in thought. "Nah. I'm not really sure why, but my mom doesn't think too highly of her."

"Huh," that was certainly new information, "So, then..."

He took my hand and lowered it another six inches. "Becca's here and everyone else," he brought my hand all the way past the table, "is right about here."

"Okay, I guess that makes sense. But what about the club? I mean, where do the Horsemen rank with all this..." I gestured out to the rowdy celebration under way yards in front of us.

Caleb held his hand up, mimicking my gestures from before. "The Horsemen are here," he lowered his hand another six inches, "the Lobos are here," he lowered his hand way down past the bench we were sitting on, "and the Cobras are way the hell down here."

I nodded slowly, trying to wrap my head around all this new information. "So if the Lobos are patching-over the Cobras, that means the Cobras are joining their charter, right?"

A wide, proud smile spread across Caleb's face and I knew I was right.

"And if Diego messed up so bad, why are they being patched over then? I know I have no idea what I'm talking about, but even to me, the logic of that just doesn't make sense."

Caleb shrugged and I wondered if he even understood the decision himself. "I guess Ortega needs some more muscle and he's puttin' his faith in Padilla. It's blind faith, that's for sure, but whatever. Doesn't matter all that much to us if the Lobos still hold up their end of the business."

"What do the Horsemen have to do with it then? If you're not the ones patching anyone over, why are you having the party here?"

"Well, the Lobos are based out of Raleigh and the Cobras are right outside of Charlotte, so they're the two closest clubs next to us in the state," he started easily. "We deal with the Lobos the most 'cuz they're our wholesaler and they run muscle for us too sometimes, so we gotta keep them happy. They invited us to the patch-over 'cuz of our history, I guess, and since their clubhouse isn't big enough for all three clubs, we ended up hosting. Besides, this just reminds everyone where they rank in the grand scheme of things, you know?"

Yeah, I got it. The way Caleb explained it at least. Still, the questions just kept bubbling to the surface.

"So when you went on that run last month, why did you go to Pittsburgh? I mean, if you were meeting with the Cobras, and they're in Charlotte, why did you have to go all the way up there?"

Caleb's lips twisted into the crooked smirk that had quickly become one of my favorite things about him. "You're pretty observant, you know that?"

"I was raised around lawyers my whole life. What do you expect?"

He just chuckled and leaned into me. "Alright, smartass. Alright. We ran the shipment to the Warlords, that's another MC we do business with. They're the ones who are in Pittsburgh. We normally make the drop on our own after we pick it up from the Lobos, but like I said, Ortega wanted to give Padilla and his boys a test run."

"And by *shipment*, you mean...?"

Caleb nodded tightly, catching my drift right away. "Guns."

Something coiled up in the pit of my stomach and that sick feeling flamed out all the way up to my throat. Well, at least now it was finally confirmed: the Iron Horsemen really were an outlaw and illegal MC. I'd always known it; I'd just never had the concrete evidence until now.

And now the questions just didn't stop.

"What exactly happens on a run then?"

Caleb's jaw clenched just enough to let me know I'd stepped into some murky waters, but there was nothing else about his demeanor that signaled I'd gone too far. In fact, all I saw in those glimmering blue eyes was resolution to give me whatever I needed.

"We transfer guns to business contacts. It's not always the same contact every time, but we switch up the day, place, and time just to keep from getting tracked. It's usually a pretty quick transaction. We're out in the open when we make the exchange, but it's always in some place where no one can spot us."

My mind was whirling in circles now. "Has a run ever gone bad? Could you get hurt?"

He smiled softly and squeezed my shoulder. "It can and I could, but that hasn't happened in years, babe. Everything we do has the potential to go bad, I guess, and if our contact wants to stir shit up, that's one thing, but we're always careful. The club has been doin' this for way longer than I've been alive, you know? We got it down."

My teeth sawed across my bottom lip in thought. "What happens if a run does go bad or if one of your...*business contacts* decides to stir up shit?"

Caleb didn't miss a beat. "The club goes on lockdown. All the old ladies, kids, friends of the club, whoever might be in danger, they all stay in the clubhouse until everything's sorted out."

This was all starting to feel pretty heavy and part of me wondered if Caleb wasn't sugarcoating this just a little because he didn't want to scare me.

"But why do you run guns though? I mean, couldn't you guys make money some other way that wouldn't get you in trouble? You've already been arrested once—why would you want to put yourself at risk like that? I'm sorry...I just don't understand why that's the *only* option."

Something flickered across his face that I couldn't place. We'd talked about his arrest record before and it wasn't like it was exactly a secret in the town, especially since he was the one who'd done most of the bragging. When they were 16, he and Dominic had swiped some beer and weed from the clubhouse, got wasted and high, and then had stormed the streets of downtown Claremont to lay claim to it.

They were arrested about two hours into their little escapade for public intoxication and disorderly conduct—not to mention nailed for underage drinking too—all in the name of proving their general bad-assery and manliness to the rest of the club.

Needless to say, they came to school that next Monday riding high and acting like they owned the place, Caleb in particular. Even though at the time I'd been embarrassingly scandalized by those kind of antics, after talking to Caleb and observing the clubhouse, I got what it really was: a rite of passage and, probably, an initiation of sorts, too.

But that didn't explain why he'd suddenly clammed up on me now.

He cleared his throat and frowned down at me, "I don't really know why or how it started to be honest with you. We've just always sorta done it this way. We've got the shop and the strip club right out of town, but that doesn't really give us enough to survive as a club, at least not comfortably. I think if we ever decided to buy up more of the Oval Office, we'd be doin' better, but Marcus isn't really interested in that right now. Guns get us fast cash and a lot of it too, so I guess I can see why he wouldn't want to jeopardize that."

"How much do you make then?"

I wanted to clamp my hand around my mouth. Stupid word vomit. Now, I'd *definitely* overstepped.

But when his mouth twisted into that crooked, lopsided grin again, I knew I wasn't completely out of line. "At the shop? With the club? Or just in general?"

"With the club," I affirmed.

"Depends on the job and how much extra income we have comin' in on the side. Every month is a little different, but it can be anywhere from 3K to 8. It'll be more when I get the VP patch."

There were other questions simmering underneath, questions I didn't have the stomach to ask, questions that involved drugs and violence and what would happen to him and to us if he was ever caught transferring a 'shipment'. I didn't think I was ready to hear the answers to those questions yet.

As if he could read my thoughts, Caleb pressed his cheek into mine to hug me into his shoulder. "Anything else you wanna know, Iz?"

This was probably all my brain could handle right now. If I tried to shove any more information in there, the whole thing would short circuit.

I shook my head, swallowing back those lingering questions and the answers to those questions that I wasn't so sure I'd be able to handle. He'd answered everything honestly, or at least, it seemed like he had, minus that weird moment when I mentioned his arrest. He'd been forthcoming, hadn't really hesitated, and had answered every question in surprising detail, too. There wasn't much more I could ask from him.

"You think you're ready to head back to the party now?" I asked, choosing to be ignorant to those lingering questions for now.

Caleb's lips curled into that familiar smirk and he leaned forward to kiss me, his hand ghosting underneath my skirt and up my thigh just enough to send shivers sliding down my entire body.

.   .   .

The grounds surrounding the clubhouse provided amble space for some interesting activities. Okay, interesting wasn't exactly the right word. Surprising? No. Shocking? Yeah, that was probably a little closer to the truth.

As we rounded the corner, a makeshift boxing ring was already in full-swing, surrounded by a loud crowd yelling and cheering as they raised their beer bottles to the action in front of them. I'd only ever seen a boxing match on TV before, but as we stepped closer to the crowd, it was clear this wasn't exactly an average fight.

Both men were bare-chested and bare-knuckled, with only their back tattoos as club identifiers and they swung viciously, aiming for any shot to the organs possible. The sick crunch of knuckle on bone, bloody sweat and spit dusting the air...it was gross.

"What is this fight club or something?" I murmured in Caleb's ear.

Despite the roar of the crowd, I could still hear Caleb's chest rumble with laughter.

"Now, Iz, you know the first rule of fight club is that you don't talk about fight club," he shook his head with a grin. "But you gotta admit, it's an easy way to entertain and make some extra cash though, don't ya think?"

A loud roar erupted from the crowd when one of the fighters swung his fist and connected with the other guy's jaw, sending a wet trail of phlegm and blood sky-high into the night air. My uneasiness and discomfort must have colored my expression because Caleb was already leading me away from the crowd and back towards the clubhouse's main doors. A high-pitched whistle had Caleb's head jerking to the side and a Horsemen I recognized as ZZ, with his sharp buzzcut and covered from the neck down in technicolor tattoos, was waving Caleb over.

"Yo, Sawyer! You wanna get in on this?" ZZ held up a particularly menacing tattoo gun with a wide grin and gestured to the empty chair next to him.

There was no hesitation. No second thoughts. Caleb just shrugged and called back, "Sure. Let's do it."

He was already heading towards the designated area, which was far enough off to the side and away from the major action of the party to allow ZZ to do his work. Apparently, they were giving away tattoos at this thing like they were party favors, and it was at this point that my brain finally caught up to what was really about to go down here.

"Wait. What?"

I tugged on his arm a little to get his attention and he frowned back at me. "What?"

"You're just gonna..." I held a hand out towards where ZZ was waiting. "Just like that?"

"Yeah, why not?"

"I don't know."

What I couldn't find the words to say was that I didn't understand how someone, even him, could just impulsively decide to get something forever tattooed on their body without much thought or consideration. Maybe that was because spontaneity and I were casual acquaintances more than anything and the only tattoo I saw myself getting in the near future was the one that forever linked me to Caleb. The idea of getting a tattoo just because didn't compute.

If anything, this was all just one more glaring reminder of how different this world was than the one I'd grown up in and how much I still had to adapt.

"It's not a big deal, babe. I've been thinkin' about gettin' more ink anyways," Caleb was reassuring me now even as he plopped down in ZZ's empty folding chair.

ZZ barely looked up from prepping that glinting needle on his gun. "What you thinkin', bro?"

Caleb pointed at me with a nonchalance he might use if he was ordering a beer. "Her call."

If I'd been sitting, I would've fallen out of my chair.

"What?"

"You heard me, Iz," he smirked up at me. "Sketch somethin' out for me."

I blinked. And then I blinked again. "Are you sure? I mean, it's not like you can just erase it if you decide you don't like it."

"If you're askin' me if I want somethin' you sketched permanently on my body, then the answer is yes."

ZZ wordlessly stood from his chair, dug around in a backpack, and then tossed me a pad of paper and pencil. I don't know how my numb limbs worked long enough to catch it.

"I can trace whatever you put on there," he told me in a gravelly voice, nodding with his head towards the pad in my hands.

When I looked to Caleb, stunned into immobility, all I could see staring back at me was complete trust and confidence. There was no doubt creeping in, no flicker of indecision. This was what he wanted and even though I didn't fully understand how he could act on a whim like this, I sat down in the chair ZZ rustled up for me to get to work.

"Okay," I started carefully. "Where would you want it?"

Caleb pushed up his flannel's long sleeve, flipped his arm over, and patted the inside of his left forearm. "I was thinkin' right here. Somewhere I can see it right away."

ZZ rolled his eyes and shook his head. "You sure you don't just wanna get her name there instead, bro? Save your girl a lot of time."

"Nah," he shrugged. "Not yet. Soon though, Z. You'll get to do that ink when she gets mine."

Caleb winked at me from where he sat and then tipped his chin to the pad of paper in my lap, signaling to me that it was time to get going. The pencil tapped against my chin almost immediately as my mind began to wander, skirting over every possibility. Soon, the cheers, yelling, cursing, music, and even Caleb and ZZ's easy chatter next to me completely tuned out until it was just white noise. My pencil skimmed across the paper, curving and pulling, dancing across the empty space until the vision in my head stared back at me.

It had to be something special. Something he'd immediately

understand and something he also wouldn't get sick of looking at. Something timeless. Something understated, but saturated with meaning.

When I held the sketch out to them, both Caleb and ZZ leaned in at the same time to get a closer look. I knew the second the significance clicked into place for Caleb because his eyes flicked back up to mine, radiating with the warmth and the unconditional love I was starting to feel confident I couldn't live without.

"Your girl's good," ZZ murmured as he slid the pad from my fingertips.

"Yeah, she is," Caleb agreed, a soft smile playing on his lips.

ZZ got to work just as quickly and transferred what I'd just sketched seamlessly onto the tracing paper. But when he moved to set the paper against Caleb's exposed forearm, I shot up from my chair.

"Wait! It actually goes like this," I took the trace from ZZ and gently turned the paper so the compass was facing down. "When anyone else looks at it, they'll think it's upside down, so they wouldn't be able to use it. But when you look at it..."

"It'll be right side up," Caleb finished for me, his voice low and hoarse in a way I'd never heard before.

"So you never lose your way again," I added, my lips curling into a smile and now, it might as well have just been the two of us sitting out here in the parking lot.

ZZ ignored the moment, taking my direction and rubbed something on Caleb's skin before tracing my design onto his forearm as instructed. He paused just long enough to let both Caleb and I inspect it before setting the used tracing paper aside and then the crowd's roar completely died out as the buzzing tattoo gun aimed right for Caleb's forearm.

As the needle grazed over Caleb's skin, I had to sit on my hands just to keep from covering my eyes. My gaze locked on the movement that permanently etched the old-fashioned, upside-down compass onto his arm with the needle's hot scratches. Caleb barely even flinched, not even a crease in his forehead from concentration. I guess this was what high pain tolerance looked like.

Now, as the tattoo began to take clearer shape, I was suddenly struck by the weight of what Caleb had just done. It hadn't really hit me before, but now that we were sitting here, he'd done nothing tonight but show me unrelenting trust.

Trust in my discretion. Trust in my abilities. Trust that, with time, I could be the old lady he needed by his side as we moved up the ranks within the clubhouse together. Now, seeing this boy staring back at me, right on the cusp of being the man I knew he could be, I knew I'd finally figured out where my place was in the clubhouse and it was right beside Caleb Sawyer.

If an old lady's job was to support and love her man, I knew I was unequivocally capable of making that happen. I was already living it. Now, like Caleb suggested, I had to own it, too.

I just had to figure out how to start doing that.

By the time ZZ wiped the excess black ink away, I saw my sketch staring back at me from Caleb's reddened skin.

"There," Caleb murmured, holding up the ink for me to see before ZZ pressed a bandage over it. "Now it's like I'm carrying you with me, right, babe?"

Maybe that was all the confirmation I needed.

I could fit in this life. It wouldn't be easy. I would encounter things that would make me uncomfortable. I wouldn't always understand what Caleb had to do and why. But this was the world he lived in and so it had to be the world I lived in, too.

He supported my passion and encouraged me to follow a dream I wouldn't have realized even existed without him being in my life. So, I had no problem diving in headfirst, even if it scared the hell out of me, if it meant I'd be able to give back what he'd already given me.

We were a team now, navigating these murky waters together, and as long as we stayed united, as long as we walked side by side, we'd be able to weather any storm.

.   .   .

Judging by the heat stifling the air, the sweaty bodies grinding into each other, and Def Leppard's "Pour Some Sugar On Me" pounding through the loudspeakers, the atmosphere inside the clubhouse had quickly deteriorated the second we'd stepped outside before.

It was all I could do to cling to Caleb's arm for dear life as he weaved in and out through the packed crowd so I didn't get tossed and pitched into the moshpit gathering at the center of the main floor. Sensory overload didn't even begin to cover it.

I didn't know exactly which direction we were headed or where we could even really stop just to take a breath it was so congested with hairy, bearded bikers and sweat-slicked half-naked women. Caleb suddenly stopped in his tracks, sending me crashing right into his leathered back, and he immediately swung an arm around my waist to steady me.

Casey, the club's sergeant at arms and from what I could tell, the resident wild card, already had Caleb by the shoulders and his beer bottle almost swiped me right across the face.

"My man!" Casey hollered in Caleb's ear. "I was wonderin' where you ran off to! Saw all the commotion before with that Cobra prick — you shoulda clocked that asshole right in the face!"

As if on cue, Casey's gaze, in all its hazy, glazed-over glory, settled on me from over Caleb's shoulder and then I was suddenly the center of his attention.

"And *you...*" Casey reached around Caleb to put a scratchy hand on my cheek and he squeezed it a little too hard for my liking. "You beautiful, beautiful woman, you. Is my boy here givin' it to you right? He better not be just keepin' a hot little thing like you on her back all night 'cuz he's gotta change it up to keep ya happy. Come here you..."

Before I really knew what was happening, Casey pressed a sloppy, wet kiss on my other cheek and gave me a little shake only to be gently pushed aside by Caleb.

"Alright, Case, alright," Caleb shook his head with a laugh, still keeping Casey away from me at arm's length. "Give her some space."

"I'm sorry," Casey bowed a little to Caleb and then did the same to me, "I'm sorry. I'm drunk. But," he clapped a hand on each of our cheeks as he spoke, "you two are beautiful together. And you know what? You're gonna make beautiful babies together too."

Caleb just shook his head because Casey's hands, beer and all, were already shooting up to the ceiling and he hollered towards the bar along with the rest of the crowd. I guess I shouldn't have been all that surprised, but I still wasn't prepared to turn my head and see my best friend spread out on top of the bar, clad in just a lacy black bra and her jean skirt, as Eli hovered on top of her, casually licking liquor off her stomach. By the time he dipped his head to take the lime from Becca's mouth, I'd already shifted back to Caleb with my eyebrows lodged high into my forehead.

He opened his mouth, but Casey cut him off.

"Get on up there!" Casey was pushing us way too enthusiastically towards the bar. "Your turn! Your turn!"

Caleb was already shaking his head and holding his hands up in surrender. "Nah, Case. I don't think—"

The words flew out of my mouth before I had time to understand what I was agreeing to: "Let's do it."

The shock that flickered across Caleb's face, almost simultaneous with the pure, unadulterated joy that spread across Casey's...absolutely priceless and totally worth what I think I was about to do.

Caleb's lips spread apart like he wanted to speak, but was just too baffled and awestruck to know how to even form the words.

Well, if I was going to live in this world, I might as well go all in. No point in doing this half-assed. No point in anyone thinking I was the lone prude in the clubhouse, especially since that wasn't who I was. I was confident in my sexuality and as far as I could tell, part of being an old lady was putting that sexuality on display every once in a while if necessary.

Time to sink or swim and damn it, I was gonna swim. If this was my initiation, I was gonna own it.

I grabbed Caleb by the arm and led him towards the bar with Casey hot on our heels.

"You sure, babe?" Caleb's warm breath found my ear.

"Just make sure no one can see up my skirt, okay?"

He leaned down as we sidled up to the bar, "That's happenin' over my dead body, Iz."

"Good," I laughed and turned on my heel so my back pressed up against the bar.

Caleb shot me a quick wink, amid the roar of the crowd and Becca's hollering right next to me, and his warm hands closed around my hips to hoist me up onto the bar. His hands locked firmly on my knees, careful to keep them closed tight as I slid my legs onto the sticky wood to settle back. Caleb leapt up on the bar right next to my feet just as the beats of "Hard to Handle" by The Black Crowes thumped from the speakers. He stalked towards my body with hooded eyes and a sexy grin twisting his lips, like he couldn't believe what he was seeing, but was planning on loving every second of it.

He hovered over me until he kneeled down between my legs as I tucked the bottom of my tank top into the space by my cleavage. Casey appeared next to us from the floor with a salt shaker in one hand and a bottle of tequila in the other and someone handed me a slice of lime from behind my head. Caleb's hands planted on either side of my stomach and his head dipped low to lick a long, hot trail from my belly right up to the edge of my bra.

I sucked in a breath and suddenly, all I could focus on was his blonde head ducked low and his body hovering in between my legs. My eyes fluttered shut at the heady contact and then I felt something sprinkling over the trail his mouth just made. The warm, wetness from his tongue slid up my bare stomach again, licking up the salt, and when I opened my eyes to find Caleb watching me, I forgot about the crowd all together. It might as well have just been us, in my bed, in his dorm, on the floor, up against a counter. It didn't matter. I could do this with him anywhere and I could own it, too.

Caleb sat up to let Casey pour tequila into my belly button and then he got a little liberal with the pour, spreading it around my stomach and curving it around my neck. I readied the lime in between my lips, eager to feel his mouth on my bare skin again and he didn't hesitate, greedily sucking up the tequila and spreading hot, little tremors down my entire body. He leaned forward to get better access to my neck and then my hands were in his hair before I could stop myself.

We might've been putting on a little show, but it really wasn't for anyone but us.

His lips closed over the lime, gently squeezing it with his teeth until the citrus liquid dripped down my chin and then he tossed it aside with his teeth so he could seal his lips over my mouth, kissing me senseless until I forgot I was even lying across a bar with a crowd of people cheering us on in the first place. As he started to pull away, I took his bottom lip between my teeth and sucked a little just because I couldn't help myself.

Caleb sat back on his knees, grinning down at me like he'd just won the lottery and I was the prize. When he jumped back down to the floor, his hands were already ghosting over my knees to clamp them together as he turned me and helped me slide off the top. His hands closed around both sides of my face, ignoring the cat calls and whistles behind us, and captured my mouth one more time, plunging his tongue through my lips until I felt drunk on tequila and him.

Initiation complete.

CHAPTER THIRTY-SEVEN
Breath of Life

Six Weeks Later

Isabelle

When I shoved the last of my boxes in the back of Caleb's truck, cold panic gripped my heart and it stuttered and skipped as I watched Caleb pull the tonneau cover down and shut the door of the cab.

It was actually starting to feel real. I was really leaving Claremont tomorrow morning and moving to my dorm at VCU.

Seeing all my personal belongings packed up and in the back of the cab like this was the final nail in the coffin of my life as I knew it.

My brain tried to talk me off the ledge and somehow convince myself that this was really the right choice. I knew I was talented enough to do well at VCU and in the D.C. art scene in general. A whole other life waited for me in Richmond and I knew I should be excited by all the prospects and new possibilities.

Caleb and I had already come so far and in these last two months we'd spent together, I'd never felt happier, never felt this safe, this whole, this *me*. The idea of upending that, of potentially chipping away at our connection with distance and time...the thought alone sent my heart flip-flopping into my stomach.

I jumped a little when Caleb's wind-chilled hands ghosted over my shoulders and pulled me into his flannel-covered arms. Everything about him surrounded me now: the soft comfort of his shirt, worn in from use, leather, gasoline, musk, grease. I wanted to bottle it up and tuck it into my purse.

Tears stung my eyes because after tomorrow, I wouldn't be able to feel this everyday like I could now. I wouldn't be able to wake up in his arms everyday, I wouldn't be able to kiss him everyday, to laugh with him, to talk to him face to face and I didn't know if I could really do this, if I could really leave and still somehow be okay.

"You wanna go back inside now, Iz?" Caleb whispered in my ear. "Head to bed? We got a big day tomorrow and everything..."

He trailed off like he couldn't bring himself to finish that thought and I knew he was struggling with this just as much as I was. While he was trying to be strong and present a resilient front that everything was going to be *fine*, we both knew neither of us were fine right now.

I wasn't Ariel and would never ask him to follow me to VCU. Granted the circumstances weren't the same, but there was no point in talking about what ifs because our only other option was to cut our losses and go our separate ways.

So here we were, on the eve of my inevitable departure away from Claremont. We weren't over, but we were also never going to be the same. This distance was going to change our relationship and we hadn't talked about that either. It probably had something to do with the fact that we were so good right now—what was the point in destroying what little time we had left to really enjoy it?

We loved each other and as Caleb had already told me countless times, that had to be enough. That had to be enough to see us through the next two years of five-hour road trips on the weekends and spending the majority of our time apart.

Suddenly, with all of this heaviness looming around us, I needed to do something for him. The last few weeks, all he'd done was reassure me and give me the confidence and resolve I needed to go through with packing up and moving. I wanted to give him the same reassurance, even if he was probably going to need a little convincing first.

"Hey, baby?" I started softly. "Can you do something for me?"

"Anything, Iz."

"Can you take me to the your dorm tonight?"

His arms stiffened around me and while this was obviously headed for an uphill battle, I was determined to do this for him whether he liked it or not.

"Babe, I don't know," he grimaced. "I mean, we're already here at your place and you know how I feel about takin' you there."

I shifted my hips a little bit closer to his waist, hoping it would help him read my message a little more clearly. "I know, Caleb, but I want to spend my last night in town there. With you. In your bed. Can we do that? Please?"

He sighed and rested his chin on the top of my head. "I haven't really been there in weeks. It's dirty. I've got shit everywhere. It probably smells. I don't know."

"I don't care about any of that. I just wanna be with you tonight in *your* bed," I jutted out my bottom lip to pout a little just for good measure.

He sighed again and lifted his eyes to the darkened sky above us. "I guess I can't really say no to you, Iz. If that's what you want, then I guess that's what you're gonna get."

I grinned widely and stood up on my toes to brush my lips against his. "That's what I thought."

I spent the entire ride to the clubhouse pressed as closely into him as possible and in turn, his arm wrapped its way around my waist, hugging me tightly into his side. It was like we couldn't get close enough and we couldn't let go for long because we both knew that, inevitably, our time like this was limited from here on out.

.   .   .

When Caleb held the door open for me, he really hadn't been exaggerating about the mess or...the smell, either. To be fair, he'd probably only really stopped in at various points in the past few weeks to grab clean clothes and drop off the dirty ones. He'd even been showering at my house, so there really hadn't been much reason for him to spend much time in this room when he'd obviously wanted to spend that time with me somewhere we could really be alone.

As I walked through the threshold, Caleb scrambled past me, shoving the dirty clothes underneath his bed and kicking some of the stray trash out of the way, but all I could really do was just chew on the inside of my cheek as he flitted around the room. He didn't need to do this because I didn't really care what the room looked or smelled like.

All that mattered was that we were here.

"I, uh, I wouldn't go in the bathroom if I were you, Iz," Caleb was saying now as he ran a hand over his face. "You're probably better off just using the one in the hallway."

I dropped my overnight bag on the floor and just shrugged. "It honestly doesn't matter, baby."

Reaching for him until both hands clasped around the closures of his cut, I pulled him closer to me, needing to do this for him more than I needed anything else tonight.

"Caleb," I whispered. "I know you don't like bringing me here and I get it. I really do. I know how many girls have been in here before me and—"

Caleb blew out a shaky breath and dropped down onto the bed. The way he was rubbing both hands on his thighs anxiously and his chest was heaving in and out—for a moment, I almost thought he was having a panic attack. So I decided to put him at ease and stepped forward until I straddled him on the bed, wrapping both arms around his neck to bring him even closer.

"Baby," I started slowly and smiled when his eyes glazed over at our closeness. "I love you and I'd be a complete idiot not to care about what's already happened in this room. I know you're not innocent. I don't even want to know how many nights you passed out on this bed with some girl next to you. I saw it too many times and I hated it every single time."

His eyes widened at this new revelation and I just hitched my legs even closer to his waist.

"I'm not saying none of that matters because you and I both know that's not true," I went on carefully. "But I'm not exactly innocent either, you know and I don't think either of us have anything to hide. So, that being said, I want you to know that from here on out, I'm giving us a clean slate. I want us to be able to be in this room and have a good time without you worrying that I'm stressing out over your past and without me actually thinking about what's gone on in this room before me. You are my future, Caleb, and because of that, nothing that happened in either of our pasts matters. When I come home on the weekends, I want us to be able to spend our time here, in this bed, and not think about anything but making the most of our time. Is that alright with you?"

He gazed up at me, his blue eyes swimming with more emotions than I could properly decipher, and then his lips closed over mine.

"Babe, that's more than alright. I really love you, you know that?"

"Yeah," I laughed against his lips. "I know and I love you, too."

I gently pushed his cut off his shoulders and tossed it on the chair next to his bed, fumbling with the buttons on his flannel as his hands went to work on my jeans. He groaned against my lips and flipped me around so he could tug my jeans all the way off. My hands were already skimming his flannel from his shoulders and then I lifted his undershirt up and over his head.

I'd thought that tonight everything would feel more desperate than normal, but it was slower, like we were taking our time, like we knew we just had tonight and needed to make the most of it.

All I needed were his lips and his hands on every inch of my skin, touching me, tasting me, loving me and then maybe I could wake up tomorrow feeling fulfilled and satisfied enough to push through.

His kisses were just as tender and gentle as I needed them to be and I felt cherished. I felt loved.

We were making new memories in this bed now and there wasn't a better or more fitting night to erase everything that had come before. My breath left my lungs in one heavy sigh as our emotional connection manifested itself into a physical one.

My hands dug into his back as our hips moved into that easy rhythm we'd found weeks ago and his hands lifted my hips up to hit the spot he knew so well by now. Every touch, every rock of his hips, every moment sent me further over the edge and I just wanted to savor this, to burn it into my memory so I could remember this feeling.

His movements were gentle and cautious like he was worried if he went too fast, I might disappear right from underneath him. And when we came down and rested shoulder to shoulder, I knew this particular moment would forever be one of my favorite memories with him.

Because in spite of everything we were about to face, in spite of everything we had already faced, he never ceased to show me just how much he loved me and this time, he'd told me everything I needed to know.

I shifted a little so that my head was resting on my elbow and grinned down at him. "So was that as horrible as you thought it would be?"

Caleb barked out a laugh and playfully yanked me against his bare, still sweaty chest. "Watch it, babe. Seriously, I think you must have some secret plans to kill me or somethin'."

Nuzzling into his neck, I nibbled his earlobe just enough to make him groan.

"I was right," he growled. "You really are tryin' to kill me, woman."

"Maybe I'm just trying to get as much of you as I can," I whispered into his ear.

Caleb sighed and turned his head so he could press a tender kiss into my forehead. "I'm not going anywhere, Iz. And I think you did a pretty good job of telling me you're not going anywhere either, babe."

"I know," I played with the edge of his comforter to distract myself. "Do you think maybe we could just stay here like this forever? I think I could lay here with you and never move from this spot for the rest of my life and be perfectly okay with that."

He chuckled into my hair and pulled me even tighter against his chest. "I know what you mean, babe. I don't think it's really hit me yet, you know? I guess it just seems like tomorrow we're gonna wake up and keep doing all the things we've been doing."

"I guess it's hard to accept that things are gonna change. I mean, I know you love me and I know you know I love you, but we can't pretend the distance isn't going to matter because it is, Caleb."

"Hey," he stiffened beside me and his voice took on a sharp edge now. "I don't wanna hear that shit from you, Iz. We've been over this already and it's gonna be hard, but you and me are gonna be fine."

A second later, he sighed again and scrubbed his free hand over his face. "I'm sorry. I didn't mean to—"

"I know, baby," I replied simply, his outburst already forgotten.

We were both on edge, which was crazy given the way we'd just expended some serious frustrated energy, and I guess I couldn't blame him for not being able to hold it in anymore.

There was really no point in arguing, especially not tonight when what we really needed to do was just wrap our arms around each other for as long as time let us.

I never should've brought it up tonight in the first place and maybe he was right, anyways. Maybe all of my pre-existing notions about how long-distance relationships worked—or didn't work—didn't apply to us. Maybe all this worry and hand-wringing was just wasted time and effort. Maybe I was just jumping the gun in assuming that our relationship would suffer because of this.

After all, we loved each other, I reasoned as I let my fingers lightly trace over the compass tattooed on his forearm. So, shouldn't we be able to withstand anything that life threw our way?

.   .   .

I trudged up the stairs towards my new dorm and barely got the heavy metal door open long enough to pass through. Caleb's tattooed arm shot out to hold it open from behind me, even though he was already balancing one of my boxes in his other hand and I sent him an appreciative glance over my shoulder as we started down the hallway towards my new room. Because I was only on the second floor, we'd decided to ignore the elevator, which, in hindsight, was a bad choice.

My heart pounded with dread as we approached room 207 and I could already feel tears stinging my eyes as Caleb stood beside me at the doorway with the box in his hands. With the way things were already going, I didn't think I'd be able to make it through the whole day without breaking down.

I'd promised myself I wouldn't cry until after he left, but now it didn't seem like I was going to find the strength to hold myself together because my bottom lip was already quivering.

I rapped on the door, checking to see if my new roommate was here, and slid the key in the door to push it open. The room was exactly what I'd expected. Boring, monotonous furniture. Cramped living space. Awesome.

"Shit," Caleb exhaled behind me. "Are college dorms supposed to be this small?"

"It's pretty much the same size as the one I lived in freshman year at Duke," I just shrugged and set the box in my hands next to the empty bed.

I didn't really know the story of why this room was open or what had happened to my new roommate's *old* roommate, but in the grand scheme of things, it didn't really matter. What mattered now was that my new roommate wasn't here, so Caleb and I would be able to move me in and say goodbye without an audience.

Caleb had already set the box on the bed and perched his hands on his hips as he surveyed the tiny square of a room.

"That's an awfully small bed, Iz," he muttered under his breath.

I smiled in spite of myself and wrapped an arm around his waist. "We've maneuvered around a twin bed before, so I'm sure we'll be able to figure it out again."

"Well, I'm always up for a challenge," he cocked an eyebrow down at me. "You know, I already got it figured out. That bed's clearly not big enough for the both of us, so I guess you're just gonna have to sleep on top of me when I'm here."

"Wow, that sure didn't take long," I laughed.

"Funny how you didn't say one word about the sleepin' on top of me part. Guess that means you're lookin' forward to it, huh?"

"Jackass," I muttered under my breath, even as my lips curved up into a grin.

For a moment there, he'd almost gotten my mind completely off the real matter at hand. And then, when I realized all those boxes were still stowed away in the back of his truck, reality crept back in.

"Well, Iz," he smiled, his lips curving up to let me know, without him having to say it, that he loved me. "I guess we'd better head down for trip number two."

About a half hour later, the last of my boxes and duffel bags were sitting in my new dorm room. We still hadn't seen my new roommate, but that was just fine. Time was running away from us and all I wanted to do was hold on to him a little bit longer.

Sooner or later, Caleb was going to have to get back in his truck and drive the five hours back to Claremont without me. While I knew I'd see him the next weekend—I'd be taking a train home so I could drive my car back to school—the thought of him driving away and leaving me here nearly had me plummeting over the edge.

"So," Caleb was saying now. "Everything's all here. Should we grab somethin' to eat? Did you still wanna show me the art building?"

Yes. Yes. Absolutely.

Anything to keep him here a little bit longer, but I couldn't say that because it really wouldn't do either of us any good. The only option I had was just to savor what little time we had left before having to separate for an entire week. I knew seven days wasn't that long, but God, it would be. It absolutely would be.

So, because my thoughts were betraying bitches right now, I just nodded and gestured with my head toward the door.

We left the dorm hand in hand and rounded the corner of the hallway. This was the only time I think I'd ever seen him without his Horsemen cut when he wasn't working at the shop, but I was grateful he'd left it in his truck today.

On top of everything else, any unnecessary attention would just be extra stress we didn't need and he was technically still representing the club with his white Horsemen T-shirt. Seeing him in his cut today would've probably been too much for me to handle anyways because it would just be one more reminder of what I was leaving behind. Not the club—just *him*. Everything he was. Everything he needed to do and be a part of in Claremont and a tiny, unspoken part of me wondered if I'd even be around to see it.

Those kind of thoughts were what my dad would call, "the devil's argument", not like he had too much of a say anymore in my life anyways. We'd barely spoken during the two months he'd been in rehab and he still had one more month to survive. He seemed to be doing well, but what scared me was what would happen when he was released, on his own, and without me around to look out for him.

Caleb would do it if I asked, but the two of them were like oil and water—they'd just never be able to mix.

We found a restaurant almost immediately after crossing the street from campus. With VCU located right in the heart of the city, you could basically turn a corner and find something you were looking for, whether it was food, entertainment, or shopping, but that wasn't why I was here.

After eating a quiet lunch and making small talk about anything to keep our minds off the inevitable, Caleb quickly paid the bill and then we were heading back towards campus. I'd actually never really been on campus before and had just seen it from pictures online, so I knew there should be some part of me jumping with joy to finally take it all in.

That part of me was smothered and snuffed out by the other part of me screaming its head off.

Still, we found the art building relatively quickly and snuck inside to get a better look at where I would be spending the majority of my time. There were studios and classrooms to spare with student work expertly on display throughout the entire building. Modern architecture oozed from every seam in the wall and I knew that an art student, or really any student, would be foaming at the mouth to get to spend any amount of time here in this building.

I wanted to be grateful Caleb was here this first time, but I just wanted to curl into his shoulder and finally let the dam break loose.

When we started the short trek from the art building back to my dorm, my feet dragged and crawled, doing everything they could to stall by the time we trudged up the steps back to my floor. The tightening in my chest felt like someone was literally reaching inside and squeezing the life out of my heart.

And when room 207 came into view, my shoulders began to tremble.

Caleb's hands settled gently over my shoulders, ever in-tune with my emotions, and it took all of my strength not to just crumble right there under his touch. It was already past 5:00 and he still had a five-hour drive back to Claremont, which meant he'd have to leave soon and I'd be here...alone and without him.

With a heavy heart, I put my key back in the lock and pushed the door open. As we started back inside, I jumped a little, startled to see someone else in the room. A short girl with wild, pixie-like dark hair turned from where she sat at her desk and then a wide, welcoming smile spread across her cute face.

"Hey!" my roommate greeted us happily and stood up from her chair to close the distance between us. "You must be Isabelle! I'm sorry I wasn't here earlier, but I had to work," she stepped closer with her hand extended. "I'm Gwen. It's so great to finally meet you!"

Her cheerfulness instinctively set me on edge. It wasn't her fault, but this was just not cool because right now, happy people were assholes.

"Hi..." I replied finally. "It's nice to finally meet you, too."

I gestured towards Caleb and if I'd been in a better mood, I would've laughed when Gwen's eyes widened the size of saucers when she got a good look at him. But I wasn't in a better mood. I was in a shit mood and so I mumbled, "This is Caleb, my boyfriend."

Boyfriend wasn't the right term for what he was to me, but in this circumstance, it was the easiest explanation I could give. He didn't waste the opportunity and hitched an arm securely around my waist to pull me flush against him, reaching out to shake Gwen's waiting hand.

"Nice to meet ya, darlin'," he winked at her and Gwen faltered a little, looking short of breath and high on my boyfriend.

I would've rolled my eyes at this entire ridiculous exchange if I wasn't already on the verge of a nervous breakdown. Thankfully, Gwen seemed to sense the shift in the air and she quickly turned on her heel to grab her bag and her jacket from the chair at her desk.

"I'll just, uh, grab some food so you guys can, um...I'll see you later, okay, Isabelle?" Gwen waved a little as she stepped around us to head out the door, graciously closing it behind her.

"Well," Caleb called out softly. "She seems nice, huh?"

I rolled my eyes. "I think she's in love with you already."

Caleb playfully tilted his head and rocked back on his heels. "Isn't everybody, Iz?"

I knew what he was trying to do, but it wasn't working. That stiff hold around my heart tightened into a vice-like grip and I had to sink down on the bed because I just couldn't handle it anymore.

Caleb dipped down next to me and wrapped an arm around my shoulders. I shifted in his arms so I could bury my face in his neck and then both his arms closed around me, reassuring me that, once again, everything was going to be okay.

"I should probably get goin', babe," he murmured in my hair. "I don't want to but..."

"I know," I nodded into his skin and then the dam broke, releasing every tear I'd been holding in since the moment we pulled out of the parking lot this morning.

My shoulders were shaking now and his fingers tangled in my hair, gently massaging my head in a vain attempt to ease some of this tension.

But I knew that it wasn't going to get better. It was only going to get worse the second he left this room.

"Iz," Caleb murmured gently. "I don't want anybody but you—you know that, right?"

Because my voice failed me, I just nodded.

He pulled my face out from his neck with gentle, tender movements and brushed some stray hair away from my face. "I'm so damned proud of you I can barely see straight. I can't wait to go to those things where they show all your work—what are they called?"

"Gallery openings?" I offered with a weak laugh.

"Yeah, those things. I'll be the first one in line and then I'll be standin' there braggin' about how I knew you before you got all rich and famous *and* how I get to take you home at night, too."

I laughed through my tears, trembling a little when his thumbs brushed away another fresh stream.

"This is absolutely the right choice, Iz," he told me firmly, both of his hands closing around my face to reiterate his point. "This is where you need to be and I don't want you to waste a second of your time here regretting it. It's just two years, Iz. We can live with anything for two years. We're good, babe. We always have been and we always will be."

His words just sent another shock wave of sobs through my body.

"I really love you," I whispered.

"I love you too, Iz."

He eased back just enough to brush his lips against my forehead and then shifted a little to dig into his back pocket. A piece of folded paper materialized in his hand and he passed it to me with a sad smile.

"Don't open it until I'm gone, okay?" he instructed, his voice soft and hoarse. "I guess I just wanted to give you something you could keep here in your room."

My fingers itched to unfold the thin paper, but I could give him this. I didn't think I'd be able to survive opening his note *and* watching him leave all in the span of a few minutes either.

He leaned down to brush his lips against my fingertips and then he rose from the bed. With my chest heaving, dangerously teetering on the edge of an all-out breakdown, I reached out for him again, desperate to keep him here a little longer.

"Iz," he whispered hoarsely, his nostrils flaring like he was struggling to stay strong, struggling to keep himself together. "I should get going."

Somehow my weak, shaky legs carried me all the way to the door. When he turned back to me, I flung into his arms and buried my face in his chest. He kissed my hair, my forehead, both cheeks, and finally my lips before gently pulling back, his heartbroken blue eyes shining with moisture.

"I love you," he whispered, holding my face with both hands.

My tears almost choked the words. "I love you too."

He kissed me one last time before opening my door and walking out into the hallway. When he pivoted back around to face me, his eyes were red, his chest was heaving, his beautiful face twisted with agony like he was about to break down right in front of me. He scrubbed a hand over his face and then yanked me to him one last time as I buried my face in his chest.

Finally, he stepped away and his lips spread in what was more of a grimace than a grin, his eyes shimmering with heartache and grief.

"See ya next weekend," he called out hoarsely. "Call me whenever you want, alright, Iz?"

I could only nod as he backpedalled down the hallway, our hands still intertwined until his fingers slipped away and my hand fell down at my side. With the rest of me helpless, I wiped away another stray tear from my cheek as I watched the only boy I'd ever really loved stalk down the hallway and push through the doors.

Remembering the paper still clenched in my fist, I quickly shut the door behind me and leaned against it to squeeze out another wave of tears from my eyes. It was only by some miracle that I was able to wait long enough to flop down on the bed before my fingers nimbly unfolded the paper Caleb had given me.

My eyes skimmed over the page and my free hand slapped over my mouth as my shoulders shook with sobs. There was just no choking it back any longer.

The page, with its rough edges and fraying on one side, had clearly been ripped out from a book, but it was the words themselves that broke down the little strength I had left.

The eloquent words of ee cummings' "i carry your heart [i carry it with me]" stared back at me and it took my brain a second to catch up to what my eyes were seeing. Next to the poem, Caleb had scrawled in his familiar chicken scratches: *Iz, I hope you're not mad I defaced a book, but I had to do it. This guy says everything I'm feeling better than I ever could. Love you, Caleb.*

My eyes flew over the words he'd underlined, *"no fate (for you are my fate, my sweet) no world (for you are my world, my true)/and it's you are whatever a moon has always meant and whatever a sun will always sing is you."*

I had to squeeze my eyes shut because it was just too goddamn painful. Tears poured from my eyes and onto the naked mattress, leaving salty stains in their wake.

This just wasn't fair.

And this just didn't feel right.

How had I ever talked myself into believing I'd really be happy here without him?

Because next to the schools in New York and Chicago, I told myself, *this is one of the best art schools in the country. You got into the number seven school in the country and you'd be stupid not to go.*

I'd earned the right to go to art school.

So many years of doing what everyone else wanted me to do and not once had I really given much thought to what would actually make *me* happy. Duke hadn't been the answer and I'd just gone through with it because it was expected of me. I'd wanted to believe that this, VCU, was the answer, but now that I was here, nothing about this appealed to me anymore.

I was starting to understand it never really had in the first place.

Because I knew, instinctively, that every moment I spent here away from Caleb would be every moment I'd begin to resent this choice.

On some level, when had this *actually* been my choice?

When I'd gotten my acceptance letters, Caleb pretty much decided VCU was it and I'd went along with it without putting up much of a fight. He had the best of intentions and that just made me love him even more, but I'd taken the choice away from myself, for the most part, the second I shoved those unopened acceptance letters into his chest.

If it was truly my decision and my decision alone, would I have really chosen VCU, in a city five *hours* away, over UNC, in a city 45 *minutes* away?

None of this was Caleb's fault. That wasn't the issue here. All he was guilty of was wanting what was best for me because he loved me.

But what *was* best? What was actually the right decision? Because the longer I sat here, the more I realized that maybe this wasn't it either. This wasn't where I needed to be. This wasn't where I *wanted* to be and I think, deep down, I'd always known that.

So, I had a problem on my hands.

I could suck it up at VCU because, well, I was already here — I'd already enrolled in classes and I'd sent in a tuition payment already for the spring semester, not to mention set up student loans to cover the rest. I could go back to Claremont and wait it out a semester to give myself a little breathing room. Or I could go back to Claremont, try to get my spot back at UNC, and commute to Winston-Salem.

The bottom line was: what was going to make *me* happy? What was going to take away this excruciating, gut-wrenching, agonizing feeling?

Being five hours away from Caleb wasn't going to make me happy. Nothing worked without him. Nothing made sense without him. Nothing felt right without him.

There was no way I'd be able to feel good about anything I achieved here if he wasn't really here to share it with me. Besides, he was the main reason I'd even considered applying for art schools in the first place. There was no way I would've had the guts to even acknowledge this dream if it weren't for his strong and supportive guidance. Doing any of this without him here to experience it with me, to share in my successes and support me in my failures...

No, I wasn't doing this without him.

But I also knew that if I put off school, even if I told myself it was only for a semester, what were the odds that I would try again?

If I didn't do this now and waited too long, would I miss my chance to become a professional artist? One who showed their work in galleries and had people pay money to not only see their work, but had those same people actually buy it? A few years ago, that hadn't even been a remote possibility, but the more I'd thought about art school and the whole art scene in general, the more I realized that that, too, was where I wanted to be.

I would always regret it if I didn't do it. I would always look back at this opportunity and wonder what would've happened if I'd had the strength and the courage to realize my dream and my passion.

And then the answer was simple. There really was no other choice.

Why couldn't I have both? Why couldn't I seek out one dream while living out another? There was really only one thing I could do that would satisfy everything I wanted and Caleb's note was the wake-up call I'd needed to get my ass in gear.

Caleb had said VCU was a once in a lifetime opportunity, but he was also my once in a lifetime love.

Ever since I'd left Duke and come home to Claremont, I'd been so adrift, searching for some sort of direction, some sort of meaning and purpose in my life. I'd wanted to take control of my life and to start living my life by my own rules, not someone else's.

Now the chance was right in front me and I could feel myself sliding into the driver's seat, revving the engine, waiting for that green light.

I'd never felt this in control of my life before. Everything had always seemed to just happen to me and all my actions as a result were just reactive to circumstances I'd never had any control over to begin with. But in this moment, I was the master of my own destiny. I was the keeper of my dreams and the pursuer of my passions.

I was done sitting on the sidelines, watching the game and cheering on the players. I wanted *in*. I wanted to *live*. I wanted to be *happy*.

The way I saw it I could choose to be miserable or I could choose to be happy. I was going to choose happy.

Anyone that disagreed with my choice could go fuck themselves.

With my resolve strong and my mind firm in this decision, the first one I'd truly made for myself in way too long, I leapt off the bed and tucked Caleb's note in my back pocket for safekeeping.

I had some calls to make and some serious work to do.

CHAPTER THIRTY-EIGHT
Carry Your Heart

Caleb

Every step that took me further away was just another nail pounding right into my already shredded heart.

Leaving the other half of my soul in room 207 was the hardest thing I'd ever had to do in my life and my only real comfort here was knowing I'd done the right thing. She had too much talent and too much potential to just waste away in Claremont and work at the shop for the rest of her life.

And I knew, as I unlocked my truck and dropped heavily into the driver's seat, that eventually, the distance would probably end up killing us.

I hadn't allowed her to even broach that subject before she left because I knew it would only make her think about staying. She wasn't giving this up because of me. Sure, she could go to school somewhere else, but this was a once in a lifetime opportunity.

All the hot galleries to showcase new artists working anywhere near here were based out of D.C. and from what I could tell and what Eli had been able to dig up, if she wanted a decent shot at getting a spot in any of those galleries, she needed to be at VCU so she could start networking. Not in Claremont and not even in North Carolina.

If someone had told me last September that I would find myself in the exact same position as when Ariel left with *Isabelle Martin* of all people, I probably would've bought that person a shot just for the good laugh.

I guess if I was being really honest with myself, I knew it all boiled down to the fact that I just didn't deserve to have someone like her in my life. She was too good, too sweet, too innocent, and too trusting to be with someone like me.

And that wasn't even the tip of the iceberg of the danger I could potentially be putting her in because of the club. Marcus' words at Dom and Lexie's reception still haunted my sleep every night since and even though I knew my old lady was strong and could handle whatever came our way, there was only so much a person could take. Someone who wasn't born into this life naturally had a lower tolerance for all things club-related and I couldn't take that for granted.

But in spite of all that, I still wished things were different. God, I would give anything to be able to spend the rest of my life with her. To be able to call her my wife and the mother of my children. For the last two months, I'd tricked my brain into only thinking optimistically, but now that reality had reared its ugly head, the trick was wearing thin. The reality was that maybe it was all just wishful thinking after all.

And the cruelest trick of all was that I'd had a taste of what my life would be like if I'd be able to actually keep her. I knew what it was like to wake up with her in my arms, to be able to kiss her in the morning and hold her at night, to be able to show her off as mine and parade her on the back of my bike, to hold her hand and revel in the time she was giving me, to laugh with her, to dance with her, to sit happily at her side as she went after her dream...it was torture knowing all this and knowing that my time with her might have an expiration date now.

She needed to leave.

It was *right* for her to leave.

Past experience had taught me there was a huge difference between *wanting* to leave and *having* to leave.

Despite initial appearances, her life had never been easy and even though I knew a little something about having a legacy to follow, it was different when the legacy wasn't one you actually wanted to follow. She'd spent the better part of her life doing everything her shitty-ass father wanted her to do and I hated that it had taken her mother's death to make her snap the hell out of it and finally find her own way.

That way, coincidentally, was going to clear her out of Claremont and shred my heart in the process. Her leaving for art school was really just the punctuation on a sentence that had already been written.

And as much as it would slaughter my heart, I wasn't angry. I wasn't bitter. I wasn't going to scream and yell. I wasn't going to beg and plead. If she was happy and safe, then that was all I could ask for and I was at peace with that.

I didn't know exactly when the tears started during my trip back to Claremont. At some point, I just stopped wiping them away altogether and let them carve a salty path down my face. No one was here to see these few hours of weakness anyways, so as long as I could pull myself together before pulling back into the shop's lot, I just didn't give a shit how much I was sobbing like a baby right now.

I'd hung on to Ariel for so long, all but chaining myself to her leg as she dragged herself out of town and now here I was, in the exact same position, but had driven Isabelle to VCU myself.

If that wasn't irony, then I guess I didn't know what was.

The real difference here, though, was me. With Ariel, I'd clung to old memories, desperate to keep my life exactly how it was and refusing to change. But the life I'd had with Ariel was a fantasy. Living in rose-colored glasses blinded me and now that I'd smashed those glasses and tossed them in the garbage, I could see what my life with her really was —absolutely painful.

There was always an argument, always something to prove, and a feeling of worthlessness always trailed after me when she was around, even though I'd never understood why I wasn't ever enough for her. The fact was: I just didn't know who I was without Ariel back then. My whole life revolved around her, almost more so than the club, and that obsession had pretty much made me miserable every second we were together.

With Isabelle, none of that mattered. She made me feel invincible and a foot taller. And when she told me she loved me, I believed her.

Loving her was like breathing. It was just instinct. You don't question breathing and you don't question instinct. You just do it.

And I loved Isabelle enough to realize when I needed to let her go, which meant selfishness and immaturity had no place in my life anymore. I needed to be strong for her, I needed to be supportive of her, and I needed to be willing to let her go if that's what was best for her.

My eyes drifted down to the compass tattooed on my left forearm and squeezed my eyes shut. I'd never regret loving her. I'd never regret the time I'd gotten to have with her, even if that time had to be short.

I wished there some way we could make this work for the long haul. The time apart, the distance...when life got crazy, I knew seeing each other every weekend just wouldn't be possible either...it could all slowly chip away at even the most solid foundation, and I knew ours was already pretty strong.

But now that I'd had her, now that I loved her, the course of my life had been forever altered and I just didn't know what I was going to do without her.

And with that thought, I pulled back into the shop's parking lot, my focus resting sullenly on the empty passenger seat next to me.

My mom was already waiting for me outside the clubhouse and I pushed out a weary breath. The last thing I wanted to do right now was deal with people, especially my mother. She'd want to comfort me and reassure me that everything was going to be fine, but I really didn't want to hear it. Still, I knew my mother and I also knew she wasn't going to leave tonight until she at least checked on me. Might as well get it over with now.

"Baby," my mom's soft voice called out to me as I shut the truck's driver side door. She was already moving towards me, so I just met her halfway. "I'd ask how you're doin' but..."

I'd never been so grateful for a loss of words in my life.

"How was your drive?" she asked finally, draping an arm around my shoulders and pulling me into a tight hug.

"It was fine," I shrugged. My voice was hoarse and heavy, which just made the fact that I'd been crying that much more obvious.

"Oh, Caleb," she whispered into my ear. "I wish there was something I could do or say to make this better for you."

"There's not," I muttered. "There's nothin' you can say that I don't already know, Ma. But thanks, though. Hey, listen, I'm tired and I just wanna go to bed. I'll call ya in the morning, alright?"

She nodded sympathetically and carefully released me, like she wasn't sure whether or not she should let me walk inside the clubhouse on my own. I shot her a weak smile in a lame attempt at reassuring her, but I knew better. My mom probably wouldn't sleep much tonight either because she too had become more attached to Isabelle than she'd ever intended.

Yeah.

I knew the feeling.

Finally, she let me walk away and after pushing through the crowd and brushing past the watchful eyes of my club brothers, I collapsed on my bed. I almost thought about grabbing the half-empty bottle of Jack buried somewhere in my closet and finishing it off, but past experience had also taught me that wouldn't solve my problems either.

If anything, it would only make this worse. I was better off just passing out face down in my bed and sleeping as far into tomorrow afternoon as I could.

As I settled back onto the mattress, my nose found the pillow Isabelle slept on the night before. It still smelled like flowers and vanilla and I immediately rolled over on my side to put myself out of my misery.

Somehow, my weary body sank deep into my bed and just, mercifully, shut down for a few hours.

. . .

I'd drifted away into a black, dreamless sleep. It was numbing and fantastic. And that was why, when loud pounding on my door jerked me awake, I just rolled over and planted face first in my pillow. I didn't care if the clubhouse was burning down — I wasn't moving from this spot.

Whoever was pounding on my door was relentless. It just wouldn't stop. One eye squeezed open and flicked over to the clock on my nightstand. Jesus Christ, it wasn't even 10 in the morning yet. What the hell was so goddamn important that they just couldn't wait until later? Couldn't even give me a full 12 hours to adjust. They just had to pound on the damn door and wake my ass up when I just wanted to be left alone.

"Caleb, open up!" Dom's voice called through the door.

I just moaned and rolled onto my back. Maybe if I ignored him, he would go away.

"Caleb, open the door!" Dom called again, his voice way too animated for this hour and that pounding just would not stop.

"What the hell do you want?" I hollered back and pulled the pillow over my head to block everything out.

"Seriously, bro, get out here!"

"Go away," I yelled back. "It's too early for this shit, Dom."

"I'm tellin' ya, Caleb, you're gonna wanna get your sorry ass out here," he laughed through the door. "Trust me, you won't be disappointed."

It was clear this wasn't going to stop until I finally surrendered.

"Alright, alright," I flung the covers off me and swung my legs over the side of the bed. "I'm comin'. Jesus Christ."

After stepping into the first pair of sweatpants I could find and throwing on a random Horsemen T-shirt from my floor, I jerked open the door, nostrils flaring at Dominic's shit-eating grin staring back at me. "What?"

He just gestured with his head towards the hallway, that grin just spreading deeper across his face. I had half a mind to punch it the hell off.

"Parking lot."

I stared back at him. "What?"

"You heard me," Dom pushed me into the hallway. "Parking lot. Go. Now."

Even as Dom shoved me again, my lead feet stuck right to the greasy, stained carpet. I was too exhausted to keep fighting it, so when my best friend gave me one more playful shove, I finally put one foot in front of the other and got on with it already. The sooner I got this over with, the sooner I could get my ass back to bed and sleep for the next week until Isabelle came home for the weekend.

The clubhouse was still completely dead, minus the two hang-arounds passed out in one of the booths next to the pool table, so there were no problems maneuvering around the main floor until I pushed through the front doors. Shielding my eyes to fend off the sun's glare, the only thing in the parking lot was a yellow cab.

Whatever Dom was smoking, I think I really needed a hit of that shit...and then I caught a flash of tanned legs and familiar long, shiny blonde hair.

What the—Isabelle was coming around the side of the cab with her duffel bags in hand as Dom moved to the passenger window to pay the driver. All the breath rushed out of my lungs and my feet cemented me right into the hot pavement.

I blinked. And I blinked again. I needed to pinch myself. This wasn't a mirage. This wasn't a figment of my overactive imagination. This was real. She was really here. What the hell was she *doing?*

Then she turned her head, her face breaking out into a wide and vivid smile, and my chest heaved as heat stung my eyes.

"Iz?" I croaked out.

My feet finally jerked out of their coma and as I stalked towards her, all my emotions slammed through me, flipping me over, and practically knocking me right on my ass and I just had to get to her before my lungs gave out on me altogether.

Isabelle dropped her bags on the pavement and flew into my waiting arms. I lifted her up, burying my nose in her hair. It was crazy—I hadn't even been away from her for a full day and yet, it felt like I was seeing her now for the first time in weeks. Her absence had cast a dark shadow over my life and now that she was here, all the light was back again.

When I set her back down, both my hands closed around her face and I pressed a hard kiss into her lips. "Babe, what...?"

"I couldn't do it, Caleb," she whispered, her ocean-blue eyes glittering with unshed tears.

"What?" I murmured hoarsely as I ran a thumb over her cheek.

"I just couldn't," she reassured me with a shrug. "It doesn't mean anything without you. I can't be really be there if you're here."

"But, how...?"

She smiled up at me. "I took a bus. It wasn't a big deal."

I exhaled with a laugh and pulled her into me again. "Why didn't you call me?"

"I knew you'd just try to talk me out of it."

I blinked again, unable to completely accept this was real. "Where's the rest of your stuff?"

She just shrugged with a small smile. "I'm Fed-Exing it all back here. Gwen was surprisingly helpful after she got over the initial shock of gaining and losing a new roommate all in the same day."

Everything was happening so fast and it took me a moment to really grasp the meaning of those words. "But what about school, Iz?"

She grinned broadly and stood up on her toes to kiss me lightly on the lips. "I'm still going. I would've been back earlier, but I had some business to take care of first."

"I just...I just can't believe you're really here. You didn't have to do this, Iz."

"Yes, I did."

I blew out a deep breath and kissed her forehead, wrapping my arms around her more tightly. "Come on, babe, let's get inside and then, you're gonna tell me what's goin' on, right?"

She just laughed and swooped down to pick up one of her bags while I grabbed the other ones. Once we were standing back inside my dorm, I dropped her duffel bags on the floor and pulled her back into my arms. My senses were aware of what was happening, that she was really here in this room again and that she was here to stay, but my brain still hadn't caught up yet.

"I'm going to commute to UNC," she told me matter-of-factly, leaving no room for argument. "I called the registrar after you left yesterday and I talked to the head of my program's department and told him what was going on. It took a while and some serious begging and pleading, but I'm enrolled at the UNC School of the Arts in Winston-Salem now. I think I might just have to miss the first week of classes until I get my schedule straightened out, but this is what I'm gonna do."

I couldn't quite compute everything she was trying to tell me. There were too many conflicting thoughts flying around in my brain. I was so happy I couldn't see straight, but did she do it because she was worried the distance would break us up? I wasn't sure if I'd be able to live with myself if she lost out on this opportunity because she'd settled for me instead.

"Babe, why?" I murmured hoarsely. "What about VCU? What about your career? You can't give that up for me, Iz. It's not fair to you."

"I'm not giving anything up, Caleb. I already told you—all that doesn't mean anything if I can't share it with you."

"But you *will* be sharing it with me," I closed my hands around her face as I spoke, still not completely allowing myself to believe that what I was hearing was true. I couldn't let myself go there, not yet. "I'm right here, babe. I'm not going anywhere and the distance doesn't matter."

"It won't be the same if we're living five hours away from each other during the week and only see each other on the weekends. I can't do that and I don't wanna live like that either."

"Babe," I was practically pleading with her now, desperate to understand what this was really about. "Don't do this because of me."

Her lips curved into a soft smile and she ran a hand over my cheek. "I'm not doing this for you. I'm doing this for *me*. Just because VCU is one of the best art schools in the country doesn't mean it's the best school for *me*. UNC has almost the exact same program. In fact, it might even be a little better for me because I get more of a say in classes and projects than I would at VCU. And I'd never really be happy there without you, Caleb."

"But—"

"There's nothing wrong with commuting," her voice grew firmer with each syllable and any hope I had at arguing dwindled with each word. "I already had the dorm life experience and to be completely honest with you, it wasn't that great the first time around so I'm sure I'm not missing anything *this* time around. I figured I'll move out of my dad's house, get my own apartment...I can't keep letting other people dictate my life anymore. I need to start living my life the way I want to and start doing what's going to make *me* happy."

We were sitting on my bed now and she crawled over to me until she was straddling my lap, wrapping both arms around my neck.

"Baby," she started again softly and I felt my chest heaving as everything she was telling me finally started to sink in. "I know you just want the best for me and I love you for that. But don't you think I should be the one who gets to decide what's really the right thing for me?"

Damn, she was right. She was so right. I'd taken the choice away from her without even realizing it. I'd been so focused on doing what I thought was right for her that I'd never even asked her what she wanted to do. All I'd heard about VCU was that it was the best and that was what I wanted for her. I hadn't stopped to think about what she really wanted for herself.

"I need to sketch and I need to work to be happy."

I nodded slowly, my chest still heaving violently.

"And I need you to be happy too, Caleb. I can't live any other way. Now that I've had you in my life, I need you to always be there."

My arms squeezed around her and I knew that this was it. *She* was it.

I hadn't wanted to get my hopes up that I could have what Dom and Lex had. That I could have a wife I would die to protect and a family I would sacrifice everything for and love until the day I died. But it was all here in my arms...all my wildest, out-of-reach dreams coming true. Maybe it was time to stop being so chicken-shit and start really living my life too.

"Babe," I whispered hoarsely. "You know I would never ask you to do any of this, right? I would never want you to feel that you *had* to."

Her hands slid lazily up my shirt until it was skimming over my head and a slow smile tugged across my face.

"I never *had* to do anything, baby," Isabelle told me. "This is what I want. You're what I want. And you're just gonna have to deal with it because you're it for me, Caleb. You can't get rid of me now."

I leaned forward until my face was buried into her soft, sweet neck. "I think I should be sayin' that to you, babe...I love you."

"I love you, too," she smiled against my lips.

There was no more argument left in me and as everything she'd laid out settled in my head, it was difficult to argue with her logic. If I was what she wanted, I wasn't going to be stupid enough to push her away. Not now and not ever. This girl—this woman—was my entire world and shit just didn't work without her in it.

"I want you to get my ink," I told her, my fingers slipping underneath her tank top and resting right at the base of her lower back. There was no point in waiting anymore. She was here, she was mine, and I needed everyone else to know it too.

Her beautiful lips spread apart into an even more beautiful smile. "Okay. You're gonna get one too, right?"

"Yeah," I nodded and lifted her fingertips until they brushed the skin right over my heart. "I was thinkin' I'd get your name right here. It's already yours. Might as well have your name on it."

And someday, I would make this woman my wife and she would be the mother of my children. She would have her art and her passion and I would support her every step of the way. The VP patch would be mine before long and I knew I had an old lady who could stand by my side and roll with whatever my life might throw our way.

We were strong. We were in love and we had our whole lives and the whole world ahead of us. With that settled, my lips found hers again as I slipped her tank top over her head to officially welcome my old lady back home.

EPILOGUE

The Claremont PD precinct bustled from the new arrivals. Nobody had to say out loud what the transplants were here for because the answer was as obvious as it was simple: the Iron Horsemen MC. So far, the local PD had been very accommodating to their needs and had pretty much adhered to anything either of them asked for from coffee to a war room to make camp.

And now, what they really needed was some space and some time to debrief.

Special Agent Matthew Jordan sipped his coffee, rocking back on his heels as he studied the pictures meticulously arranged before him. While it had taken him several hours to piece all the connective dots together, he felt confident in his understanding of the hierarchy within the Iron Horsemen motorcycle gang.

Experience had taught him never to judge a book by its cover and so, there was no use in sugarcoating what the Horsemen really were. They were by no estimation simply motorcycle enthusiasts. They were a street gang. Violent, ruthless, and deadly. And it was time they were finally taken down.

His partner sighed next to him and tilted her head to the side in deep thought.

"What are you thinking, Summers?"

Special Agent Grace Summers crinkled her forehead as she took a step closer to the black and white surveillance photo of Skyler Sawyer. "I wonder how much she knows."

"What do you mean?"

"She's not just an old lady, you know. She's *the* old lady. Been married to the MC's first president. She's banging the current one. Her son's next in line for president. That's gotta be a goldmine, you know? Can you imagine getting to pick her brain and poke around at everything that's inside? I think it would be fascinating."

"And probably incredibly incriminating," Jordan finished for her with a nod.

Summers sighed again and ran a hand through her shoulder-length, auburn hair. In the three years they'd been partners, he'd never known her to be unnecessarily cold-hearted or mean-spirited about their investigations. Instead, she was a brilliant interrogator and one of the sharpest detectives he'd ever been in contact with. Working with her was a pleasure, especially when she was struck with an idea like this.

He'd only been with the ATF for four years and even though that was an incredible accomplishment at 29, he still felt like he hadn't quite proven himself to his colleagues. At times, he wondered if Summers even completely trusted him, but he had to believe that, given the opportunity, she would always have his back. This take-down would lift both of them to the next level and so, neither of them could even think about resting until every single member of the Horsemen were behind bars.

No holds barred. Any means necessary.

With that thought, his eyes drifted over to the other well-known old ladies within the culture of the Horsemen and an idea struck him.

"Skyler Sawyer would never talk. It wouldn't matter what we did or what we threatened her with. She'd never rat."

Summers nodded without tearing her eyes away from the wall covered in their notes and surveillance photos. With a gleam in her eyes that he knew well, she gestured with her head towards the pictures to their right. "What about new generation old ladies? Think they'd crack?"

"Okay. So, there's Lexie Fletcher."

"Who's got a newborn at home now," Summers reminded him quickly.

"Right and then who are we really left with? Becca Ullmer and Isabelle Martin. Those are the only three I think anyone in the club could actually count as an old lady, next to Skyler Sawyer."

Summers cocked her head to the side as she studied their photos, each lined up with their respective 'old man'. "I wonder how much they know?"

"And how much would it take?"

"Well," Summers murmured thoughtfully as she moved around the photos, pacing like a predator stalking its prey. "Lexie Fletcher's a newlywed and a first-time mother. Lots of new responsibility. Lots of stress. Lots of bills. The last thing she needs right now is her husband in federal prison."

"And we know Becca Ullmer's been nursing her coke habit down at The Sundown Saloon," Jordan added, nodding towards a surveillance picture of Becca Ullmer leaving the bar. "I can't imagine Harris would appreciate finding out his woman is a closet junkie. At the very least, she seems to be doing a pretty good job of hiding it, but secrets don't stay hidden for long. Especially not if it's spreading over to the clubhouse too."

Summers grinned back at him and then moved on to the next photo. "And then we've got Isabelle Martin. She just enrolled at the UNC School of the Arts in Winston-Salem. What's she majoring in again?"

He rummaged around on the table behind them, quickly flipping through Caleb Sawyer's file for the information. "Majoring in Fine Arts for Drawing and Painting."

"An artist," Summers huffed. "These people and everyone around them baffle me sometimes."

As Jordan glanced back at the grainy black and white surveillance photo of Isabelle Martin, which had been taken just a few weeks ago as she'd left Sawyer Auto Repair's parking lot after spending the night at the clubhouse, he felt something stirring in his stomach. She was achingly beautiful. Long, athletic legs. Crystal clear blue eyes. Smooth, curly blonde hair. And a smile that could smash your insides into pieces.

"Well," Summers went on, unaware that he'd just drifted off into dreamland again. "She's got a dad in rehab and a potential career as an artist."

After a short pause, probably for effect, she charged ahead.

"You know, when you think about it, you take any man, doesn't matter who he is, and you'll find that his greatest weakness is his woman. Just look at history: Adam and Eve. Samson and Delilah. Caesar and Cleopatra. Antony and Cleopatra. Bill Clinton and Monica Lewinsky. All brought to their knees because of a woman. Some of them literally. Anyways, what I'm saying is why not use the Horsemen's women? Maybe we have to tail them for longer to really get somewhere, but with gangs like this, the insiders have the most information out of anyone not officially a member and usually, that's almost always the women."

"The women relieve their stress and the men tell them all their dirty secrets. That's usually the way it works, isn't it?"

"As misogynistic as it is, yes, that's usually how it works," Summers nodded tightly. "So we turn their culture against them. Sure, it wouldn't be the first time an agent's done this, but the Horsemen are the perfect target. Skyler Sawyer wouldn't talk even if we tortured her within an inch of her life. But the younger women, this new generation, are a different story. They haven't been around quite as long to have the kind of built-in, take-it-until-I-die kind of loyalty that Skyler has."

"Lexie and Dominic Fletcher have been together since they were in high school," Jordan pointed out.

"Sure," Summers brushed that aside with a shrug. "But that doesn't mean she wouldn't crack, especially not with everything else going on too. And then you've got Becca Ullmer and Isabelle Martin, still pretty fresh to the lifestyle, but their men seem to be pretty serious about them, Sawyer especially. Didn't they all go to high school together?" Summers wondered out loud. "And Becca and Isabelle are just recent additions to the *family*, so to speak?"

Jordan flipped through some more pages in their files just to make sure. "Yeah, that sounds about right."

"I say it's an angle to play," she concluded. "We've got the time. And if we play this right and play them all *off* each other right, we could have the whole club crumbled in less than a year. Toppled by their own barbaric hierarchy."

Jordan snorted out a laugh and his eyes inadvertently found their way back to Sawyer's file, particularly the information about his old lady, Isabelle Martin. Sawyer was a real piece of work with multiple arrests at the ripe old age of 21. Nothing had been serious enough to give him any significant amount of time—disorderly conduct, petty theft, and assault, but still—and as Jordan took in a surveillance photo of Sawyer with his arms wrapped around Isabelle Martin, his desire to see this particular Horsemen patch behind bars for the rest of his life only heightened.

She was just so beautiful. And from the digital portfolio he'd lifted from her art school applications, an extremely talented artist. This was a person who had something truly worthwhile to offer the world. This was a person who was better than the lowlifes she surrounded herself with. Even her best friend was a junkie and he was positive she had no idea because she just didn't seem like the type of person to ever suspect that about someone.

She didn't deserve this life. She didn't deserve the constant danger that being involved with Sawyer would inevitably put her in. She deserved the best—happiness, safety, security, and all the things a life with Sawyer would never give her, if he kept her around long enough to actually get that far.

And as his eyes roamed over the picture in his hands, he wondered what someone as beautiful, as talented, and as decent as Isabelle Martin was doing with a criminal like Caleb Sawyer.

About the Author

K. Ryan is a former English teacher, who graduated from the University of Wisconsin-Stevens Point in 2009. She lives in the Green Bay area with her crazy-supportive boyfriend and the best decision of her adult life, a not-so-stray cat named Oliver.

Follow her on Twitter (@authorkryan), Instagram and Facebook (@kryanauthor) or visit authorkryan.com for updates and news.

Also by K. Ryan

Finding Emma

The Carry Your Heart Duo

Carry Your Heart

Carry You Home (Releases February 9, 2016)

Here's a look at *Carry You Home,* the conclusion to Caleb and Isabelle's story...

Prologue

Hey Iz,

I honestly have no idea if you've been getting my letters. I think I just want to believe that you're reading them, so I just keeping writing. It's weird being in here, where time pretty much stands still, and knowing that life just keeps moving forward without you. Honestly, writing these letters to you is the only thing that keeps me sane. The only thing that makes me feel normal. The only thing that makes me feel close to you.

If you're not reading this, I guess I can't blame you. If I were you, I don't know if I'd be reading this either. I'm such an idiot, Iz. I know I'll never be able to say that enough. I don't deserve you and I deserve to be exactly where I am. Hell, I'm not even worth this piece of paper I'm writing on right now. I'm kinda surprised they even gave me a pencil.

I miss you, Iz. I miss your smile. I miss your laugh. I miss the way you always bite down on your bottom lip when you get nervous. I miss how soft your hair is when I touch it. I miss your lips. I miss your eyes. I miss the way you used to look at me. I miss everything, Iz.

I wish you would visit, but I get why you won't. I wouldn't want to visit me either. I think if we could see each other face to face, maybe we'd be able to talk this through, and I'd be able to explain better than I've been able to in my letters. You know I'm shit with words, but this is all I've got right now. I wish there was another way I could reach out to you, to talk to you, but since you won't take my calls and you won't visit, you're just going to have to get used to me sending you these letters.

I'm not going to give up, Iz. I know what I did. I know how much I hurt you. But I'm not going to give up.

Love you always,

Caleb

Acknowledgements

First of all, I think a book is really only as good as its cover, so I owe a huge thank you to Matt at The Cover Lure. Not only did you create something that was vibrant, full of life, and beautifully eye-catching, but you also managed to capture exactly what was in my head. You were also, by the way, super patient with me and all my newbie questions and I felt like it was true collaboration in every sense of the word.

To Jamie McGuire and Karina Halle—I'm pretty sure you're not aware I exist, but without your fearless bulldozing of the new adult genre a few years ago, I doubt I would've went through with self-publishing. When I read Jamie's book, Beautiful Disaster, and Karina's book, Sins and Needles, my hopes and dreams of becoming a published author were just a pipe dream. When I read those books, I thought to myself, God, I wish I could do that too...maybe I can do that too. So thank you, Jamie and Karina, for inspiring me to see this thing through to the end and proving that it can be done.

To Michelle and Heather, my awesome betas—your time and your thoughtful feedback has been invaluable to me. I can't tell you how helpful it was to have someone to bounce ideas off of that really understood what I was doing and the changes I needed to make in order for this to work. Let's do it again.

To my first readers—you know who you are. It's been such a scary, fantastic ride two years in the making and you guys were there from the very beginning, challenging and supporting me to keep going. Caleb and Isabelle wouldn't be here without you.

To my parents—thank you for supporting me even when you weren't entirely sure what I was doing and even when I wasn't entirely sure I wanted to explain it. Thank you for trusting me and for encouraging me to chase a dream instead of a paycheck.

To Oliver—best writing partner ever. Just saying.

To Andrea—my best friend and my first official reader. I don't think you have any idea how hard it was for me to turn this over and let you actually read the thing. I've never been more nervous and I really shouldn't have been. You've been supportive since day one and I can't wait to hand over books two and three next!

And finally, last but not least, to Michael—I don't think there are a lot of people who would accept their girlfriend being let go from her job and then making writing her new career plan with so much peace. I think it's just because you've always understood what this has meant to me without me really needing to explain it. You've always known my original career path was really just a placeholder for what I really wanted in my life and without your unwavering support, I would not have been able to do this. I guess maybe some of this was a little bit of art imitating life, huh?

Playlist for Carry Your Heart

1. "Use Somebody" by Kings of Leon
2. "See How I Run" by Jessie Baylin
3. "Come Pick Me Up" by Ryan Adams
4. "Wicker Chair" by Kings of Leon
5. "Pumped Up Kicks" by Foster the People
6. "Walk" by Foo Fighters
7. "Follow Your Arrow" by Kacey Musgraves
8. "Shut Up and Dance" by Walk the Moon
9. "She Will Be Loved" by Maroon 5
10. "Can't Help Falling In Love" by Ingrid Michaelson
11. "All I Want Is You" by U2
12. "I'll Be Your Man" by The Black Keys
13. "Will You Still Love Me Tomorrow?" by Amy Winehouse
14. "Somebody That I Used To Know" by Gotye
15. "Maybe I'm Amazed" by Paul McCartney
16. "American Girl" by Tom Petty and the Heartbreakers
17. "Roadhouse Blues" by The Doors
18. "Hard to Handle" by The Black Crowes
19. "Fight Song" by Rachel Platten
20. "Cannonball" by Damien Rice

<<<<>>>>